DEAD AT FIRST SIGHT

Peter James is a UK number one bestselling author, best known for writing crime and thriller novels, and the creator of the much-loved Detective Superintendent Roy Grace. Globally, his books have been translated into thirty-seven languages.

Synonymous with plot-twisting page-turners, Peter has garnered an army of loyal fans throughout his storytelling career – which also included stints writing for TV and producing films. He has won over forty awards for his work, including the WHSmith Best Crime Author of All Time Award, the Crime Writers' Association Diamond Dagger and a BAFTA nomination for *The Merchant of Venice* starring Al Pacino and Jeremy Irons for which he was an executive producer. Many of Peter's novels have been adapted for film, TV and stage.

Visit his website at www.peterjames.com
Twitter 🐦 @peterjamesuk
Facebook 📘 facebook.com/peterjames.roygrace
Instagram 📷 Instagram.com/peterjamesuk
YouTube ▶️ Peter James TV

DEAD AT FIRST SIGHT

PETER JAMES

PAN BOOKS

First published 2019 by Macmillan

This edition first published 2019 by Pan Books
an imprint of Pan Macmillan
The Smithson, 6 Briset Street, London EC1M 5NR
Associated companies throughout the world
www.panmacmillan.com

ISBN 978-1-5098-1641-5

5 7 9 8 6

A CIP catalogue record for this book is available from the British Library.

Map artwork by ML Design
Typeset by Palimpsest Book Production Ltd, Falkirk, Stirlingshire
Printed and bound by CPI Group (UK) Ltd, Croydon, CR0 4YY

MIX
Paper from
responsible sources
FSC® C116313
www.fsc.org

Visit www.panmacmillan.com to read more about all our books
and to buy them. You will also find features, author interviews and
news of any author events, and you can sign up for e-newsletters
so that you're always first to hear about our new releases.

TO ROB KEMPSON

My ski buddy and very dear friend

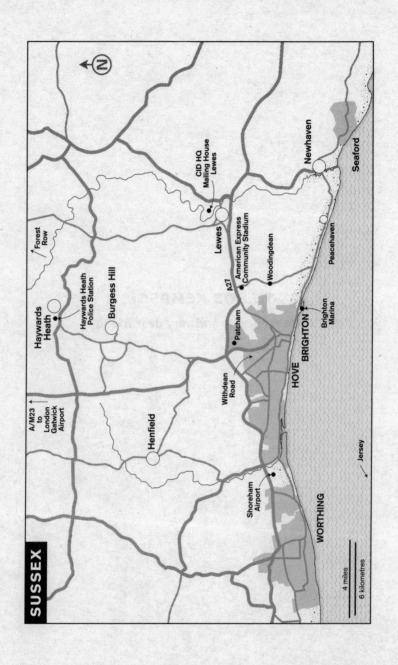

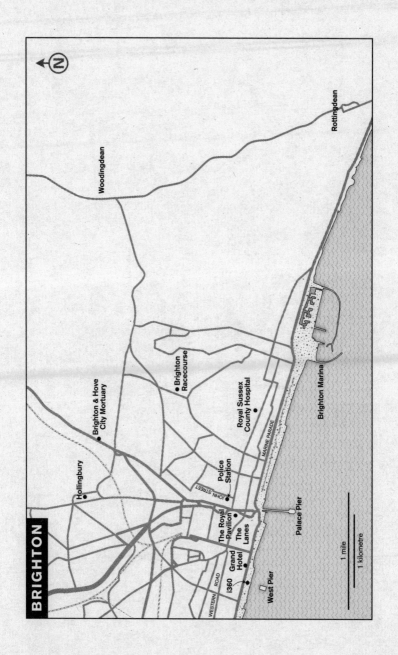

1

Life may not be the party we'd hoped for, but while we're here we should dance, Gerald Ronson used to say. It was Gerry who had put him up to this, the reason he was standing in the arrivals hall of London's Gatwick Airport. A bit difficult to dance at this particular moment, but inside him, boy, was his heart pounding away!

She would appear at any moment.

His upright military bearing, conservative tweed suit, suede brogues and neat grey hair barbered earlier today were at odds with the sheer, utter childlike joy on his face. His whole body was jigging with excitement. With anticipation. His stomach was all twisted up. He felt like a teenager on a first date, except he was approaching sixty, and he knew it was ridiculous to be like this, but he couldn't help it. And, hey, this day had been such a long time coming – almost a year – he could scarcely believe it was finally here – that *she* was finally here!

Most of the people massed alongside him were chauffeurs, holding up placards bearing the names of their pick-ups, peering hopefully at the throng emerging through the sliding doors. But Johnny Fordwater, instead, clutched a massive bouquet of pink roses, so big he needed both arms to hold it. Normally the former soldier might have

1

been embarrassed about carrying a bunch of flowers, he wasn't really a flowers kind of guy, but today was different. Today he didn't give a monkey's what anyone thought. He was walking on air. And he only had one thought.

Ingrid. She would be coming into the arrivals hall any second. The love of his life. Who had told him she loved pink roses. And rosé champagne. A fine bottle of that was on ice, awaiting her, back in his flat in Hove. Laurent Perrier, vintage. Classy.

For a very classy lady.

The wait was tantalizing. The butterflies were going berserk inside him. Butterflies he'd not felt since that first date with Elaine, over forty years ago, when as a teenage student he'd nervously climbed out of his rust-bucket of an old Mini and walked up the garden path of her parents' house close to Brighton seafront.

A cluster of people emerged through the doors. An elderly couple being driven on a buggy, their luggage stacked behind them. A large Middle Eastern family, accompanied by a porter with a loaded flatbed trolley. A mother wheeling a suitcase with a small boy trailing behind her, pulling a little suitcase striped like a tiger. A group of serious-looking suits. Two nuns. A man in shorts, a Hawaiian shirt and flip-flops with a woman wearing a sombrero the size of a tepee, each pushing along gaudy, wheeled cases.

Come on, Ingrid! My darling, my love! Mein Liebling, mein Schatz!

He glanced at his watch: 7.08 p.m. Fifty minutes had elapsed since the Munich flight had landed. He looked at the arrivals board, then pulled out his phone and double-checked on the flight tracker app for the fifth or maybe sixth time to make sure he wasn't mistaken. Definitely. Fifty-two minutes ago, now. Probably a delay with the baggage coming through, which often happened here. He looked at the luggage tags of passengers who had just emerged and were walking past him along the cordon. Looking for the tell-tale easyJet tags, which would show him they were probably on the flight from Munich, along with his beloved.

Ingrid Ostermann.

He loved everything about her, including her name. There was something mysterious about it, something exotic. A woman of the world!

A blonde in her late thirties, with cool dark glasses, a short leather jacket and ankle boots appeared, striding confidently, pulling an expensive-looking suitcase.

Ingrid!

His heart did a double flip. Then another!

Then sank as she came nearer and he realized it wasn't her. Was it?

She walked straight past him. He was about to check her photograph on his phone when she waved at someone ahead. He watched her step up her pace and fall into the arms of a tall guy with a ponytail.

At least the Munich flight was coming through now, he thought. Hoped. He waited. Another fifteen minutes. Twenty minutes. Plenty more easyJet tags. But no Ingrid. He checked his phone. She had promised she would text the moment she landed, but maybe she had a problem getting her German phone to connect here. He sent a text.

> **I'm here waiting, mein Liebling!**
> **XXXXXXXXXX**

He watched the display, waiting for a text back. Had she forgotten to switch her phone back on?

Then he heard a male voice right behind him say his name. 'Mr Fordwater?'

He turned to see a shaven-headed, stocky man in his fifties, wearing a suit and tie, accompanied by a woman in her late twenties, with sharply styled fair hair, in a dark trouser suit.

'Yes?' Johnny said, alarmed by their sudden presence. Had something happened?

'John Charles Fordwater?'

'Yes, that's me.'

The man held out a warrant card. 'Detective Sergeant Potting and Detective Constable Wilde from Surrey and Sussex Major Crime Team, sir. We've had a phone call from your sister, Angela, who's been concerned about you since one of my colleagues spoke to you a couple of months ago. Your sister told us you would be here and who you are meeting. Could we have a word with you, sir?'

Johnny felt a moment of utter bewilderment. Then his insides were like a lift plunging down, as the terrible thought struck him. 'Oh God, please no, please don't tell me Ingrid's had an accident. Please don't.'

'Would you mind accompanying us to the airport police station, Mr Fordwater?' DS Potting said. 'It's only a five-minute drive.'

'Please – please say she's all right. She hasn't had an accident, has she?'

'There hasn't been an accident, sir, no,' DC Wilde said as they went outside and reached the parked police car.

'Thank God, thank God for that,' Johnny said, relief surging through his confusion. 'You see I'm worried – I've been waiting for – waiting to meet her off the flight.' He looked down a little sheepishly at the bouquet he was carrying.

'I'm afraid Ingrid Ostermann wasn't on the flight, sir,' she said.

4

Johnny turned to her, feeling that plunging sensation again. 'Why – what happened?'

There was a brief moment in which both police officers glanced uncomfortably at each other before DC Wilde spoke again, deeply sympathetic.

'I don't know quite how to put this to you, sir,' she said. 'I'm really sorry to have to tell you, as I think it's going to come as a shock. From our intelligence, the lady you are waiting for, Frau Ingrid Ostermann, does not exist.'

2

Monday 24 September

A text pinged in.

Take your clothes off, meine liebe Lena, I want to see your beautiful body!

In her sixth-floor apartment in Munich's Müllerstrasse, Lena Welch was feeling an erotic tingle and desire she had not experienced in a very long while. Fortified by three glasses of Prosecco, her normal inhibitions were all but gone. The forty-seven-year-old divorcee was flattered by the attentions of the handsome man who had responded to her ad on an online dating agency, who had been engaging with her for the past three months, but whom she had not yet met.

She liked to think she was still attractive, and through keeping rigorously fit in the gym and by running three times a week, she knew her body was still in great shape, particularly for someone who had given birth to three children, now all at university. But five years on, she was still wounded by the break-up of her twenty-year marriage to her Peter Pan of a husband, who preferred the company of younger women to herself and to the responsibility of his growing children.

Some of her old confidence was beginning to return and she had finally taken the advice of her sister, who had joined an online dating agency after being widowed, and pressed her to do the same. And her sister had been right, these past months of flirting online with a number of men had done wonders for her self-esteem. But after enduring years of Jorg's behaviour, it was still taking the former PR executive time to trust any man. And she had good reason, just recently, to be suspicious about this one. Although Dieter Haas was the only one of her current suitors that she actually really fancied.

Until she'd discovered that he wasn't real.

Propped up on her desk in front of her was a row of photographs of a fair-haired hunk. In one he was modelling a Prada suit on a catwalk. In another, all rippling muscles, he was wearing the briefest of swimming trunks on the quay of a Mediterranean harbour, against a background of yachts. In a third, he was in a cool black jacket and Ray-Bans, leaning on a bar, being admired by a very beautiful girl.

And in a fourth, he was posed in a pornographic shot, stark naked.

None of these images quite gelled with the advert he had placed on the German dating agency site, ZweitesMal.de.

> Thirty-five-year-old divorcee, Air Traffic
> Controller, seeks friendship with a feisty fair-
> haired lady for fun, frolics, and who knows
> what beyond?

She took another sip of prosecco for Dutch courage and texted back:

> **You'll have to wait to get here to see what I'm
> wearing ;-)**

Moments later he replied:

> **Meine liebe Lena, I cannot wait!**

She looked again at the photographs of Mr Too-Good-To-Be-True. Thinking how much she had been enjoying their email correspondence, but at the same time getting increasingly concerned that some of the things he had said to her and his excuses for not meeting just did not correlate. And then came the bombshell of asking her for a loan of 25,000 euros for his sick mother's hospital bills.

That had made her suspicious enough to begin extensive research on the internet. With her background in IT and with the help of a former work colleague who was a border-line hacker, she now believed she'd uncovered his true identity.

She hadn't yet updated her sister about what she had found out earlier today, and before she went to the police she needed to have some evidence. Which was why she'd invited him here tonight, under the pretext of handing over the money he'd asked for. She'd set up a hidden camera and recording device.

But would he take the bait?

3

So far, a no-show.

His intelligence was wrong. Crap. And he was feeling crap, again. His head was swimming from the symptoms that kept recurring, randomly, and mostly when they were least welcome. Behind the tinted glass of his grey Passat parked on Munich's residential Müllerstrasse, Andreas Vogel continued his vigil, drinking a tepid can of Coke and frequently lighting another cigarette, which, each time, made him feel even worse. A steady drizzle was falling, coating his windows, helping make him even more invisible, but not helping his view of the entrance to the small apartment building a short distance ahead, on the other side of the street. A typically Bavarian building, painted yellow with red roof tiles and dinky balconies.

Lena Welch, the woman he had been sent here to watch, had arrived home over four hours ago. Definitely her. In her forties, with blonde hair, a smart raincoat and high boots; from the photograph on his phone there was no mistaking her. She'd opened the gate in the spiked railings, let herself in the front door of the building and had not come out again, that he was certain of. The rear entrance was only a fire escape that would trigger an alarm. He might not be feeling up to the job at this moment, but he was professional enough not to have let her slip out unnoticed. Vogel could see lights on in the sixth-floor apartment that, from the plan he had been given, he was pretty certain was hers.

Suddenly, he stiffened. Headlights in his rear-view mirror. A car was crawling along the street as if looking for an address. A dark-coloured sedan. An Audi. It passed by and in the glow of a street light he saw the silhouettes of two men inside. African-looking.

Them?

An instant later his view was blocked by a large motor-home that pulled up alongside him.

'Get out of my way!'

The passenger door of the camper opened and a dumpy woman climbed down, then stood in the road talking loudly to the driver. Another car pulled up behind and, after some moments, gave a blast of its horn.

The woman carried on talking, in German, to the driver. 'Get out of my way!' Vogel repeated, frustrated.

The horn from the car behind blasted again.

4

Monday 24 September

Johnny Fordwater sat in silence in the back of the car during the short drive from Gatwick's North Terminal to the airport police station, anger rising inside him. He stared at his phone, willing a text to appear from Ingrid. The police had no idea. Of course she existed! He and Ingrid were crazily in love with each other. About to start a new life together. She had been selling up everything in Germany, preparing for her move to be with him in England. He'd had his flat redecorated, with new carpets in some rooms, and he'd worked hard making it feel homely.

The male officer in front of him put his window down as they reached a barrier and held a card against the reader. The barrier rose and they entered a wire-mesh compound containing several police vehicles. They pulled into a bay and the female officer opened the door to let him out.

They walked through the September warmth, the male officer having a quick vape on the way, and entered a nondescript two-storey building that smelled of old linoleum. They went up a flight of stairs, along a drab corridor past several notices stuck to the wall and into a small, functional, windowless room with two chairs on either side of a metal table. A CCTV camera, mounted high on one wall, was aimed down at them.

'Would you like something to drink, Mr Fordwater?' Velvet Wilde asked. 'Tea or coffee?'

He felt sick with worry. Numb. He didn't know what he wanted. 'Just some water, please.'

As the two police officers left the room, he checked his phone again. Then again. There was clearly a terrible mistake here. Had Ingrid missed the flight? There could have been any number of reasons. Most likely the road to the airport closed because of an accident, or something of that nature. He texted her again. Perhaps the police were mistaken and she was still in the baggage area, waiting for her luggage? Or filling in a lost-baggage claim?

No reply.

He dialled her number.

All he got was a message in German which he did not understand. But it sounded like there was some kind of a problem with the number.

Was the network down? Had she lost her phone? Had the battery died?

The woman officer, DC Wilde – he remembered her name – came back in, followed by her colleague. She placed a plastic beaker of water on the table in front of him. He thanked her. 'Mr Fordwater, would you be comfortable if my colleague, DS Potting, and I recorded this conversation?' she asked.

'Sure, why not,' he said, bleakly.

'We met you at the airport as a result of a phone call from your sister, Angela, and we believe you have been targeted in a fraud case that we are investigating. You may remember my colleague DC Helen Searle coming to see you a couple of months ago. She was concerned that you were a possible victim of an internet scam, but you disagreed,' she said. 'We believe the situation now has changed and want to ask you a number of questions. It will be easier to have those on record, so thank you for agreeing to us recording it.'

The two officers sat down opposite him. She pressed a button on a control panel and tilted her head up towards the camera. 'The time is 8.10 p.m., Monday, September 24th. DC Wilde and DS Potting interviewing Mr John Charles Fordwater.'

She gave him a look of reassurance. Johnny didn't touch his water.

Potting began, 'Mr Fordwater, can I ask how you first met *Ingrid Ostermann*?'

He blushed. 'Online, on a German dating site.'

'When was that?'

'Almost a year ago.'

'Does October 22nd sound right?'

'Honestly? I don't remember. Perhaps, yes.'

'And you placed this advertisement? "Widower, mid-fifties, former army officer, fourteen handicap golfer, keen hiker, likes fine wine and good food, can do *Times* crossword in ten mins, seeks like-minded lady for companionship and perhaps romance."'

Johnny shrugged. 'I did. You see, I've been on my own for the last four years since my beloved Elaine died. Years back I served in the army for a time in Germany and – frankly – I really liked German women, although I was married at the time and never strayed. But there is something about them that always appealed to me – so many of them seemed strong and confident and full of life.'

'When did this lady begin asking you for money, Mr Fordwater?'

'Why do you want to know?'

'It might be relevant, sir.'

Johnny shrugged. 'About a month after we first made contact. She was going to come over for a weekend, but someone rear-ended her car on the way to the airport. She told me her ex-husband had cleaned out her bank account. So I sent her 3,000 euros to get her car fixed – oh, and another 2,000 for her medical bill, for her whiplash investigation – MRI scan and stuff. Apparently, her husband hadn't told her he'd not been paying her medical insurance.'

'That was all you sent her?' Potting asked.

'Initially, yes – as a loan. About three weeks later she paid it all back – and sweetly added two hundred euros, saying that was interest!'

'She paid it back?' Potting queried, surprised.

'She did, yes.'

'Did you send any more money after that?' Wilde asked.

Johnny hesitated. 'She told me she wanted to come over to see me, but her two sons were going to be removed from private boarding school because, same problem, her ex hadn't paid the fees. I sent her 30,000 euros to cover their schooling for the next term – as a loan, as was the car-repair money. She said she would pay me back as soon as her divorce was settled, and they'd sold the marital home – she's entitled to a fair chunk of it, under German law.'

'Did you make any further payments to this lady, Mr Fordwater?' Wilde pressed.

Beginning to feel irritated by them, he replied, 'Look, frankly, this is very embarrassing, I don't really want to talk about it any more. Can you take me back to the airport to get my car, please.'

From her recent work with the Financial Crimes Unit, Velvet Wilde knew there were a number of phases that a victim of fraud went through. They would begin with denial, followed by doubt, then partial acceptance. Then would come realization, next anger and finally accusation, blaming anyone. Mr Fordwater was following just this deeply tragic pattern now.

'We'll drive you back,' Norman Potting said. 'But can you tell us if you made any more payments to Ingrid Ostermann, Mr Fordwater?'

'It's *Major* actually,' he said testily. 'But why do you need to know?'

'As I've said before, it may be relevant, sir – Major.'

'Well, OK, yes, a couple.'

'And these were?'

Johnny was silent for some moments, then he said, 'Well, quite substantial, actually.' He lapsed into silence again, studying his blank phone. 'You see, she needs money for a top brief to fight her manipulative ex-husband. That doesn't come cheap. I loaned her 60,000 euros for her legal battle. On top of that, the poor lady's mother has advanced Alzheimer's. In Germany, apparently, they don't have the National Health care facilities we have here in this country. Her mother was living at home with her, you see. The only way she could be free to come over to be with me was to put her mother in a home, so I helped her out with that.'

'Very generous of you,' Norman Potting said. 'To what extent?'

'I paid for a year's care for her mother – 120,000 euros.'

Johnny ignored the gasp from the female police officer.

'So if I total that up, sir, by my reckoning that comes to a grand total of over 200,000 euros – is that correct?' Norman Potting asked.

'More or less. There are a few further bits and pieces,' he said, blushing. 'It's all just a loan, she's going to pay it all back, as she did before. But what does this have to do with anything?'

'Quite a lot, sir. May I ask a personal question? Are you a wealthy man, Major Fordwater?'

'Wealthy? No, I was a career soldier. When I left the army, I worked in the charity sector, until my wife became sick – motor neurone disease. I had to quit my job to care for her full-time. I needed round-the-clock nursing care for her during the final two years, which financially drained me – that and private medical care. We didn't have insurance, you see.'

'But you were able to pay this lady, Ingrid Ostermann, over 200,000 euros?'

'Actually, I – took out bank loans, and did one of these equity-release plans on my flat. I'm pretty much hocked to the hilt. Sold a rare Bentley I inherited from my father. But it's fine, because Ingrid's going to pay it all back from her share of her house in Munich.' He shrugged. 'You know? If you love someone, you help them, right?'

The two detectives were giving him a strange look.

'I love her. We're going to spend the rest of our lives together. The money is irrelevant. She's going to pay it all back and we can live on the income from her divorce settlement.'

'We told you earlier, sir, that this lady does not exist, but you don't believe us, do you?'

'No, you've got this all wrong – I think you must have crossed wires somewhere along the line.'

Norman Potting slid a photograph across the table to him. 'Is this the lady you believe is Ingrid Ostermann?'

Johnny studied it for a fleeting second and his face lit up. 'Yes! But hold on, old chap, I don't *believe* it – I *know* it!'

'You are absolutely sure?'

'No question, that is her, yes. What exactly are you implying?'

Potting hesitated. When he had been a young cop, working on Traffic, the one job he had hated was delivering what the police called a 'death message'. Knocking on a door at 2 a.m. to tell them a loved one had died. What he was about to tell Major Johnny Fordwater was going to be just as bad.

In some ways, maybe, worse.

5

Monday 24 September

Lena texted.

Hurry up! Your surprise is ready ;-)

The reply came instantly.

30 seconds!

As the text pinged on her phone, the doorbell rang. Nerves began to set in.

She gulped down the last of the glass of prosecco and pressed the intercom. '*Ja?*'

'It's Dieter!'

She buzzed him in.

A minute later, there was a knock on her apartment door. She strode along the hall and carefully checked the spyhole, but the light was out on the landing and it was too dark to see clearly. She removed the safety chain and opened the door, cautiously.

Then when she saw the figure, she hesitated.

Before she could close the door again, a powerful hand clamped over her mouth, stifling the scream. He pushed her backwards, one foot kicking the door shut behind him. He then hooked his foot around her ankle, sending her crashing backwards onto the bare wooden floorboards.

He stared around, surveying the flat. 'Where's the money?'

'There is none,' she said defiantly. 'You told me your name is Dieter Haas and that you're an air traffic controller, but I know who you really are. Your name is Tunde Oganjimi, right?'

He froze. She saw sudden rage in his face.

'The police would very much like to know where you are, Mr Oganjimi. I have a friend in the Munich police.'

'That's too bad,' he replied.

6

Monday 24 September

The goddam camper van finally moved off. The Audi had pulled over just past Lena Welch's front door. Had he missed anything? Andreas Vogel, sweating profusely and feeling nauseous, opened the Passat's door and stumbled out. A passing taxi missed him by inches.

Trying to pull himself together, he straightened up, unsteadily, supporting himself against the side of the car. Just in time to see a dark shape high above him, falling.

Plummeting from the balcony of the sixth-floor apartment. Her apartment.

There was a dull thud like a fallen sack of potatoes. Momentarily detached, as if observing a scene in a movie, he saw the motionless body of a woman impaled on railings directly beneath Lena Welch's balcony. Before he could even gather the energy to run over to her, he saw the driver's door of the Audi open, a wiry black man jump out holding what looked like a large blade, glinting in the street lighting, run over to her, grab her face, slice with his blade and sprint back to the car, clutching something in his hand. As he reached the vehicle, the front door of the apartment building opened and another man, much more powerfully built and wearing red shoes, raced out and across to the car with something bulky under his jacket.

Within seconds the Audi was pulling away.

Vogel hesitated. Then he got back into the Passat and drove after them. They drove straight through a red light and he was forced to jam on his brakes as a stream of traffic passed across in front of him. It was a full two minutes before the lights changed and he could accelerate. He drove recklessly fast for some distance, but there was no sign of the Audi. For ten minutes he drove around, searching up and down side streets, feeling no better.

He gave up and headed back to his apartment, cursing. And wondering just what the accomplice with the large blade had done.

He'd find out soon enough, he figured. Shit.

He'd failed. He swore loudly, shouting at the windscreen. He didn't do failure.

7

Detective Superintendent Roy Grace was reflecting on the words in one of Gilbert and Sullivan's comic operas.

A policeman's lot is not a happy one.

Not entirely true, he thought, although just now, when he'd taken a rare two weeks' break, he'd still had to come into the office on several of those days. This was his first official day back and he was getting up to speed with current investigations.

During his time off he'd arranged a barbecue for friends and some members of his team, as well as a number of his senior colleagues in the force, though with one notable omission. He was particularly pleased that his eldest son, Bruno, who had been showing some signs of behavioural difficulty, seemed to interact with the adults. He also noted, with some amusement, how well his young DS Jack Alexander seemed to be getting on with his and Cleo's nanny, Kaitlynn. The barbecue had also been an opportunity to introduce his team to its newest member, Vivienne, the wife of the American detective Arnie Crown, who had been seconded to Roy from the FBI. She had recently taken up a post as an analyst.

Back in the early days, as a detective constable at Brighton's busy John Street police station, where he had handled everything from burglaries to drug dealers, vehicle thefts, street crimes and violent assaults, Roy had loved the constant adrenaline rush of his job and the building itself. When he'd been transferred to Major Crime, housed on the Hollingbury industrial estate on the outskirts of the city, he'd loved that job even more – and still did, most days – but he'd loathed the building, like just about everyone else who worked there. Among its numerous faults, of which lack of parking was just one, the heating only seemed to work in summer and the air con only in winter and there was no canteen. But after nine months in his cramped, horrid little office in the former student accommodation buildings at the Police Headquarters in Lewes, he would have given anything to be back in his spacious one in Hollingbury.

And to have had his old boss, Assistant Chief Constable Peter Rigg, back in place of his current one, ACC Cassian Pewe.

And to not feel, as he and all other officers did these days, that they were all the time walking on eggshells. Scared of putting a single politically incorrect foot wrong. Somewhere along the line, during the past decade, something called common sense had gone AWOL. Along with the world's sense of humour.

At least the past few months had been a rare quiet period for the Head of Major Crime, with just a handful of murders in Sussex. Two of them had been domestics – fights or killings within a relationship – and the other three drugs-related. Each had been cleared up within days by other detectives in the Surrey and Sussex Major Crime Team.

This had given him badly needed time to spend evenings and weekends with his family. Until recently the family unit had been his wife Cleo, toddler Noah and their rescue dog, Humphrey. Earlier this year they had been joined by the ten-year-old son he never knew he had, Bruno, who had been born and brought up in Germany. Bruno's mother was Roy's missing, now deceased estranged first wife, Sandy. Over the last few evenings Roy had also had the opportunity to prepare for the forthcoming trials of murder suspects his team had arrested, and at most of which he would be required to give evidence.

Roy Grace knew a lot of officers did not enjoy being in court, but he genuinely did. At least, when the trial was going his way. What the public didn't realize was that the process of an investigation, and the ultimate successful outcome of the arrest of the prime suspect, was only the beginning. The many months that followed, of laboriously piecing together the evidence to make it watertight for presentation in court, was so often an even harder task than solving the crime itself. The tiniest slip in the chain of evidence would be pounced on by a smart defence brief, enabling an offender the police knew was guilty as hell to walk free. Free to perpetrate all over again. Few things were more demoralizing to his team than that.

Together with his colleague and mate DI Glenn Branson he was currently poring over the vast amount of trial documents relating to a Brighton family doctor who had turned out to be a serial killer. The man deserved to spend the rest of his life behind bars, and Grace was determined that was going to happen.

In addition to this case, he was working closely with a civilian financial investigator, Emily Denyer, on preparations for another trial, the so-called 'Black Widow' who he was certain had murdered at least two husbands, and possibly more.

As his job phone rang, the display showing *Caller ID Withheld*, he had no idea that, when he picked up, his period of respite would be under threat.

'Roy Grace,' he answered. Then immediately recognized the voice at the other end, of his friend and German equivalent Detective Marcel Kullen from the Munich Landeskriminalamt or LKA.

'Hey, Marcel, how are you doing?'

They exchanged jibes and pleasantries, briefly catching up on each other's lives since they'd last seen each other, earlier this year in Munich. Then Kullen became serious.

'Roy, we have a situation I am thinking you might be able to help us with. You are still Head of Major Crime for Sussex Police?'

'I am.'

'*Gut.* We have a murder enquiry you may be able to help us with. Does the name *Lena Welch* mean anything to you – or to anyone in Sussex Police?'

'Lena Welch?'

'*Ja.*'

'No. Not immediately, anyway.' With Kullen spelling the name to him, Roy Grace wrote it down on his pad. Putting the phone momentarily on mute, he turned to Branson. 'The name Lena Welch mean anything?'

The DI, wearing a sharp waistcoat with his suit, looked pensive for an instant. 'Nope. She welched on someone?'

Grace shook his head. 'Be serious.'

'Lena Welch?' Branson thought for a few seconds. 'Nope.'

Un-muting the phone, Grace said, 'Why do you ask, Marcel?'

'She died on Monday night, and is originally from England – from your city. Her birth name is *Williamson.*'

'Lena Williamson?' Grace added a note and looked at Branson. Again his colleague shook his head. 'Doesn't ring any bells, Marcel. Tell me?'

'Although Lena's laptop and phone seem to have been

taken, we have found a back-up hard drive. From initial examination, it seems she discovered that her photograph was being used by internet romance fraudsters. One of the identities is an Ingrid Ostermann. It is looking as if this fictitious character was purporting to be in love with a man in Sussex, England, called John – or Johnny – Fordwater. A former army officer, a major. We understand he has transferred considerable amounts of money to a München bank account in the fake name and identity of Ingrid Ostermann – a total in excess of 200,000 euros. And now we have Lena Welch found dead and the money long cleared out of the fictitious Ingrid Ostermann's account.'

'How did she die?'

'Not very pleasantly.'

'Dying isn't generally a very pleasant experience, Marcel.'

Kullen laughed. 'Glad to know you still have your dark humour, my friend. This was definitely not a pleasant death.'

'Tell me?'

'She fell from her sixth-floor apartment and was impaled on railings beneath.'

'Was it suicide?'

'No. She lived on her own after a divorce. But we have very good reason for doubting suicide.'

'Which is?'

'She had most of her tongue cut off.'

'Her tongue?'

'*Ja*. A witness reported that moments after she landed on the railings, a man ran from a car over towards her holding what looked like a machete. He hacked at her face and ran back to the car. A few seconds after, another man ran from the apartment building into the same car, an Audi A4, and they drove off at high speed.'

'Did your witness give you any descriptions?'

'She was pretty shaken up. She said both men were black. She gave us a couple of digits from the Audi's licence plate, but as you can imagine there are many thousands of these cars here in Germany. And probably the plates are false. She said something else that might be of interest. The man who ran from the apartment was wearing shiny red shoes.'

'Red shoes? What man wears shiny red shoes?' He looked at Branson, imagining him in a pair.

But even the DI, with his sometimes questionable taste in clothes, looked askance. 'Not sure I'd trust any bloke wearing red shoes, boss.'

Grace glanced down at Branson's feet. 'Wouldn't go with those socks anyway.' They were lime green.

'It's how you wear 'em.' Branson grinned. 'Could be a case for our foot man, Haydn Kelly.'

'Can I see the forensic report, Marcel?' Grace asked.

'Sure, I will send the autopsy report when it is finished. The photographs are not so nice, probably not ones for her family album.'

He smiled, grimly. 'What is your hypothesis, Marcel?'

'What we know so far from our investigations is that this lady had discovered her identity is used by a "romance fraud" gang. She confided in a friend of hers, recently, that she was suspicious of a man she had met online after joining a dating agency herself. She told her friend that she was going to meet the man and confront him. Then she is found dead, missing half of her tongue.'

Grace shuddered. 'Which dating agency was it?'

'As I said, her computer and phone are missing – presumably taken by her attacker – and we are examining CCTV coverage from a hidden camera we found. But there seems to be a lot of information on the back-up drive relating to names, photographs and emails, which we are trying to piece together, to see whether this is connected with her death.'

'We have a dedicated "romance fraud" team operating here in Sussex, Marcel,' Grace said. 'It's a growing menace. There are very big sums involved in this country. We estimate about thirty million pounds in the past twelve months in the county of Sussex alone, based on those we know about and an estimate of those we don't from people who've been too embarrassed to come forward.'

'Here also a similar amount. We are aware there's an organization operating internationally, with one of their bases somewhere in Germany. They are taking people's identities from online dating agencies and using them to defraud people. This unfortunate lady, Lena Welch, had discovered the truth and was perhaps threatening to expose them. Our hypothesis is they might have killed her in order to discourage other victims from trying to do the same. Perhaps there is some symbolism with the tongue. We are trying to establish who else has been targeted with Lena Welch's identity around the globe. But, so far, the only person we have is Major Fordwater, in your country.'

'What details can you give me about him?'

'At this stage very little, I'm afraid. We have his name. And his date of birth – which makes him fifty-eight. And we believe he is from your city, Brighton and Hove. If you could find out anything about him, that would be extremely helpful to us.'

'Leave it with me, Marcel. By the way, that hangover I got when I stayed with you in April?'

'*Ja?*'

'I'm still suffering.'

The German detective laughed. 'You poor antique. You

are over forty. Maybe you should retire and go live in an old people's home. With some nice bright-red slippers, perhaps?'

'Ha, ha! I'll book the room next to yours, Marcel!'

Ending the call, Grace entered the name, 'John, Johnny, Fordwater' into the NICHE – the Sussex Police Combined Crime and Intelligence System search engine.

Within seconds he had a result. He picked up his phone.

8

Wednesday 26 September

Johnny Fordwater, unshaven, in his dressing gown, hair unkempt, sat at the dining table, on which lay his uneaten breakfast and his unopened copy of today's *Times* newspaper. Normally he would have done the crossword first thing, but today he had not even glanced at it.

Instead he stared glumly out of the living-room window of his home, a spacious fourth-floor apartment on Hove seafront – or rather the bank's apartment, since they effectively now owned it. He was in hock to them up to the hilt. And, if the police were right about Ingrid, he wasn't going to be able to meet many more of the monthly payments. He'd been too embarrassed to tell the police that it was, actually, substantially more than 200,000 euros that he'd loaned Ingrid. It was closer to 400,000. He'd raised that by cashing in most of his pension and shares, releasing equity from his property, selling his classic car and going cap-in-hand to his bank.

Drops of rain slid down the glass and a cold wind blew in, despite the double-glazing, a reminder that summer was over and winter was not far off. Below, on the promenade, a woman in an anorak was being tugged one way by her umbrella and the other way by her grey Spinone dog. It was high tide and the turbulent sea threw spray and pebbles over the pastel-green railings.

Turbulent, like his mind. The heaving water at its greyest. Also like his mind. It was 11 a.m. He'd lain awake most of the night, his phone beside him. Waiting for a text from Ingrid. A call. Neither of which, he sensed increasingly in his heart, was going to happen. The photographs Detective Potting had given him, which were laid out on the breakfast bar behind him, attested to that.

Yet he still could not believe it. Did not want to believe it.

Could not afford to believe it.

In front of him was a lined notepad with calculations scrawled on it. Sums. Maths. The interest and repayment amounts on the money he owed. What remained of his army pension coming in.

Strewth, before Ingrid he'd been comfortably enough off. He was able to afford to live in this flat, with the mortgage paid off, and to enjoy plenty of luxuries – not that he had ever been an extravagant person. Now he faced ruin. The prospect of having to go to a military charity perhaps and beg for help mortified him.

Still in semi-denial, as he watched a seagull swirl a short distance from his window, he drained his coffee and stood up. He needed to eat something, but he had no appetite. He sat back down on a bar stool and stared again at the array of photographs of Ingrid Ostermann. Nine of them. Except in only one of them was she actually called 'Ingrid Ostermann'.

In each of the other eight she had a different identity. The same woman, no question. But different names and profiles on different online dating agencies. He sent her yet another text.

> **Please call me, Ingrid. Please say the police have**
> **it wrong, that this is all a dreadful mistake. I love**

you. I love you so much. I'm looking forward so
much to us spending the rest of our lives
together! Call me! Please.

Moments later a text pinged in. His heart fleetingly rose,
until he looked at it. And saw it was from Amazon, informing
him of a delivery delay of a book on military strategies he
had ordered. It was an expensive book. Maybe he should
return it when it arrived?

He stared at the damned silent phone. Back at the photographs, his heart flip-flopping between love, hatred and
disbelief.

Denial.

The love of his life did not exist.

All the money he had in the world, and much more
beyond, was not coming back. He was going to lose his
home.

How at his age could he ever make back the money he
had now lost? The headline of the newspaper read:

CURBS ON TOP BANKERS' PAY?

Bankers, he thought, erratically. Bankers with bonuses
of millions of pounds. None of those fat cats would miss a
few hundred thousand. The sum would mean almost
nothing to them. But it was everything to him.

Bastards.

A lifetime of careful savings and prudent investments,
to ensure a decent lifestyle when he retired. Gone. The police
told him there was little hope of ever recovering even one
penny of it.

Gone.

No one was going to employ him in anything other than
a menial job. His life was over.

He stared at the silver ice bucket on the coffee table, in front of the blue sofa. At the bottle of Laurent Perrier rosé still lying in there, with its soggy label floating free. At the vase of roses he had placed beside it. Was it his imagination or were they wilting, like himself?

Duped. Conned.

How stupid and gullible had he been?

On the wall beside him was a framed winged dagger badge of his former corps, the SAS. And beneath, its legend.

Who Dares Wins.

It was there as a permanent reminder of the best ten years of his life. He'd been at the peak of his fitness back then – something he'd endeavoured to get back to recently by doing two challenging hours of weights and interval training every day in the gym. Because he'd determined, successfully, to lose his pot belly and have as much of a six-pack as was possible for a man of his age, for when he and Ingrid were finally in bed together.

He'd better cancel his membership, to save some money there.

Beyond his army pension he had no income. He remembered, years ago, being pinned down in a foxhole in Iraq with a bunch of squaddies under his command. They were against impossible odds and running out of ammunition. If they stayed where they were they would eventually be taken out by a shell. If they climbed out, they'd be cut down by machine-gun fire.

He remembered the words he had shouted out to the men under his command.

'OK, we're all going to die. Let's just take out as many of them as we can before we do.'

Then they'd gone over the top.

To his astonishment, somehow with the loss of just one

of his team, they'd made it through to the enemy gun emplacement and neutralized it by killing all five Iraqi soldiers manning it.

He had later been decorated with the Military Cross for valour in combat. It hung in a frame on the living-room wall. His proudest achievement, and the last thing he would ever sell.

Now he had been destroyed, with no bloodshed, by an unseen enemy.

And he was thinking to himself, *Is this what I nearly died for? Only years later to lose my home to another enemy?*

I thought I was smart. How could I have been so stupid?

Before going into any combat situation, some soldiers drank, some took drugs, others just pumped themselves up with fury-based adrenaline.

He stared down at the photographs again. Thinking. Anger, like the livid sea beyond his window, surging through his veins.

I fought so this could happen?

His phone rang.

9

Wednesday 26 September

The single-engined Cessna bumped and yawed through the grey cloud swirling past the windscreen in front of him. Through his headphones, Andreas Vogel heard the calm exchange between the English pilot, seated to his left, and the St Helier tower on Jersey. The little plane reminded him of his time, years back, as a sniper in the US military in George Bush's Iraq, being flown places in Black Hawks. Not the greatest of memories. Sitting on his helmet to avoid losing his nuts if someone fired at their helicopter from the ground.

For most of the journey they'd flown in silence. The pilot, who used to fly for Qantas, he'd told him, and who had flown him from the little private airfield outside Rennes for a very large wad of cash, had attempted to chat to him, but Vogel had said little in response. He didn't do small talk.

And he was still thinking about Munich, which he had left on a private flight to Rennes early this morning. What a screw-up that had been. He'd never normally have let something like that happen – his current illness was really impacting on his judgement.

Moments later the cloud became wispy, then was gone. Below them appeared the grey, white-flecked water of the outer extremity of the English Channel. He saw a couple of

35

rocky outcrops. Then the green, hilly land mass of an island ahead. Clusters of houses; a town; a tall smokestack; a harbour mole.

Vogel saw the long, straight tarmac of the runway. The pitch of the engine changed and the plane began losing height rapidly. It bounced on the runway, veering right then left, then the wheels touched down again and settled. After a short taxi, the pilot turned right towards a series of hangars, in which there were parked several executive jets. They turned left and he saw a batman ahead, waving them forward with paddles. Finally, they stopped. The pilot killed the engine and removed his headphones. Vogel removed his.

'Welcome to Jersey,' the pilot said.

Vogel did not reply.

'Nice talking to you.'

He didn't respond to the sarcasm in the pilot's voice.

The pilot reached across him and yanked on a door handle. 'The best way to get out is put your right leg on the rubber strip on the wing, kneel, turn around and put your left leg on the rung just behind the wing.'

Vogel did what he was told and jumped down onto the tarmac. Then the short, wiry man with an angry face waited in the strong, gusting wind that billowed his camel sports coat as the pilot removed the brown holdall from the luggage locker behind the rear seats and handed it to him. Vogel always travelled light.

As he took the leather bag and turned away from the aircraft, limping from an injury earlier this year, he looked around warily for any signs of an official. But, as he had been previously reassured, there was none in sight. A woman in her thirties strode out of a building beside the hangars and greeted him. 'Mr Vogel, welcome to Gama Aviation. Your car is here for you.'

He followed her through the building, passing a couple of empty baggage carts in a corridor, and then outside, where a black, long-wheelbase Range Rover was parked. A bald-headed giant of a man, in wrap-around sunglasses and a sharp suit, jumped out and strode towards him.

'Mr Vogel?'

He gave a short nod.

'Welcome to Jersey, sir. Your first visit?'

Vogel did not respond.

'Mr Barrey sends his regards. You will see him at midday tomorrow. It's important to be punctual, Mr Barrey does not like people who are late. I'll be here to make sure you are not late.'

Again Vogel did not respond.

The man took his bag and ushered him into the rear of the car. As they swept away from the airport, Andreas Vogel glanced through the darkened glass. No one knew he was here. Just as no one knew he had left Germany. That was how he needed to travel. No checked baggage, no record of where he was. His mobile phone had been in airplane mode since before leaving Munich. It would remain in that mode until he returned.

Munich was his new home, for now. For the next few days he would be using a phone that had been placed on the seat beside him for his convenience. Programmed into it were all the telephone numbers he would need. It had no GPS capability. He wasn't exactly *persona grata* on English soil these days. Maybe it was dumb to be accepting a job that took him back there. But the truth was, word had gotten around in the US that he had murdered one of his previous paymasters – and that hadn't been great PR for him. Clients weren't exactly tripping over each other to hire him any more.

Maybe it was time to quit. Cash in his chips.

'You been to the Channel Isles before, Mr Vogel?' the driver asked. Vogel did not reply.

He didn't particularly like his current name, Vogel, either. It was a make of healthy bread sold in supermarkets, and not his choice. But it would suffice for now.

10

Johnny Fordwater saw on his phone display the words *No Caller ID*.

Instantly, his spirits rose. Was it Ingrid at last? Excitedly, he answered.

The voice at the other end said, 'Hey, buddy, how you doing?' His old mate, Gerald Ronson.

Masking his disappointment, he replied, with as much brightness as he could muster, 'Gerry! Good to hear you!'

'You OK, buddy?'

'Yes, fine.'

They'd been in that foxhole together, almost twenty years back, and had both, somehow, survived the rest of their time in Iraq. They'd remained good friends ever since. Both couples had visited each other back in the good old days when Elaine was fit and well.

After his divorce, Gerry, who had become a firefighter when he quit the military, sounded like he'd been having a ball trying out online dating agencies. Gerry had been encouraging him to do the same. For over three years, still mourning Elaine's death, Johnny had resisted. Almost a year ago, with wording provided by Gerry, he'd finally put a toe in the water. He'd chosen a German dating site, partly to avoid embarrassment if anyone in the UK found out, but just as much because of his liking for German women.

'You don't sound OK, buddy. You sound a little down.'

'Around £400,000 down, if you want to know the truth, Gerry. I'm about to lose my home – thanks to my stupidity.'

'Hey, hold on! What do you mean about what you are going to lose?'

'My home. I'm about to lose my home.'

'Your home?'

'All of it, buddy.'

'How – like – why – what's happened?'

'Want me to spell it out?'

'Letter by letter.'

Johnny spelled it out. When he had finished, he sat in silence, waiting for Gerry's response.

When it finally came it was succinct. 'Shit, buddy.'

Within seconds of ending the call, his phone rang again. Once more he answered with his hopes raised.

It was Detective Sergeant Potting.

11

A sharp rap on Roy Grace's office door, then it opened before he could say anything, and detectives Potting and Wilde appeared.

There had been a time, last year, when the four-times married Potting, approaching normal police retirement age, had been on the verge of marrying – yet again – this time to a police officer who was subsequently killed in a fire. He had really spruced himself up during the time he had been dating her, and he continued to take pride in his appearance after her death, which would have pleased Bella, Grace reflected.

Although he was still dressing well, some of his spark seemed to have left him, his face was drawn and pale and he seemed downcast. Grace wondered if that had anything to do with the prostate cancer treatment Norman had begun back in May, after which he had lamented privately to him that his libido was on the floor.

Unable to cope with the changed world he was in, the detective constantly upset people with his politically incorrect remarks and attitude, but Roy Grace resolutely kept him on his team, despite requests from ACC Pewe to the contrary. He fought Norman Potting's corner for two reasons. Firstly, and most importantly, he was an immensely capable detective with years of invaluable experience – something, Grace rued, people seemed to value less and less. And secondly, he fought to keep him because he cared for the man. Compassion was another value that had gone missing during the country's austerity measures.

Grace no longer had space for a conference table in his office, so Potting and Wilde had to sit in the two swivel chairs at the empty desk facing his own.

'Good to see you, Norman,' he said. 'It's been a while.'

'Not enough blooming murders,' Potting grumbled. DC Wilde smiled politely.

'Good to see you, too, Velvet,' Grace said. She was a feisty character, with short, spiky blonde hair, though conservatively dressed, like most detectives. 'How's everything?' he asked.

'Good, thank you, sir,' she said in her Belfast accent.

He turned to Potting. 'Norman, what can you tell me about this man John – Johnny – Fordwater?'

'If you want my opinion, chief, for a retired high-ranking soldier he's pretty dim. Allowed himself to be defrauded by a woman he met on a German dating agency. I think he's a sandwich short of a picnic.'

Grace looked at DC Wilde. 'Would you agree with that assessment, Velvet?'

'Well,' she said, guardedly. 'He's a nice fellow, but he seems to have been pretty naive, as Norman says, sir.'

'In what way naive, Velvet?'

'To hand over every penny he has in the world to a complete stranger he's never actually met in person. I call that naive, sir.'

Grace glanced quizzically at Norman Potting for being quick to criticize Fordwater. Potting's own record wasn't much better. His third marriage – or perhaps it was his fourth – had been to a Thai gold-digger. After just a few months, Potting had come to see him wanting advice. She'd returned to Thailand to be with her supposedly sick father. Within days, the first request for money had come through. The amounts had steadily risen. Grace had told him to stop, and Potting had, wisely, heeded his advice. But not before the DS had paid over many thousands into her bank account.

Potting never saw the money or his bride again.

'Like I said, chief,' Potting added, 'a complete idiot! Unbelievably gullible.'

'We're talking about an amount of 200,000 euros, right?'

'I don't think he told us the whole story, sir,' Velvet Wilde cut in. 'I suspect it's even more than that. We're going to talk to him again, in an hour's time.'

'Let me ask you a question. Do either of you think he's capable of murdering someone – or ordering them to be killed?' Grace asked, looking at each of them in turn.

'Murdering someone – seriously, chief?' Potting quizzed.

'Very seriously, Norman.'

'You want my humble opinion?' Potting looked at his colleague for reassurance. 'I don't think he's capable of making toast.'

'But he was a soldier, right? SAS regiment. Decorated for bravery,' Grace said. 'We're talking about pretty capable people, Norman.'

Potting looked at Wilde again and shook his head. 'Maybe once he was a tough soldier, but not now. The only soldier in him these days is the kind you dunk in an egg.'

'I agree with Norman,' she said.

'This is the lady Major Fordwater has been in a romantic flirtation with – or so he thought,' Grace said. He leaned over and pushed three photographs across the desk. 'I just received these from the Munich Landeskriminalamt. I'll be getting a full set shortly.'

Potting and Wilde looked at them, in shock.

'If you're wondering about all the blood running down from her mouth,' Grace said, 'it's because half her tongue was sliced off when she was lying impaled.'

12

Wednesday 26 September

Toby Seward, a motivational speaker – and recent early loser on the television programme *MasterChef* – was happily occupied with one of his two passions, preparing meals for his husband, Paul. His other was tending the tiny garden at the front of their home. Playing on the television in the kitchen of their house in the North Laine district of Brighton was a recording of the programme, with contestants on the show who had got further than he had managed.

Few things in life gave the distinguished-looking, silver-haired, soon-to-be forty-eight-year-old more pleasure than to cook a fine dinner for the man he loved. And he was at a critical stage in the early preparations for tonight. Lobster ravioli with avocado and garlic, broccoli, almond and quinoa salad. Paul's favourite. The almonds, frying in coconut oil in the pan, were on the verge of burning. He drained them, all the time watching the television programme, as he was copying a recipe from it. He was also in a hurry. In less than two hours he was due on stage at the Brighton Centre to talk to five hundred delegates from a pharmaceutical company.

His mobile phone rang, and he very nearly did not answer. Usually, when he saw the message *ID Withheld*, he ignored the call, because almost certainly it was spam,

45

someone trying to sell insurance, a fake car-crash claim or some other bit of flotsam from the digital sewer. Then he remembered that Paul was having problems with his new iPhone and was taking it to the shop to exchange it. Perhaps it was him?

Hitting the remote to freeze the television, he answered perkily, 'Toby here!' And heard a cultured, middle-aged female voice. 'Is that Toby *Seward*?'

'It is indeed!'

'I'm very sorry if this sounds strange, Mr Seward,' the woman said. 'My name is Suzy Driver. You see, you don't know me, but the thing is, I thought I knew you.'

13

Twenty-five minutes after he'd left the airport, the receptionist at the Radisson Blu hotel on St Helier harbour front photocopied his passport, took an impression of his Amex card, told him how to connect to the Wi-Fi and handed him his key card. 'Enjoy your stay with us, Mr Vogel.'

Tooth scooped up his passport, Amex and the key card in its little envelope and headed to the lifts, he walked down the fourth-floor corridor and entered the suite his paymaster had booked for him. Hotels like this suited him. Big, modern, anonymous. The windows looked down onto a commercial port. A tall incinerator chimney, fishing boats, a ferry marked CONDOR and a harbour basin of small private motorboats and yachts. The tide was a very long way out. Over to the right was a causeway to a rocky island on which was some kind of an old fortress.

He removed his laptop from his bag, set it on the desk and connected to the Wi-Fi, then removed his washbag and the small amount of spare clothing he travelled with, along with the encrypted, ex-military phone he'd bought for $10,000 on the dark web, as well as his pre-paid 'burner' phones and the one he'd been given earlier, and placed the items in drawers. Next, he removed a roll of gaffer tape, stood on the desk and masked the smoke detector. He made himself a treble espresso coffee from the capsules and, using the spare mug as an ashtray, lit a cigarette.

An email pinged in on the phone he'd been given:

> **I will see you at midday tomorrow. You screwed up. This will not happen again. This is where he and his accomplice are living, and I believe this is his next target. You will stop them. Frighten them.**

Beneath was an address in the city of Brighton and Hove, in England, as well as a JPEG attachment.

He didn't like the tone of the email, the thinly veiled threat. Nobody threatened him, ever. Tooth had fed the testicles of the last person who'd threatened him to his dog. Yossarian had licked his lips and looked up at him for more. Maybe soon, if he had any further emails like this, the dog would finally be getting a second helping.

He looked again at the address. It didn't make him happy.

If there was one place in England he did not want to return to it was there. The lair of that smartass detective, Roy Grace, who had been such a big pain in his life in recent years. Although, he considered, it would give him a kind of perverse pleasure to outsmart him yet again. And an even bigger pleasure to kill him.

Just the thought of Roy Grace's name made him angry. He'd like to get even with him. And take his dog a little Detective Grace goody bag. But that was not for now. He had a job to do and needed the money, paltry though it was compared to the fee he normally commanded, to fund the new life in Ecuador he was planning. Somewhere he could have his 'associate', Yossarian, flown out to join him. The only friend he'd ever had in this shitty world.

He removed the SIM card from the phone, went into

the bathroom, shut the door and switched the shower on hot. Then with his lighter he burned the card. Steam from showers, he had learned, dissipated smoke and prevented the alarm from going off.

Tooth flushed the charred card down the toilet. He was feeling hot, he realized. Clammy. He walked over to the air-con control on the wall to turn it down. Saw it was already down low, 16 degrees. And it wasn't even a warm day outside.

He needed another cigarette. He sat down heavily at his desk, perspiring. Again.

He drank some coffee, lit a Lucky Strike and instantly felt worse. Jesus.

He wobbled his way across to the minibar, peered at the rack of miniatures inside and pulled out a Jim Beam. Not his favourite bourbon, but better than nothing. He twisted off the cap, necked half the contents and sat back down.

For a few seconds he felt better, then his head was swimming again. The same flu-like symptoms he'd had repeatedly over the past six months. Back in March, due to his own stupidity and Detective Superintendent Roy Grace's actions, he'd been trapped in a room full of venomous creatures. He'd been bitten by spiders, snakes and suffered a sting from a deathstalker scorpion, one of the world's most venomous critters. He'd been close to death for some while, so he'd been told by medical staff at the Royal Sussex County Hospital when he'd eventually come round.

He managed to escape, evading the dumb police guard on his room, and make his way under one of his false identities to Germany, where he had work contacts. The specialist doctor he had consulted subsequently, in Munich, was a world authority on tropical diseases and reptile venom. He told him he'd been lucky to survive the scorpion sting, but as a result he was likely to suffer severe flu-like symptoms on a regular basis for the rest of his life. He was experiencing another of these episodes now, he realized.

There was another side effect the doctor informed him of, the bastard barely masking a smirk. That he might find his manhood had shrunk.

Which, to his embarrassment, it had.

Thank you, Detective Superintendent Roy Grace.

One day, I'm just biding my time at present, but one day, I'll get you – I promise you that.

He badly needed to lie down, but he daren't. Last time, a month back, when he had felt like this, he'd lain down on his bed and woken, soaking wet and shaking, three days later. Remembering his military training as a sniper, which had enabled him to stay concealed, motionless, behind enemy lines for days at a time, he allowed himself to catnap, seated. Five minutes' shut-eye and he'd be good to go again. That had been part of his training. He used to be able to function for days like that. Weeks if he had to. But those catnaps were vital. Deprive a cat of sleep and it would die in two weeks. Deprive a human and he would become psychotic.

He was remembering something else about that sniper course all those years back, too. Almost the first thing his instructor had said. 'Most times you get just the one chance at your target, one shot. There's no second chance. The target needs to be dead at first sight. And if he ain't, you might be.'

Five minutes later he opened his eyes and necked the rest of the tiny bottle, then, forcing himself to concentrate, opened the JPEG. A sequence of photographs. A blowsy-looking woman in her mid-fifties. Long dark hair. Still doing her best to look sexy. And no doubt did, to some. Might have been a beauty in her younger years, but probably spent too much time in the sun, judging from her tanned, wrinkled skin. Or a heavy smoker, perhaps. Or both.

Whatever.

Next was a photograph of his target – his employer's former business partner who had gotten greedy and gone rogue. A tall, large-framed African, his hair cropped to a neat fuzz, wearing an Armani bomber jacket over jeans, a bling watch and loud red trainers. He was leaning, propri-etorially, against the driver's door of a red Ferrari, his expression confident and arrogant. A long way from his impoverished roots as a boy soldier in a war-torn nation. When he'd moved to the West he'd ditched his old name, Tunde Oganjimi, in favour of Jules de Copeland, a name he had seen on the credits of a television show, and which he wore with a swagger.

This was the man Tooth had seen running from the front door of Lena Welch's apartment building and jumping into the passenger seat of the Audi.

There was another photograph, this one of Copeland's colleague and distant cousin, Dunstan Ogwang, whose real name was Kofi Okonjo. Tooth instantly recognized the shorter man with the machete who had hacked out the tongue of the dying woman. According to the file, this man had formerly been a child soldier along with Copeland. He read on.

Both men, at the age of fourteen, had been taught how to rape and then mutilate or cut the throats of their victims. What kind of moral compass did either have, he wondered? More fool his paymaster, Steve Barrey, for thinking he could be in business with them.

Tooth liked always to know who he was actually dealing

with, in a world where few people went under their real names. Barrey at some point in the past decade had relocated from his native city of Brighton and Hove to Germany, where he had made his base, and from there to Jersey. Barrey seemed to be his real name, but Tooth was never sure.

After being transplanted from Ghana to Bavaria by Barrey, Copeland had then moved, with a forged passport, from Germany to Brighton, England, where he had an uncle and a cousin who ran an internet café and safety deposit box business. It was behind that front he had set up his own internet scamming business, and brought over his cousin as his lieutenant. He'd taken into his employment, back in Ghana, several of the notorious Sakawa Boys internet scammers, whom he'd been running for Barrey, and he was now both targeting his former employer's chosen victims, as well as fishing for new ones. Tooth was well aware that, through Copeland's clumsy approach, the dumb, greedy, arrogant idiot was risking blowing apart his employer's entire carefully crafted and managed empire. Two of the targeted women had already rumbled the scam. Both had threatened to go to the police. One was now dead.

If Copeland had anything between his eyes other than sawdust and pound signs, he'd have moved on and ended all contact. There were enough firewalls and digital trails for it to take any cop a year or more to drill down through them, and still end up at a dead-end. And no cop had that time to spare. Copeland should have just moved on to the next targets – there were plenty of them out there online, thousands of men and women looking for love, all of them rich pickings. But Tooth knew Copeland's type, blinded by greed and hubris.

He was so dumb he hadn't even realized that Barrey was monitoring his computer, phones and his every move. He'd never even thought to throw away the laptop Barrey had given him and get a new one.

Tooth had been hired in Munich to follow the men and stop them. But, stupidly, he had failed, because of all that venom inside his body making him feel crap. Now the first woman was dead.

You will stop them. Frighten them.

His work was killing people. How was he supposed to *frighten* these guys? Run up behind them in a Halloween mask and shout *boo*?

The way he was feeling right now, sick in the pit of his stomach, giddy, too hot, he wasn't in the mood to frighten anyone. Everything had turned to rat shit. His health, his judgement, his future. He'd been reduced to taking a job paying way beneath his skill set. Way beneath his dignity. At this moment he envied scorpions. They had it sorted. Scorpions had a gap between the armoured scales that covered their backs. When a scorpion wasn't happy it would commit suicide by stinging itself through that gap. Simple. End of. If he'd had his gun with him, he'd be gone, too.

But he had no gun with him now. Just a view across St Helier harbour.

He never saw the point in views – what did it matter if it was an ocean or a brick wall you were looking at? People travelled hundreds, sometimes thousands of miles to commit suicide some place with a beautiful view. They flew or drove across America, and sometimes even from further afield, to jump off the Golden Gate Bridge facing the bay of San Francisco. Or a place called Beachy Head in Sussex, facing the English Channel. Or the Aokigahara Forest in Japan.

What was all that about?

Did a view matter when oblivion beckoned? They could put him in a garbage bin after he was gone, for all he cared. That's all the human race was anyway. Garbage with attitude.

He stared at the photograph of Suzy Driver. Then at her address in the city of Brighton – a city which over the past few years he had come to know well. And which in turn knew him a little bit too well.

This had to be a fast in-and-out mission. In and out before Detective Superintendent Roy Grace would have a chance to know he'd been there.

He stared at the photograph of the African again. As he did so, an email came in. A phone number. The pilot he was to call. The one who would fly him to Shoreham Airport, just outside Brighton. There were few customs and immigration controls there. All being well he would slip back into England without anyone noticing. Especially not Detective Superintendent Roy Grace.

And, job done, out again. And then?

Perhaps Mr Barrey would know, when he met him for the first time tomorrow. Mr Barrey, who had threatened him.

Consequences.

Already, he didn't like Mr Barrey. He didn't like anyone who threatened him. Mr Barrey wanted to see him at midday. Mr Barrey's goon had told him his boss did not like people being late. Well, tomorrow was Mr Barrey's lucky day, Tooth thought.

He didn't do *late*.

14

Intrigued by the woman at the other end of the phone, but anxious not to ruin his dish, Toby Seward said, 'I'm sorry – Suzy, right? Did you say you *thought* you knew me? What do you mean, exactly?'

'Well, Toby – if you don't mind my calling you that – we've been chatting each other up for the past eight months – or I thought we had. Until you asked me to lend you £20,000 for your sick grandmother's hospital bills.'

'I'm sorry – a sick *grandmother*? I don't have a sick grand-mother, touch wood. Are you calling the right person?'

'Oh good, is she better?'

'She's just celebrated her one hundred and fifth birthday last week, I was at the party. A wonderful lady, smokes ten fags a day, drinks a large whisky and is still flirting!'

'I want to be her!'

'So now you know the recipe for a grand old age. What exactly do you mean, that *you thought you knew me* – and what's your last name again?'

'Driver. Suzy Driver. I think you might be interested in what I'm going to tell you.'

'I'm already interested.' With the phone still jammed to his ear, holding a small knife, he began removing the meat from the body of the pre-cracked lobster and putting it into a bowl. Was he talking to a nutter?

'Did you know, Toby, you are in love with me?'

Definitely a nutter, he decided. 'I'm sorry, I really think you've dialled a wrong number.'

'You are Toby Seward, of 57 North Gardens, Brighton? Successful motivational speaker?'

'I'm in a real rush – what are you trying to sell me?'

'Please listen to me, I'm a fifty-five-year-old widow and I'm not selling you anything. I'm telling you because you're a victim of identity theft. Please believe what I'm saying. There are eleven women – here in England and in other countries around the world – who are in love with you.'

'In love with me? I've no idea what you are talking about.'

'I'm talking about eleven women who think you are God's gift to them! I'm guessing you don't know that?'

'No, but I'm flattered,' he replied, applying his knife to a large, cracked-open claw.

'I would imagine that depends on how you define *flattering*,' she said, sounding amused.

'Eleven women, I'd consider that's pretty flattering! Wait until I tell my husband!'

'They all think you are fifty-eight years old!'

'What? I'm not telling my husband that bit!' He nearly gouged a chunk of skin from his finger. 'Fifty-eight? I'm just coming up to *forty*-eight!' He put the knife down.

'Not on the internet, you're not. Fifty-eight, rather dishy, and soon-to-be a multimillionaire – from the sale of your company that operates a fleet of seismic oil exploration ships around the globe!'

'A soon-to-be multimillionaire in my dreams.'

'And their dreams, too.'

Something in her voice gave him a reality check. 'What are you saying exactly, Suzy? Suzy Driver, right?'

'Yes.'

'OK, Suzy.' He glanced at the frozen television screen, then down at the lobster. 'Fifty-eight years old, you said?'

'I'm aware you are only forty-eight!'

'I think I'm falling in love with you!' he said, jokily.

'You've been in love with me for months.'

'I have?'

'And you've been sending me flowers – mostly orchids – every week.'

'Seriously?'

'Very beautiful they are, too. They must have cost you a fortune.'

'Maybe we should wind back, Suzy, start from the beginning?'

'Good idea. I think you'll find what I have to say a little uncomfortable. Just to warn you.'

'Well, my darling, if we've been lovers for the past few months, bring it on!'

'I'd hate to make your husband jealous.'

'He'll get over it!'

She laughed. He liked her laugh. In another life, hey, who knew what might have been?

'OK,' she said. 'Let's wind back.'

'I really am in a rush,' he interrupted politely. 'Can you give me the short version?'

'Of course. My darling husband, Raymond, died four years ago, from a heart attack. Coming up to fifty-five, I decided I still had some living – and romance – left in me, so I enrolled in a couple of online dating agencies – ones for the more mature person.'

'Very sensible of you,' Toby Seward said. 'Fifty is the new forty, it's all about attitude.'

'Totally. So, online I kissed a lot of frogs, and then I met *you*.'

'Me?'

'Uh-huh. Or so I thought. Except your name wasn't Toby Seward. It was Norbert Petersen. Or Richie Griffiths. Or one of several others.'

'It was?'

'Yes! You and I really hit it off, Norbert!'

'We did?'

'Trust me! Online, we were going at it hammer and tongs. I was sure I'd met the man of my dreams. We were planning the rest of our lives together. And then you asked me for a loan. That's when I had a major reality check – and decided to do some investigating. Hence this call.'

'I'm so sorry to be a disappointment.'

'Don't worry, you're nothing compared to the Niagara Falls,' she said.

'Niagara Falls? What do you mean?'

'You never heard what Oscar Wilde said about them?'

'Clearly I've led a sheltered existence.'

'He said that, sooner or later, every American groom takes his bride to see the Niagara Falls. And that they must surely be the second greatest disappointment in American married life.'

Toby laughed. 'Do you mind if I call you back, I'm in the middle of cooking?'

'Of course,' she said and gave him her number.

Ending the call, he sat in silence. Thinking. He'd built up his reputation as a motivational speaker over many years. What impact was this going to have on his life?

15

Glenn Branson, Norman Potting, Velvet Wilde and DC Kevin Hall crowded around Roy Grace in his office, looking at sets of photographs printed from the email sent by Detective Kullen of the Munich LKA.

The first photograph was of two women in evening gowns and looking very glamorous, one in a white outfit, with fair hair, the other in red, with dark hair.

'Marcel said the woman in the white dress is the victim,' Grace told them.

The next photographs were grim. Each was professionally taken from a different angle by a Crime Scene Photographer. The first group were taken in the street showing the victim in situ. One was a wide-angle shot showing the whole scene, the others were all close-ups. The subject, a blonde-haired woman in her forties, dressed only in shorts and a blood-stained T-shirt, was impaled on railings. Blood, the colour of oil, pooled all around her. Congealed blood masked her chin, like a beard.

The second set was taken in the mortuary. One was a close-up inside the dead woman's mouth, showing the blackened stump of her severed tongue.

Grace glanced at their blanched faces and was reminded

of the comment of a senior officer some years back: *Wearing a uniform does not protect you from trauma.*

For one of the few moments in all the years Grace had worked with Potting, the DS was silent.

Wilde's face was ashen. Kevin Hall was silent, too.

'Not pretty,' Branson commented.

'Cutting off her tongue has to be symbolic, don't you think, chief?' Potting said.

'A warning not to talk, perhaps, Norman?' Grace replied. 'Could be.'

Kevin Hall, who had begun his career as a bookseller before joining the police, suddenly spoke. 'Gottit!' he said loudly, then looked around apologetically. 'Can't remember who wrote it, boss, but it might apply here. Something like, "A cutting word is worse than a bowstring. A cut may heal but a cut of the tongue does not."'

Norman Potting pulled out a long slim black object from his pocket and vaped, several times in succession, blowing the steam at the ceiling. Then he tapped the device on the table.

Grace looked at him, about to chide him, then let it go. Looking at these images was making him crave a smoke himself. 'For sure there's some symbolism going on here. Maybe some kind of a warning to others. My understanding is this lady is the one to whom Johnny Fordwater had handed over his life savings – at least the one he thought he was handing them over to. The one he believed to be called "Ingrid Ostermann", who we now know to be the Munich victim Lena Welch, who in addition to having her identity taken was also being scammed herself.'

Potting looked at the date and time printed on the first set of photographs. 'Chief, these were taken at around 10.30 Monday night. At that time DC Wilde and I were interviewing Major Fordwater at Gatwick Airport. Which would give him a pretty good alibi, wouldn't you say?'

'Yep, I guess it would,' Grace replied.

'How much do we know about what happened, sir?' DC Wilde asked, looking at the photographs again, clearly uncomfortable with the images. 'What was her cause of death?'

'We might know more after the postmortem,' Grace replied. 'The LKA are concerned by a comment from a neighbour, who saw a man in her corridor, approaching Lena Welch's apartment, shortly before she was found dead. Apparently this woman has given a good description – including his red shoes – and the Crime Scene Manager there is working with her on an identikit.'

'Chief, as I said, Fordwater might be a former soldier, and could just about go to the toilet unaided, but I don't think he'd be capable of killing anyone these days, and certainly not in Munich on Monday. Unless of course he's a time traveller.'

Potting looked again at Velvet Wilde. Again, she nodded in agreement.

'I think we can rule time travel out, Norman.'

'I'm with you on that one, chief.'

16

'So, Suzy Driver, how exactly did you check on me?' Toby Seward, amused and concerned at the same time, asked. He had put his phone on speaker so that he could carry on with his cooking.

Seated on the sofa in the living room of her large, detached Victorian villa in Hove's Somerhill Avenue, with a view across the street to St Ann's Well Gardens, with its tennis courts and well-tended gardens, Suzy stroked her Yorkshire terrier, Buster, curled up beside her, and stirred her coffee before replying. 'Well, it wasn't too difficult – with the help of a friend of mine's son who's a bit of a geek. You'll find you have a lot of admirers – more than admirers, actually, women, including myself, who are besotted with you and planning to spend the rest of their lives with you.'

'Lucky me!'

'Lucky you – not!' she retorted. 'Do you remember our Skype conversation?'

'Our what?'

'I thought as much, it wasn't you. *We* had a Skype conversation about ten days ago – just before I went on holiday.'

'No way.'

'On Saturday, September 15th. You – or rather *Norbert Petersen* – declared your undying love for me.'

'On Saturday, September 15th, my husband and I were sailing in the Aegean, with no internet.'

'That's what you think!' she said, good-humouredly. 'But I know different. You told me how much you liked my eyes, my hair, my face. You told me you were in Bahrain on business and could not wait to come to England to sweep me up in your arms. You actually got quite fruity, Dr Petersen – or is it Mr Griffiths?'

'Dr Petersen?'

'You are a geologist, right?'

'Hey, wind back. I'm a geologist?'

'Yes.'

'I'm not a geologist, I don't know the first thing about it. I'm a motivational speaker. I do seminars for businesses.'

'Well, you say that.'

'What do you mean?'

'Would you like to see the conversation? I recorded it on video. Shall I send it to you?'

'I'd very much like to see it.'

'It's a big file, I'll have to use file transfer.'

'I'm looking forward to seeing it.'

'I think you'll find it interesting!'

'Yuck!' he shouted.

'Pardon?'

'Sorry,' he replied. 'I just cracked a bit of lobster and got juice squirted over my face.'

'That's a lot classier than egg all over your face!'

'I'm feeling the latter.'

'Wipe it off, all your other lovers wouldn't be impressed. They haven't handed over their life savings to a man with lobster juice running down his chin.'

17

It was parents' evening. Roy Grace and Cleo stood in the large common room of St Christopher's school, Roy holding a cup of coffee and a saucer, Cleo a glass of mineral water. There were plates of biscuits all around, and parents with their children, none of whom they knew, engaged in conversations with the teachers. Bruno should have been here too, but he had refused to come.

Roy glanced at his watch: 7.30 p.m. They'd need to leave in fifteen minutes, for their dinner reservation at 8 p.m. The taxi would be waiting outside. So far, they'd talked to Bruno's geography, maths, biology and English teachers. None of them had been negative but, equally, none had been exactly glowing about the boy.

Out of the corner of his eye, Grace saw the headmaster, a smartly suited man in his fifties, tall and nearly bald, making a beeline for them.

'Mr and Mrs – or should I say, Detective Superintendent and Mrs Grace?'

'Either is fine, Mr Hartwell,' Cleo said pleasantly.

'Very good of you to come.'

'Well, of course,' Cleo replied. 'We're very interested to know how our son is doing, and whether he is fitting in?'

'Yes, well – I – we . . .' Hartwell hesitated, then moment-arily looked lost for words. 'Well,' he said, 'Bruno is a *nice* chap. No question. A very polite boy.' After another brief hesitation he added, rubbing his hands together as if soaping them, 'Quite independent, his teachers are finding.' He wrung his hands in silence for a few seconds. 'A little bit of a loner, perhaps. That's hardly surprising, given the back-ground, losing his mother – a lady who lived a rather – shall we say *chaotic* lifestyle – from what you told me?'

Roy Grace grimaced. 'I think that's a fair description of his mother, certainly in recent years, from what I've been able to establish.'

'Let's look at the facts. Bruno's having problems adjusting, which is hardly surprising. He's lost his mother, who wasn't the best role model to him, it would seem. He's moved country. From being an only child he's having to contend with a sibling, a stepmother, a father who was never previously part of his life and a new language and culture.'

'It's something we're very aware of,' Cleo said. 'Our hope is that by giving him a stable and loving home life, together with the caring nature of your school, things will become normalized for him.'

'Indeed.' Again he hesitated. 'There are still, unfortu-nately, some prejudices about Germany, and we have noticed a couple of instances of bullying, which of course we are doing our best to put a stop to, very firmly. Has he mentioned this?'

Grace looked at Cleo, who shook her head. 'No,' he said. 'Not a word.'

'I think he's dealing with it in his own way. And he is actually a very confident boy in some ways.'

'He is,' Cleo said.

The headmaster looked pensive. 'I had a private chat with him a couple of days ago and he did rather surprise me with something he said.' He seemed unsure he should now repeat it.

'Which was?' Cleo prompted.

Hartwell wrung his hands together again, now looking rather bemused. 'Well, I asked him a question I ask all the boys here of his age, to give me an idea of where their interests lie and to give their teachers direction. I asked your son if he had any thoughts on what he would like to do for a future career. For many of our pupils it is of course far too early. But Bruno was very definite – and, frankly, his response took me a little bit by surprise. Have you ever asked him this question?'

'No,' Grace said. 'What was it?'

'Well, he said that he would either like to become a chemist or a dictator.'

Grace smiled, briefly, until he saw the shocked expression on Cleo's face.

'A chemist or a *dictator*?' she said.

'Exactly those words.'

'Did he elaborate?' she asked. 'If a dictator, of which country?'

'I asked him that very question,' the headmaster said. 'He told me, quite solemnly, he hadn't yet decided, but that he favoured Venezuela.'

'Venezuela?' Grace said. 'Why Venezuela?'

'He said so that he could create similar conservation ethics to those of the Galapagos Islands and encourage other countries across the world to do the same. Pretty impressive thinking, wouldn't you say, for a lad of his age?'

'Is Venezuela a dictatorship?' Cleo asked.

'A good question,' the headmaster replied. 'It isn't, it's a democracy.' He looked bemused. 'I suspect Bruno is too young to understand the difference.'

Grace reflected for a while, saying nothing. He just hoped Ted Hartwell was right.

He wasn't sure.

18

Roy Grace and Cleo stopped for a meal at a country pub and restaurant on their way home, the Ginger Fox. Seated at a corner table, he got a gin and tonic and Cleo an elder-flower cordial, then they glanced at the menus.

When they had ordered – a starter of scallops with black pudding for Roy and lentil soup for Cleo, followed by roast cod for him and plaice for Cleo, and a large glass of Albarino for him – they began to discuss what Ted Hartwell had told them about Bruno.

'Is it normal for a ten-year-old to have ambitions to be a dictator?' Cleo asked him. 'I mean, did you have ambitions of world domination at his age?'

A basket of bread arrived. 'I'm not sure what clear ambitions I had, but certainly not that, no!'

'We know so little about the first ten years of his life, don't we?' she said.

He shrugged, tipping some oil then balsamic into a bowl. 'Virtually nothing.' He broke off a piece of bread, dipped it in the bowl and ate it, hungrily. 'I suppose—' He shrugged. 'We haven't really talked seriously with him. We put him in a nice school and hoped for the best – that he would make friends and settle in. It's not happening, is it?'

'No.' She twirled her glass in her hands. 'I've tried to talk to him, but apart from the time he talked to our neighbour about his Porsche, I've hardly seen him engage with anyone, let alone people of his own age. He doesn't seem interested in making friends – when he went to the football with your colleague Jason and his son, Stan, it didn't go well. We have to sit down and have a heart-to-heart with him. About his issues at school, about food – his likes and dislikes – and about, you know, just everyday life with us. He seems to like Noah and Humphrey, but that's about all. He's never had a father – at least from what we know. Maybe you can get through to him?'

Roy dipped another piece of bread into some olive oil. 'Sure, I'll try. I think we need to make a plan. Let's start with my trying to make a real effort with him. See how that goes?'

'Yep. He's got your genes in him, Roy. You have good person genes. Maybe you can mine those out of him.'

Their starters arrived, along with Roy's glass of wine. He realized, to his surprise, that he had finished his gin and tonic. And by the time they'd eaten their starters, he'd finished his glass of wine also. He ordered another.

'We'll prove him to be a nice kid,' Grace said. 'I'll do everything I can to work on him – or rather, with him.'

'I know you will.'

When his second Albarino arrived, they clinked glasses. 'To Bruno,' he said. Cleo gave him a strange, hopeful look.

19

'Toby, darling, you really do look quite dishy – for a fifty-eight-year-old, anyhow!' Paul Sibley ribbed his husband. He was seated at the kitchen table glancing through the images of him that Suzy Driver had found on her internet search and emailed him.

'I can't believe the bastards made me fifty-eight!' Toby Seward, wearing his kitchen apron bearing the legend *My sausage is on fire!*, was keeping a weather eye on the water heating in the saucepan. He took a sip of his glass of wine. '*Fifty-eight* – I mean, how dare they? It's outrageous, they've added ten years to my age!'

'Eleven, darling, actually – Norbert!'

'Yep, well, my birthday's next week so it will be then, Mr Pedantic.'

Paul poured himself another glass of wine from the bottle in the fridge and lit a cigarette. 'I do have to say, you look pretty good for your age.'

'Not funny!'

Paul clicked on the keyboard to bring up the profile photograph of Suzy Driver from the dating site. He studied the fifty-five-year-old for a few moments. 'Not bad, not bad at all for her age. Nice hair, attractive face! You know, I really ought to be jealous. All these lovely ladies fawning over you, craving your body. Eleven of them, no less.' He sighed. 'Well, I've got to admit they all have something in common!'

'Which is?'

'They have good taste.'

Toby blew him a kiss.

As steam started to rise from the pan, Toby's phone pinged with a text. Almost simultaneously, the laptop pinged, signalling an email. The text was from Suzy Driver.

Sent it!

He took the pan off the heat, hurried to the table and clicked to open the attachment. Both of them watched the screen. An image appeared.

Toby.

With his handsome, tanned features and short, salt-and-pepper hair he looked every inch the charmer. Then they heard a cultured, very correct female voice that Toby recognized instantly as Suzy Driver.

'Hello, Norbert, very nice to talk to you face to face, finally!'

The image of his face became a spider's web of cracks, then froze. Toby watched, fascinated, as in a staccato voice that was very definitely not his own, with an accent he couldn't place, the man replied, 'My darling, you look even more beautiful than in all your photographs. Wow, I must be the luckiest man on the planet!'

'You look very nice, too,' she replied.

Animated again, his head moving, his lips formed a smile. Then the screen froze, once more breaking into cracked, jagged segments.

'I apologize, my love. There seems to be a problem with the internet, I'm having to connect through my mobile phone.'

'That's OK, it's been nice to meet at last!'

Paul stabbed the *pause* button and turned to Toby. 'This is not your voice – it's not you speaking.'

Toby was staring in shock. 'No, it isn't.'

For the next twenty minutes, riveted, they watched the conversation, which became increasingly personal and fruity. Throughout, with the image constantly freezing or fragmenting, there had only been a couple of moments of actual lip-sync. In both, Toby Seward – or rather his avatar – had said, very sincerely, 'I love you'.

The same words he had used to the other ten women he was also flirting with, Suzy added in the accompanying text. Except, she explained, *he* wasn't a Norwegian geologist. He was a nineteen-year-old student in Ghana. A 'Sakawa Boy'. She urged Toby to look up 'Sakawa Boys' on the internet.

He googled the name and the two of them spent the next half-hour in complete astonishment.

'Well,' Paul said. 'I've heard of conmen, but this is like nothing, ever!'

What they were watching was little short of a university in Ghana for internet scammers. One pupil said, to camera, 'We are just taking back from the West what belongs to us.'

The Sakawa students were all from poor, underprivileged backgrounds. Sakawa was a mix of religious juju and modern internet technology. They were taught, in structured classes, the art of online fraud as well as arcane African rituals – which included animal sacrifice – to have a voodoo effect on their victims, ensuring the success of each fraud, of which there was a wide variety.

The majority involved preying on vulnerable, unsuspecting targets in the Western world, such as those placing lonely-hearts ads, as well as bank scams on the elderly and just about anyone else. The money they were making was beyond what would have once been these young men's wildest dreams. Now, on the financial and emotional ruins of lives in the Western world, they were buying mansions for their families, the latest designer clothes, and driving around in flash new Range Rovers, BMWs, Mercedes and Ferraris.

'Unbelievable!' Toby said.

'But can you blame them?' Paul replied.

'What do you mean? You think it's OK what they are doing?'

'I do, actually.' He lit another cigarette.

'How can you say that? It's outrageous.'

'It's outrageous how successive European countries raped their nation from the fifteenth century onwards, with England ultimately being the worst offender. This is their payback and good for them!'

'I can't believe what you're saying.'

'Read your history, darling.'

'That was governments, not innocent members of the public. How can that possibly justify these horrible scams today?'

'The British Empire spent five hundred years plundering the world. Is it any wonder it's such a mess today? Get real. I'm actually finding it quite amusing.'

Toby looked at him. 'I'm not sure someone who's just been conned out of their life savings would agree.'

'Mmmm, maybe not. Some of them are quite fit, though,' his husband said. 'Maybe we should have a holiday there?'

'Do you want a nice dinner tonight?' Toby said, then pointed at the saucepan. 'Or do you want me to tip that over your head?'

20

Electric gates opened in front of the Range Rover. Wrought iron, black, with gold spikes, between two pillars topped with stone acorns. The car drove through and up a long tree-lined avenue of a drive designed to impress. It didn't impress Tooth.

The incline increased sharply as they approached a turreted granite mansion in the style of a French chateau. A vista opened up to the left of the Atlantic Ocean and a lighthouse on a rock at the end of a causeway.

'Some view!' the driver said. 'Got great views everywhere on this island.'

Tooth said nothing.

Mr Barrey, who was his current employer, had summoned him. This was Mr Barrey's place. Good for him. Mr Barrey was a rich man, with the same kind of taste in showy grandeur as many rich men who had hired him in the past. One day Mr Barrey would have the honour of being one of the richest men in the graveyard of his choice. The showiest mausoleum. Black marble, carved angels and cherubs, that kind of shit. If Mr Barrey annoyed him, he could help speed up that process.

A shaven-headed bodyguard, all in black, with the physique of a walk-in safe and the charm of a mortuary slab, led them inside, followed by the driver. Tooth didn't care for the suits of armour in the hallway, nor the fine art on the walls, as he was led through the house.

Another bodyguard stood outside double doors, with a bulge in the left breast of his collarless jacket where his piece was. Tooth could have taken it off him in seconds, leaving both this one and his driver lying on the floor with broken spines, but he reminded himself that he needed the shitty money this job was paying – and the temporary refuge Mr Barrey had provided for him in Munich.

The one with the piece spoke to him in a foreign accent he couldn't place. 'When I take you inside, you do not look at Mr Barrey. Understand? No one is permitted to look at Mr Barrey. Nor do you look at the men in there with him. You do not look their faces. None of them. Yes?'

'Kind of them to spare me the sight because they're all so ugly, is that what you're saying?' Tooth retorted.

The man did not react.

But Tooth was only half jesting. He had done his research on his employer, which had not been hard – it never was. Steve Barrey had a badly disfigured face, despite two decades of regular plastic reconstructive surgery. His press release was that it had happened in a helicopter crash, but Tooth knew the truth. It was a revenge sulphuric acid attack by a Romanian lover who had found him in bed with her best friend.

'So where do I look?' he questioned.

'At the floor. If you look up, you dead.'

Tooth bristled. He allowed himself to be frisked by the gorilla guarding the doors, then led through into a room which was dimly lit, with blinds drawn. He heard the doors close behind him. The room smelled of smoke and all he could see, from his peripheral vision, was the tiny red glow of a cigarette in the far distance. He continued looking down, as he was bidden. Anger festered inside him. He thought about lighting up himself, but he needed to keep his hands free.

'So, my disobedient friend, Mr Tooth,' a man with an English accent said in a voice that was utterly devoid of charm. 'It is very good to finally meet you.'

Tooth did not reply.

The man he presumed was Steve Barrey continued. 'Mr Tooth, you are not in any position to negotiate terms with me. You know that you cannot return to your home in the Turks and Caicos without being arrested. You cannot return to the United States without either the FBI arresting you or the members of a crime family seizing you for what you did to your last employer there. And you are not exactly flavour of the month with the police in England.'

'But you want me to go there,' he answered, testily.

'Of course, because you know it so well, Mr Tooth. You are an excellent choice for the task. But first explain to me, why did you disobey my orders and fail to protect Lena Welch and warn off the Ghanaians?'

'I did not disobey your orders,' he said flatly, attempting to wriggle out of the truth that for the first time in his career he had failed in his mission. 'I was given wrong information. No one told me Copeland would have his shitbag accomplice, Ogwang, with him. Maybe you should choose your intelligence sources better in future.'

Barrey roared with laughter. When it subsided, Tooth saw a flare of light. Barrey had lit another cigarette. 'Of course. You are such a scary man, Mr Tooth. On your next job for me, Mrs Suzy Driver in Brighton, you will protect her from my former partner, Jules de Copeland, and his sidekick, Dunstan Ogwang. That's all. End of. Do you understand? You protect her in any way you need. But try not to kill these two. With the police there, killing people in England is never a good idea, as I think you have found out previously, no?'

Tooth risked a glance up. It wasn't much of a risk, in reality. He had one bodyguard behind him, two in front of him and Mr Barrey behind his desk. He didn't like being here.

'You are trying to look at me, are you not, Mr Tooth? You are curious to see my face. Do you not know about curiosity and the cat?'

Tooth felt the tension in the room. All his time as a sniper in the US military, where he'd had to remain hidden for days at a time, had taught him awareness of the slightest movement around him. He could feel the flunkey coming closer behind him. Saw the two in front taking an almost invisible step towards him.

He did not like that.

The gorilla was right behind him now and that was really not good. He focused, tuning out everything except his three potential enemies, two in front, one behind. What he was about to do would not endear him to his employer, but he really didn't care.

If he had been a scorpion he'd have denied them the pleasure of his company, he thought, by simply exiting the world with a flick of his tail. Instead he had other choices, and only one suited his current mood. He focused hard and fast. One, inches behind him. Two, a couple of yards in front.

Surprise was an element that had always served him well.

He arched his neck back, delivering a fierce reverse headbutt to the man's face, striking him in the nose, hearing the crunch. He sensed him reeling back, giving him enough space to fire out a powerful reverse kick to the man's liver, which sent him crashing to the floor in spasm. Then for good measure, with a quick glance, he brutally stamped on his head, knocking him unconscious.

As the two men guarding Barrey advanced towards him, Tooth ducked under a clumsily swung punch and put one guard in a choke hold, using him as a human shield against the punches being thrown by his colleague. As he felt the man he was choking go limp, he dropped him to the floor, leaving him one-on-one with the remaining guard. With clinical precision, Tooth threw out a violent low leg-kick and heard the faintly audible crack of snapping knee ligaments. As the guard fell to the floor, shrieking in pain, Tooth delivered a bludgeoning blow to the temple with his elbow.

Then, with the three guards out of it, he looked at the shadow of his employer. Or rather, at the shadow of the barrel of the Sig Sauer handgun his employer was holding.

'Nice gun, Mr Barrey,' he said. 'Why don't you shoot me?'

Barrey said nothing.

Tooth opened up his arms, presenting his small frame as the biggest target he could make himself into.

Barrey switched on his desk lamp, turning it towards Tooth, then illuminating the three unconscious men on the floor. 'What the hell have you done?'

'You want a detailed medical report or just the press release?'

'I would happily shoot you,' Barrey said. 'But, for the moment, you are useful to me.'

'I know that. You hired me on my reputation, because you knew I'd get the job done. But your bad intelligence is making everything a lot more complicated than you'd told me. That's why I feel a renegotiation of terms is due.'

'Really?'

'You see, Mr Barrey, I don't care if you shoot me. But I know you won't because your scuzzy empire is already starting to fall apart at the seams due to your bad choice of business partner. Didn't your mother – if you have one – ever tell you that you judge a man by his shoes? If you don't mind me saying, this Copeland guy was a bad choice, man! And, you know, some of your victims are not stupid people. All over the globe they are doing Google searches and rumbling the scams. You don't want to be found out, with all the millions you are raking in, do you? All those men and women who are salivating over you around the globe. Or over who they *think* is you or one of your dozens of phoney images. All those alter egos you have, male and female. The twenty-eight-year-old Colombian fashion model. The thirty-seven-year-old blonde sports trainer. The fifty-eight-year-old seismic shipping guy, soon to be a multi-millionaire. The sixty-two-year-old former US Marine.' Tooth lunged forward and twisted the desk lamp until the beam shone directly onto Barrey's ravaged face.

Barrey wore a Stetson tipped low. Wisps of fair hair protruded from either side of it. His eyes were bloodshot and his facial skin was all contorted into ridges and troughs, like a partially stretched and deflated balloon. He barely had any lips. His body was large, bordering on obese. He continued holding the gun, but the threat had gone.

'Does it make you happy to destroy lives, Mr Barrey?'

'Mr Tooth, after surviving my helicopter crash and spending the next two years on and off in the burns unit at Queen Victoria Hospital in Sussex, England, I had a lot of time to reflect. Do you want to know what I concluded?'

Tooth looked at him. 'What?'

'That life is a game. You win, you lose. Lots of people never understand that. But that's all it is, just a dumb game.

I'm helping all those poverty-stricken Ghanaian kids who never had a bean to count in the world, or an opportunity, because for five hundred years European colonialization enslaved them and plundered their country. Now, thanks to me, some of them are rich beyond their wildest dreams.'

'From scamming decent folk in the West and ruining their lives? And now your *trusted* business partner has scammed you. You want me to stop him, and his charming lieutenant, Dunstan Ogwang. The machete boys, right? You know their background, don't you? Boy soldiers. All they understand is brutality. Humanity's not in their make-up. That's why you brought them to Germany, right? To run your nasty little training camp.'

'*Academy*, Mr Tooth.'

'*Academy*. Right. *Academy* for internet scammers. You know, you have a very skewed moral compass.'

Tooth had visited the place, housed in the fortress of a hilltop *schloss* in Bavaria, the former residence of one of Adolf Hitler's least charming buddies, who'd been executed at Nuremberg. Steve Barrey had exploited Chancellor Angela Merkel's open-doors policy to asylum seekers, bringing in over one hundred so-called Sakawa Boys. He arranged coach trips to England for them to help them better understand the culture and hone their skills at targeting their victims.

'You're a good one to talk about moral compasses, Mr Tooth.'

'What we have to talk about, Mr Barrey, is renegotiation of contract terms. You hired me to protect Lena Welch against someone who was a threat to her. You told me to frighten them but you didn't tell me it was two psycho crazies. The *game* is changing. For your business to survive, you may need me to take out Copeland and Ogwang, correct?'

'That's about the size of it.'

'But not the size of my fee. Protection is one thing, eliminating is another. My fee is one million dollars per hit. Up front. You know where to find me. When I hear from my bank the payment's made, I'll start work. This Mrs Suzy Driver looks a nice lady. Your former business partner and his pal seem to think by applying the rules of violence they grew up by, they can protect their business. You're worried they're going to bring down their business – and yours, too, as collateral damage.'

'Mr Tooth, I have over one hundred decent kids from Ghana who've been studying hard to try to better themselves and make a nicer life for their families. Copeland's greed and violence is going to destroy all that.'

'You really believe your own press release, don't you, Mr Barrey? You glamorize your disfigurement and you try to justify your shitty business. *Steve Barrey, Saviour of the Dispossessed Third World.*'

'So give me your press release, Mr Tooth – I'm all ears.'

'Not really,' Tooth replied. 'Both yours were burned off by sulphuric acid.'

21

The baby-faced sixty-three-year-old, with a boyish mop of greying hair, looked more like a cuddly grandpa than a man with Ryukyu Kempo ninth-degree black-belt status. Sitting at a wobbly, beaten-metal table in the outside area of the Gas Monkey bar, on buzzy Duval Street in Florida's Key West, wearing his best seersucker coat and reeking of his best cologne, Matthew Sorokin swallowed the remains of his Space Dust IPA draught beer, watching the early-evening holidaymakers strolling by. Watching more keenly than ever. Waiting, increasingly impatiently, for his date to show up.

She was over an hour late.

He had a surprise for her tomorrow: he was taking her down to the Wounded Nature Organization's Coast Preservation Day. He thought she would be impressed by his concern for the environment and wildlife, and it would show her another side to him other than just being a cop.

Sorokin had put on weight in the seven years since he'd retired from the New York Police Homicide Department and moved down south. Actually, quite a lot of weight – thirty-five pounds of the stuff last time he'd looked at the scales. He knew what surplus weight looked like from the numerous autopsies he'd attended over the years. It didn't look pretty. It was a greasy yellow colour. Most of that weight he'd put on had come during the past two years, since leaving Rozanna – or rather, her leaving him.

She'd just woken up one morning and told him she hadn't liked him for at least ten years, and didn't want to be with him any more. Their two daughters had long left home and started their own families, and there was nothing left in their bankrupt relationship, she had said, except for them to grow old hating each other more and more.

Rozanna was a very private person, who had, throughout their long marriage, kept a lot to herself. Including the serial affairs she'd been having, which he'd only discovered when he took her cell phone to work by mistake, one day, instead of his own – dumbly, they had the same model and cover. It had rung soon after he'd left their house in Queens and he'd answered it to hear a male voice saying, 'OK, babe, I can see on Friend Finder you've left home. I'm so horny today. I'll be at the hotel in forty. Are you wet?'

'Not really,' Matt had replied. 'This is her husband, want me to ask her to take a shower?'

He liked to imagine the guy at the other end had shat his pants. The noise he had made had sure sounded that way.

For all her faults, Rozanna was a brilliant cook, and aware of just what rubbish cops ate most of the time when on duty, she had always done her best to ensure they both ate healthily. At fifty-five, she still had a terrific figure. And thanks to her discipline over food, throughout their married life he'd remained in trim shape, with virtually no middle-age spread at all.

All that had now gone out of the window – or, more accurately, into his belly and then elsewhere around his body. He had no idea how to cook and wasn't even much good at heating meals up in the microwave. He always forgot to remove the foil or the lid, ending up with the oven looking like Old Sparky, or the food exploding. It was because he was impatient and could never be bothered reading the instructions, he knew. But hey, at sixty-three years old, if you hadn't discovered your limitations, you weren't ever going to. For Matt Sorokin, a kitchen was forever going to remain a place where he cooled beers in a refrigerator, unwrapped and ate takeaways, and opened tins for his surly cat that had come with him because Rozanna didn't like the creature.

Most of those extra thirty-five pounds were from burgers and pizzas, and bingeing on the French fries that Rozanna had never allowed in the house. He didn't like all this weight – it felt like he was walking around with hammers sewn inside his skin, and he had to buy bigger pants. On top of that, as his weight had increased, he realized he was no longer as fit as he had once been. He still kept up his Okinawan karate, which he had been practising for just short of fifty years. But he was starting to find some of the youngsters he was up against in the gym a struggle these days.

One of his former NYPD buddies, Detective Investigator Pat Lanigan, had been down here last summer and cheekily ribbed him that he looked like he had gone to seed.

Huh.

But the barb had prompted him into action. After several years of doing little except fishing, hunting duck and drinking beer on the deck of his condo, bored out of his mind, he had joined the Hernando County Sheriff's office as an unpaid Reserve Deputy. Once more with a badge and a gun, he'd felt he had his life back. And within twelve months he'd made himself indispensable to the Sheriff by solving two cold cases, the first a serial rapist who targeted older women and the second a murdered schoolgirl.

Then, eight months ago, another old buddy, Gerald Ronson, a former New York firefighter he'd met during the aftermath of 9/11, and who had since moved to Minnesota, came to visit with his new wife, a delightful lady whom he had met through an online dating agency. Gerry had convinced Matt that he should try it, too. So he had, and met the woman, online, he was convinced he was going to marry.

Evelyne Desota.

A Brazilian restaurant manager who was from São Paulo, she had been left in financial ruin by her rat of a husband who'd deserted her. For the past five months she'd been stuck back in her home city, dealing with family problems. Her mother, suffering from cancer, had been unable to afford the medication she needed, so he'd helped get her decent treatment. He'd also helped out her brother and his wife – her brother had lost his job soon after having their first baby, Evelyne had sobbed, telling him they were destitute. Then Evelyne had been in a bad car wreck, and he'd funded her hospital bills and bought her a new car. But Matt didn't mind. Hey, what was a loan of ninety thousand bucks – his fun money – to help this amazing lady. She was going to pay it all back, and interest too, but he'd generously told her he would not accept any interest.

And, finally, they were going to meet. Tonight!

He just hoped with all his heart that when she saw him she wasn't going to be disappointed – he'd fibbed a bit with his photograph, posting one of himself some years back when he'd been a lot leaner and just a little younger – by ten years. But, hey, he would charm her. He was pretty good at that. Slipping his hand inside the front of his jacket, he pinched a roll of flesh on his stomach. It wasn't too bad. He'd managed to shed three pounds this past week. More to come. Just had to remember to hold his tummy in tight when he stood up to greet her.

One thing that rather surprised him was her choice of venue for their first date. She'd told him this was her favourite bar on the planet, that it served the best cocktails and was the coolest – uber-coolest – place ever.

Right. Yeah. This was a bar that served a range of beers, but there was nothing cool about it, other than the name, in his view.

When had she last been here? Had she gotten the name wrong? Was there some other place here in Key West where she was sat, drinking a Martini, waiting for him?

He looked at his watch. One hour and ten minutes late now. He texted her, for the second time since he had arrived from his home in Brooksville, Hernando County – 'Home of the tangerine!' – a six-hour drive. But worth every damned mile for what lay ahead.

Here waiting for you, craving you, my honey-bunch!

Then he left his perch, ambled over to the bar and ordered a second Space Dust, feeling pleasantly woozy, but unpleasantly anxious. Potent beer at 8.5 per cent, so he needed to be careful, but at the same time he needed the courage it gave him. This was, truth be known, his first date in over forty-five years, since he had first taken Rozanna to the prom.

As he headed back to his table, the calm of the early evening was shattered by the reverb of a bunch of tattooed, mostly shaven-headed beefcakes in singlets, throbbing by on Harleys, all thinking they looked pretty macho.

'Dickheads,' he murmured under his breath, and checked his phone. No response.

Evelyne Desota. What a babe. So sweet. He loved how much she cared about her family. So much more concerned than Rozanna had ever been. And what a night lay ahead! He'd blown a wad on the ocean-view honeymoon suite at the Hyatt Centric. Champagne on ice was waiting up there. He'd blown another wad on filling the suite with flowers. Petals on the bed read out, *Evelyne, I love you!*

He couldn't wait to see her face when she walked in there.

He flipped down through the recent texts from her, the last one 12.02 p.m.

> **Matt, I cannot wait, finally to be in your arms! Tonight! At last.**

> **My darling, my love, Matt. I'm not going to be able to keep my hands off you for long ;-)**

> **God, why didn't you and I meet years ago? My heart is exploding to meet you, finally! XXXXX**

His phone pinged.

He looked down, hopefully. The display had a message in red below the one he had sent a few minutes ago.

Not Delivered

He tried again.

Almost instantly the same message appeared.

Not Delivered

Some of his recent casework had involved internet fraud, and he'd familiarized himself with all the workings of computers and phones. Familiarized himself enough to understand what was happening.

She had blocked him.

22

Jack Roberts had been at his desk, in his comfortable office, since 6 a.m., as he was most days. A tall, muscular man in his forties, with a shiny head and a light beard, he exuded natural charm which always inspired confidence in his clients. But he could be tough as nails at the flick of a switch, when he needed to be.

He retained the same enthusiasm for his work as he had as a youngster, when his dad had taken him to see *The Spy Who Loved Me*. He had been immediately captivated by James Bond, and determined, one day, to be like him.

At the age of twenty-one he began working for a firm that traced people, and four years later started his own private investigation agency, Global Investigations. His company, based in a modern low-rise office block, offered a range of services including carrying out background checks, tracing missing persons, surveillance of suspected unfaithful spouses and investigating fraud. During the past few years, much of their business was with online scamming, and increasingly with the new menace of so-called 'romance fraud'.

With three beautiful daughters and a wife he still adored every bit as much as when they had first married, he loved the photographs of his family on his desk. They gave him an often-needed reassurance of normality in what seemed to him to be an increasingly toxic world – all the more so with the shameless targeting of the vulnerable and elderly by online predators.

He liked the early morning, the sense of being ahead of the world. In the silence of his company's otherwise empty first-floor office suite with a view across the quiet high street, he caught up on his emails and the overnight reports filed by his field agents. He was smiling as he read through a surveillance report emailed from one of his agents.

The man had spent two days concealed in a tree, in pelting rain, watching a secluded cottage in Dorset, the suspected illicit love nest of a couple having an affair. It reminded Jack of a case early on in his career. He had spent three days concealed in a hedge bordering a lay-by, watching and photographing a man who had been claiming disability benefits, who was out every day, digging in his cottage garden. Jack had worn his ghillie camouflage suit to reduce the chances of being spotted. Around midnight on the first day a car had pulled into the lay-by, and a man got out and walked straight towards him. Convinced he had been spotted, he braced himself. Instead the stranger unzipped his flies, urinated on him, blissfully unaware of his presence, and drove off.

Some parts of being out in the field he really did not miss, he reflected.

'Good morning, Jack, what are you looking so cheerful about?' his long-standing secretary asked, breezing into the room.

He decided she might take it the wrong way if he said, 'Being peed on,' and instead simply replied, 'Oh, nothing, Lucy.'

'Your 8.30's here.'

He glanced at his calendar on his screen. 'Elizabeth Foster? Romance fraud issue?'

'That's her.'

'Fine, show her in.'

He stood up as a smartly dressed fair-haired woman in her mid-thirties entered. She was a lot younger than most victims of romance fraud, who were more usually in their fifties and upwards. He shook her hand, ushered her to the black leather sofa in front of his desk, then sat down in a chair beside her and picked up a lined pad and a pen. It always put his clients at ease to sit beside them rather than the more confrontational position of facing them. 'Would you like some tea or coffee, Ms – Mrs – Foster?'

'Liz is fine – and just some water would be good, thank you.'

He gave the instruction through the intercom, then asked her if she would be OK with him recording the interview. She was. He placed the recorder on the coffee table in front of her. 'So, Liz, how can I help you?'

Wringing her hands nervously, she said, 'My mother is being conned blind by someone she met a few months ago on an internet dating site, and won't believe the man's not real. She's in thrall to him. She's already paid some cash and I'm scared stiff he'll keep going until he's bled her dry and she's lost her home and everything.'

It was an all-too familiar story. 'Cat-fishing', the Americans called it. He did his best to put her at ease, mentally adding that she was probably worried about her inheritance, too. 'OK, can you tell me about your mother – start from the beginning.'

She paused, as if gathering her thoughts. 'Her name is Lynda Merrill. She's fifty-nine and was totally devoted to my – our – father, who died four years ago after a horrible time with early-onset dementia. He worked in the Diplomatic Service and we lived abroad, moving around for much of our lives – my two brothers and I. When he retired, my parents came back to England and settled in Surrey, just outside Godalming, near Guildford. When he became ill they moved to Hove, to be near myself and my husband.'

Jack jotted down a note.

'Dad did everything, taking care of all the bills, and Mum was totally dependent on him. She was lost for a long while after he died and they didn't have many friends here. Both my brothers live abroad – one in California and the other in Australia – so it sort of fell to myself and my husband, Don, to take care of her. She wasn't that tech-savvy, so Don pretty much taught her how to use her computer for more than just emails and changed her old phone for a smart one. The next thing I knew was that she very excitedly told me she'd joined an online dating agency. A recently widowed member of her book group had told her about a wonderful man she'd met online. So Mother decided to join one.' She hesitated.

'As a lot of single people do,' Jack encouraged.

'Absolutely. Next thing, she told me she'd met someone. At first I was delighted – I thought he was probably a retired professional, someone like Dad, until one day I went round to the house and saw a picture of this – er – fellow – on her computer screen. A very good-looking man, younger than my mum, whose name, she told me, was Richie Griffiths.'

'Richie Griffiths?'

'Yes. I discovered that what she'd done was put up a photo of me, because the earlier ones of her looked out of date – we looked very similar when she was my age. I told her that the moment they met, he was going to realize she had lied.'

'How did she respond?'

'She got angry with me and told me I was being *ageist*. That what did an age gap matter? She said she'd read about a sixty-nine-year-old man in Holland who'd gone to court saying his doctor had told him he had the body of a forty-nine-year-old, so that's what he wanted to change his age to. He argued that if you could change your name or your sex, then you could change your age – he wanted to be twenty years younger to help his chances of getting a job. Mum said that when they met she knew Richie would forgive her little white lie. She said they were madly in love and that she slept with his photo under her pillow.'

'OK, so then what happened?' Jack prompted.

'Well, I help out with her paperwork – I go over there every week. A couple of months or so ago I opened a bank statement and saw a whole bunch of payments to an account in Munich. Small at first – £250. Then £500. Then £800. Then £2,000. I asked her about them. My mother told me that Richie Griffiths was a film-maker, originally from England, and married to a German actress in Munich. They'd recently split up and were going through an acrimonious divorce, and he'd had his bank account frozen by a German lawyer. He was strapped for cash and if she could help him out he would pay her back when he got his life sorted out. I wasn't happy about this, obviously.'

'It's a familiar kind of pattern.'

'Next time I visited her, I was alarmed to see a much bigger payment, £15,000. This man had told her his sister had been diagnosed with ovarian cancer and needed immediate treatment. He was in despair and could she lend him the money to pay for her treatment until he got his affairs sorted out? Then yesterday morning I went over to her and she told me he'd offered her a great investment. His marital home, in the best area of Munich, was worth a lot more than his ex-wife was claiming from him. If my mother loaned him the money to buy out his wife's share of their home, they would both make a killing when he sold it.'

'How much is the loan he's asking for?'

'In the region of £450,000.'

Roberts whistled. 'Does she have that amount in cash available?'

'She has, invested. Luckily it's going to take a while for her to get all the money because much of it is in bonds. I've told her she needs to get her solicitor to make sure it's all done correctly with this fellow – hoping any lawyer would realize pretty quickly it's a con. I've spoken to her bank manager. She was sympathetic but said she was powerless to stop her. But she said she would speak to her to try to dissuade her. What is even more alarming is that the manager told me, in confidence, that my mother had enquired about remortgaging her house. When she told Mother that she was unlikely to get a mortgage due to her lack of income, my mother said she had been looking into equity-release plans. So this Richie – whoever he might be – is clearly not going to stop at £450,000. That's when I decided I needed urgent help and found you, on the internet. You seem to be specializing in this kind of fraud – if that's what this is.'

'You did the right thing,' Jack Roberts reassured her. 'When I got your message, via my secretary, I did some background checks on this "Richie Griffiths" and found out he's a pretty busy guy out on the internet. At least half a dozen different ladies are all in love with him – and several of them in the process of helping him buy his ex-wife out of their property.' He grimaced. 'Not bad for someone who doesn't actually exist.'

23

Matt Sorokin sat on a huge sofa in his hotel suite, feeling small and lost. He stared, blankly, at the ghost of himself in the window that stared back at him, and at the darkness of the night and ocean beyond. Darkness that felt like it was leaking in through the glass and seeping deep into every vein and pore of his body.

His brain was wired. His stomach felt hollowed out. Four a.m.

He was a long way from sleep. A long way from anything, oh God, from what this night should have been.

He reached over and grabbed his wallet. Flipped it open and stared at the photograph. Evelyne's beautiful face, with her big, trusting eyes, the laughter creases around her mouth, her long, silky dark hair. Half his age. *Punching above his weight*, a couple of buddies back at the Sheriff's office had ribbed him. But they were just jealous – any guy would be when they saw that picture. And there were plenty, way more sexy photographs that she'd sent him on their private Facebook link. Some wickedly so indeed, driving him wild with anticipation!

This was to have been the night of his dreams. Sweeping into his arms the woman of his dreams.

Instead he sat alone in the wreckage of a train crash.

Surrounded by vases of flowers. Big, vibrantly coloured and insanely expensive flowers. Thinking what a close call he'd had to giving her more money. She'd tried to get him to lend her over half a million bucks, ostensibly to buy out her husband's share of their house in São Paulo. But it still hurt to lose ninety thousand bucks. What his NYPD pal Pat Lanigan called his *fun money*.

Money he'd put aside to help his brother, who was unable to walk because of a muscle-wasting disease, to make his home more wheelchair friendly. Money he was going to use to help his granddaughter rent premises for her new fashion business. And the rest he'd been going to spend enjoying life with Evelyne.

Gone.

Evelyne and the money? Not possible.

He looked at his phone, as he did every few minutes. In the forlorn, fading hope that . . . That . . . ?

He was too gutted to open the champagne in the fridge – and toast what? Instead he was drinking his way steadily through the contents of the minibar. The bourbons. Then the Scotch. The gin. And now he was on the vodka.

On the screen of his laptop beside him was the real estate agent's brochure of the white, colonial-looking house. Evelyne Desota's home. He had nearly taken out a mortgage to help her buy out her husband's share.

Except, from an exhaustive trawl of the internet an hour or so back, it had become evident the real estate agency did not exist.

It was all an elaborate scam and he had been suckered in.

How?

How had he been such a fool?

At least he'd not been a complete idiot and given her all

the money. But even so, he felt a raw, ulcerous pain in his stomach. He was sixty-three. He'd had it all figured out. Maybe twenty years of active life left if he was lucky and, boy, had he been planning to make each one of those years count – even more so in the five months since beautiful Evelyne Desota had responded to his advert on findMefindYou.net.

He'd learned very early on in his career as a cop never to trust anyone and to check every story. How had he allowed himself to blindly believe Evelyne? To send her money without even a signed piece of paper between them?

Because he had trusted her – or maybe it was his dick that had trusted her. All those Facebook messages. Texts all day long and late into the night, telling him how much she loved him. The long and often very intense phone conversations. Ever since she had come into his life he'd been fired with a zest he never knew was in him.

The woman he was certain he would cherish to the ends of the earth. In his dreams.

Where was she now? Who was she?

He'd done a reverse Google search on her. The one he should have done the moment he'd first seen her, when he'd have found out right away she wasn't a restaurant manager at all. Her image was on the website of a Brazilian escort agency, under a different name. He recognized her from the erotic pose; the exact same photograph she had sent him a while back.

He'd found her five more times, under five more different names, on other dating websites.

His eyes were watering with tiredness, with sadness, with anger. Anger at himself.

You dumb asshole.

24

'That's him,' Elizabeth Foster said, peering over Jack Roberts's shoulder at the screen on his desk. At the face of a handsome, amiable-looking man with short silver hair. He was smartly dressed in a suit jacket, shirt and tie.

His profile gave him as a Munich-based film producer, formerly from England.

'You're sure, Liz?'

'Positive.'

'I looked him up on the IMDb – the Internet movie database which lists everyone in the world in the movie business,' Roberts said. 'The only Richard Griffiths listed is the chubby actor best known for his role in the *Harry Potter* films – who died in 2013.

'Take a look at this,' he continued. He tapped his keyboard and another image of Toby Seward appeared, this time in military uniform. His profile gave him as Colonel Rob Cohen, aged forty-seven.

Elizabeth Foster narrowed her eyes.

'Same fellow?' Jack Roberts asked.

'I think so. Yes.'

He tapped the keys again and another image of the same man appeared, this time in a British Airways pilot's uniform, complete with cap. This profile was of a Peter Olins, fifty-one, airline captain.

Roberts looked over his shoulder. 'Want to see any more of this busy chap? He has plenty of other different personas.'

'How?'

'Photoshop?' He shrugged.

'Can you give me the links – maybe that will help convince Mother.'

'Of course.'

'So, who is the real identity? Which one of these?'

'I'm guessing it's Colonel Rob Cohen. But that's just a hunch.'

'And presumably he has no knowledge of this?'

'I doubt it. When they target ladies, these scammers tend to pick military types because they look trustworthy. Look at him, he seems a regular guy, decent and upright.'

They went back over to the sofa and sat down again.

'I want to get that money back for her, Mr Roberts. My mother's not a wealthy woman – by today's standards. When my father died he left her the house mortgage free and just under half a million pounds in cash and stocks and shares. It's a nice house, a semi, close to Hove seafront, but it's not a mansion. That money, combined with her state pension, would have enabled her to live comfortably – she's never been an extravagant woman.' She hesitated and smiled, nervously. 'She's pretty thrifty by nature. She's always looked for a deal when she's been food shopping, buying stuff at the end of its sell-by date and hunting down the cheapest supermarket offers. In the past few years she's done most of her grocery shopping at Lidl, and she's always proud of her bargains. Only a couple of months ago she phoned me, excitedly, to tell me about an amazing offer Lidl had on prawns. What she's doing now is so out of character. I need to somehow convince her of what is really happening here. Can you help me do that?'

'Liz, I'd love to tell you I could, but I don't want you throwing good money after bad.'

'I don't care what it costs, Mr Roberts. My husband's a very successful businessman, with deep pockets. He's as angry as I am. I've come to you because I've been told you are the best in this field. Don and I don't care what it costs or what it takes, I want to find the bastard – or bastards – behind this and teach them a lesson they will never forget.'

He gave her a sardonic look. 'I like your spirit, Liz. And I never like to turn down business or a challenge. But before my charge clock starts ticking you need to be aware just how slim the chances of success are. Most of the master-minds behind these scams operate from jurisdictions that aren't easy for our police forces to get any help from. Ghana, Nigeria and Eastern Europe are the three most common ones. They hide behind firewalls in the dark web. Any money that's sent to them is either spent almost right away or placed in accounts in countries – admittedly getting fewer these days – that aren't willing to hand over information to police authorities.'

'So a shitty little conman in one of these countries can screw my mother – and anyone else in the Western world – out of every penny, and none of our law-enforcement agencies can do a damned thing about it? Is that what you are saying?'

'Not for want of trying, but in a nutshell, yes.'

'Well, I'm going to do something about it. Are you in or out?'

Roberts looked back at her confidently. 'I'm in.'

25

Monday 1 October

DS Sally Medlock looked around the room at the members of the recently formed Financial Crimes Safeguarding Team. It had been her initiative to set it up, with the enthusiastic support of the Chief Constable and Police and Crime Commissioner, to take new approaches in guarding the vulnerable – and sometimes just plain gullible – against the myriad predators lurking out there in the digital sewers.

In 2005 romance fraud accounted for just seven per cent of all financial scams perpetrated in the UK. Today it was close to eighty per cent. Sums varied from a few thousand pounds up to a staggering four and a half million. And romance fraud was just one area of the growing menace of financial crime.

The situation had become so serious they now had a daily management meeting, Monday to Friday. Seven officers, a mixture of detectives and uniform, sat around the table in the first-floor conference room at Police Headquarters in Lewes. They were housed, along with Major Crime, in one of the former dormitory buildings at the rear of the HQ campus, directly above Detective Superintendent Roy Grace's office.

'Safeguarding' was a vital but largely unseen duty carried out by British police forces. Monitoring and protecting people who were suffering domestic abuse. Children who were victims of sexual abuse. Young people from overseas, mostly Nigeria, Romania and Albania, who were brought over as slaves and forced into being sex workers or working in other jobs for a pittance. And more recently people who were under observation as victims of internet fraud – many of whom were elderly.

A wide number of both men and women of all ages, but mostly over forty, were currently being targeted by perpetrators of romance fraud. This new, specialist unit, expensive to run, was performing a crucial service, carrying out safeguarding assessments, along with social workers, and working with financial institutions to identify victims – and potential victims – and work with them and their families to try to prevent them parting with their cash.

Many of the victims were elderly and vulnerable with mental health issues, such as dementia and other age-related illnesses. Among the questions facing the team was whether targeted victims had the capacity to make informed decisions or were they just making unwise choices. Increasingly the police were being helped by the staff of money services bureaux, post offices and supermarket banks. There were protocols in place involving all high-street banks and post offices on reporting suspicious transactions. There were likely to be few good reasons, in this team's view, for any elderly Sussex resident to be sending large sums of cash to Ghana or Nigeria.

The exponential growth of telephone and online fraud had resulted in a step change for the police. In the past, policing policy had been 'let's go after the offender'. But with romance fraud, in particular, mostly originating overseas, there were simply not the resources to send officers out to those countries. Too often police forces would have to close their files, marked 'Undetected'. It was Sussex Police's Operation Signature that had led the way forward.

The biggest task for the Safeguarding Team was to try to persuade individuals to take a step back and look at the evidence and reality of the situation. One recent such fraud had suckered in a staggering thirty-seven women around the globe – three of whom were in Sussex, their ages ranging from sixty-five to eighty-nine. It was easy for the fraudsters to give a plausible story. All of the women were in love with a hunk of a tattooed bike-fanatic US soldier, whom they thought was in love with them. It had been relatively easy to persuade the three Sussex victims simply by showing them the source photograph of the soldier.

One of the main reasons for victims not coming forward, the team knew, was embarrassment. Many of the victims were smart, professional or former professional people who were supposed to know what they were doing. It was hard for a worldly-wise person, who had handed over every penny they had, to admit this to friends and family. Just as it was equally hard for police officers to have to break the news to someone that their internet lover, who had spent a year rinsing them, did not actually exist.

Behind DS Medlock was a large monitor on which, in turn, examples of the latest sophisticated banking scams identified by the team's researchers appeared. Emails purporting to be from the high-street bank HSBC warning the recipient their online account was being hacked and to immediately enter their password and change it, along with all other details. Another, similar, from Apple. And another, seemingly from their own Sussex Police Financial Crimes Unit, looking totally authentic, until two spelling errors were pointed out along with the bogus email address, carefully masked.

Next, the people currently on their radar appeared, with

a few lines of background. As each one came on the screen, the DS asked her team for any updates.

After twenty minutes of going through the list, they reached the romance fraud category, and a photograph of a handsome, distinguished-looking silver-haired man in his late fifties appeared. His name, below the image, read Major John (Johnny) Fordwater. Financial Crimes Safeguarding Officer DC Helen Searle, a woman in her thirties, raised an arm on which were several chunky bracelets. 'A bit of a sad story here, boss, I'm afraid. His name first came to our attention two months ago, during Intel's surveillance of Sakawa Boy social media traffic from Ghana. I actually went to see Major Fordwater myself to try to convince him that he was the victim of fraudsters, but he was, frankly, very rude to me, and refused to believe me. Unfortunately, at that time, I didn't have the photographic evidence that might have convinced him. So far as he was concerned he was very much in love with a German lady called Ingrid Ostermann, and we were mistaken. Subsequently he has been interviewed twice by DS Potting and DC Wilde, and I understand he has now been presented with the evidence and has accepted the situation – at least I hope he has. He's paid out about £400,000.'

There was a gasp from the room.

'Four hundred thousand?' DS Jon Exton said. He had been seconded from Major Crime because he had previously been in banking before joining the police.

'Correct, Jon,' Searle said. 'He's in despair. I understand he faces losing his home. He is now cooperating with us.'

The next photograph and name appeared, 'Betty Ward'. Below was a brief description. Another officer raised his hand – DC Kevin Hall, also seconded to the team from Major Crime.

'Guv, we've had a lot of help on this one from Tesco's Service Bureau. This is an elderly widow in Brighton, who struggles to get out of an armchair, a blue-rinse granny who is convinced she is in love with the man in the next image and sleeps with a photograph of him beside her.' He pointed at the screen and everyone in the room turned towards it.

The image was of a young black man with a six-pack and a smiling face, naked apart from a pair of skimpy budgie-smugglers that left little to the imagination.

'He has been telling Betty for several months that he cannot wait to come to England and make love to her. I won't go into the graphic details of all the sexual things he's told her he plans to do with her. But what I can say is that this lady can only walk with the aid of a Zimmer and, fair play to her, the photographs she's posted of herself to him don't exactly make her out to be a Page Three girl.'

As photographs appeared of a frail-looking lady in her finery, there were a few raised eyebrows.

Hall went on. 'A member of staff at Tesco in Shoreham contacted us to say they had concerns. This lady, Betty Ward, had sent two MoneyGrams to Ghana, the first to a "Mickey Mouse", the second to a "Michael Jackson".'

The sniggers turned into a ripple of uncomfortable laughter.

'Seriously,' Hall said, 'this guy, whoever he is, convinced her it is just a loan to help with his hospital bills after a car accident, and to pay for treatment for his mother who has cancer. He told her to send the money to these names, otherwise the government would take fifty per cent of it in tax. And she believed him. She's totally besotted with him. She's sent him £27,000 to date. Tesco have agreed not to process any more of her MoneyGrams and to let me know if she shows up again wanting to send another. I've also alerted Western Union and all the other MoneyGram service bureaux in the area.'

Medlock thanked him and moved on to the next victim on their radar. The name 'Ralph Beresford' appeared. 'This is a new one.'

'Yes, ma'am,' a young DC from Brighton, Preena Gadher, said. 'A widower, reported by his daughter who is very concerned. Mr Beresford is seventy-seven, a retired chartered accountant, and has early-stage dementia. She visits her father every week and noticed two days ago that he had an image of, shall we say, a somewhat curvy woman on his computer screen. When she asked him who it was he very proudly said it was his new girlfriend, that she was Romanian and he'd met her on the internet three months previously. He told her the poor woman was in trouble, with nowhere to turn to, and he was helping her to get her life straight. The daughter has access to his computer and checked out his bank. Turns out over the past three months he's been cashing in stocks and shares, buying Bitcoins and making substantial transactions with them.'

'How substantial?' Sally Medlock asked.

'The biggest was £250,000.'

'Is he loaded, Preena?'

'No, but he's comfortably off – or was. He's now in the process of doing one of those equity-release schemes on his house.'

'And the daughter sees her inheritance vanishing down the khazi,' Exton said.

'Along with all his plans for a comfortable old age,' Gadher responded. 'The Romanian woman in question, Sorina Vasile, spun a story to Mr Beresford about her brother being wrongly accused of murder and banged up in a terrible jail. She asked if Beresford would loan the bail money, which of course he would get back.'

'Of course,' Medlock said.

'I've done some background checks with Interpol and with the British Embassy in Bucharest and there is no record of this supposed brother at all. I believe she is using a false name, as well.'

'What actions are you taking?' Medlock asked.

'I've contacted Adult Social Care. I've also spoken to his bank manager, but with all the new data protection regulation – the GDPR – it's not easy to intervene there. The manager is sympathetic and aware of the situation, but says that beyond warning his client that the money may not be going to whom he thinks, there is nothing he can do to stop him. I think the daughter's taken more dramatic intervention – she's changed the password on his computer, effectively locking him out, and hidden his chequebook. I'll know more after social services have visited him.'

Sally thanked her and they moved on. A photograph of a neat-looking man in his late thirties in a business suit came up. The name beneath read 'John Southern'.

DS Exton raised a hand. 'I'm dealing with this one, and there seem to be a growing number of cases like this coming to us, boss,' he said. 'It's a bit sad. Southern was put through to me and asked to see me in confidence. He's a Brighton solicitor, married with three kids. For whatever reason, he signed on to an internet dating agency for married people seeking affairs. He met a lady who told him she was also married and their exchanges, over a few weeks, became increasingly – er – fruity.'

The very strait-laced detective blushed then went on. 'She started sending him pictures of herself in a state of undress and asked him to reciprocate. Which he did. Then she asked him to show her pictures of his – er, member – aroused.'

'Member of Parliament, would that be?' Kevin Hall quizzed. Several of the team laughed.

'It then progressed further. She sent him a video of herself masturbating and asked him to send her one of him doing the same. Which, unfortunately, he did – very foolishly, he now realizes. The next thing that happened was her threatening to expose him on Facebook to all his followers. To circulate the video. His followers included his wife and three children. She started with a demand for £5,000, which he paid. Then one for £10,000. It was followed by one for £25,000. He's not a wealthy guy, he's only a junior partner, but he managed to find and send the money. But now he's had a demand for £100,000 and that's when he contacted us – fortunately. The only way he could raise this would be by remortgaging his house – which couldn't happen without his wife consenting.'

'What have you advised him, Jon?'

'I've told him to string her along for the moment, tell her – whoever *her* is – or the people behind her, more likely – that it will take him time to raise the money.'

'I think this is definitely one for Digital Forensics,' Sally Medlock said. 'But he's going to have to take the risk of the threat being carried out.'

'He's petrified of it getting out there.'

'He shouldn't be such a wanker!' Kevin Hall said.

'Watch out, Kevin,' DC Charlotte Williams said. 'You're sounding like Norman Potting!'

Next, a photograph of a striking woman in her mid-fifties with long dark hair and a provocative expression appeared. The name beneath was 'Suzy Driver'.

Williams signalled to the DS.

'Yes, Charlotte?'

'This is an interesting one, ma'am. Mrs Driver is a fifty-five-year-old wealthy widow in the city – her late husband was an antiques dealer. She's sussed that she's being scammed and has done quite a lot of work checking out her scammer on the internet, before contacting us. I interviewed her at her home. She has challenged her apparent "lover" to meet her in person. The email trails that Intel have come up with point to Germany.'

'Germany again?' Sally Medlock said. 'This is getting interesting, a new area for us. Historically we have mostly Ghana, Nigeria and Eastern Europe.'

'Mrs Driver's been very cooperative,' Charlotte Williams said. 'Fortunately, she's not parted with any money – it was the request for a loan that triggered her suspicions.'

Unlike most of our victims, the DS rued, privately. 'What's the latest with her?'

'Well, she's given us the name of her scammer, a Dr Norbert Petersen, who claims to be a Norwegian geologist, residing in Oslo. Digital Forensics have found his name, and same identity, on five European internet dating sites. He's using images of a gay Brighton man, Toby Seward, a professional motivational speaker married to an architect, Paul Sibley. Digital Forensics are currently working on trying to uncover his real identity with the lady's help. Mrs Driver has been very smart.'

'In what way?'

'She's keeping up the pretence to Petersen. Although she's told us she is certain the man's ID is phoney, she's pretending to him that she accepts his explanation, and that she is going to arrange the money – the £20,000 loan he's asked to borrow for his grandmother's hospital bills.'

'Brilliant!' Medlock said. 'How long can she keep up the pretence?'

'I think for a while. She has a daughter in Melbourne who's due to give birth to her first grandson and she's booked on a flight next weekend to go out to stay with them for a few weeks. Petersen has been very clever too. He told her he was coming to England to see her. When she replied that she was going to Australia for a while, he begged her to stay on in the UK for a bit longer. She said she'd bought a non-refundable air ticket and he immediately offered to reimburse her if she cancelled it.'

'What would happen if she called his bluff, Charlotte?' DS Exton asked.

'He'd probably come up with one of the excuses they all use,' said DS Phil Taylor, who had headed the fledgling former High-Tech Crime Unit some years back. 'A car crash on the way to the airport. Or problems with his visa requiring a huge bung. Or a sick relative. They know how to yank the heart strings. They learn that on their first day.'

'Twenty grand is a big chunk of change,' Medlock said. 'Not many people can come up with that amount of money instantly. Can't she say it's in an account where there's a period of notice?'

'I've suggested that. But as yet she's not responded. I'm sure she will use every excuse she can, she's a feisty lady. And it will be a lot easier for her if she is in Australia.'

The DS thanked her and they moved on to the next of the names on the list. As they did so, DC Charlotte Williams looked at her phone, checking for texts, then emails. During the past few days, Suzy Driver had been in constant communication with her, either by phone, text or email. But it was worrying her that she'd heard nothing from her since Friday evening.

She sent her a text.

PETER JAMES

Hi, Mrs Driver, have you any more news for us?
Could you update us before you leave? All best,
DC Williams

By the end of the meeting, twenty minutes later, there
had been no reply. She made a note to try calling her later.

26

Roy Grace generally had an even temper and lost it rarely, but this evening he was close to boiling point, with a raging toothache not helping. The day had started well: a glorious early-morning jog with Humphrey across the fields, through an autumnal dawn – their rescue Labrador-Border Collie cross was loving their move to the country.

Then it had begun going downhill soon after, when his beloved Alfa Romeo wouldn't start. It had a flat battery, for no apparent reason. He'd jump-started it and it had got him to the office, then wouldn't start again. The RAC had duly arrived and cheerily given him the good and bad news. The bad was that the battery was knackered. The good was that they had a spare on board, for which they relieved him of nearly £200.

He'd then had a two-hour meeting with a solicitor at the Crown Prosecution Service, who was pedantically questioning Roy's identification of a Brighton GP, Edward Crisp, a suspected serial killer. How much *veracity* did you need to identify a man who had fired a twelve-bore shotgun at you from ten feet and nearly blown your leg off?

Next he'd had to endure a performance review by his immediate boss – and nemesis – Assistant Chief Constable Cassian Pewe. There had been, unsurprisingly, high-level repercussions over a kidnapping case Grace had handled six weeks ago, Operation Replay, because of the high body count, mostly within the Brighton Albanian community. Pewe wasn't interested that Roy had nearly died in the process of achieving a successful outcome, saving a fourteen-year-old boy from what would otherwise have been certain death. He was only concerned to personally come out smelling of roses from the Independent Office for Police Conduct enquiry into seven deaths related to the kidnap.

On top of it all, it was his week to be the Duty Force Gold Commander. This was a responsibility that came around every four months, on a roster that included the Chief, Deputy and Assistant Chief Constables, as well as all the force's Chief Superintendents. It was the role of a Gold Commander to take strategic charge of any major incident in the county, and to authorize, if required, the deployment of firearms.

It meant no alcohol all that week, and he was badly in need of a drink at this moment. A large one. A very large one. He craved an ice-cold vodka Martini, which would do the trick nicely. But that wasn't an option all the time he was on-call.

Instead, being home from work in time for once, he read to Noah, their fourteen-month-old son, his favourite book, about a hungry caterpillar, and put him to bed. He'd done this every night during the past fortnight he had been off, and he loved it. Loved the trust in his son's eyes. Noah's giggles and little laughs, and his naughtiness, splashing his arms in the bathwater, soaking himself and Cleo, and giggling even harder each time he did it.

Oftentimes during this he found himself reflecting on Bruno, all the missed childhood years. It made him even more determined to spend as much time as he could with both his sons.

When Noah was finally settled, Cleo, himself and Bruno had supper in the kitchen. Tonight, Bruno sat at the table, very upright, in a clean T-shirt, eating, but, as normal, saying nothing. Humphrey did his usual routine of moving around the table, sitting beside each of them in turn for some minutes in the hope a scrap would fall his way. Grace was less tolerant of the boy's silence than his wife. It seemed to him it was, in his son's mind, a way of getting back at them – punishing them – for uprooting him from Germany. Except what choice had they had? Boarding school was one but they didn't feel that would be right. The only other option for Bruno would have been to go and live with his ghastly grandparents in Seaford – and life in their home, with their legendary meanness, would have been hellish for him. But Bruno did not seem to appreciate anything. At this moment he was toying with a piece of vegetarian sausage he had cut off and pronged with his fork, examining it suspiciously like a pathology specimen.

'They're Linda McCartney's, Bruno,' Cleo said.

'Who is that?'

'She was married to Paul McCartney.'

He looked blank.

'One of the Beatles. Maybe you don't know them – you're too young.'

Ignoring her, he sniffed the morsel, turning it round with his fork as if concerned it might escape if he took his eye off it. 'This does not even smell like meat.'

'It's not meant to,' Cleo said. 'It's vegetarian.'

The boy smirked, but there was more supercilious mockery – and almost pity – in his expression than humour. 'If people want to be vegetarian they should eat vegetables that look like what they are. My mother would never have eaten something as ridiculous as this. A beetle would taste better.'

Out of the corner of her eye, Cleo saw Roy was about to react, and she mouthed for him to hold off. 'You told me your mother was vegan,' she said.

'She was a correct vegan. She cared about not eating animals. *Meine Mutter* would never have eaten a fake sausage or a fake hamburger,' he sneered. 'That's just silly. If you want to be a vegetarian or a vegan, do that, but don't make it look like meat and mess with everyone's heads.'

Roy and Cleo shot a glance at each other. 'So you didn't become a vegan yourself, Bruno?' Grace asked.

'I'm blood-type A,' Bruno said, solemnly. 'It is important to eat according to your blood type. If you are type A you need proper meat.' He pushed his plate aside and stood up, abruptly. 'I go to my room.'

Again Roy Grace was about to rebuke him, when Cleo signalled for him to be quiet.

'You've not eaten anything,' she said. 'You must have something.'

Bruno stared at his stepmother strangely. It was a look Roy Grace had seen many times before, during his career. It was the gleam in the eyes of a prosecution counsel, in court, who is just about to deliver a crushing rebuke to a key defence witness.

'If you get me some proper food, I will,' he said. 'Why did you think I would wish for vegetarian?'

Smiling, as if determined not to be riled by him, Cleo asked, 'What kind of *proper* food would you like me to get you, Bruno?'

'Sausages,' he said. 'Proper German sausages: Weiss-wurst, Frankfurters, Bratwurst, Blutwurst, Bockwurst,

Bregenwurst, Knackwurst, Gelbwurst, Teewurst, not the crap you have in butcher's here.'

'OK,' she said, brightly. 'German sausages it will be. Which kind would you most like me to get you?'

'Weisswurst and Bratwurst.'

'OK, I'll get some in for you.'

Without a word of acknowledgement, Bruno turned his back, walked away from the kitchen table, through the open-plan living room and up the stairs.

'The word is *thanks*,' Roy Grace murmured, so quietly only Cleo could hear. He looked at her and she gave him a *what-can-you-do* look back. Then she reached out a hand and covered his.

'Gently,' she said quietly, almost whispering. 'Gently, gently, gently.'

Almost whispering back, Grace said, 'Yes, that's how I'd like to throttle him. Gently.'

She grimaced.

To add to his bad mood, there was a bunch of bills that had arrived in today's post, which he always liked to settle promptly. He glanced through them. The first was for new netting for the chicken run. 'Blimey!' he said, wincing at the amount. 'I hate to think how much each egg costs us!'

'At least we know where they come from – and that the hens have a nice life, darling.'

'From the cost of this netting it would be cheaper to keep them in a suite in the Ritz.'

The second invoice was a stage payment request from Starling Row, their bathroom fitters. 'Yikes!' he said. 'We've got our hens in the Ritz and I hope Bruno appreciates his swanky bathroom – let's hope he doesn't tell us he had a bigger one in Germany!'

The final invoice was from a company whose name he

didn't recognize. 'Who are Lloyds Environmental Services?' he asked, showing Cleo the invoice.

'They're the people who come twice a year to suck the sewage from the cesspit.'

'To remove our shit,' he added. 'Hmmmm. I might have a job for them at Headquarters.'

His job phone rang. Apologizing to her, he answered with a curt, 'Roy Grace.'

And immediately his spirits sank even lower as he recognized the nervy voice of Inspector Andy Anakin, known to most of his colleagues as 'Panicking Anakin'. Tonight Anakin was the Golf 99 – the Duty Critical Incident Inspector at Brighton police station – and a person with a temperament less suited to handling critical incidents would be hard to find, Grace thought. The vast majority of his colleagues, at all ranks, were good people, but just occasionally someone like Anakin would slip through the cracks – or rather, rise through them. He often wondered how on earth Anakin ever managed to make it into the police force, let alone get promoted to inspector.

'Roy, ah, good, you are there!' He sounded out of breath, as ever.

'I am, yes, Andy.'

'Ah, good.'

There was a brief silence. Grace took advantage of it. 'Well, if that's all you wanted to ask, I'll sign off now. Cheerio, Andy.'

'No – no, no, no, I – I – I just wanted to alert you. The thing. Well, sir, you see, I think we may have a situation. Thought I'd better forewarn you.'

'OK, tell me?'

'It could turn out to be nothing, of course, a false alarm.'

Grace waited patiently for Anakin to get to the point. It

was a long wait. 'It's this guy's wife, you see – ah – as I understand they had a pretty big bust-up eight months ago – quite a long history of abuse. His name's Liam Morrisey – long history with us, small-time drug dealer, sacked as a bouncer for excessive violence, once did three years for GBH after stabbing someone in a pub.'

'Nice chap,' Grace said.

'No, not really,' Anakin said. 'Not at all nice, sir. Thing is, he's under a court order not to go near her – his former wife – Kerry – he has to remain half a mile distant. She phoned earlier this evening apparently, dialled the nines, because she'd seen him driving up and down her street.'

'Where does she live, Andy?'

'Hadden Avenue, just off Freshfield Road, up near the racecourse.'

'I know it.'

'An hour ago he threw something from his car into her front garden. She thought it might be a bomb or something. We sent a unit to investigate and it turned out to be what looked like a roadkill fox in a bin liner. The bastard sent her a text saying the next thing the police will find in a bin liner will be her body.'

'What reassurances have you given her, Andy?'

'I've told her that all the crews have been alerted, and they will drive past her house as often as they can throughout the night. But we haven't got the resources to do a proper job, you know that, Roy. I've got four cars out covering the whole city, it's ridiculous!'

'OK, so all's calm at the moment?'

'At the moment.'

'OK, good.'

'I've got a bad feeling about this one, Roy. I think it's going to kick off.'

'OK, I'm here if you need me. What you should be thinking about is putting a team of officers together who may have to effect a forced entry. Where are your ARVs at the moment, if required, and do you have someone on Division, other than yourself, overseeing this? Do you have a sergeant monitoring the situation for a quick response if required? I suggest you ensure you have a plan to respond quickly if the situation escalates.'

'OK, I will, I will,' he said. 'I definitely will. It's going to kick off, I know it.'

27

Monday 1 October

Tooth was feeling ill again, despite having seen the specialist this morning in Munich. Dr Wolfgang Riske was considered to be the top man in the world in the field of venoms. It was an appointment he'd waited two months for, and he'd been desperate not to miss it. He seriously believed that the poisons inside him were killing him, slowly, steadily, and the effects he felt were worsening by the day.

A German actor who lived on the floor below him in the Breisacher Strasse apartment building was not helping by playing his goddam piano again. Some piece of operatic crap. The same piece over and over.

Plink-plink-plink, plink-plink-plink, plink-plink-PLONK.

And every few minutes the jerk would start singing along to it, in English, in a baritone voice, changing the inflection each time as if trying to find the right emphasis. Maybe he had a good voice, Tooth didn't know or care. Country and Western was the only music he listened to, and he didn't listen to much of that.

It was eleven-goddam-thirty at night. He was singing again now – 'All my *DAYS* of philandering are over!'

Plink-plink-plink, plink-plink-plink, plink-plink-PLONK.

The actor's name was on the panel by the front door. *Hans-Jürgen Stockerl.* Tooth had seen him once downstairs, coming out of his apartment. A mediagenic guy in his fifties with foppish hair. He'd googled him, out of interest. He was quite famous, it appeared. A stage, screen and television actor, singer and musician.

Tooth had felt lousy the whole short time he'd been in England. Now back here in Munich, he'd not eaten since yesterday morning. Lying on his bed, giddy, a lot of circling around happening inside his head. The room heaved about like he was in the cabin of a ship in a rough sea. Every sound weaved through his nerves. He was trying to sleep.

Plink-plink-plink, plink-plink-plink, plink-plink-PLONK.

'All my days of *PHILANDERING* are over!' He was singing even louder now.

Anger was growing inside Tooth. Anger at himself for failing in Munich and now failing in Brighton. Both because of useless intelligence from Steve Barrey.

'Shut up!' Tooth said. 'Shut the—'

His phone began vibrating and buzzing on his bedside table.

Tooth knew who it was and he didn't want to answer it. He didn't have the energy or inclination to listen to Mr Barrey yelling at him.

The only inclination he had was to go downstairs, kick open Hans-Jürgen Stockerl's front door, break all the fingers on both of his hands and ram a sock in his mouth.

The phone stopped buzzing. A few seconds later, it started again.

Maybe he'd take the phone downstairs and ram that in the crooner's mouth.

See what his voice sounded like without any teeth.

Plink-plink-plink, plink-plink-plink, plink-plink-PLONK.
Again.

The voice, even louder now. 'All my days of philandering are *OVER*!'

The phone fell silent again. For a brief while. Then it pinged with a text. He picked it up and glanced at it. As he expected, it was Mr Barrey.

> **What happened, asshole? Call me. NOW!**

Tooth texted back.

> **The other asshole got there first. Maybe you should employ a better quality of assholes on your surveillance. And learn some manners. Asshole.**

28

After ending his call with Panicking Anakin, Roy Grace sat at the kitchen table in silence, toying with his food. 'I just don't know what to do about Bruno's rudeness.'

'We have to give him time,' Cleo replied after a short while.

'That's what you keep saying.' He drank some water. 'It's over six months now he's been with us, and he hasn't made a single friend – that we're aware of. You heard what the headmaster said last week.'

'I'm still thinking about what the headmaster told us about Bruno's ambitions,' she said.

Humphrey nuzzled Grace's leg. 'I might find it funny' – he leaned down and rubbed the dog's head and neck – 'if I didn't think he was actually serious about it.' Mimicking Bruno's broken English, he said, '*I'm going to be either a chemist or a dictator.*' He shook his head. 'Did any kid you ever met in your life have that ambition?'

'Well, he's thinking big!'

'Really? Are you happy to know we have a budding Saddam Hussein or Muammar Gaddafi or Kim Jong-un living under our roof?'

'Darling, I think you are reading too much into it. Probably just Bruno having a laugh. Anyhow, what were your ambitions when you were his age? Did you know what you wanted to do when you grew up?'

Grace drank some more water, wishing again it could be something stronger. 'Yes, I did – kind of. I just felt I wanted to do something to help make the world a better place.'

Cleo laid her hand over his. 'I love that about you – that that is important to you.'

He shrugged. 'My dad inspired me. He'd come home in his uniform and enthral me with stories of what had happened during the day – or the night before – when he'd been out on the beat. How he'd found a missing kid, or helped calm down a fight in a pub, or chased and arrested a burglar. Or went in the sea and saved someone's life. And the time he'd been shot at. I kind of knew I wanted to go into the police, but for a while before then I had an ambition to be an eye surgeon and help people who had become blind to see again. But I was rubbish at all the sciences – and flunked biology, as you know – so going into medicine was never an option.' He shrugged. 'When you were at your posh school, did you ever think one day you would be a mortician?'

She shook her head. 'Never, in my wildest dreams, although I was always fascinated by death. Mum and Dad definitely thought I was pretty weird. We were on holiday in Ireland one time and we came across this graveyard which had all these grand Catholic mausoleums. I ran around, getting down on my knees and peering through the holes in them to see if I could spot any bones lying at the bottom of the graves!'

'So you never thought of trying to qualify as a doctor?' he asked.

She shook her head. 'God, no. After Roedean, the trad-itional route was uni or college. Mum and Dad encouraged me to go into the City and become a high-flyer. I couldn't see myself as a hedge-fund gazillionaire, so I took my nursing degree!'

'And you ended up married to an impoverished copper, and helping dismember dead bodies for a living. Funny how life turns out.'

She leaned over and kissed him. 'Who was it who said, "Start with big dreams and make life worth living"?'

'I dunno, who?'

'I don't remember. But that's what my job does, and it's what being married to you does.'

'So I guess I lucked out!' he said.

'Remember that. Don't ever let any creep – like Cassian Pewe – persuade you otherwise.'

He stood up and kissed her on the lips. 'I'm going up to see if Bruno's gone to bed.'

'OK! But be understanding if he's still up. Imagine yourself in his situation.'

He climbed the stairs. At the top he trod along dust sheets on the carpets, towards Bruno's room. Work on the bathroom conversion had begun. A smell of dust and sawn timber hung in the air.

As he entered, Bruno, wearing headphones, was lounging on his bed, dressed in the red-and-white shirt of Bayern Munich football club. He was holding a gaming control box in his hand, focused with such concentration he did not turn round as his father entered.

A virtual football game was in progress and Bruno was intensely involved, his fingers dancing on the keys of the box, moving his players around. Grace worked out, from the 2–1 score in the left-hand corner, that his son's team was winning.

'Bruno!' he said. 'You know the rules, it's nine on a school day. You should have been asleep an hour ago. Turn it off now!'

Bruno did not react to his presence in any way. As he carried on, focused on the machine, Grace felt his earlier anger rising again. Anger at his son's total lack of interest in him.

You do not know what a nice life lies ahead for you, do you, lad?

None too gently, he lifted the headphones off Bruno's ears. 'Hello!' he said.

Bruno did not react. He kept staring, rigidly, at the screen. As if he was playing some separate game with his father – *Who Blinks First.*

Bruno had a midfielder with possession. Ignoring his father, he used the controls to have the player kick the ball out to the right, to a winger, who then ran down the touch-line with it.

Roy Grace snatched the box out of his son's hands.

'Hey!' Bruno said. 'You just stopped—'

'Don't you *hey* me, ever,' Grace said furiously. 'You were very rude to your stepmother about the meal she prepared. That wasn't very nice.'

'She doesn't know how to cook,' Bruno retorted. 'Vegetarian crap tonight. Last night I said I wanted schnitzel and she gave me some stupid chicken dish.'

Grace looked at him in astonishment. Thinking how his own father might have reacted if he'd behaved this way. His father would have given him a clip round the ear.

'Bruno, you don't talk to us like that, ever. Understand?'

They were going to have to be very much tougher with the boy, he decided. Equally, he was well aware how difficult it must be for Bruno, to have his life transplanted from

Munich to here. All the time, he tried to bear that in mind, but the boy was constantly pushing him – and Cleo – to the edge of their patience. 'This is not a hotel, Bruno, OK? Neither Cleo, nor I when I'm cooking, have a menu of options. If you tell us what you don't like to eat, as Cleo said, we'll make sure not to give you it. And if you give us time, and you want something specific, give us notice, all right?'

Bruno was staring at the screen, ignoring him again.

'Did you hear me?'

Bruno turned reluctantly towards him.

Grace sat down on the edge of the bed, not facing him at first. 'Look, I know it can't be easy for you. You lost your mother, and then you got taken away from your homeland into a completely new country, with a different language. Your stepmother and I want to understand what we can do to make your life better.'

Some of the anger drained from the boy's face and seemed, to Roy, to be replaced with sadness.

'Bruno, we know so little – pretty much nothing – about the ten years of your life before you came to us. Perhaps we can talk about it – you know? You can tell us what kind of life you had – it might be helpful for all of us—'

At that moment, Grace's job phone in his jeans pocket rang, interrupting them.

With an apologetic nod to Bruno, he answered it. 'Roy Grace.' It was Anakin, and he was definitely panicking.

Walking to the door, he mouthed to Bruno, 'We'll talk later.'

'Boss, as I warned you, the situation has developed!' Anakin said excitedly, half shouting.

'Give me some details, Andy?'

He went out onto the landing and closed Bruno's door.

'That Liam Morrisey. He's in his wife's house in Hadden

Avenue and he's not coming out. He's threatening to kill himself.'

'Is his wife with him? Kerry, is that her name?'

'Yes, Kerry. No, she got out, and has her two kids with her. She's gone to her mother's place in Hollingbury.'

'So what exactly is the situation?'

'Morrisey. Liam Morrisey. He's in there and not coming out.'

Grace was rapidly thinking this through. 'Morrisey's in her house, on his own, no one else is in there – not his wife or kids?'

'That's right, Roy. Oh God, it's a siege!'

'Andy, just calm down, this is not a siege, OK?'

'It is! He won't come out. He's locked himself inside and won't come out.'

'How does that make it a siege, Andy? Has he got a gun? Is he threatening to fire at your officers?'

'No, chief, no threat – not yet, anyhow.'

'So in what way, exactly, does this make it a siege?'

'That's what it is, Roy! He won't come out, he's locked the doors! What if he self-harms, Roy? I mean – what if he kills himself?'

'I'll have to take him off my Christmas card list.'

'That's really not funny.'

'Listen to me very carefully, Andy. I want you to get the unit from the Public Order Team to go into the house. Can you see him?'

'Yes-yes.' Anakin's voice was sounding even more tense. 'I can see him, upstairs, looking out through the window!'

'Right,' Grace said, his patience running on empty. 'This is what you are going to do. You're going to put the front door in and show Liam Morrisey the back of a cell door within the next thirty minutes, do you understand?'

'What do you mean, Roy? How, why?'

'Why?'

'Yes, why?'

'I'll tell you exactly why, Andy, OK? You're going to do it because I'm telling you to do it. This is our town, we're the cops and tonight I'm the fucking sheriff.'

An hour later Grace was out in the garden, in the darkness, waiting for Humphrey to finish doing his business, when his job phone pinged with a text. He looked down at the screen. It was from Andy Anakin. The message was short and meek.

One in custody.

29

PC Holly Little, nicknamed the Pocket Rocket because of her small stature and cluttered kit of gadgets and protection that made her look like a walking machine, was partnered on B-Section with John Alldridge, a six-foot-four, eighteen-stone rugby forward, fondly known as the Gentle Giant. They were two hours into their shift, cruising around the city of Brighton and Hove, *hunting* as they called it. Windswept rain lashed down, which meant most of the city's scrotes would be tucked away inside their lairs, staying dry. Good old PC Rain doing its stuff. Although it made for a boring morning for the two Response officers itching for some action.

All they'd had was a call to a domestic at the eastern end of the city in Kemp Town, which they had just left. Two gay women were slugging it out, but by the time they'd arrived at the scene there were already three other cars – with crews as bored as they were – in attendance.

'Bloody Q,' Alldridge said to his colleague, who was driving.

No police officer ever said the word 'quiet' intentionally. It was a jinx. They were heading along the seafront, passing Brighton Palace Pier to their left and the angry grey sea around it.

'Back to base and grab a coffee?' Holly suggested.

Just as Alldridge said, 'Good plan,' the driver of a beaten-up Astra heading past in the opposite direction suddenly drew Holly's attention. 'That looked like Leetham Greene!' she said. 'Little shitbag's got a ban. I nicked him for driving while disqualified just a couple of months ago!'

Looking swiftly over his shoulder, John Alldridge clocked the registration and tapped it into the computer. Moments later it came up as registered to Leetham Greene, flagged as untaxed and uninsured. 'Spin her round,' he said, leaning forward and switching on the blues and twos.

A taxi coming in the opposite direction obligingly slowed and flashed its headlights. As Holly made a sharp U-turn and accelerated, the voice of a female controller came through the radio. 'Charlie Romeo Zero Five?'

'Charlie Romeo Zero Five,' Alldridge answered.

Holly rapidly caught up a two-lane bottleneck of traffic at the roundabout in front of the pier. The rogue Astra was some cars in front. No one could move out of the way so she switched off the siren, leaving the blue lights flashing.

'Charlie Romeo Zero Five, we've had a couple of calls about the same address, in Somerhill Avenue. A concerned daughter called us from Australia about her widowed mother. She's not been able to contact her since the weekend, says she's not responding to calls, texts, emails or Facebook. We've also had a report of a yapping dog at the same address, from a neighbour. Are you free to attend? Grade Two.'

John answered. 'Yes, yes.'

He turned to his colleague. 'See which way Greene, went?' She shook her head.

'Let him go, we'd better attend at Somerhill.'

Grade Two was not an emergency, which meant, to Holly's disappointment, it wouldn't be a blue-light run.

'What do we know about the occupant?' John asked the call handler.

'Owner is a Mrs Driver, first name Susan. She lives alone with a Yorkshire terrier called Buster. Her neighbour says she's concerned because she's been round a few times, knocking on the door and getting no reply, other than the dog going nuts. The dog has barked off and on for three days, which is very unusual. She's phoned Mrs Driver, also, and she's not picking up.'

'We're on our way.' John leaned forward to punch the address into the satnav.

'It's OK,' his partner said. 'I know the area.' She made a left into Old Steine and another left into North Street up towards the Clock Tower, and then on, uphill, to the Seven Dials. She shot John a glance. 'G5?'

'Sounds likely.'

Holly wrinkled her nose. 'Not my favourite.'

'At least it's not summer. Went to one a couple of years ago, a seafront flat where an old lady had put a Sainsbury's bag over her head – and been there three months before anyone noticed she was missing. Called in by a neighbour who said there was a funny smell. I thought she was still alive when I went in the door – that she was moving – then I realized it was her body covered in maggots.'

'Yech! I attended one, an old man, dead for a month, locked in a room with his cat. The cat had eaten half his face.'

'Says it all about cats, doesn't it?'

'I'd like to think my cheeky cat, Madam Woo, wouldn't eat me,' she replied. 'Probably best not to give them the chance.'

In front of them, a tiny Honda with what looked like two old ducks in it halted at the roundabout. And stayed halted. A taxi came round; a van; a car; a lorry; then a long, long gap before another car and then another interminable gap. The Honda did not move.

'What are you waiting for? Go!' Holly yelled through the screen. 'For God's sake!'

John chuckled at her impatience. Another car came round.

Holly hammered on the steering wheel in frustration. 'GO!'

Finally the little car pulled forward, straight into the path of a BMW which blasted its horn, narrowly missing the back end of the Honda.

A couple of minutes later they drove slowly along Somerhill Avenue, looking at the house numbers.

'Nice street,' Holly Little said. 'Lovely park opposite. I think I could live here.'

'All you need is a rich old uncle to die and leave you a couple of million quid and you'd be sorted.'

'Or win the Lottery,' she replied.

'I wouldn't bank on that buying you anything much. I almost won it once.'

'You did?'

'Well, sort of – five matches. Same day that half of England had the same numbers. I ended up with a few hundred quid. Seven hundred and eighty-five, to be precise.'

'Bummer.'

'That wasn't actually the word I used, but you're on the right track.' Then he pointed through the windscreen. 'There!'

They pulled up outside a handsome, red-brick Victorian house in good condition. There was a short, neat front garden with a tarmac drive up to what was previously an integral garage that had, at some time, been converted to a room. As they got out they could hear yapping.

stood by her story, and he had the restaurant
her evidence.

had discovered something significant. AT&T
ed their phone records. Alexander Graham
nted the telephone in 1879, established the
phone and Telegraph Company in 1885. It
oly on the US telephone service until 1982. As
olicy, they kept all phone records for twenty
n archived them. But when Homeland Security
ed in the aftermath of 9/11, a request was
S phone providers to retain call records indef-

had managed to obtain the complete call log
Lamont's mobile phone from 1998. The calls
lorida, at the family home, at the exact time of
urder. The Sheriff's task now, in order not to be
by a defence brief, was to try to establish that
had the phone in his possession at that exact
was a tough one. A real challenge.

was grateful for it. For taking his mind off the
of the past week.

aking nightmare that had become his new
His life.

ne rang.

y Sheriff Sorokin,' he answered.

rand. Does Deputy Sheriff Sorokin have time to
old buddy?'

' he said.

you doing?'

e to say *great*, Gerry! I'd like to say *it's good to hear*
but right now, if I saw you, I'd happily plug you.'

whoahhh! Wind back, pal!'

, there isn't any *winding back*.'

They hurried through the rain up to the shelter of the
entrance porch. John rang the smart, in-period, bell push.
They could both hear, clearly, the loud ring from the interior
of the house. The yapping became frenzied.

He knelt down, opened the letter box and peered in.
The floor was littered with newspapers and mail. He pressed
his nose in and sniffed, instantly recoiling.

The one smell all police officers could instantly recognize. And loathed.

The two officers looked at each other. They'd been
partnered up for long enough to know each other's body
language. And Holly Little was reading his loud and clear.

They walked down the side of the house, past the bins,
and into a very well-kept urban garden that could do with
the grass cutting. There were patio doors leading out from
a conservatory at the rear. John rapped on the window. The
dog came racing through, putting its paws up against the
glass, near demented.

'Think we should call for a dog unit?' he asked.

'You wuss!'

They went back round to the front. John hurried over
to the car, removed the heavy battering ram and lugged it
up to the imposing front door. 'You happy about this?' he
asked her. 'We're not contravening any of the new bloody
privacy laws? We don't need to get a warrant?'

'Would it make you feel better?'

'No.'

'Good. Let's go round the back and do the patio doors
– less expensive to repair.'

They hurried round. He swung the ram at the door,
shattering it, then again, punching a big enough hole for
them to crawl through. The dog snarled at them and then
ran out into the garden. Laying the ram down, John called

out, futilely, he reckoned, 'Mrs Driver? Hello! This is the police! Hello!'

The dog came running back in. Holly Little tried to stroke it, but it shot past and ran up the stairs.

The smell was even stronger now they were inside the house. The distinctive, putrid, cloying smell of decaying human flesh and blood. There was no smell on earth more horrible to either officer.

'Mrs Driver!' Holly called out, with little expectation of a response. 'Hello, this is the police!'

They split and dutifully checked out the ground-floor rooms. There were stains of dog wee on the white carpet, and several dried dog messes. Then they looked in the separate garage. It contained a modern Mini and a silver classic Mercedes 500SL, from the 1980s. No sign of anyone.

Then they ventured upstairs. The dog was frantically yapping and pawing at a closed door. John turned the handle and tried to open it, but it would barely budge. He pushed hard against it, opening it just a few inches, the stench even stronger now. Then he threw all of his considerable weight against it and it opened wide. He burst through, stumbling across the room, closely followed by Holly.

An instant later a pair of stockinged legs, high in the air, one foot wearing a velvet slipper, the other bare, struck him in the face.

Matthew Sorokin sat i
had been allocated in
by the Sheriff's Departm
He sneezed, feeling and
was freezing his nuts off,
Florida. Outside it was
inside it was an icebox. H
sweating or shivering, an

He was leafing throug
graphs of another cold ca
1998, Dara Lamont, a beau
of a mansion on a gated
her head blasted away by a
to the cops like a burglary
changed.

Her husband, Arron, the
process of filing for divorce,
of his infidelities, his wife w
she could get. His real estate c
after a large, unwise investn
millions, was struggling to su
died, Arron had a cast-iron ali
in New York, having dinner wit

'Buddy, what's the problem?'

'That dating agency you put me on to?'

'Uh-huh?'

'It just cost me a packet, OK? Ninety thousand bucks.'

'Holy shit. That's why I was calling you, to see how it was going. Say you're joking?'

'I'm not joking.'

'I was calling to warn you. I've got another pal I put on to online dating – a guy in England, he got stiffed for an insane amount of money. I met Karen, my wife, online. Thought I'd do you guys a favour. But it seems it's been hijacked by total shitbags since. Ninety thousand bucks? What do you mean, ninety thousand bucks?'

'I mean, Gerry, *ninety thousand bucks.*'

'How in God's name did you part with that kind of dough?'

'Probably the same way your pal in England got suckered. I thought she was for real – her name was Evelyne Desota. A babe. We got on so well, and I felt – you know – I really cared for her and trusted her. She had a whole load of issues, with a nightmare of a husband and family – so I thought. I don't know what to believe any more – I don't think I believe any of it. I was just spun a load of total baloney.'

'Pretty convincing baloney,' Gerry said.

'I've lost all my fun money. Every extra dime I worked for is gone.'

'Any chance you can recover any of it?'

'You sitting near a window, Gerry?'

'Near a window? Sure, right by a window.'

'Can you see the sky?'

'Uh-huh. Got a clear view.'

'See any pigs flying past?'

31

'Follow the money,' Financial Investigator Emily Denyer said. 'That's what we need to do.'

The phrase, Roy Grace well knew, had become a mantra for the police in every case where money was involved. Following the money would, hopefully, lead you to the villain or villains.

Glenn Branson, seated alongside Emily in Grace's office, stared gloomily at the paperwork stacked in front of him. Two mountains, in fact, one getting smaller as the other grew taller. Evidence. All in sixteen-point type on the advice of the lawyers, because they might be unlucky enough to come in front of an elderly judge with deteriorating eyesight and failing patience.

A bronze statue of Lady Justice stood outside the Old Bailey, the building housing the Central Criminal Court of England and Wales. She carried a sword in her right hand and scales in her left. In Roy Grace's view, for accuracy the scales should be replaced with a pair of dice or a roulette wheel. Every prosecution, even the most watertight one, was a gamble, a game of chance in which the prosecution might be up against a smart defence brief, a perverse jury or a blinkered judge. You did all you could to arrest the right suspect and once that was done the even bigger battle of the paperwork started – with the chain of evidence being one of the most important elements.

The paperwork in front of the three of them related to the impending trial of Jodie Bentley, a woman who had sent at least two husbands as well as a prospective one to premature graves, and pertained in part to proving the money – and potential money – she had to gain from her machinations.

With all three unfortunate victims, the physical proof that she had murdered them was entirely circumstantial, even after laying a honeytrap for her with an undercover operator. As Emily Denyer said, following the money was their best hope. But Jodie Bentley was a clever woman and operated under a string of aliases, with bank accounts in different names spread around the globe.

'What a bitch,' Glenn Branson said, studying one document, evidence from a Home Office pathologist, Dr Colin Duncton. 'Even if her last victim had survived the snake venom she used – from a saw-scale viper – his willy would have shrunk! I'm sure there was some movie about that.'

'*The Shrinking Man* or something?'

'Yeah, right,' said Branson, a movie buff. '1957, *The Incredible Shrinking Man*, directed by Jack Arnold and starring Grant Williams and Randy Stuart. But it wasn't just his manhood that shrunk.'

'Grant Williams and Randy Stuart?' Grace looked perplexed.

'A man of your vintage? Surely you remember them?'

'Respect your elders, Detective Inspector Branson!'

'That was a TV movie in 2012.'

'Is there anything you don't know about films?' Grace shook his head with a smile and returned to the stack he was working through, covered in annotations from a Crown

Prosecution solicitor. He read through them, trying to answer each of the queries about Jodie Bentley's then fiancé, an American called Walt Klein. The solicitor was asking for corroboration on the following points.

Why were they in Courchevel?

What time did they leave the hotel?

Exactly what time did she lose sight of him?

How long after his disappearance before she notified the police?

There weren't just hours of questions, there were days. He had been working on the queries since 7 a.m. this morning and was starting to lose the will to live. Then his phone rang.

'Roy Grace,' he answered.

It was an old colleague he hadn't spoken to in a while, Inspector Bill Warner from Brighton CID. 'Roy, how are you doing?'

'Good, Bill, you? How's your back?'

Warner, a former professional boxer, taxi driver then international water polo player, was suffering from a disintegrating spine condition, which he was not letting interfere with his work. He was today's on-call detective inspector for Brighton and Hove.

'Crap, if you want the truth, mate! But I'm fine otherwise. I've just attended a suicide, but I'm not happy with it. I think someone from Major Crime should go and take a look.'

'OK,' Grace said to him. 'What are your thoughts, Bill?'

'Lady by the name of Susan Driver, age fifty-five. Widowed four years ago. Her husband, Raymond Driver, was a big name in the Brighton antiques world – started life as a knocker boy, then became a player in brown furniture until that market collapsed and he moved into antique jewellery. Left his old lady properly loaded. Her daughter in Australia was worried because she hasn't been able to contact her for several days. There's a number of reasons why this looks suspicious to me. CSM Alex Call's at the scene and he can fill in your officers.'

Bill then went on to describe the scene and what he had found there.

'I'll go myself,' Grace said.

Warner thanked him.

'Fancy a peep at a swinger?' he asked Branson after he ended the call.

'Not really my thing, but I'll come and hold your hand, boss.'

Apologizing to Emily Denyer, telling her they would be back as soon as they could, the two detectives left, both trying not to look too happy about the welcome, if grim, distraction.

32

To dream of death is good for those in fear, for the dead have no more fears.

Johnny Fordwater kept returning to that quote he'd heard, years back, trying to recall the source.

Death, as it had for the past week, felt like the best solution. Suicide.

Any other option meant complete loss of face.

In front of him lay his neat and elaborately written notes to his three children and eight grandchildren. In them, he apologized for being unable to leave them the bequests he had always planned for them. He told them the reason, perhaps too much information, but so what? Maybe it would serve as a warning to them to never do what he had done. However desperate their lives might have become.

He walked over to the safe in his study, entered the six-digit code and swung open the heavy door. Inside lay his old service revolver, which he should have handed in years ago, when he'd left the army. But no one had actually requested it so he'd just thought 'sod it' and kept the weapon. Next to it lay several rounds of ammunition. With a steady hand he filled each of the six chambers, in turn, with a live round. An old army chum who suffered from depression had told him that he occasionally toyed with shooting himself with his service revolver, and each time he changed his mind at the last minute it felt better.

It felt to Johnny that the only way out of his financial ruin was to do the honourable thing. When he pulled the trigger it wouldn't matter which chamber ended up in front of the firing pin. The relief of death was a certainty. He completed the task, then put the gun in his mouth, pointing upwards, and with his right index finger found first the trigger guard, then the trigger itself.

Staring out through the window at the afternoon sun low over the calm water of the English Channel, he saw a container ship sitting up high on the horizon and, closer to shore, a paddleboarder. He squeezed the trigger, gently at first, then steadily increased the pressure.

33

'It's not pretty, sir,' Crime Scene Manager Alex Call said. Roy Grace, accompanied by DI Glenn Branson, both gowned up in protective suits, overshoes and gloves, signed the scene guard's log outside the substantial, detached Victorian house.

A row of police vehicles, including a Crime Scene Investigation van, were parked along the residential street.

'What do we have, Alex?'

The CSM was a slightly built, intensely serious man, with a sharp eye for detail that had earned him rapid promotion. 'The home owner – who we believe is the victim – is Susan – Suzy – Adele Driver, widowed four years ago, sir,' Call said. 'Her late husband was an antiques dealer who moved into jewellery after the market in brown furniture collapsed. Apparent suicide by hanging, but the Coroner's Officer who attended agrees with DI Warner.'

'Who was that?'

'Michelle Websdale. She's gone to attend a fatal – RTC – but she's coming back.'

Michelle Websdale was someone Grace trusted. As he did DI Bill Warner. 'Where's Bill now?'

'He's just left on a shout – a woman holding a baby threatening to jump from a fourth-floor balcony.'

'So, what are your initial findings?'

'The height of the noose is one thing – which I agree with. Her feet are a good six inches above the chair she stood on. There's a bruise on the back of her head. My CSIs have already found hairs on the floor a short distance away, which could be evidence she'd fallen or been pushed backwards, prior to hanging.'

'Are you aware of anything missing in the house? Any sign of it being burgled or ransacked?'

'No, sir, everything looks orderly. Nothing immediately obvious missing – there's what seems like some quality art on the walls and a lot of antiques, statuettes and stuff. Difficult to know if anything has been taken at this stage, but my impression is this is not a burglary.'

'She's still in situ?'

'Yes, I spoke to the Home Office pathologist, who should be here in an hour or so.'

'Who is it?'

'Your good mate, Dr Frazer Theobald.'

Grace rolled his eyes and said, 'Great, that's my evening gone.' He thanked Call, then both detectives ducked under the taped barrier.

As they entered the front door into a large, handsomely furnished hall, they wrinkled their noses at the reek of human decay. They walked up the stairs, the smell becoming more distinct, and the heat rising; the central heating had been left on full blast. On the first-floor landing a gowned-up Crime Scene Investigator stood outside a closed door. Recognizing Roy Grace, she said, 'You'll have to push hard, sir, it's a heavy fire door.'

Entering the stiflingly warm room, pushing hard as he was told, Grace saw two Crime Scene Investigators on the floor, with gloved hands, doing a fingertip search, one of whom, Chris Gee, he recognized, and CSI photographer James Gartrell, videoing the scene. Above them was a woman in her mid-fifties, with dark hair, dressed in a loose sweater and jeans, hanging from what looked like a bathrobe cord looped round a massive, gilded chandelier. All around the fixing the ceiling was badly cracked, with some chunks of plaster fallen away. Among the debris on the floor was a black velvet slipper embossed with a gold crest. The other was still on her foot.

Her neck looked elongated. Her contorted tongue, dark blue and pink, protruded from her mouth. Her eyes were bloodshot and flat. Her face was blotchy, mottled with green, and there were several early bluebottles gathered around her eyes. Her hands were purple and there was dried foam around her mouth.

Grace held the door, to stop it swinging back, as his colleague entered.

Glenn Branson looked up. Despite recoiling with the shock and horror of what he saw, and the smell, he felt a twist of sadness inside his heart. The same he'd felt each time in his career when he'd attended a suicide. Wondering about the victim's life, what had led to them taking this terrible step – and who might have been able to talk to them and convince them there were other choices.

Grace was feeling many of the same emotions. He looked at the woman's eyes, wide open as most hanging victims he'd ever encountered were. Staring. *Windows of the soul*, he thought.

Unless you fell through a hangman's trap, breaking your neck, death by hanging was not an instant process. He'd learned this from numerous pathologists' reports. You would still have some air coming through and could dangle there for a long while, struggling for breath.

Thinking about what you had done? Maybe regretting it?

Where is your soul now, Suzy Driver? he wondered, deeply saddened.

He looked down at the gap between her feet and the chair beneath. Then looked back at her. Thinking. This scene was telling him one thing, but in his mind he was seeing something else. Something not quite right. As if in some meagre form of compensation, he pulled out his phone and took several photographs of her. He knew that Gartrell would cover everything thoroughly, but he still liked to have some photographs of his own to study before the CSI ones were distributed.

Looking up at her again, he thought, *This wasn't your choice, was it? I'm sorry. I know it's not much comfort, but I promise you one thing: I will do everything I can to find out who did this to you and make sure they never do this to anyone again, ever. Probably not what you want to hear.* He shrugged his shoulders and looked, apologetically, into her eyes. They stared, accusingly, back at him. Like they were saying: *Do something!*

34

Tuesday 2 October

Johnny Fordwater continued standing, holding the cold muzzle of the revolver against the roof of his mouth, his finger curled securely around the trigger, squeezing it. His hand was shaking. This was not easy. He squeezed a little more. His gaze lingered on the container ship on the horizon, then on the paddleboarder gracefully gliding across the almost preternaturally calm sea. A seagull swooped down to the promenade and seized something from the pavement in its beak. The last things he would ever see.

Any moment the gun would discharge. Any moment.

This really was not as simple to do as he had thought. Was he holding back from giving that trigger the one final bit of pressure it needed because he was petrified, he wondered? When all the chips were down, was he really a coward at heart? Scared of what lay beyond? Frightened of not doing the job thoroughly enough and waking up in hospital with his eyes and half his face blown away, as had happened to one of the squaddies out in Iraq, suffering from post-traumatic stress disorder? The poor bastard was still alive, in the nearby Blind Veterans' home.

His hand was shaking, tiring. He couldn't hold the gun up there much longer.

Get on with it, do it, be a man.

He closed his eyes, tried to think of Elaine's face, to take her memory with him, but the image wouldn't come. His brain refused to print it out for him. Just a blank.

Too bad. He jerked his finger hard, decisively, straight back against the guard. *THONK.*

A sharp, metallic sound. Silence.

Somewhere below him a car horn hooted in anger. He opened his eyes. The paddleboarder was still there, moving serenely. The container ship was still out on the horizon. He was still alive.

Or was he imagining it?

He lowered the gun and stared in disbelief at it.

He felt the paddleboarder laughing at him. The ship's crew mocking him.

The whole world enjoying his embarrassment.

Johnny Fordwater's so useless he can't even kill himself!

He spun the cylinder, but it barely moved. 'Useless as a chocolate teapot,' he muttered. He hadn't oiled the damned thing in years, he realized, maybe that was the problem.

He laid it down on the table behind him and went through into the utility room behind the kitchen to see what he had. There on a shelf above him, nestling between the Mr Muscle and a canister of Brasso, was a small can of 3-in-One Oil. As he reached up, his phone rang.

Ignore it.

It rang several times then stopped.

He returned to the living room with the oil and a rag and began lubricating his weapon until the cylinder spun freely.

The phone rang again. He looked at the display:

International. In a sudden moment of black humour he was reminded of an old favourite film of Elaine's, with Peter Sellers and Peter O'Toole – and the actress Ursula Andress.

What's New Pussycat? There was a scene beneath a bridge across the Seine in Paris, when one of them had said to the other – he couldn't remember which – 'How can I eat my dinner while you are trying to commit suicide here?'

He picked up the phone and answered with a quiet, 'Hello?'

A man with a foreign accent he couldn't place, possibly German, said, 'Major Fordwater?'

'Speaking.'

'I am Mr Jules de Copeland, I am Ingrid's brother.'

'Pardon?'

'Ingrid – Ingrid Ostermann – I am her brother, you see.'

Johnny wasn't sure what he was seeing – or rather, hearing. The man's accent was strange, now sounding more African – Nigerian, perhaps – than German.

'Jules?'

'Yes, Jules.' He gave a strange little laugh, all good-natured.

'Nice to speak to you, Jules.'

'Well, yes, you see I have some news about Ingrid. She should have come to England – she was looking forward so much, she was so excited for her new life with you! But very misfortunately, her taxi on the way from Munich to the airport was in a bad accident on the highway. The driver was killed. She was in a coma, you see. It has taken me a while to track you down and tell you this very bad news, sir.'

'I see. She is still in a coma?'

'Yes, but they say she will wake soon. We are praying for her. But there is another problem – she has no medical insurance. The hospital needs to transfer her to a private clinic to continue her recovery, but without funds they will not accept her. I am thinking you would want to help her.'

'There's no one else in the family who could help her financially, Jules?'

'No, unfortunately, there is just me.'

'So none of the money I sent over previously for you is left?'

There was a moment of hesitation, then the man laughed again. 'No, there's not unfortunately, no.'

'And how are the boys doing at school? You did use that money I sent to pay their fees, I trust?'

A brief hesitation then he replied, 'Oh yes, indeed.'

'I'm glad to hear it.'

'So perhaps, Mr Fordwater, you could arrange a bank transfer of £30,000 to cover the initial medical bills?'

'Thirty thousand – will that be enough?'

'Well, perhaps not really, sir. Maybe £50,000 might be better.'

'Fifty thousand, yes?'

'Yes, I will give you new account details.'

Inside, Johnny was bristling, but he kept his calm. 'That's very good of you. I have just a few problems, Jules.' He deliberately fell silent, waiting for a reaction.

After several seconds the man prompted him. 'Problems?'

'Well yes, you see, firstly you say you are Ingrid's brother. But her brother's name is Rudy, not Jules. Secondly, in Germany they don't have *highways*, they have *autobahns*. And thirdly, I believe Ingrid Ostermann, whoever she is, has been suckering money out of umpteen other mugs like me. I suggest you try your luck elsewhere. Now if you'll excuse me, I'm right in the middle of something important.' He ended the call with a grim satisfaction, then looked back at the gun. The phone rang. Again, *International* showed on the display.

He nearly didn't answer it.

35

Roy Grace stared warily up at the fixings of the large chandelier the woman was hanging from. Decorated with carved, gilded birds and dripping with teardrop pendants, it looked like it belonged in a stately home, as did the stucco work on the ceiling. He was trying to assess the danger from the evident strain on the ceiling, which had caused the cracks and fallen chunks of plaster. Was it going to hold, he wondered, or was the ceiling about to come crashing down under her added weight? From a safety standpoint, the sooner her body was cut down, the better. Another flake of plaster fell as he watched.

'What do you think, Glenn? Cut her down?'

Branson, several inches taller and closer to the ceiling than him, was looking equally concerned. 'I reckon the whole chandelier's going to come down soon if we don't,' he said. 'Like that massive one in the Royal Pavilion, when we were on Operation Icon – the one that came down during our investigation, killing Gaia's stalker, Drayton Wheeler.'

'That didn't have the help of a dead body.'

'Right, boss.' He looked up again, nervously. 'Didn't one come down in the *Phantom of the Opera* as well?'

'I wouldn't know – I'm not a lover of musicals.'

'You're such a cultural philistine, you know?'

'A philistine? Me? What's cultural about a bunch of luvvies in ridiculous costumes bursting into song? Cleo took me to the opera once. I spent the whole time praying for a fat lady to come on stage and start singing. Or a heart attack – whichever came sooner.'

'I rest my case,' Branson said. 'There's no hope for you.'

'There's no hope for either of us if the ceiling comes down while we're arguing. Shall we focus?' He instructed Alex Call to have someone cut down the dead woman immediately, but to preserve the knot. Knots often yielded fingerprints or DNA, and in the case of serial offenders, the style of knot could be a vital clue.

He scanned the bedroom, not wanting to stay in there too long. Evidence that he was in the home of someone in the antiques world was all around. The grand two-poster bed, the beautiful inlaid dressing table adorned by silver and porcelain ornaments, the chaise longue scattered with cushions. Through the window he could see white marble statues dotted around the lawn of the well-kept garden. They looked vulgar, as if trying to give the place the airs and graces of a stately home. Not his taste. There were framed oil miniatures on the walls, fine curtains and antique rugs, and an exquisitely upholstered bow-backed chair directly beneath the dead woman.

His focus was on the elements that might make it a crime scene, as Bill Warner had suspected. The DI had good reason to be suspicious. The top of the seat cushion was a good six inches below Suzy Driver's feet. Roy assessed the cushion. If she'd been standing on it, attempting to hang herself, it would have squashed down even more. There was no obvious way she could have hauled herself up the extra distance.

On her right foot was a black velvet slipper with a gold

crest. Her left foot was bare and the left slipper lay on its side on the far side of the room, against the skirting board. He speculated on how it had got there. Had she kicked out her legs in her death throes, in her final desperate struggle for air? Or had she been carried unconscious by her assailant and had the slipper fallen off and, in a red mist of panic, had he – or she – not noticed?

Had she even died from hanging, he began to wonder? Or was she dead some time before being strung up there? Hopefully, the pathologist would be able to answer that. But however she had died, he was already pretty certain in his own mind that she had not taken her own life. Someone else had.

An iPhone lay on the floor, beneath the chair at the dressing table. An odd location – had it fallen there? Possible sign of a struggle? He called one of the scene investigators over and instructed him to seize the phone as evidence. Then the two detectives left and carried out a room-by-room walk-through. Downstairs in a sumptuous den were two chesterfields, face to face across a handsome coffee table, and a tidy roll-top desk. The clue that something was missing from it was a Mac power cable lying on the floor. Grace followed the cable under the desk, where it was plugged into a wall socket. The switch was in the *on* position.

Had her computer been taken? By her killer?

There were no other signs that this was a burglary. No cupboard doors or filing-cabinet drawers left open with the contents scattered everywhere. The whole house looked neat and tidy. The offender might have just taken her computer. Because of what was on it? But if so, why hadn't he – or she – taken the phone also? Not noticed it under the chair, perhaps, in the heat of the moment? What else had they not noticed?

He walked into the hall, with busts on plinths, framed antique Brighton prints on the walls and a very ancient high-backed hall-porter's chair. He carried on through into the kitchen, which was fairly modern in comparison. And saw the iPad immediately. It sat on a work surface on the far side of the room, next to a toaster and a coffee machine, plugged into a socket.

Had Suzy Driver's killer also missed this?

He called Aiden Gilbert at the Digital Forensics Team and asked him if someone could take a fast look at Suzy Driver's phone and iPad, to try to see who she had been in contact with in recent weeks. Next, he radioed the Force Control Room and requested a bike or car from the Road Policing Unit to pick the items up and rush them to Gilbert in nearby Haywards Heath.

On a handsome oak Welsh dresser was a wedding photo in a silver frame. He presumed it was Suzy Driver and her husband. She was standing in the front porch of a church, in a wedding dress, her hair tumbling in ringlets around her shoulders, and wearing a short veil. Raymond Driver, in a morning suit with wide trousers and sporting a red carnation, a fancy gold brocade waistcoat and big hair, stood proudly beside her. Alongside was her maid of honour, a fair-haired woman who looked familiar to Roy.

Next to it was another silver-framed photograph, one he was immediately certain he had seen before. Identical to the one he had received from Marcel Kullen in Germany. The photo of the two ladies in ballgowns. The fair-haired one was the maid of honour.

They weren't identical but they looked so similar they had to be sisters. Suzy and Lena, Roy thought. Both dead.

He looked at Branson, who had joined him and was staring intently at a yellow Post-it note stuck to a work surface. Something was handwritten on it, in blue ink. 'Jack Roberts,' the DI said, pensively. 'Why do I know that name?'

'Is he a movie star?' Grace said, mischievously.

'Ha ha. If he is, he's from back in the silent movie era – you're more likely to remember that, old-timer.'

Grace gave him two fingers and opened a drawer in the dresser. He could see without touching anything that it contained a roll of Sellotape, scissors, a couple of ballpoint pens, a stapler and a photograph of three young children playing on a beach that he recognized, from a trip to Australia with Sandy many years ago, as Bondi. He slid the drawer shut, then opened the next and glanced in, but saw nothing of interest, nor in any of the other kitchen drawers.

Then he looked at a cork noticeboard fixed to a wall. There were a couple of taxi firm business cards pinned to it; a Thai takeaway menu; a cartoon drawn by a child of a beach, sea, a sailing boat and a big, low sun.

Then he saw another business card. 'Bingo!' Branson said.

'Perhaps?' Grace added with a note of caution. The card read:

Jack Roberts

Investigations Director

GLOBAL INVESTIGATIONS

1st Floor, 44 Richmond Road, Kingston,
Surrey KT2 5EE

'Pay him a visit?' Branson suggested.

Grace glanced at his watch. Kingston was a good hour away; longer, probably, as they would be heading into rush hour. 'Better see if he's there, and willing to wait for us.'

He dialled the number on the business card.

36

'Hello?' Johnny Fordwater answered cautiously, his hands reeking of oil.

'Hey, buddy, how you doing?'

It was Gerry. Sounding irrepressibly cheerful.

'Not that great, actually, but thanks for asking.' Johnny glanced at his watch and did a quick calculation. Gerry was in the Midwest. Six or was it seven hours behind the UK? Mid-morning for him. He looked down at his gun. It lay there, taunting him.

Try again, Major Failure!

'Look, buddy, I'm feeling pretty gutted myself, for suggesting online dating.'

'Well, you were only trying to be helpful, Gerry – and you had a great experience – you found a beautiful lady in Katrina.'

'Karen,' Gerry corrected him.

'Karen, yes, sorry. You're a lucky guy.'

He fell silent, fixated on his gun. Tempted. So tempted to pick it up and end it all whilst still talking to Gerry.

Interrupting his chain of thought, Gerry said, 'Thought you might want to know the same's happened to another buddy of mine, a former NYPD detective who went through one shitstorm of a divorce and then thought he'd met his

157

PETER JAMES

soulmate. Instead, she rinsed him. I feel terrible, buddy –
like, I'm the idiot who made all this happen.'

'Gerry, I don't blame you in any way. I know you meant
well, and it's not your fault, I was just incredibly stupid. I
just – I – I should have seen it. Blinded by love, I guess.'

'These internet scammers are smart. They know how to
yank someone's chain every which way.'

'Very neatly put.'

'OK, here's the thing. My ex-NYPD buddy, Matthew
Sorokin, isn't gonna take this lying down. I hope you don't
mind, but I told him about your situation and he'd like to
talk to you – can I hook you guys up?'

*Well, I'd like to but I'm just about to blow my brains out,
as soon as you get off the line, if that's all right with you,
Gerry?* Johnny was tempted to say. Instead he found himself
saying, 'Sure, Gerry, I'd be really interested to talk to him.'

37

'So, how can I help you, gentlemen?'

Jack Roberts, getting up from behind his desk to greet Grace and Branson, still exuded energy and charm, despite it being the back-end of his working day. The PI's dark tie was slack, the top button of his creased purple shirt unbuttoned, his grey suit jacket hanging over the back of his chair. As he beamed, he revealed a youthful set of gleaming white teeth.

Showing their warrant cards, Roy Grace said, 'We are investigating the death of Mrs Susan Driver. We found your business card at her home, and possibly your name on a note in her kitchen.'

Roberts looked visibly shaken. 'Dead? Suzy Driver?'

'You knew her, sir?' Glenn Branson asked.

Roberts ushered them to a leather sofa, and then sank into an armchair beside it. 'Suzy's *dead*?' He clenched his knuckles.

'I'm afraid so,' Grace said.

A woman brought in a tray with tea, coffee, bottled water and a plate of digestive biscuits, which she set down in front of them, then left.

'How – when – when did this happen – what happened?' Roberts asked. 'How did she die?'

159

'I'm afraid we can't tell you at this moment, sir. May I ask how you knew this lady?' Grace asked.

The private investigator said nothing for some moments. 'Well, she first contacted this agency about three weeks ago – hold on a sec and I'll tell you exactly.'

He jumped up, went over to his desk, stood over it and tapped the keys on his computer. 'Yes, September 7th she came to see me. She was quite agitated. She told me she'd been widowed four years previously and had joined an online dating agency.' He shrugged, walked back over and sat down again.

'I'm afraid, gentlemen,' he said, 'it's a familiar kind of story that we deal with here constantly. She'd met a man purportedly from Norway, giving his name as Norbert Petersen. And using a photograph of a gentleman lifted from the internet. But she was unaware of this at the time.

'She was attracted to him and they chatted online for several months – just steadily getting to know each other. He told her he was a geologist in the petrochemical industry, working on oil exploration in Bahrain. They got on so well, she said she was starting to fall in love with him.'

'Despite not having met him?' Grace asked.

'Correct.' Roberts paused and dropped a sweetener in his tea. 'Then one day he gave her the usual kind of cock-and-bull sob story, some bullshit about his grandmother having cancer and needing treatment in a special clinic in the USA, and asked her if she could give him a short-term loan of £20,000 to pay her costs. He explained he was going through an acrimonious divorce and his wife had had his bank accounts frozen. Could she lend him the money to tide him over and he would pay her back as soon as the divorce was settled and he was able to sell his home. Luckily, Mrs Driver was sceptical and did a reverse Google search on his image – something her sister had explained to her. You just put in an image and do a Google search on it and it will come up with any matches. Mrs Driver found his same profile on a number of different online dating sites. When she challenged the so-called "Norbert Petersen", he assured her that he was genuine and that some bastard had stolen his identity and was using it to scam lonely women around the world.'

'She was clearly a smart lady,' Glenn Branson said. 'How did she get suckered in – or, at least, nearly suckered in?'

Roberts shrugged. 'I can't explain what it is, but there is something strangely powerful – almost magnetic – about internet romances. A connection that is far stronger than a traditional meeting of two people. Maybe because on the internet you can lie all the time, each person gives the other only their good side. It's intoxicating. That's one of the things which makes it so dangerous – and such easy pickings for fraudsters.'

'Can you tell us more about Suzy Driver?' Grace asked.

'Suzy came to see me because she was in love with this Norbert Petersen, but had been smart enough to want someone to check him out before sending him any money.'

'You checked him out?' Grace asked.

'That's one of the things my agency specializes in,' he responded. 'The Norbert Petersen that Mrs Driver is – was – in love with, I'm afraid, is an invention. Our investigations led to two dead ends – one in Jersey in the Channel Islands, the other, Munich. They led us to the true identity of the photograph this Norbert Petersen was using. He is quite a high-profile Brighton resident, a motivational speaker called Toby Seward. He's gay and happily married.'

Grace frowned. 'What do you know about Suzy Driver's sister, Lena?'

'Very little, but they both appeared to be on to something.'

'Are you aware that she's dead?'

'Her sister? Lena?' Roberts exclaimed, looking shocked.

'She was killed in Munich last week,' Grace continued.

Roberts shook his head in disbelief. 'Whatever it was they were on to must have something to do with why they're both dead now.' He was silent again for a moment. 'This changes everything. Our IT guys have been digging as hard as they can, but they've hit firewalls in both places they haven't been able to penetrate, yet. I'll gladly share any information we do get to help your investigation, as their client confidentiality is no longer an issue here. You might be interested to know that we've had two other clients who seem to have been targeted by this same group.'

'Can you give us any of their details?' Grace asked.

'I'm afraid with the new privacy regulations I can't disclose much about them. What I can tell you is that one paid out over £300,000 and the other close to two million.'

'Two million?' Glenn Branson exclaimed.

'I've had one client who paid out just over *five* million.'

Grace stared at him. 'How could—'

'I know,' Roberts interrupted him. 'Incredible, right. We're in the grip of an epidemic. These scammers are smart professionals.'

'Five million pounds?' Glenn Branson said, incredulous.

'A charming old boy, a retired investment fund manager with a beautiful mansion and fifty acres. Had a nice, comfortable retirement all mapped out. Now he's living in a bedsit on his state pension, while some kiddo in Ghana or Nigeria is wearing a Rolex and riding around in a top-of-the-range Porsche or Ferrari or Range Rover Sport my client's money has bought him, as well as probably his grandpa, his cousins and all his mates. Meanwhile, what are you guys doing about it?'

'All we can,' Grace said.

Roberts looked at him the way he might study a wounded animal. 'Really? Thanks to our former Home Secretary, you don't have enough officers to chase the moped and knife gangs who've turned London into a war zone. Right?' he added, pointedly.

'I think you'd have to look pretty far and wide to find a copper with a good thing to say about her,' Grace admitted.

Roberts shrugged. 'I love her! I raise a glass to her every night. "Thanks, darling Theresa," I say, "for all the business you've handed to me."' Then he shook his head. 'But I tell you something. I built much of this business out of exposing rogues. It hurts me deeply to have to tell nice, decent people the truth about the person they've met online. The *love of their life*, who doesn't actually exist.' He looked at them both. 'Is that why Suzy Driver is dead? Killed herself in desperation?'

'I'm afraid I can't comment,' Grace said.

Jack Roberts nodded. 'I respect that.' He looked at each detective in turn. 'I'll say one thing. Unless you get on top of this situation, there's going to be an epidemic of suicides in the months and years to come.'

'You said your agency is specializing in so-called internet romance fraud,' Grace said. 'Is there any intelligence you can share with us?'

'Well, there is something you may be able to follow up on. A possible mastermind operating out of Jersey.'

'Do you have his name?'

'I will have soon, with luck.'

The man was lying, Grace could tell. He already knew the name and wasn't going to give it to them.

'Anything else I can do for you, gentlemen?'

'No, not for now,' Grace said. 'You've been very helpful. We'll need to take a formal statement in due course.'

'You know, the best thing you guys can do is get the word out to the public. Make them aware. Maybe use Crimestoppers – get them running a national campaign.'

'We're working with the local Sussex branch on this,' Branson said.

Roberts nodded. 'It needs to be nationwide.' He shrugged. 'Suzy Driver. I don't know how she died and I understand you gentlemen aren't able to tell me at this moment. But I tell you this, you should be treating anyone who dies after being scammed online as murder victims, whether they take their own lives or not. Scamming an elderly person out of their life savings is tantamount to killing them. I've had three clients who got wiped out, who eventually took their own lives. What's left for people in their seventies or eighties, who've always been used to having a little money, who are suddenly facing losing their home? They're not going to be able to go out and start earning – at least nothing other than pin money, you know?'

The two detectives shot an uncomfortable glance at each other. 'I hear what you're saying, Mr Roberts,' Grace said.

'I'll give you one piece of advice. You'd better act fast and hard on this. Otherwise you're going to find vigilantes doing your job for you.'

'Really?'

Roberts gave him a strange look he could not read.

Grace and Branson stood up to leave. As Roberts shook their hands, he said, 'Guys, I know a lot of police officers are currently pretty disenchanted with their lot – several have joined my team. If you ever decide to quit the police, my door will always be open. And I pay a lot better.'

'We'll bear that in mind,' Grace said.

'You do that, gentlemen. The pleasure will be all mine.'

After the two detectives had left, Jack Roberts opened a file on his computer.

It was titled: LYNDA MERRILL – DAUGHTER, ELIZABETH FOSTER. SCAM. He had an idea that was steadily taking shape.

38

Johnny Fordwater dialled the number Gerry had given him.

It was answered almost immediately, in a brusque, businesslike, American voice. 'Sheriff's office.'

'Is it possible to speak to Matthew Sorokin?'

'Completely possible, you got him now.'

'Ah, right, hello. My name is John Fordwater. I was given your number by our mutual friend, Gerald – Gerry – Ronson.'

'That son of a bitch?'

It wasn't the response Johnny had been expecting. He wasn't sure if it was humour or anger in Sorokin's voice.

'You know what I would do to Gerry if I had him in range?' Sorokin said, ending Johnny's uncertainty. 'I'd squeeze his scrotum so tight his testicles flew out hard and fast enough to win me a coconut. OK?'

'OK,' Johnny echoed, uncertainly. 'Should we talk?'

'We sure should. How much you been suckered for?'

'Close to 500,000 dollars, in your currency. You, er – Matt?'

'A lot less, but all my savings.' He hesitated then he said, 'Ninety thousand give or take. I've been a goddam fool.'

'I think you and I are members of a very big club.'

'Tell me about it. So what's your story? Apart from having the same misfortune as me to know Gerry.'

Johnny told him. Sorokin listened in silence until he had finished. Then he said, 'You and I – we're in the same deep brown stuff. I'm down a little less than you but that don't make the pain any easier. Thing is, John, I don't take crap lying down. You don't strike me, from your background, as a guy who does either. Are you in my boat?'

Johnny Fordwater didn't know the expression. But he had a good idea what it meant.

'I'm in your boat,' he replied.

'An old colleague, Pat Lanigan, is still working in law enforcement in New York. He has connections, know what I'm saying?'

'What kind of connections?'

'You got enough dough left to buy yourself an air ticket to New York?'

'Just about.'

'Good. We have a plan. I'll meet you there. Next Monday too soon?'

'Not soon enough.'

39

Roy Grace stood in front of Assistant Chief Constable Cassian Pewe's absurdly large desk – which he was about to lose, Grace thought with some satisfaction, due to austerity forcing more and more senior officers to have to share office space. The ACC, still seated, was daintily sipping from a china cup of coffee. He offered Grace neither a seat nor a drink, pretty much par for the course. The time to be worried, Grace knew, was when he did.

Pewe, perfectly groomed as always, was, in Roy Grace's opinion, sailing close to a nervous breakdown. The sooner the better, he thought. The man had been on a management training course earlier in the year, and ever since, at their twice-weekly morning meetings, had been spouting unintelligible gobbledygook.

Pewe gave him an unnaturally warm – near-dementedly warm – smile, staring at him intently. The look reminded Grace of an expression he had always liked: *The eagle eye of the inefficient.* Then, the ACC's voice, half snide, half patronizing, asked, 'So, Roy, are all your spreadsheets green?'

'I actually wouldn't know, sir.' The *sir* came out with the reluctance of a dental extraction.

'You are aware, are you not, Roy, that I'm an advocate of the multi-systems approach?'

'Completely.'

'Good. So may I enquire why, in midst of preparing for three important murder trials, you've decided to take time out to waste your valuable energies – doing nothing to move the needle on our homicide statistics and stretching police financial resources on what is clearly no more than an unfortunate suicide?'

'I beg your pardon, sir?'

'You know exactly what I'm referring to, Roy. You are allowing yourself to be distracted from your important trial work out of sheer hubris.'

'Hubris?'

'Yes, *hubris*. You always need to be at the forefront of any major investigation, don't you, in order to see your name in the papers?'

'In my role as Head of Major Crime for the county I'd be derelict in my duties if I wasn't involved in an overseeing capacity in our major investigations, sir.'

'Perhaps it would help you focus if I removed you from that role?'

Struggling to contain his anger, and thinking to himself, *I once saved your life, more fool me*, Grace replied, tersely, 'That would be your prerogative. But I cannot agree with you that Suzy Driver's death is suicide. You've seen the pathologist's initial report, that she had suffered a blow to the back of her head from a blunt instrument prior to hanging – or rather, being hung.'

'A blow to the back of her head that matched marks and hair found on her carpet by the CSIs which indicated she might have fallen over backwards sometime before her death. Old people do fall over sometimes.'

'She was not an old lady, sir, she was only in her mid-fifties.'

'I don't care, Roy, I don't see enough evidence here to launch a murder enquiry. You are aware of our tight budgets these days, aren't you? The average cost of a murder enquiry currently stands at £3.2 million.'

'What about the emotional cost to a victim's loved ones? Have the bean-counters calculated that, too?'

'Everything has a cost, Roy, unlike the dreamland where your head seems to spend most of its time.'

'Fine, sir. So from now on you want me to tell the families of murder victims that we're not going to be investigating them because we can't afford to?'

'That's not what I'm saying at all. We just have to be absolutely certain before we launch any investigation and start incurring costs.'

Grace was struggling to keep his temper. 'Is it really that you don't want to spend the money on an investigation, or is the truth that you are mindful of massaging your crime statistics and we are already over our murder rate for the year?'

Pewe wagged a warning finger.

Ignoring it, Grace said, 'Christ, you were once a detective yourself. Would you have looked at a body hanging from a cord around the neck with her feet six inches above anything she could have stood on and not wondered how she could possibly have done that by herself?'

'No,' Pewe replied, flatly.

'Do you want to tell me she stood on a block of ice, like that old locked-room puzzle?'

'I'm not playing puzzle games with you, Roy, I'm looking at the evidence, the facts. We have a bereaved and lonely woman. She's looking for love online and all she finds is conmen. Then her sister dies, the final straw. Did she know? Maybe she got drunk, fell over, bashed her head. Had enough, ended it all. End of.'

'Very few women hang themselves, sir, that's a known fact. It's extremely rare.'

'Good, so you have an extremely rare situation. As you are into known facts and presumably statistics, too, let me throw a few at you. Last year in the UK we had a total of 585 homicides. We had 1,730 road traffic deaths. Those figures pale into insignificance when you look at the number of suicides: 6,188. How does that weight the odds, Roy?'

The Detective Superintendent shook his head in disbelief at his boss's attitude.

'Anything else I can help you with today?' asked Pewe.

'You're really happy to leave it there?' Grace stared at him with a mixture of frustration and anger.

'Until I see better evidence to convince me she might have been murdered, I am, Roy. Perhaps you should be wondering to yourself, Roy, how come – when we were both the same rank less than two years ago – you are exactly where you were and I'm now an ACC? Maybe there's a reason for it which is now becoming self-evident.'

It was all Grace could do not to punch his boss's supercilious face. He stood, simmering. 'And what about her dead sister in Germany?'

Pewe replied, 'Is that information confirmed yet? It's for them to investigate, not us.'

'It's not confirmed one hundred per cent, but it's looking like the two sisters were killed and their deaths are linked.'

'Not in my mind, they're not. And while you've been out there garnering more newspaper column inches, you've been totally ignoring another directive I gave you, Roy.'

'I have?'

'You don't think so?'

'Which directive are you referring to, sir?' Pewe threw so many at him, he had lost track.

'I'm referring to one from the latest Home Office report, Roy. Can you tell me exactly how you have delivered, supported and inspired your team in a way that's led to an increase in diversity?'

Grace stared back at him, almost incredulous. 'Sir, at this moment we are facing a crime epidemic. Sussex citizens on dating agencies were scammed out of £30 million last year. Our murder rate in the last twelve months is at a fifty-year record high, as are burglaries and street crime. And you are worrying about diversity? I'm extremely proud of the diversity in my team, sir. I'm afraid I don't have any field officer in a wheelchair because unfortunately, in my wide but admittedly limited experience, not many victims are considerate enough to always be murdered in access-friendly locations.'

'You're sailing very close to the wind, Roy,' Pewe said.

All of it coming from your backside, with a very nasty smell, Grace would dearly love to have said.

As he left the ACC's office a few minutes later, closing the grand door behind him, he was thinking about the words an embittered colleague had said to him recently, over a pint: 'It's not the down-and-outs and the criminals on the outside that you have to worry about, Roy, it's the ones on the inside who'll cut your throat and hang you out to bleed dry.'

His phone rang.

'Roy Grace,' he answered, standing in the corridor; Pewe's assistant sat typing in her booth, opposite him.

It was DC Kevin Hall, a member of the small Major Enquiry Team he had assembled to investigate Susan Driver's death.

'Boss, we've just heard back from the Landeskrim-inalamt in Munich. Could be quite significant.'

'Tell me?'

'Lena Welch, the woman who went over her balcony in Munich, and Suzy Driver, are definitely confirmed as sisters. It took them a while to make the connection because both of them have married names. And there's more, boss. Velvet's just spoken to a close friend of Mrs Driver. She'd been telling her, very excitedly, about the dating agency she'd joined about a year ago. The friend told Velvet that recently the sisters had been concerned that a man Suzy had been talking with, who she found very attractive, had asked her for money and she was becoming suspicious about him.

'And now both sisters are dead,' Grace said.

'It gets better. Munich police recovered from Lena's flat a digital recording device, which shows images of her killer. There might be more to this than meets the eye, boss – in my humble opinion.'

Roy Grace was feeling a sudden burst of elation. 'Humble is good, Kevin!' Ending the call, he spun round and knocked on ACC Pewe's door, a *rat-a-tat-tat* riff on the classic policeman's knock, and loud enough to annoy him. He was more than a little pleased that he was about to ruin his boss's morning – and, with a bit of luck, his entire day.

40

Monday 8 October

Johnny Fordwater, nursing a stinger of a hangover, was feeling tired and fractious. It was 9 a.m. in New York but his metabolism was elsewhere, in another time zone. It was 2 p.m. UK time, he calculated, which would be fine if he'd managed to sleep last night, which he hadn't. He'd dozed for a while on the flight over from London, but it had been hard in the cramped economy seat. Then he and Sorokin met and hit it off like old mates. They'd sat drinking far too much whisky in his hotel bar late into the evening.

Now, in the open-plan offices of the Conviction Review Team, on the second floor of the handsome building of the Brooklyn District Attorney's office, Johnny sat perched alongside his new comrade-in-arms on a wobbly swivel chair. Facing them, arms outstretched on top of his cluttered desk, was the tall, broad-shouldered figure of Detective Investigator Pat Lanigan. In his mid-fifties, the Irish-American had begun his working life in the US Navy, before becoming a stevedore in the docks and then joining the NYPD. He had a pockmarked face with greying brush-cut hair and a light beard. He exuded charm and seemed genuinely concerned for their predicament.

The Conviction Review Team shared the floor with the Mafia-busting Team. A short distance behind Fordwater and

Sorokin was a large whiteboard on which was charted the family tree of one of the most notorious New York crime families.

'So, Johnny,' Pat Lanigan said in a strong Brooklyn accent, 'I wanna tell you something about how I feel about all vets, OK? The American flag that you see on our roof and every other place does not fly because the wind moves past it. Our beautiful flag flies from the last breath of each military member who has died serving it. And that goes for the flag you served under, too, Johnny. I don't like to see anyone screwed over, but most of all someone who's put their life on the line serving all that we believe in and stand for.'

'Thank you,' Johnny said. He had liked Lanigan instantly, the moment he met him, just fifteen minutes or so ago. Matt Sorokin, dressed in jeans, a leather jacket over a turquoise polo shirt and cowboy boots, looked like a guy who had been born angry and had just got even angrier with each passing year.

'Good old Lanigan horseshit!' Sorokin retorted.

'You'll have to excuse my pal,' Lanigan said. 'He never took too kindly to life creeping up and biting him on the ass.'

'I only protected your ass for thirty-two years in this city, buddy! But I appreciate your sentiments.'

Looking serious now, Lanigan said, 'So, I wanna do everything I can to help you guys. Where do we begin, how do you wanna play this?'

'Pat,' Sorokin said, 'Johnny Fordwater here is a decorated war hero. He served his country, rank of major in the military, and put his life on the line, then lost his beloved wife. He deserves happiness in his twilight years. Having dedicated forty years of my life to serving my country, mostly through the NYPD, I kind of feel the same. Instead, both of us have been hit pretty hard. How do we wanna play it? Hardball, is what I say.' He looked at the Englishman for confirmation.

'Detective Investigator Lanigan,' Johnny Fordwater said, 'the thing is—'

'*Pat*, please,' Lanigan interjected.

'OK, Pat. Thank you. Matt and I know there is little – if any – hope of ever recovering what we've lost. We've both been damned fools, in our own ways. But if there's to be any good out of all this mess it will be to – somehow – use our experience to help prevent others from becoming victims. And just maybe, in the process, find a way to recover some of our losses.'

Sorokin was looking studiously at his phone. 'What we'd like, Pat, is for you to use whatever contacts you have in the NYPD, currently, to track down the shitbags behind this. I'll do whatever it takes.'

Johnny stared at the family tree behind him. 'Are the New York Mafia involved in this area, Pat?'

'I'm sure it's a business they'd love to be in,' Lanigan said. 'These guys hate to miss out on any opportunity. But mostly they carry on their business the way they always have done – with one foot in the past, and they're being overtaken. They've not moved into technology. They're still doing mostly their same protection racketeering shit but with smaller traders now, because none of the big ones have cash these days, it's all credit cards and online. So now it's the corner stores, the little guys who are struggling who are their prey, as well as the same old smuggling cigarettes and alcohol, fake designer goods and prostitution. The Mob are behind the eight-ball when it comes to internet crime – for now, anyhows.'

'Probably not for long,' Sorokin commented.

Lanigan nodded. 'So, I talked to a couple of Secret Service guys who are housed right here in this building, just one floor up, and they say internet financial fraud comes mostly under Homeland Security or the FBI depending on jurisdiction.' He looked at them. 'So, here's the thing. I've spoken to internet fraud guys in both these outfits here in New York and they tell me the ringleaders are almost all based either out of Africa or Eastern Europe. The major player in tackling internet fraud is the City of London Police Economic Crimes Unit, but they're creaking under the strain. We're talking about an epidemic here. Over one billion dollars in this country in the last year alone.'

'One billion?' Johnny said.

'One billion that they *know* about. The true figure could be way above that. A lot of people are too embarrassed to admit to anyone they've been scammed. And large corporations, too. It's party time for the con artists. Banking, credit card fraud, romance fraud, mortgage fraud, and still, after thirty years, every day of every week someone falls for an email telling them their uncle in Nigeria has died leaving a fortune of a hundred million bucks they can't get out of the country, and all they have to do is send four blank sheets of signed letterhead notepaper to get a share of it. Every damn day of the week some poor damned sucker is standing in a hotel lobby, somewhere in the world, waiting for a guy to turn up with ten million bucks in a suitcase who is never going to appear. And they're gonna find out they've just been cleaned out of every cent they have in the world. I hate to have to tell you, but you guys are small beer in this shitstorm.'

'Well, that's just great to hear, Pat,' Sorokin said, bitterly.

Lanigan raised his arms placatingly. 'I have someone who may be of help to you guys.'

'You do?' Johnny's hopes rose.

'Uh-huh. Someone the FBI Cybercrime Unit has worked with in the past. This is one smart guy – he's been an advisor to both Apple and Microsoft on cybersecurity.' Lanigan looked directly at the Englishman. 'And he must be near where you live, Johnny. Ray Packham. Recently retired from the Sussex Police Digital Forensics Team due to a health issue. Set himself up as an independent consultant investigating internet fraud. The guys here say he's the top banana, knows how to drill down through pretty much any internet exchange. My advice to you guys is to go talk to him.'

'I've flown all the way to New York for you to tell me this?' Johnny said, angrily. He looked at Sorokin, who shrugged. 'We could have done this in a phone call – instead I've forked out over £500 I no longer have to fly out here. This expense I really did not need. I'd rather have given the money straight to this Packman fellow.'

'*Packham*,' Lanigan corrected. Fordwater snorted.

'Johnny, we needed you here in person to share the intelligence – that's something we could only do face to face. We had to meet, this was not going to happen over the phone or via email. OK?'

Fordwater shrugged. 'OK, so be it. But I'm not exactly happy.'

'What time's your flight?' Sorokin asked.

'I got the latest one out I could, to give us plenty of time,' Johnny replied. 'Nine o'clock this evening, I think it is. I might as well try to get an earlier one.'

'Tell you what, Johnny,' Lanigan said. 'It's a beautiful city. You've not been here before, right?'

'Right.'

'How about I take you guys on a ride around, since you've come all this way. Would you like to see the Dakota?'

'The what?' Johnny asked.

'The apartment building that was used in the movie *Rosemary's Baby*. It's where John Lennon lived – and was murdered. I'll show you the place where poor John was shot. Terrible. I'll take you across to the memorial in Central Park, Strawberry Fields – would you like to see that? Were you a Beatles fan?'

'Not particularly.'

'We're talking the greatest musicians of all time, Johnny.'

'That's what you think.'

'We all got our opinions. That's what Francene and I think about John, anyhows. What else would you like to see while you're here, Major? Any place you'd like me to take you?'

'The airport.'

41

Success is the ability to go from one failure to another, with no loss of enthusiasm.

Toby Seward, who was sitting at his desk reading through his filed collection of quotes, liked to tell that one from Churchill to salesmen. He was searching for appropriate ones for a motivational speech he had to give on Wednesday, to 400 double-glazing sales people at their company's annual conference. He cut and pasted it into his speech as a possible, then searched for more.

In the background was BBC Radio Sussex, his regular daytime companion when he was working at home. He knew his local station well, and did an occasional afternoon slot on it, talking about how to motivate oneself. He came to another quote that was particularly appropriate to sales teams.

The most dangerous phrase in the English language is, 'We've always done it this way.'

That always amused him. And when he used it, he would see a large number of his audience amused, too, just for a moment, before they squirmed at the uncomfortable truth.

Then he added another, more because it, too, was an audience pleaser.

Stay away from negative people. They have a problem for every solution.

It was coming up to 3 p.m. He dutifully stood to do his hourly stretches, as his chiropractor had instructed. Then he left his tiny den, which was little more than a cupboard with no door, and went down into the kitchen to make a cup of tea. As the kettle came to the boil he heard, through the overhead Sonos speakers, the familiar jingle of the Radio Sussex theme tune heralding the news. He only half listened to yet another dreary item about more overrunning engineering works on Southern Rail. But as he poured water onto the teabag in the mug, he froze as he heard the words:

'Sussex Police have confirmed they now believe the death of a woman found dead in her house in Hove, last Tuesday, is suspicious. Susan Driver, aged fifty-five, was the widow of the well-known Brighton antiques dealer and charitable benefactor, Raymond Driver, who died four years ago.'

Dead? Murdered?

By who – why?

He felt gripped by a sudden terrible sense of dread. Who would have killed her? Why?

The female newsreader said, 'We talked to the Senior Investigating Officer, Detective Superintendent Roy Grace of Surrey and Sussex Major Crime Team, just a few minutes ago.'

A man came on the radio, talking with a straightforward, blunt voice. 'We would like to hear from any members of the public who were in the vicinity of St Ann's Well Gardens or Somerhill Avenue over the weekend of the 29th and 30th of September and saw anything unusual or suspicious – in particular an unfamiliar vehicle. If they would please call the Incident Room on 0800 747 3651 or Crimestoppers, anonymously, on 0800 445 6000.'

The news moved on to sport and an important football fixture this evening for Brighton and Hove Albion.

Ignoring his tea, Toby hurried back up to his den and logged on to the *Argus* newspaper's online site to see what up-to-the-minute news they had of Suzy Driver. A photograph of her came up immediately. The one she had sent him only a short while ago. Her pleasant, warm face, with large blue eyes – a hint of sadness in them.

WEALTHY BRIGHTON WIDOW'S DEATH SUSPICIOUS

Dead.

He'd spoken to her less than a fortnight ago.

He read the article. It was an elaboration of what he had just heard on the radio, with further comments from the investigating officer and his request for witnesses to come forward. But the detective gave no clue how she had died, other than to say she was found dead in her own home. The article said, as he remembered Suzy telling him, that her husband had been one of the city's most prominent antiques dealers.

Did they have some priceless gems in the house that a gang knew about? Or cash, Toby wondered?

Or?

Was it possible there was any connection to the request for money from her determined, fraudulent online 'lover'? Should he tell the police about that or would they already know? He debated for some minutes, then picked up his phone and dialled the number, at the bottom of the *Argus* column, for the Incident Room.

As he waited for it to connect, he wondered if he should also call his friend, Danny Pike, presenter of the Radio Sussex morning show. Danny was always interested in issues, and Suzy's targeting by a fraudster in the months before her death was a story in the public interest, a salutary warning about the perils of internet dating.

Had he known the consequences that were to follow, he would never have picked the damned phone up.

42

Roy Grace sat with his assembled team in the first-floor conference room of the Major Crime suite. There were seven detectives including a new member of the team, DS John Camping, who had been seconded to them from the City of London Economic Crimes Unit, and three civilian staff – an analyst, an indexer and the Crime Scene Manager.

Grace rested his elbows on the oval table, feeling tired and with two days' growth of stubble. He'd spent most of the weekend here, apart from a few hours at home each night snatching some sleep. His shirt was crumpled, the sleeves rolled up and the top button undone, his tie slack. He tasted some of the tepid, stewed coffee in a mug stencilled SHERIFF that Glenn Branson had given him for his birthday, wrinkled his nose at it and put it down. A light bulb was buzzing and flickering above his head, annoying him, but he let it ride, trying to keep his focus on the case. Driven as much by a desire to show Cassian Pewe just how wrong he had been, as he was to deliver justice to Suzy Driver and her family.

Next to the wall-mounted monitor behind the conference table were three whiteboards on easels. On one were crime scene photographs of Suzy Driver's hanging body in her bedroom, as well as a couple of her taken when she was alive. On another was a family tree of both her and her sister, Lena Welch. On the third was an association chart. One section of that contained the names, along with photographs, of six different men Suzy Driver had had contact with on the internet dating site. These had been recovered from her phone and iPad by the Digital Forensics Team. Five of the photographs were small, the sixth, of a man with silver hair, much larger. There was a second photograph of the same man, but with a different hairstyle, next to it.

Grace stifled a yawn and swallowed a guarana pill from the bottle Cleo had got him, to try to help him cut down on his coffee intake. 'OK, everyone, this is the seventh briefing of Operation Lisbon, the enquiry into the suspicious death of Suzy Adele Driver, so we will be running through all the information to date. With new members of the team, we need to bring everyone up to speed. What we know at this juncture is that Suzy had joined PerfectPartners.net in the hope of finding a soulmate to share the latter years of her life with. She engaged in online dialogues with six different men, five of whom have now been contacted and eliminated from our enquiries, but we've drawn a blank on the sixth.' He pointed at the large photograph. 'This person gave his name to Suzy Driver as Dr Norbert Petersen. He told her he was a Norwegian geologist from Oslo, working in the petro-chemical industry in Bahrain. But so far he hasn't been traced. A double-check at the Norwegian Embassy confirms Petersen is not a real person. They have no one of that name working either in the petrochemical industry or in Bahrain – or anywhere. This might chime with recent information that's just come in from our media appeal, right, Simon?' He looked over at DS Snape.

'Very much so, sir. This afternoon I took a call from a

Brighton resident, Toby Seward, a professional motivational speaker. He said Mrs Driver had contacted him out of the blue on September 26th, telling him his photograph was being used for what she believed to be an internet scam. He said she'd told him that eleven different women, including herself, thought they were in love with him.'

'Lucky him!' Norman Potting said.

'I don't think so,' Snape, who was not a Potting fan, retorted. 'Toby Seward is gay.'

'He could pass these ladies on to me, then!'

'Thank you, Norman,' Grace said, sharply.

Snape went over to the whiteboard and pointed at the larger photographs. 'These two are of Toby Seward. On the left is one he emailed me this afternoon. The one on the right is the online profile photograph with the name Dr Norbert Petersen.' He paused to let this sink in.

'Do all the other women Suzy traced have this same name and identity of Petersen, Simon?' Kevin Hall asked.

'All different,' said the newly promoted Detective Sergeant Jack Alexander, who was running the Outside Enquiry Team. 'According to Mr Seward, who I went over to see with Arnie. He'd subsequently spoken to Suzy Driver on several occasions and she'd given him pretty much chapter and verse.'

Arnie Crown was a diminutive, wiry American of thirty-six. Due to his height he had been nicknamed Notmuch, as in 'Not Much Cop'. It was a soubriquet he appeared to revel in. His wife, Vivienne, now a member of the enquiry team, was proving extremely effective as the analyst.

'Mr Seward is a smart guy,' Crown said. 'No question he had absolutely no idea his identity had been taken. He was devastated that Suzy was dead. He certainly didn't think she was remotely suicidal – he said she was a feisty lady who was rather enjoying her sleuthing, and she was hatching a plan to turn the tables on the scammers.'

'That's helpful, thanks, Arnie,' Grace said. 'Now, we have another significant development regarding her sister, Lena Welch. We have established from talking to relatives and friends of Suzy that they were close. Suzy was widowed, Lena Welch was a divorcee. The two ladies both joined online dating agencies – Digital Forensics have looked at email exchanges between them in which they compared notes on the replies from men they received. Where this gets particularly interesting is that in the weeks prior to their deaths, each woman had become suspicious about a man they were communicating with.'

'The same man?' Simon Snape queried. The Detective Sergeant, an intense and very keen officer in his early thirties, was a new addition to Roy's team. With his elongated neck that left his shirt collar snagged on his Adam's apple, and small head with eyes close together, he had the look of a reptile constantly poised to strike. An effect further enhanced by his sometimes hissy voice from the way he pronounced his 'S's.

'No.' Grace hesitated. 'Actually, Simon, that's a very good question. Certainly neither women thought or suspected that. But from what Digital Forensics have learned, and from what we've been told by Munich, each of them was in communication with someone who had gone a very long way to hide his – or even her – identity.'

He paused to turn the page, momentarily distracted by Norman Potting who was tapping his vaping device on his worktop. Then he continued.

'On Monday, September 24th, Lena Welch plunged to her death from her sixth-floor apartment in Munich, landing on railings which impaled her. Moments after her fall, according to witnesses, a man ran up to her wielding a machete and hacked at her face with it, which accords with the subsequent forensic report in which the front part of her tongue was severed. A week later, Suzy Driver was found hanged in the bedroom of her home here in Hove. Although it was meant to look like suicide, in my opinion and supported by forensic evidence, she was murdered. Kevin has some details on this.'

Despite his confident figure, DC Hall looked a tad nervous addressing the team. 'Thank you, guv. Well, two primary reasons for believing Suzy was murdered. The first as the boss says is the forensic evidence. She had a blow to the rear of her head – sufficient in the pathologist's view to have rendered her unconscious prior to her being hanged. This was backed up by further forensic evidence – traces of her hair and blood found on the carpet of her bedroom. Secondly, we have new information from the Landeskriminalamt in Munich. A neighbour of Lena Welch reported seeing a man acting suspiciously outside her flat in Munich, sometime before she fell to her death. Her description of this man matches closely a report from one of Mrs Driver's neighbours who saw a person of his description in a car near her house several times over the weekend she died. This is possibly the same man who stars in very blurry CCTV footage the LKA have obtained from a convenience store opposite Lena Welch's apartment building.'

'How blurry, Kevin?' Grace asked.

'The quality's rubbish, I'm afraid.'

The team watched on the monitor, in poor, hazy colour, with constant flare-out from the street lighting, a man of African origin pacing up and down the street, past Lena Welch's front door. He appeared to press the door panel and disappear inside. The image was too blurred to make out his face, but he was wearing bright-red shoes of some kind. After a gap of several minutes, he reappeared and walked out of frame.

Suddenly, a second African appeared, holding something, possibly a blade, that glinted in the light. After a brief gap, a dark-coloured car raced past at speed.

'It gets better, guv. Here's footage from a concealed camera in Lena's flat.'

He hit a couple of buttons on his laptop and on the screen appeared an African man, blurry at first, and there was the sound of a scuffle, followed by a woman's voice crying out, then stifled. Something, possibly two figures, moved past the camera. There was a loud thud. The woman was silent. They saw the African again, in better focus now, walking hurriedly around as if looking for something. Then he ran out of the room.

Hall stopped the recording.

'Nice work, Kevin. Have Munich police said anything about getting this analysed?'

'Only that they're working on it, guv.'

'OK,' Grace said. 'Last Tuesday, DI Branson and myself met with a PI, Jack Roberts, of Global Investigations, whose company has carved a niche in the romance fraud area. He told us that the biggest current player in this field is an outfit with links to Ghana, Nigeria, Munich and the Channel Isles. He believes there is a possible mastermind currently based in Jersey. I've made contact with a Detective Inspector Nick Paddenberg of the Jersey States Police Financial Crimes Unit. I understand from him that with a large number of elderly, wealthy residents, they're experiencing, proportionately, just as big a problem in the field of romance fraud as we are. I'm tasking you with making contact with them to see what you can find out.'

'I'll get straight on it, sir,' Camping replied.

Grace thanked him, then saw DS Alexander had raised a hand. 'Yes, Jack?'

'I have something that may be very relevant, sir. A neighbour of Mrs Driver told one of my Outside Enquiry Team officers this afternoon, DC Patel, that she too had noticed an unfamiliar car drive up and down the street several times over the Friday and Saturday of the previous week. The Saturday was the last time Suzy's daughter in Australia spoke to her. There has been no phone or internet activity from Suzy since early Saturday afternoon, and no transactions on her credit or debit cards since then either.

'At around 9 p.m. on the Saturday evening, this same neighbour was putting a lead on her puppy in the front garden of her house to take it across the road into the park, St Ann's Well Gardens, when she heard someone running down the road – a jogger, she assumed. She was distracted by her puppy, which was playing up and not letting her get the lead on, but she glanced up and noticed the man was African-looking. A minute or so later she heard a vehicle start up and drive off at speed. She didn't immediately connect this jogger to the two men she'd seen in the car during the previous two days, because she was focused on her dog at the time. It was only when DC Patel spoke to her that she started making the connection.' Alexander glanced at his notes, then up again. 'And she said something which I think now might be highly significant. She noticed that this jogger – runner – passing under a street lamp had bright-red trainers.'

43

Monday 8 October

'Fatso!' Ray Packham called out. 'HUDSON! FATSO!' he shouted, even louder, the wind instantly whipping his voice away as he dutifully traipsed across the hilly fields behind his Woodingdean home, on his evening constitutional walk with the dog.

The disobedient, overweight beagle had lumbered off, in one of his eternally futile chases after a rabbit. The thing was so plump it would struggle to catch a tortoise, Packham thought. Although he was only too well aware that until recently he would have struggled to catch a tortoise, too.

In his late forties, mild-mannered and polite, Packham always dressed more corporately than the more-casual average tech guru. He was on the mend from a debilitating spinal condition that had caused him to take early retirement from the Sussex Police Digital Forensics Team. After years of crippling pain, he'd now been given a new, almost miraculous treatment, and on his doctor's orders was walking five miles a day, recording them on his Fitbit.

He was revelling in his second career as an independent IT consultant, working with police forces and banking security advisors around the world, although tonight he was feeling a bit gloomy at the prospect of going back to an empty house. His wife, Jen, was on a Mediterranean cruise with her sister. It was one they should have been on together, but two days before departure an urgent job had come up from the City of London Economic Crimes Unit, currently his biggest paymaster, which he and Jen agreed he should not turn down.

'FATSO!'

The blooming dog was nowhere to be seen in the rapidly deepening darkness. A few miles to the south he could see, intermittently, two pinpricks of light: a fishing boat or a container ship far out on the choppy water of the English Channel.

'FATSO! HUDSON!'

He was wishing he'd worn a heavier coat tonight, the bitter wind freezing his nuts off. Suddenly the display of his phone lit up. An incoming call.

International was all the display revealed.

'Ray Packham,' he answered, tenting his head with his anorak to try to keep out the noise of the wind so he could hear.

There was a brief delay then he heard a very correct-sounding English voice. 'Mr Packham? My name is Johnny Fordwater. I've been given your name by Detective Investigator Lanigan of the New York Police Department. An associate of his in the FBI – Bradley Warren – suggested you might be able to help me.'

'Bradley Warren? I met him a few years ago at Quantico. He's a good chap, how is he?'

'I've not actually met him himself – he passed on the recommendation.'

'Very good of him, I'd be happy to try. What can I do for you?'

Fordwater filled him in on his and Sorokin's situation.

'I'm sorry to hear this, Mr Fordwater.'

'It's *Major*, actually. Retired.'

'Apologies, Major. Did I hear you say £400,000, Mr – Major – Fordwater?'

'Correct – and change.'

Hudson came lumbering out of the gloom towards him.

'Good boy!' he praised.

'Pardon?'

'Sorry, I was talking to my dog!'

'Ah. I'm getting a lot of roaring sounds, can hardly hear you – don't think this is a very good line.'

'I'm halfway up a hill and it's blowing a hooley,' Packham said. 'Might be best if you call me in half an hour when I'm back home.'

'Good plan.'

When he did call back, Johnny Fordwater related the whole story in detail. As he finished, from the sound of it Ray Packham was now scraping food into a dog bowl. There were several loud, deep barks. 'Hudson, quiet!' More clattering, then he said, 'I'm afraid, Major Fordwater, yours is not a unique story. I have a whole caseload of similar tales. If you're hoping I might be able to recover your money I'd like to save you any further time and costs right away. I'm sorry to tell you this bluntly, but there isn't a hope in hell.'

'I know that,' the Englishman said, bleakly. 'But myself and my chum, Matt Sorokin here, from the Hernando County Sheriff's office in Florida, would like to use our experiences to at least warn others not to end up in the same situation as ourselves. And I – we . . .' His voice tailed off.

'Yes?' Packham prompted.

'We have a proposal we'd like to discuss with you. I'm flying back to London tonight. Can we meet – as soon as possible? Tomorrow morning, I could come straight to you from the airport.'

'Are you sure you want to spend the money?'

'Oh yes, very.'

44

The Elvis Presley track was coming to an end.

Radio Sussex presenter Danny Pike said, over the music, 'From the King! The one and only Elvis Presley! "Can't Help Falling in Love". Great song, eh? But it comes today with a health warning. My next guest will be familiar to regular listeners of BBC Sussex, and we've all learned something positive from him – Brighton's very own motivational speaker, Toby Seward. Me, I learned from him how to be motivated enough to wake up early in the morning. Then my son, Josh, was born and my wife and I didn't need an alarm clock any more! But today Toby Seward is here to talk about something quite different. Thanks for coming along, Toby.'

'My pleasure, thanks for having me on, Danny.'

'Just to set the scene, Toby is a handsome fellow, forty-eight years old with nice hair and great teeth. He is so handsome in fact that his image has been used, without his knowledge or consent, to chat up no less than eleven different ladies who've signed up to internet dating agencies in search of a soulmate. He is in the studio with me to talk about the dangers of online dating. Sussex Police today released figures on internet crime, showing it to have reached epidemic status, and online dating is the biggest of all in this current crime wave. In Sussex alone, during the past twelve months, over forty residents have been scammed out of £30 million by people they had met online and fallen in love with. The smallest loss was £40,000 and the largest scam relieved one person of an incredible four million quid. Toby, you've recently had a pretty shocking experience. Would you like to tell our listeners about it? I should repeat, this comes with a health warning. So, Toby, you must have had lots of success internet dating?'

'Thank you, Danny,' Toby Seward said with a grin. 'I've got no need at all to go internet dating now. My husband, Paul, and I are very happy – we did actually meet on a dating site some years ago. But since then I've had an experience I felt I needed to publicize because, as you rightly say, online romance does indeed come with a very serious warning.'

'Tell us what happened to you, Toby.'

'Sure. Well, it was about a fortnight ago I got a phone call out of the blue from a well-spoken lady called Suzy. It's a call I will never ever forget. She asked if I was Toby Seward. When I said yes, she said, "I'm very sorry if this sounds strange, Mr Seward. My name is Suzy. You see, you don't know me, but the thing is, I thought I knew you."'

'Wow!' Pike interjected. 'And you didn't, right?'

'I'd never heard of her, no. She went on to tell me that we'd been in love with each other for the past eight months, having met on a dating website.'

'In love – but you hadn't actually met, right?'

'Right. She'd signed up to this agency, putting up a photograph of herself and her profile. She was the fifty-five-year-old widow of an antiques dealer, looking for a new life-partner. One of the replies she'd received was from a gentleman giving his name as Dr Norbert Petersen, a geologist from Norway working in Bahrain in petrochemicals. And he used my photograph!'

'Your photograph? Where did he get it from?'

'He must have pulled it off the internet. He also said he was fifty-eight, which is a bit insulting as I'm only forty-eight!'

'I'd be a bit annoyed by that, too, I think! So how did she rumble this person?'

'Well, it seems he strung her along for several months, all the time professing to be falling more and more in love with her.'

'Although they hadn't actually met?'

'Not physically, no. I think there is something very powerful about internet flirtations. I remember the excitement when I first met Paul over the internet. There's something both mystical and compelling about it.'

'And dangerous?'

'Exactly. Very. If you meet someone through friends, you have a frame of reference, you'll know something about that person's background by the fact that they're a friend of a friend – that's a kind of automatic vouching for them. When you meet a complete stranger online, it's a very different situation.'

'Don't online dating agencies check out their clients carefully?'

'I'm sure that some do, Danny, but there's a limit to how far they can, and all the more so with the current data protection legislation in place.'

'OK, so go on.'

'Well, a few weeks ago, Norbert Petersen told Suzy that his grandmother was desperately ill and needed expensive hospital treatment. He explained that his wife, whom he was divorcing, had had their bank account frozen. Could she lend him £20,000 to help with the medical bills, which he promised to pay back as soon as the divorce was sorted and he could sell their home. Fortunately, Suzy is – was – a smart lady. She became suspicious at this point and did a reverse Google search.'

'A what?'

'She popped Norbert Petersen's photograph into Google and basically did a search on it – it's very simple. Through this she discovered that "Norbert Petersen" was one of a number of different names under which this same photograph of myself appeared across different dating sites.'

'Blimey, so what happened?'

'She confronted him, saying she believed she was being scammed and she was going to report it to the police. He came back at her with a story about his identity being taken by an internet scammer, which again she was smart enough not to believe. Then yesterday I heard the shocking news that she is dead and Sussex Police have begun an investigation. It begs the question of whether there is a connection.'

'What do you know? What do you believe, Toby?'

'I don't know anything more than I read in the *Argus*. Two officers came to interview me, but they wouldn't give me any details. All I can say is that from my conversation with her she was a very nice lady. I can't think of any reason why someone would kill her other than to silence her.'

'She was the widow of a very successful antiques dealer,' Pike said. 'Might it not be simply and tragically a burglary gone badly wrong?'

'It might indeed be, but I don't think it's that.'

'So what's your theory, Toby?'

'I'm speculating wildly here, Danny, but knowing how much money is at stake with internet fraud, I think it's possible Suzy was killed to stop her investigating any further. She had also hinted to me the last time we spoke that she had found out something really damning about the person who'd been trying to scam her.'

'What do you think that might have been, Toby?'

'I don't know. I suspect it was something to do with his past – about who he really is.'

'And do you think that could have got her killed?' Pike pressed.

'It could have, yes.'

'So the dark side of internet dating,' Pike said. 'Do you have any message for our listeners, Toby?'

'I do, yes. I want people who go online looking for love to understand the potential dangers they're exposing themselves to.'

'So people should stop online dating? Is that what you'd like to see, Toby?'

'Not at all. But for anyone out there listening, who is either internet dating or contemplating it, please just be aware.'

45

Tuesday 9 October

They *were* aware. Very aware.

Only too aware.

'Like, you should be aware, too, Toby *Seward*-sounds-like-*Sewage*,' Jules de Copeland muttered back at the radio. 'You know, going live on air and saying this shit.' Tossing his cigarette butt out of his window, he glanced at his colleague in the passenger seat. Ogwang was playing a game on his phone, concentrating intently. 'Right?'

'Yeah.'

Ogwang glanced at his watch. His large, shiny, £15,000 Breitling Navitimer that was his pride and joy. And more swanky than Copeland's smaller Vacheron Constantin.

The wipers squeak-clonked in front of them, shovelling away the pelting rain. 'You're not even listening to me, man. Local radio, that's where you find what's going on. That and the local paper, right? They're your eyes and ears, yeah?' Copeland pointed to his own eyes, then ears.

A gusting sou'westerly straight off the English Channel rocked the car. Copeland had rented the little black Hyundai deliberately, figuring they would look less conspicuous than in something bigger and flashier. But with his hulking frame making him look like he had been shoehorned into the small vehicle, his penchant for shiny clothes and his sidekick an angry bonsai version of himself, they were about as inconspicuous as two sharks in a toddler's paddling pool.

Ogwang had recently picked up urban street language and had taken to using it. 'I'm hearing you, bro, got you mega. Mr Toby Seward, OK, right? This dude's dangerous. We should teach him a lesson.'

'Like, not to go on radio and shoot off his big fat mouth?'

Ogwang stuck his tongue out, pinched the end of it between his forefinger and thumb, then made a chopping motion with his free hand. He looked at Copeland expectantly.

Copeland turned left away from Hove seafront as the lights changed, without replying. They headed up Grand Avenue, past tall apartment blocks. 'Lotta rich people in them apartments,' he said. 'Lotta older folks, widows, widowers. Looking for love. Rich pickings, here, Eastbourne, Worthing. Rich and lonely, looking for love. This is the place to be.'

He was completely unaware of the small, grey Polo, four cars back, that steadfastly followed them.

'Where we going, bro?' Ogwang clicked his cheap lighter and moments later the interior of the car filled with ganja smoke. He glanced at his watch again, admiringly. He'd had it for over two years, but it still gave him a thrill.

'Yeah? Well, I'll tell you where we're not going. Prison.' Mimicking his friend's street accent he said, 'Now put that weed out before we gets our asses busted and we gone have to 'splain what we doing here.'

They were returning to base, their gated mansion on Brighton's leafy, secluded Withdean Road, from a shopping trip. Ogwang took another drag on the joint, inhaled deeply and removed it from his mouth. He held it in front of his face, staring at it, as if weighing up his options. Copeland closed them off for him. He snatched it and tossed it out of the window.

'That was good shit, man!' Ogwang protested.

'You get good shit by staying out of prison, dumbfuck. I made that bitch in Munich look like a suicide, until you gone crazy and cut her tongue off. Now here we have a suicide, they not gonna prove nothing.'

'Gotta leave warnings,' Ogwang said. 'See? Gotta leave them, bro, else they talk. Gotta stop this Tony Sewage man talking. Dissing our agency.'

'So we go frighten him, right?'

'Right.'

'But that's all. We don't hurt him, we don't want the police coming for us.'

Ogwang slipped his hand inside his parka and closed his fingers around the wooden handle of his sheathed machete. He pulled it out a few inches and felt the cold steel of the blade. He sharpened it every day of his life, keeping the edge like a razor.

'You hearing me?' Copeland said. 'I don't think you're hearing me.'

Ogwang tested the sharpness of his blade again and said nothing.

46

There wasn't much about being back in Brighton that pleased Tooth, but the heavy rain did. Rain was always good for surveillance – it distracted people, making them less alert to their surroundings, less aware. The rain was obligingly misting up the windows of the little rental Hyundai, four cars in front, further obscuring the rear view of the two men inside it. Although in Tooth's opinion, what was mostly obscuring the view was their combined lack of intelligence. They ignored speed limits, pinging camera after camera they passed. What were they doing inside that little shitbox ahead of him? Playing a game of *pass-the-brain-cell*?

He had the radio tuned in to the local station, BBC Sussex. Over the years he'd learned that local radio gave you stuff that could be useful, and he was curious to hear any news reports about Suzy Driver. And he had been right to tune in. A man, whose name he hadn't caught, was talking in a mellifluous voice, by sheer coincidence about how his identity had been used in attempted romance frauds on eleven victims. One of whom was Suzy Driver.

Tooth had flown into Shoreham yesterday morning, one of his alias passports at the ready in case he was challenged, but no one from Border Control was around. Then he'd been dropped off, by a driver Steve Barrey had arranged, at a car rental place at Gatwick where he'd hired this Volkswagen, turning down the offer of a free upgrade. He told the surprised Budget reception guy that if he'd wanted a bigger car he'd have rented a bigger car. He wanted small.

And inconspicuous.

Wary of spending too much time in the city itself, he'd checked into a Ramada at Gatwick Airport. Tomorrow, he'd switch to another hotel in the area. For security reasons, he never liked to spend more than one night in the same location. And as yet he didn't have the firearm Barrey had assured him he was fixing for him. As soon as he got it, he'd do a double-tap on Jules de Copeland and Dunstan Ogwang and be on a plane, back out of Shoreham Airport.

The Hyundai Getz shot an amber light and he pulled up his little Polo for the red. Didn't matter he wouldn't lose them. Earlier this morning, after they'd emerged from the gates of their fortress-like residence, he'd followed them into Brighton where they'd parked in a multistorey, giving him plenty of time to place a magnetic tracking bug under the rear of the car.

And at least his employer had finally come to his senses. He no longer had the lame instruction to *frighten*. He had an updated order from Barrey.

Eliminate.

It was like he'd been walking around for days with a limp dick, and now he'd been given a shot of Viagra. He'd checked the money was in his account.

He was going after them. On it.

Where were the dopeheads going? He looked at the blue dot on his phone. They had turned right, east.

The interview with the man, Toby Seward, ended and the midday news came on.

When the lights turned green, he accelerated hard.

47

The presence of Haydn Kelly at the noon meeting Roy Grace had convened brought a smile to his face. A wicked one. Kelly, a former Professor of Podiatry at Plymouth University, was the world's leading authority on Forensic Gait Analysis. And he was, as the Stella Artois lager adverts used to say, 'reassuringly expensive'.

Expensive enough to give ACC Cassian Pewe some serious pain.

Mid-forties, solidly built, with thinning, close-cropped hair, the Forensic Podiatrist was smartly attired as ever, today in a navy suit, crisp white shirt and striped tie. There was little about shoes he did not know, although, amusingly to the team, his own were usually in need of a clean. Kelly had pioneering software, which Grace had used on previous cases to considerable effect, enabling him to identify suspects from the way they walked, from just a single foot-print.

Kelly travelled the world, much of the time in Asia, and was in constant demand by police forces everywhere. Grace needed him on his team for this investigation, and knew he was lucky the podiatrist had a gap in his schedule and was available to come down today.

'I don't think Professor Kelly needs much introduction

to most of you,' Grace said. 'So, Haydn, what can you tell us about our suspect and his apparent liking for red footwear?'

'Well,' Kelly said, 'it's early doors, but from the very poor CCTV footage I've seen from Munich there appears to be a distinctive "N" on the shoes. That indicates the brand is New Balance. I've established they did produce a shoe in this colour last year. I see from your CSI luminol spray of the area that there are footprints in the front garden of the deceased Mrs Driver's house which match the tread pattern of New Balance shoes manufactured in this red colour.' He pointed at the wall-mounted monitor above the conference table, on which was displayed the zigzag tread pattern of a trainer, obtained from the Police National Footwear Database. 'But as a caveat, this trainer was made in a range of colours. You have no CCTV from the area of your crime scene?'

Grace shook his head. 'Mrs Driver's immediate and near neighbours have been questioned. All we have to go on, at the moment, is a statement from one of the witnesses that she saw a man, who in her words looked African, running fast in red trainers shortly before hearing a car drive off at speed.'

'Anything else that jumps out at you, Roy?' Haydn Kelly asked. 'Or any of your team?'

He faced a sea of shaking heads.

'Professor, you've just seen the CCTV footage from Munich,' Glenn Branson said. 'What, as Sherlock Holmes might say to Watson, can you deduce from that?'

'I'm afraid, at this stage, nothing too *elementary*. But I did deduce that the subject might easily be picked out in a crowd. He has a rather peculiar exaggerated arm swing and very distinctive rolling gait. Prior to this meeting I ran the

footprints, taken from the deceased's garden, through my software. They indicate a very similar gait, which would produce that same kind of arm swing. You have hundreds of CCTV cameras in your county, right? Of which close to one hundred are in this city. If your camera operators could pick out anyone in red trainers, I could analyse their gait from what I have, and very probably get a match that way.'

Roy Grace took on board what Kelly had to say, but he knew the immense size of the task. With just four operators on at any one time, how on earth could they trawl through all that footage effectively? But equally, he knew, this was the best shot they had. At least they had some criteria to narrow it down.

'That was a famous movie, boss,' Branson said.

'Famous movie?'

'*The Red Shoes*, 1948. Starred Moira Shearer.'

'Is this relevant, Glenn?'

'Not really, boss. Just saying.'

48

The blue dot, now only a few car lengths ahead of Tooth, continued threading its way east, in the direction of Brighton's Clock Tower. Then it turned north up into the maze of residential streets above Queen's Road, heading in the general direction of Brighton Station. He closed the gap until he could see the Hyundai ahead, separated from him only by a turquoise taxi.

It made a sharp right, losing the taxi. He slowed down, following at a safe distance. Large terraced houses on either side. The Hyundai made a right at a T-junction at the end of the road, in front of a pub, then headed down a steep hill towards a busy one-way system with a queue of traffic. Just before reaching it, the car made another right.

Holding back again for a brief while, he then followed where the Hyundai had gone, turning into a narrow, one-way street. To his right were dinky-looking terraced cottages, Victorian, he guessed from the architecture, set back from the road behind trellis-fenced gardens and narrow car ports. To the left were more modern-looking terraced houses and an old, traditional-looking pub. The Hyundai had stopped a short distance ahead, outside a canary-yellow cottage that looked even cuter than all its neighbours, the front garden a riot of flowers despite the autumnal season.

Tooth halted the car, curious. Watching. Waiting. One of those little Suzuki Cappuccinos, in an almost matching canary yellow, was parked in the driveway. He waited, letting the wipers swipe away the rain. Watching.

The Hyundai drove on.

They were casing the place. Why?

He continued waiting until they had rounded the bend at the end of the street and were out of sight, then drove up to the yellow house, passing it slowly, clocking the number. He stopped a few houses on and texted his paymaster, Steve Barrey.

Within seconds, his phone software told him his message had been read.

The blue dot was now heading north-west, the direction of their base, he guessed.

A reply pinged back.

Why do you need to know?

Tooth responded:

Your buddies are interested.

Another text arrived.

So figure it out. That's what you're paid for.

Tooth put two wheels on the pavement so as not to block the street, got out of the car and hurried back through the rain. He checked there was no CCTV, then sidled up past the little Suzuki to the porch and rapped the big, brass lion-head knocker.

He had a story prepared, but no one answered.

He tried again, then again. Satisfied no one was in, he retreated to his car, started it and drove around the block until he was back at the entrance to the street. He pulled over, again partially on the pavement, and settled down to do one of the things he had been trained for in the US military, and did best. Waiting and watching.

It wasn't long before his vigilance was rewarded. A man hurried past in a trenchcoat, his face obscured by a black umbrella. He turned into the driveway, past the Cappuccino, and let himself in through the front door.

Tooth waited for a decent interval, then climbed out, approached the house and rapped the knocker again. The door was opened a few moments later by a casually dressed man in his late forties, wearing a tight-fitting jumper and holding his wet coat. He looked at Tooth inquisitively. 'Hello?'

'Have I got the right address? I'm looking for fifty-seven Campden Terrace?' Tooth asked.

The man said, almost apologetically, 'No, I'm afraid this is fifty-seven North Gardens.' He frowned. 'Campden Terrace? I'm pretty sure that's a little further up the hill.'

'I'm sorry to have bothered you,' Tooth said.

'You're American?'

'Uh-huh. Just in town for a few days, looking up an old buddy.'

'Up the hill. It's no more than five minutes away.'

Tooth hurried back to his car, arriving moments before a traffic warden. He climbed in and drove off. Thinking.

He recognized the voice of this man, and now he was guessing why Jules de Copeland and Dunstan Ogwang were so interested in him.

The distinctive voice.

The man he had been listening to earlier, the motivational speaker whose identity had been used to attempt to scam the late Suzy Driver and numerous other women. Who was now concerned to warn others.

Toby Seward.

There was a sharp *ting* from his phone. A new text. He waited until he could pull into a lay-by before looking at it. It would be dumb to get stopped – and then identified – by the police for looking at his phone while driving.

It was from Steve Barrey.

> **My pal Eddie Keys wants to buy you a drink tonight. The Stag pub on Church Road, Hove, 7.30 pm.**

Above the wording was a photograph. An unsmiling, shaven-headed man wearing a singlet and a single earring. His heavily tattooed arms were folded in a defensive pose.

Eddie Keys didn't look like the kind of guy who would want to buy anyone a drink.

Ever.

49

Johnny Fordwater could not have made that trip to New York a year ago, he reflected. Not while Nero, his Labrador, had still been alive. He would never have left the elderly, arthritic creature home alone for almost two days, and he could never bear the thought of incarcerating him in kennels; he loved that damned, loyal creature too much. In addition, Nero had been a kind of a link between him and his late wife, Elaine. She'd adored that dog, too. During those last months when she was bedridden, before she had moved into the hospice, the dog would spend hours at a time by her side.

Some miles after leaving Heathrow Airport, he turned his fourteen-year-old Mercedes E-Class south off the M25. Until just a few weeks ago he'd been planning to replace it with a more recent model, but now he knew, sadly, he never would.

He yawned, the bright, low sun shining straight through the windscreen, hurting his eyes which were raw from lack of sleep on the transatlantic flight. He'd tried a few stiff drinks to knock him out, but all they'd done was make him thirsty and drink a lot of water. As a result he'd had to clamber, several times, over the legs of two increasingly irate passengers between himself and the aisle to make his way to the toilet. He'd tried watching a movie, but couldn't concentrate. All he could think about was the mission he was now on, and trying to make a budget for his future. Something he dreaded most was the humiliating thought that he might need to turn to the Soldiers, Sailors and Airmen's charity for help.

The angry blast of a horn behind shook him; he realized with a start he was drifting across into the fast lane. He swerved back as a van travelling fast shot by, inches from his door. He should pull over somewhere, get some shut-eye for half an hour, he knew. But he didn't have the luxury of time to do that. The flight had been over two hours late arriving, due to delays at JFK, and then they were stacked for half an hour over Heathrow. His plans to go home first, shower and change were out of the window, because he did not want to miss his appointment.

After an hour, the soft green hills of the South Downs loomed ahead – the sight of which always lifted his spirits. A further twenty minutes later, entering the hilly Brighton suburb of Woodingdean, his satnav announced, 'You have arrived!' He halted on a steep residential street, outside a sprawling modern house with a sporty-looking black Audi under the car port.

Five minutes later he was seated in a snug room, surrounded on all sides by books, a veritable library of military history. He had a mug of tea in his hand, a plate of plain digestive biscuits on the low table in front of him and an overweight beagle at his feet looking up at him expectantly. Suddenly the dog jumped up at him.

'Fatso, down! Down! DOWN!' Ray Packham said.

Reluctantly the beagle lowered its paws, then gave his master a baleful look. 'Sorry about him, I didn't ask – are you OK with dogs, Major?'

'Love them. And please – call me Johnny.'

'OK. So, Johnny,' the IT consultant said, 'I understand you have a bit of a problem?'

'You could say that.'

'How would you like me to help you?'

'How long do you have?'

'As long as you need.'

Johnny repeated the whole story, from the start, bringing in Sorokin's plight, too. When he had finished, he handed Packham his laptop and guided him to the site where he had met Ingrid Ostermann.

'A very nice-looking lady,' Packham conceded, looking at her photograph. 'Whoever she *really* is.'

Fordwater gave a wan nod.

'I'm afraid you've joined a very big club, Major – Johnny.'

'So I realize,' he said glumly, feeling his chin. Feeling the growth of stubble and aware he probably didn't smell that great.

'Let me ask you a direct question. What are your expectations from me, or anyone else you're approaching for help?'

Johnny shrugged. 'At best, to recover my money, which I know isn't going to happen. At worst, for my American chum and I to at least nail the bastards who did this and stop them from destroying any more lives.'

Ray Packham looked at him sympathetically. 'I appreciate your sentiments. I'd love to help you for free, but since leaving the police I have to make a living – I've a mortgage over my head – so I do have to charge for my services. But the thing is, I don't want you throwing good money after bad. To be very blunt, in my experience your chances of recovering a single penny are remote, as I think you understand. The scammers could be anywhere in the world – most likely Ghana, Nigeria or somewhere in Eastern Europe – Romania, Albania. My honest advice to you is to treat this as a life-lesson, bite the bullet, try to forget all about it and move on. Don't let it destroy the rest of your life.'

'I can't do that, Mr Packham, I'm afraid that's not in my DNA. What is it they say – you can take the man out of the army, but you can't take the army out of the man? I'm a soldier through and through. One of the reasons I joined the army was because I wanted to correct injustices. These bastards have suckered me out of just about every penny I have. What's left in the kitty is yours. I'm happy to pay you. I want revenge on these bastards. I need you to understand that.'

'Revenge? That's your driver?'

'Yes.'

Packham looked hard at him. 'Can I just remind you of the words of Confucius, a very wise man: *Before you seek revenge, first dig two graves.*'

'I'm comfortable with that. I'm wiped out, my beloved wife is dead, my eldest child lives in Canada and I'm buggered if I'm going to go and live there, sponging off him until I die. I have nothing to live for. If any good can come out of this appalling mess, I'm happy to dig two graves – and pay for them up front. At least I'll have one certainty to look forward to.' Johnny gave him a wistful look, then stood and reached up to one of the bookshelves for a volume he'd spotted. Sun Tzu's *The Art Of War.* He pulled it out and handed it to Packham. 'Ever read this?'

'Absolutely.'

'*Stand by the riverbank for long enough, and the bodies of all your enemies will float past,*' Johnny recited.

There was a brief reflective silence by both men, before Johnny continued.

'Do you have any idea how it feels to be such a mug as I've been, Mr Packham? I've served my country to the best of my abilities, always tried to do the decent thing, always treated people fairly, and always put a little bit aside for a rainy day. Now I'm faced with losing my home and every bean I have in the world – and going cap in hand to charity. Shall I tell you what my future holds?'

Packham looked at him expectantly.

'At my age I have no chance of building up any kind of nest egg again. I'm wiped out. I face a future of living on benefits, in council accommodation. Then at some point in the future, I'll probably die in an overcrowded hospital corridor with some bloody hung-over medical student jumping up and down on my chest because they can't find a defibrillator. That's the future I face. Not a great prospect, is it? All because of my own stupidity.' He shrugged. 'Look, I'm not blaming anyone. I was lucky, I didn't take a bullet or lose my limbs in the desert. I suppose sooner or later everyone's luck runs out. I'd just rather mine had run out when I was a younger man, at an age when I could have started over and rebuilt my life. Now I'm an old fart. The best I can hope for, to supplement my meagre income, is a job on a supermarket checkout.'

Packham scribbled a note on a pad. He tore off the sheet and handed it to Fordwater. 'I don't want to take your money, there's no charge for today's session. This is who you should go and talk to, he knows more about this field than anyone. Save your money for him.'

Johnny Fordwater looked down at the sheet.

On it was written a name – Jack Roberts, Private Investigator – and a phone number.

'If he likes you, Mr Fordwater, he's your man.'

'How do I get him to like me?'

Ray Packham shrugged. 'Can't help you on that one, mate. But good luck.'

50

The Force Control Room was the nerve centre of Sussex Police. Located in a modern building on the HQ campus it housed, in a vast open-plan area, all the emergency call handlers and radio dispatchers, as well as the CCTV surveillance hub, from where any of the county's cameras could be monitored.

The CCTV hub was manned 24/7, with each shift comprising a team of four operators. Much of their time was spent scanning randomly through the cameras, watching for anything unusual or suspicious, or any accidents. During major incidents and crimes in action they would provide visual guidance to the police on any activity within camera range. Occasionally, as they were tasked now, they carried out a search.

Haydn Kelly, accompanied by DS Jack Alexander, sat staring at a bank of monitors. Next to them was the senior CCTV operator assigned to assist, Jon Pumfrey. Each of the screens showed different street views of Brighton. On one was the seafront at the bottom of West Street. Another a section of the Lanes, the lunchtime crowds shuffling along. The rain had eased off and many were carrying furled umbrellas. Another showed the busy shopping area of North Street, with the Clock Tower in the background. A further one showed a steady trickle of people heading down Queen's Road from the station.

Jack Alexander remembered the stuffed fish Roy Grace had on the wall of his office in their previous building, Sussex House. When he'd asked the Detective Superintendent about it, Grace had told him it was to remind him always of one of the essential qualities you needed to be an effective detective. Patience. Good anglers had endless patience and detectives needed that, too. Jack was understanding that only too well, now. For the past hour and ten minutes, his lean, beanstalk frame had been perched on an uncomfortable chair as the four operators cycled, randomly, through live images from various of the plethora of CCTV cameras covering the central area of Brighton and Hove.

It was a long-shot, he knew. All they had to go on was the blurry footage from Munich Police, and the description from Suzy Driver's neighbour. They were looking for a tall black man with a distinctive swagger, wearing red shoes. Since the surveillance had started there had been over a dozen sightings of males in red shoes, but none of the images had remotely matched their target. They had no knowledge who the suspect actually was, nor if he was indeed still in the area. Even less so whether he would be brazenly out and about on the streets.

After another thirty minutes, badly in need of a drink, Jack was about to get up and stretch his legs when Haydn Kelly suddenly called out, urgently, 'Camera Five! Can you stop it!'

Pumfrey froze the image. 'Want me to rewind a bit?' he asked.

'Yes, until they first appear, please,' Kelly said.

Pumfrey wound back, then played it again. The camera showed a pedestrianized street of what looked like fashion boutiques on both sides. Two black men suddenly came into view. One was tall, in a shiny suit and bright-red shoes, striding along like he owned the pavement. His companion was a much smaller, morose-looking man, in a bomber jacket and jeans. They stopped outside a men's boutique, peering at the window display. The tall African pointed at something and the other nodded.

'That's his gait – and his shoes!' Kelly said, excitedly.

'Dukes Lane, right, Jon?' Jack Alexander said.

'Yes,' Pumfrey replied. 'The shop is called OnTrend. Very expensive, high-end.'

The two men walked forward to the edge of the frame, then entered the shop.

The door closed behind them.

Alexander called the Operation Lisbon Incident Room. Emma-Jane Boutwood answered. 'Is the guv there, EJ?' he asked.

'He's just stepped away to get a sarnie. Glenn's here.'

'Put him on!'

Moments later Glenn Branson said, 'Jack, what's up?'

'I'm with Professor Kelly up at CCTV. He's just identified our suspect going into a boutique in Dukes Lane with another guy – it's called OnTrend.'

'I know that shop. Is he still there?'

'Yes.'

'Nice work, Jack. It's only a short street, ask Oscar-1 to see if he can get a unit at both ends.'

Oscar-1 was the Duty Inspector in charge of the Force Control Room. The imposing figure of Keith Ellis, in his white uniform shirt with epaulettes, hurried across from his high perch. Jack Alexander quickly brought him up to speed.

Ellis immediately radioed the Duty Inspector at John

Street Police Station, Dan Hiles, and requested response crews to cover both ends of Dukes Lane, relaying the description Alexander had given him.

Less than five minutes later the two men emerged. The tall guy was holding a large carrier bag, on which they could see clearly the shop's logo and name. The pair walked rapidly out of shot. Ellis gave urgent instructions to the camera operators to try to pick them up again. A minute later another camera picked them up leaving the end of the lane and turning into Ship Street. They walked out of shot once more.

After several minutes there were no further sightings.

'Maybe they got in a taxi?' Alexander suggested, his eyes still glued to the screens.

'I'll call Streamline and Radio Cabs,' Ellis said. 'Get someone from the Incident Room to call the shop, see what information they have on them, what credit card details they have from the transaction.'

Ten minutes later, DC Boutwood rang Jack Alexander back.

'I've spoken to the shop, Jack. He paid cash. They have CCTV inside the shop and will have footage of them.'

'Good!' Jack Alexander said. 'OK, call them back and tell them not to touch the bank notes, we can lift prints from them.'

'Yes, Jack.'

Alexander looked at Haydn Kelly, who was busy typing on his iPad. 'What do you have, Haydn?'

'The tall guy, his gait is an exact match to our man in Munich – and to the footprint analysis from Suzy Driver's house in Brighton – or, technically, Hove.'

'So what you're saying is it's the same man who was at the scene of Lena Welch's death in Munich and Suzy Driver's in Brighton – or rather, Hove?'

'No question.'

'So, where do we find him?'

'You and your team, you're the detectives. I'm just a humble podiatrist, Jack. I file down corns and bunions and cut toenails for a living.'

'Bullshit!'

51

Paul said he would be late home tonight, 8 p.m. at the very earliest, and Toby Seward was happy about that. He'd only got back an hour ago from a meeting with a multinational tech company that had offered him a dream ticket. A series of motivational speeches around the globe. They would fly him and Paul – if he could join him – business class and put them up in swanky hotels. What he was required to do was a cake-walk. Give a series of talks he'd done a thousand times before and could do in his sleep.

On the television on the wall beyond the kitchen island unit, a recording of *MasterChef* was playing. A contestant was explaining his particular recipe for scallops with chorizo and black pudding. Toby had blanched the scallops, the black pudding ready on the side on the warming plate. He was now occupied dicing tomatoes with his cheffing knife on the chopping board, whilst keeping an eye on the shallots softening in the pan on the induction hob. The oven timer tinged. He needed to take the chorizo out.

The doorbell rang.

Toby glanced at his watch: 7.05 p.m. Who was it? Paul, locked out? Too early for him to be back.

The bell rang again.

Oh, for God's sake!

He debated whether to take the chorizo out or answer the door first. He wasn't expecting anyone. Probably some dimwit pizza delivery guy with the wrong address. He walked into the hallway and over to the front door. He should have checked the spyhole, he knew. Should have checked it, he rued, in the months and years that followed. If someone had asked him why he hadn't, he would not have been able to give them a rational answer.

It was a question that would haunt him for the rest of his life.

52

Driving to his house along the rutted car track made Roy Grace happy every time. Moving to the countryside from their home in the centre of Brighton had been a gamble for both of them, but so far the only question he had was why had he not done this sooner?

The house came into view, lights blazing in the windows, and he felt a sudden moment of profound joy. As he climbed out of his car into the strong, chilly wind, he heard Humphrey bark and a clanking from the scaffolding on the far side. The workmen were now halfway through installing the en suite for Bruno. And not a day too soon – he'd never known it was possible for a young boy to take quite so long over his appearance or to have quite so many skin- and hair-care products. Some days he would be in there for the best part of an hour with him and Cleo getting more and more exasperated. It would be better in a couple of weeks, when his son had his own private bathroom. He could spend all day in there, if he wanted.

Grace looked at the house, still finding it hard to take in that he actually lived here now. Their home, their sanctuary. The rural air, tinged with woodsmoke, smelled so good. It was strange, he thought, standing here in almost pitch-blackness. He used to be afraid of the dark when he was a kid, but now he felt safe in it. Secure. Far more so than he'd ever done living in the centre of the city with all the street lights – and shadows.

Built in the 1930s for a farm labourer and his family, it wasn't the prettiest, picture-postcard cottage in the world. It had been built on the cheap, with plain, rendered exterior walls, and every window was a different size, making it look slightly lopsided. But he and Cleo loved both the house and the isolation, a place where she could escape from her duties in the mortuary, the never-ending task of receiving and preparing bodies, and trying to find words of comfort for each newly bereaved relative as they faced probably the worst moment of their life – identifying their loved one's body. And a place where he could get away from the pressure-cooker environment of Major Crime Investigation, chill with his family and recharge his batteries, if only, often, for just a few hours.

Ten minutes later, changed from his suit into jeans and a quilted gilet, he went downstairs, removed his laptop from his bag and plonked it down on an armchair opposite Cleo. She was on the sofa, surrounded by her coursework papers for the Open University degree she was taking in philosophy – which she had been steadily working on ever since he'd known her. Snug in a loose-fitting jumper, with the fire blazing, she looked cosy and contented. But Roy knew just how frustrated she was that she wasn't getting through the course more quickly. A combination of both a demanding job and home life made it hard to find the time to study, and with no classroom to turn up to, self-motivation was challenging.

They'd yet to go through a full winter here, and on the advice of other friends who'd made the move to the countryside, they'd invested in a wood-burning stove to supplement their heating. And tonight, with a draught blowing through the single glazing, he was glad they had. He took a log out of the basket, opened the door of the stove and pushed it into the flames, shutting the door again immediately. Then he looked enviously at Cleo's glass. But it wasn't an option, not even one small glass – he wouldn't take the risk. If there were any developments on the case he could be called back out.

'Supper in half an hour?' Cleo said.

'Sure.' He sat down and opened the lid of his computer.

'You seem very distant tonight,' she said.

'I'm sorry, love,' he replied. 'Pewe is down my throat over Suzy Driver.'

'He's still angry at you for making it a murder enquiry?'

'Yes.'

'For God's sake, Roy, Suzy Driver *was* murdered, no question. She did *not* hang herself. Frazer has no doubt at all. EJ was at the post-mortem, along with Michelle. Tell Pewe to speak to either of them or read the interim report!'

'I know. I'm on it. My team had the prime suspect sighted in the centre of Brighton this afternoon, but he disappeared.' He shrugged. 'Anyhow, sorry I've not asked – how was your day? How are the kids?'

As if on cue, there was a faint gurgle from the baby monitor on the table beside her. 'Noah's fine, he's asleep. Bruno's upstairs playing that game again. Him and half the youth of this nation.' Then she brightened. 'But hey, he's made a friend at school!'

'What? He has?'

Bruno's lack of friends had been a big worry to both of them. He'd not seemed interested in making any friends at all. Their attempts at introducing him to similar-aged sons of friends had not gone well and there had been no further contact with any of them. For these past six months that Bruno had been living with them, he never spoke of contact with anyone else.

'He's been invited to a birthday party in a gaming bus!'

'A what? *Gaming party bus?*'

'It's a new craze, apparently. Parents can hire this bus which rocks up at your house and all the kids get into it and play games!'

'OK,' he said, dubiously. 'Games? Like hide-and-seek and pass-the-parcel?'

'Don't show your age! Children's games are a bit more sophisticated these days, methinks – electronic – mostly video games. Don't you think it's brilliant, Roy – just the fact that he's been invited and seems keen to go?'

'Sure.'

'You don't sound that excited.'

'No, I am, absolutely. It's just . . .' His voice tailed off.

'I know what you're going to say, but I think we should give him more time before we – you know – take him to any kind of specialist. Going to a party is a really big step forward for him, perhaps a turning point in getting him more socialized.'

'Yes,' he said, walking upstairs, wishing he could believe it. He stuck his head into Noah's bedroom, lit with the weak glow of the nightlight, and tiptoed over to the cot. The boy was sound asleep, on his side. He would do anything for this little chap. But, he wondered guiltily, would he do the same for Bruno? He quickly dismissed the thought. As the animal mobile above him tinged in the draught, he blew Noah a kiss and stepped back and out of the room, closing the door silently.

Then he went along to Bruno's room.

Outside the door, he could hear gunfire, explosions and

Bruno shouting out loud, one moment in joy then the next in anger. He went in. Bruno was in his usual pose, lying back on the bed in jeans and a T-shirt, staring at the screen in fierce life-or-death concentration, his fingers moving in a blur on the control unit.

On the screen Grace saw an old bus, high in the sky, functioning as the basket for a hot-air balloon; a crouched man in military gear with a pickaxe sticking out of his backpack, aiming an automatic weapon. Swooping down aggressively out of the sky was a man on some kind of powered hang-glider, fashioned from what looked like an old window frame and shutters. There were explosions everywhere around a strange landscape with weird architecture and some ruins.

He walked round the side of the bed into his son's line of sight and said, 'Hi, Bruno, how are you doing?'

Bruno gave him a dismissive wave, furrowing his brow in even deeper concentration, either feigned or real, Roy couldn't be sure, and either way it angered him.

He stood for a moment. Just to let Bruno know he wasn't going away simply because he was being ignored. But, within seconds, he could see that Bruno was completely absorbed again, living and breathing the game. Life or death.

The sheer intensity of the boy's focus disturbed him a little. It was as if he'd gone through a parallel universe and was inside the set himself. Maybe that was the aim of the modern game creators. A kind of simulated or virtual reality that was more real than life itself.

A few minutes ago Cleo had implied he was a dinosaur. Only partly in jest. He was aware how little he knew about the culture of youngsters today, and that there was no point at all, he realized, in trying to draw from his own memories of being that age. During the time when he had been off, he'd tried very hard to engage with Bruno and learn a little more about his likes and dislikes, but virtually nothing had been forthcoming.

Bruno suddenly surprised Roy by muting the sound and turning to face him with a softer, more vulnerable expression than he'd seen before.

'I know we still need to speak, Bruno – but I've been very busy with work.'

'So how many bad guys did you catch today?'

Grace laughed. And suddenly they were chatting easily for a good fifteen minutes, more like mates than a father and son.

After he left the room, he stood for a while on the landing, reflecting that maybe he and Cleo had really started to make progress on building their relationship with the boy.

He went down to the kitchen, poured himself a glass of water and sat back down opposite Cleo, telling her the good news. Then he began the task of scanning the deluge of emails that had poured in, most of them irrelevant. But one caught his eye.

It was from his former boss, Assistant Chief Constable Alison Vosper. He'd not heard from her since the day she'd left a couple of years ago to join another force, and from the signature on her email, she now appeared to be with the London Met. Their relationship, although never easy, had been a lot better than his current one with Pewe. She'd been so mercurial in her moods, sometimes charming and sometimes acidic, that she'd been nicknamed No. 27, after the menu of a local Chinese takeaway, which had listed that dish as 'sweet and sour pork'.

She was being sweet now.

Dear Roy

I hope this finds you well. You may have heard that I'm now appointed to a Deputy Assistant Commissioner role in the Met. Could we meet for lunch sometime soon? Do you have any time free in the next couple of days, perhaps? There is something I would like to discuss. I will have my staff officer, DI Sparking, contact you to arrange a date convenient to you.

I look forward to seeing you again.

Alison Vosper

Deputy Assistant Commissioner.

Astonished, Grace read it out loud.

'Interesting,' Cleo said. 'What's that all about?'

He shrugged. 'I've no idea.'

'Are you going to meet her?'

'Sure, I'm curious. I've got to go to London later this week for a meeting in counsels' chambers with a CPS solicitor and the prosecution counsel they've engaged – I could maybe combine the two.'

'Sounds to me like she intends offering you something in the Met,' Cleo said. 'Unless she's finally realized she fancies you!'

He tried to brush it off, but Cleo was giving him a strangely penetrating stare and he was aware he was blushing slightly. In truth, although Alison Vosper had been an icebox, there were times, on the days when she was warm towards him, that he felt a connection.

'Have I touched a nerve?' she probed.

'Not my type, and I am certainly not hers. No way. Never.'

'Would you want to go to the Met? Why – why would

you want to do that? With the commute it would probably mean even crazier hours than you work here.'

'I know. But a lot of Sussex officers have – better pay there. It would really piss off Pewe if I left, he'd have no one to beat-up on.' He shrugged. 'But seriously, ever since that asshole's come to Sussex, I'm not enjoying the job any more – at least not the way I used to.'

She gave him a mischievous look. 'Why don't you tell Alison you have the perfect person for whatever role she has in mind – Cassian Pewe. She takes him on, he moves back to London, problem gone. Simples!'

'Then I'd know there really was a God.'

53

Through the crack in the door, Toby Seward saw two men with hoodies low over their faces. Gripped with terror, he tried desperately to slam the door shut.

Too late. One had a foot inside. A bright-red shoe.

An instant later the door flew wide open with the force of an express train, cracking him hard in the face and propelling him, stumbling, backwards. He crashed against the newel post at the bottom of the stairs.

Calmly, casually, as if they had all the time in the world, the two men entered and closed the front door. One, the red-shoe man, was tall, wearing a long, expensive coat; the other was short, in a shapeless parka, sporting a large, bling watch. Both wore black leather gloves. The tall one slid the safety chain home in a matter-of-fact way, as if he always did this when he entered a stranger's house. Then they turned towards him.

All he could see of their faces below the hoodies was the lower half. 'Who – who – are – who are you?' His voice came out as a petrified croak.

From inside the front of his parka, the short one suddenly pulled out a large, gleaming machete.

Toby turned and fled up the stairs, heart pounding, throat tight with terror. He ran into the master bedroom, slammed the door behind him and turned the key. Neither he nor Paul had ever locked the door in all the time they'd lived here, but he thanked God for that key now.

Phone. He ran to the landline phone on his side of the bed. As he reached it he heard a *blam* and a splintering crash behind him. Turning, he heard another loud *blam* and the thin oak door seemed to balloon inwards. The lock held. Just. He picked up the receiver, but his hand was shaking so much he dropped the handset. It clattered to the floor and bounced under the bed.

Frantically he dropped onto his hands and knees.

Blam. Blam. Blam. The walls felt like they were shaking.

Then he saw something he'd forgotten all about. Low down, just above the skirting board. Some years ago, the police had advised them to install it after they'd been victims of homophobic hate mail, followed by a petrol bomb that had been thrown through their front window, but fortunately hadn't ignited.

The black panic button.

BLAM. BLAM. BLAM.

Behind him he heard the sound of the door bursting open and crashing back against the wall.

He stabbed the button. Nothing happened.

No, please. Please. Oh God.

Then he remembered. The alert was meant to be silent. That way the police had a chance of arresting intruders before they ran off.

But was it still working?

His two assailants dragged him to his feet. There was a reek of cologne and cigarette smoke.

'What – what – what do you want, please? Do you want money?'

'Motherfucker shooting your mouth off on the radio this morning. Yeah?' the shorter man said.

They propelled him back down the stairs and into the kitchen. 'I don't understand – what do – what – what do – you mean?'

'Tell us what that bitch told you! What do you know about us?'

'Nothing – just the fraud. Nothing else.'

'Gimme your hand, bro,' the shorter one said. 'That one, the right one, yeah.'

On the screen the *MasterChef* contestant said, 'Now with a sharp knife, I am separating the coral from the flesh of the scallop, but I don't throw it away, I'm going to use it for my sauce.'

'Like cooking, do you, bro?'

'Please don't hurt me. Please don't. She didn't tell me anything. Please believe me. Please, just tell me what you want from me? Anything! I can give you my cards, pin numbers – please, what is it you want? We don't have anything in the house, we don't have jewellery, money. What do you mean, shooting my mouth off? I don't know anything.'

'You know what we mean, bro,' the short one said. He forced Toby Seward's hand down flat on the chopping board, grabbed the long-bladed knife Seward had been using to dice tomatoes and plunged it hard through the back of his hand, just behind the knuckles, crunching it through bone, pinning his hand to the board.

Seward screamed in shock and agony. 'Oh my God, you bastards, you bastards! Oh, oh Jesus. Why? Why?'

Deep crimson blood ran down his hand. The pain was excruciating. He was gasping, panting in shock. 'Why are you doing this?'

'You don't go mouthing off no more about Suzy Driver, are you hearing me?' the short one said.

'Suzy Driver?'

'Are you hearing me, bro?'

'Yes, yes, yes, I'm – I'm hearing you. Oh Jesus.'

'You say one mo word to anyone, any media, any cop, and next time the knife won't be in yo hand, bro, it's gonna be across your pretty husband's throat while you watch. You understanding me?'

He was shaking, in agony, shock kicking in. He nodded vigorously. The two men turned and walked out of the kitchen.

Toby Seward stared at the rivulets of blood pouring down around the blade of the knife and running along the board. He hovered his left hand over the handle of the knife, wondering if he had the courage to pull it out. Shaking too much to think straight.

Got to stop the bleeding. Got to phone. Phone for help.

The phone was on the far side of the kitchen. Should he pull the knife out?

He touched it with his left hand. Gripped it. Closed his eyes.

Footsteps. He opened his eyes.

The shorter man hurried back in, holding his machete. 'You got a problem there, dude, right?'

Seward shook his head, eyes bulging in pain and fear. There was nothing back. Just blackness. Dead eyes.

'Can help you out there, bro.'

'Thank you,' he gasped, the pain becoming more unbearable by the second.

The man lifted his machete and brought it down hard, severing Toby Seward's wrist cleanly, a few inches up from his hand.

54

Tuesday 9 October

Tooth strode out of the blustery wind into the Stag pub and a smell of stale beer and old carpet. He was fifteen minutes early. He was always early.

Early gave you advantages. Time to look around, check out the faces and the body language, locate the exits.

The pub wasn't busy. A handful of men were seated at the bar. A group of three men sat around a table, and one banquette was occupied by a couple, a glum-faced man and a hard-bitten brunette. All of them studied him, some overtly, some surreptitiously. It felt like he'd entered some private members' club for lowlifes, where no one was welcome, and which only a total loser would ever want to join.

There were plenty of big watches, gold medallions and vulgar rings on display, and just about everyone in here looked like they might be up for a fight with little provocation.

He spotted Eddie Keys in seconds. A tattooed mass of advanced muscle and less advanced brain. Dressed in a leather flying jacket, holding a straight glass of beer in his hand, the pair of slim, dark glasses perched on his head made him look about as stupid as stupid gets. He was talking to a guy beside him who was the wrong side of seventy, with a fake tan and orange hair.

Tooth strode over to the bar, his military posture as ever adding a few inches to his short stature, and eased himself onto a stool next to his date. There was no acknowledgement. He waited a couple of minutes, then ordered a double Jim Beam on the rocks from the barman, an old guy with a seen-it-all face. Without a sideways glance Tooth said, 'Thought you were meant to be buying me a drink?'

'I gotta take a piss,' his date said. 'Know what I'm saying?'

'I gotta take one, also.'

'Wait two minutes.'

Tooth obliged, paid for his drink and drank half of it. Then he walked across and into the stinky Gents toilet. He sidled up to the next urinal to Eddie Keys. Moments later, Keys dug his hand inside his jacket and handed Tooth a carrier bag. A very heavy carrier bag.

Tooth stuffed it into his belt and closed his jacket over it. 'What do I owe you?'

'Nothing. Sorted. Now fuck off.'

55

Tuesday 9 October

PC Holly Little, accompanied by her partner, John Alldridge, drove the Mondeo north from the Clock Tower, heading slowly up Queen's Road. The B-Section Response crew was on lates this week, the 6 p.m. to 2 a.m. shift. Thursday, Friday and Saturday were the busiest nights generally in the city of Brighton and Hove. That was when everything tended to kick off, but equally, as the two experienced officers well knew, you could predict nothing. It was the big buzz of the job for all officers working response, that you didn't know what was going to happen in five minutes' time.

Or in this case, thirty seconds.

A female voice from the Control Room came over their radios. 'Charlie Romeo Zero Five?'

'Charlie Romeo Zero Five,' Alldridge acknowledged, calmly.

'We have a reported panic alarm from a residence that's had a previous homophobic attack. Five-seven North Gardens. Can you attend, please, Grade One.'

'Five-seven North Gardens, yes yes,' Alldridge said. 'On our way.' He leaned forward and switched on the blue lights and siren.

'Just off the top of this road,' his colleague said, accelerating hard and pulling over onto the wrong side of the road to overtake a bus.

56

Jules de Copeland stood out in the dark street, his hoodie pulled even lower over his face, waiting for his idiot companion who had dashed back into the house. Suddenly Ogwang appeared, holding his machete, which was now dripping blood.

'What you done, man?'

'He's gotta learn.'

'What you done, you douchebag? What the fuck you done?' He could hear the piercing scream from inside the house.

Then a different scream. A police siren.

'Split! Gimme your blade!'

'No way.'

The siren was getting closer.

Copeland looked around in panic. His brain was spinning. This was a one-way street.

Right was against the traffic. Left was with it. He sprinted to the left. Ogwang followed.

Moments later, the siren louder, they were lit up by headlights.

57

As they swung into North Gardens, at speed, the officers saw the two figures sprinting away. Holly Little accelerated hard again, gaining on them.

'That's fifty-seven!' John Alldridge called out.

She stood on the brakes. 'Check the house, I'll stay on them.'

'OK.' He unbuckled his belt.

She halted for just the fleeting second it took for him to jump out, then accelerated off.

He crossed to the front door. As he reached it a figure staggered towards him wearing an apron over a pullover, holding his right wrist with his left hand, blood spraying everywhere as if his arm was a hosepipe, a catatonic look on his face.

For an instant it was like a scene from a horror movie. Except, Alldridge realized, this was real.

The man's wrist had been severed.

If he didn't do something immediately the man risked bleeding to death. All his training kicked in. He put his hand higher up on the man's arm, pushing his sleeve up, and squeezed hard. Blood spurted into his face.

'Help me,' the man was whispering. 'Help me, oh Jesus, help me.' He sounded faint.

John pressed his phone button. 'Charlie Romeo Zero Five. I urgently need an ambulance and back-up.'

'Charlie Romeo Zero Five, copy.'

The man's face was draining of colour as he looked at his wrist. Had to get a tourniquet on him, he knew. And fast.

Tightening his grip on the man's arm, he steered him back into the house, thinking desperately, *What to do, what to do, what to do?* There was blood everywhere, on the floor, the walls, the ceiling.

The man led him into the kitchen and to his horror he saw the reason for the severed wrist. A hand, looking like something from a joke shop, was skewered to a chopping board by a knife.

What could he use?

He spotted a tea towel. And a wooden spoon with a long handle. 'There's an ambulance on its way,' he said, trying to reassure him. The man was now looking a deathly pale.

How much blood had he lost?

Somewhere in the distance John Alldridge heard a siren. Getting closer.

Hurry.

'What's your name, sir?'

'Toby,' he said, weakly.

'Toby, I'm going to sit you down at the table, OK?'

Seward looked at him with barely comprehending eyes.

Alldridge grabbed the tea towel, wound it once round Toby's wrist, then jammed the handle of the wooden spoon into it and, using it as a lever, began twisting until it was as tight as it would go.

The spurting blood dwindled to a trickle, then almost stopped altogether. The siren was getting louder.

Two Response officers came running into the room.

'Oh my God,' one of them said quietly. He was looking at the severed hand, his face going green.

'Have you called an ambulance?' his colleague asked.

'The ambulance could take an hour. Take us to the hospital. NOW!'

58

One man disappeared up an alley. The other, holding the glinting machete, dodged onto the pavement as Holly Little, frantically radioing for back-up, drew level with him. She was debating whether to keep pursuing in the vehicle or jump out and run after him on foot.

Pepper spray and a baton against a machete. Swing onto the pavement and run him over? What if he was innocent?

An innocent man doesn't run through a city centre holding a machete. With blood on it.

But the IOPC might take a different view.

All these thoughts running through her head. A black man with a bloody machete versus, potentially, her career.

Screw you.

They reached the main road, just below the old Royal Alexandra Children's Hospital building. He turned left, down the hill, going like the wind.

She overtook him. Swung the car onto the pavement. Screeched to a halt, blocking his path, and jumped out.

He dodged past her.

'Stop, police!' she shouted. Then she sprinted after him. He stopped. Turned towards her.

Holding his blood-stained machete high.

'One step towards me, lady, and you are dead.'

She took ten steps, pulling out her pepper spray, aware the wind was behind her, and fired off its contents.

In his face.

The machete hit the pavement. His hands hit his eyes. He was screaming in agony.

Two seconds later she had him face-down on the pavement. Using her fast-cuffs she snapped one wrist, then the next.

Two guys walked past, up the hill. One said, in passing comment, 'Racist pigs.'

Another time she might have rounded on them and startled them, but not now.

'What's your name?' she said to her prisoner, pressing her emergency location button.

'Mickey Mouse.'

'So what's your alias?'

'Donald Duck.'

She slipped her hand inside his jacket, found a wallet and phone and pulled them out. Holding him down with her knee, she flipped the wallet open and saw a couple of credit cards.

Both said *D. Duck.*

'Work in Disneyland, do you? Or Disneyworld?' she asked. He said nothing but continued to struggle.

She dug her kneecap into his left kidney to restrain him. He screamed in pain.

'Sorry,' she said. 'I didn't hear your answer. What's your name?'

He was silent for a moment. 'Duck,' he gasped, thinking about the false Ghanaian driving licence in his wallet.

'Duck? As in Donald Duck.'

'That's my name. Donald.'

'Nice to meet you, Donald. My name's PC Little.'

He grunted.

She told him he was under arrest and cautioned him. Although she knew that, whatever crime this piece of scum had committed with his lethal knife, he would never get an appropriate sentence.

'Come on, sista, we're both black, lemme go!'

'It's not going to happen.'

He suddenly struggled violently, trying to pull free. She kneed him in the kidney again.

He yelped in pain.

'Sorry,' she said. 'Not nice, is it? I'll keep doing it until you stop.'

59

Something Cleo had insisted on from the earliest days of their marriage was that, no matter how busy either of them might be, they would make time to sit down at the table, with no television on, and have their evening meal together. She had also been steadily trying to wean Roy onto a healthier diet than he'd traditionally eaten as a police officer. A lot more fish than meat, vegetarian and sometimes even vegan meals.

He'd once had a pathological aversion to the very notion of vegan, but after she'd created some seriously tasty recipes he had now started to enjoy it. Tonight they'd had nut burgers, with baked beans and sliced avocado. Afterwards they both returned to the living area, Cleo to continue with her studies and Roy to start work on his best-man's speech for Glenn Branson's wedding to *Argus* reporter Siobhan Sheldrake.

He googled the subject on his laptop and found a number of websites. He needed a good joke to start with, something perhaps a little risqué but inoffensive. He found a whole stack of them, most of them terrible. Then he came across one he quite liked. 'Darling, sorry to interrupt you, what do you think of this?' he asked.

She looked up.

'*I would strongly advise the newlyweds to be cautious*

about buying their marital bed from Harrods. Apparently, they always stand by their products!'

She rocked her head from side to side as if weighing the balance. 'Yuk, that is so cheesy. No, no, no!'

'I quite like it,' he said defensively. 'I mean, hey, Glenn is cheesy, right?'

'You can do a lot better.' She peered at him. 'Roy, you look exhausted. I'm knackered, too, and I've a full-on day tomorrow, nine post-mortems.'

'Be nice if people stopped dying for a couple of days to give you a break!'

'Maybe you should ask the *Argus* to put out a request.'

His job phone rang.

Cleo raised her eyebrows.

'Roy Grace,' he answered.

It was Arnie – Notmuch – Crown. 'Sir,' the American said, 'thought you'd appreciate an update. We've arrested one of the suspects, but Red Shoes got away and has disappeared.'

Instantly, Roy sat upright. 'Tell me?' Crown filled him in on events. 'Jesus, his right hand? How is he?'

'Lost a lot of blood. He's in ITU at the Sussex County, but they think he'll pull through. The Response Team had the presence of mind to get instructions from the hospital on how to pack the hand and keep it cold. Surgeons are going to attempt to reattach it.'

'What do we know about the suspect?'

'Very little, sir. Apparently he's keeping resolutely *schtum*. All they have at present is a burner phone and two credit cards and a driving licence in his wallet, both cards in the name D. Duck – from two different private banks in Lithuania. No address in the UK that he's giving out. He wouldn't say a word to the custody sergeant.'

'So we need to make him quack.'

Notmuch gave a nervous, 'Ha ha.'

'Anything on the phone?'

'It's been biked over to Digital Forensics as an urgent priority.'

'Good. What about the missing one – any progress on finding him?'

'We've alerted Oscar-1 and CCTV are reviewing all footage of the area where he was last seen.'

'Did we get anything from that boutique they went into? OnTrend? How did they pay?'

'Cash, I'm afraid. There's some CCTV from inside the shop but it doesn't give us much more. The officers attending seized the banknotes Red Shoes paid with for fingerprint and DNA analysis. There's no print match. We'll have DNA sometime tomorrow.'

'Nothing back from Europe or Interpol?' Grace asked him.

'No, sir.'

'Was the victim able to speak? Did he say anything?'

'Only one thing, sir. In the car on the way to the hospital he told the officers that the guys who did this said they were upset by his radio appearance this morning.'

'Radio appearance?'

'He was on the Danny Pike show, talking about Suzy Driver.'

'Shit,' Grace said. His brain spun, rapidly connecting the dots. At least this latest development, horrific though it was, gave him whatever further ammunition he might need – if indeed he did still need it – to convince Cassian Pewe of just what they were dealing with. The woman dead in Munich after threatening to expose her online 'lover'. Suzy Driver dead after threatening to do the same. Now Toby Seward, the man Suzy Driver had gone to, whose identity had been taken, viciously attacked in his home hours after talking on the radio.

One of the assailants still at large.

Who was the next victim going to be?

Where did they start looking?

'Arnie, who's with you in the Incident Room tonight?'

'DS Snape, Norman, EJ, Alec and Velvet.'

Grace debated whether to go in, but decided there was little he could accomplish that he couldn't do over the phone. And, as Cleo rightly observed, he was knackered, and would be a lot more use to the investigation after a night's sleep. They had thirty-six hours to keep the man in custody before they needed to formally charge him. He didn't know how secretive Lithuanian banks might be, but they had enough time, hopefully, to establish his real identity. What he now needed was two trained advanced suspect interviewers. 'Nice work, Arnie. I want you to make sure that the suspect has a lawyer – if he doesn't have one of his own, arrange a legal aid solicitor. We're going to interview him at 9 a.m.'

'Right, sir.'

'Put Norman on, will you?'

Grace briefed Potting, then called Glenn Branson. 'Sorry to disturb your love nest.'

'Very funny.'

In the background he could hear the television. 'What are you watching? A replay of *Love Island*?'

'The news, actually.'

'Getting your rocks off to the latest on Brexit?'

'Sometimes, Roy, you are really sad.'

Grace told him the recent development. 'I want you and Norman to interview the suspect at 9 a.m. I'll watch from the observation room.'

'I always perform better in front of a voyeur.'

60

As he walked away from the pub, the heavy package still tucked in his belt, safely concealed by his jacket and parka, Tooth checked his phone.

The blue dot was heading north on the A23, the main road out of Brighton towards London, passing Gatwick Airport.

He hurried back to the Polo, which he'd parked down a side street a short distance away, and jumped in. Under the glow of a street lamp, he peered cautiously inside his coat at the contents of the brown carrier. Inside was an unbranded handgun that looked like a backstreet copy of a Beretta, a silencer and a plastic bag containing some bullets – around twenty, he guessed, he didn't have time to count them. More than enough for his purposes.

He balanced the phone on the seat beside him, stuck the bag with its contents in the glovebox, looked at the moving blue dot again and calculated that the Hyundai was around fifteen minutes in front of him.

He drove carefully through the city, then once he was out of the 30-mph zone and on the A27 dual carriageway he accelerated hard up the hill and down the far side, before peeling off left, onto the A23 north.

Taking a risk on the quiet road, he increased his speed

251

until the needle was nudging the 90-mph mark. Steadily, over the next fifteen minutes, he narrowed the gap with the blue dot. He maintained his speed. It was reckless, he knew, but he watched out for police cars like a hawk. The gap continued to close.

A few miles on, the A23 became the M23 motorway. He continued maintaining his speed. Less than ten minutes between them now. The blue dot was turning left, off the M23. Onto the Gatwick Airport slip road, the map showed him.

Shortly after, the blue dot stopped moving. Why?

Tooth almost shot past the Hyundai. He spotted it pulled over in a lay-by a few hundred yards ahead.

He slowed right down and switched off his headlights. A couple of taxis overtook him as he was wondering where to pull in. But he didn't need to as the Hyundai suddenly began moving again, crawling round the perimeter road. Tooth followed behind it at a safe distance, wondering what they were doing. Were they returning the car? Flying out?

The Hyundai drove all the way round, through the Departure drop-off zone and back round the perimeter road. Then it entered the short-term car park.

Tooth felt a beat of excitement. The car park would be pretty quiet at this time of the night. Perhaps, if they parked in a dark area, he could get them both as they climbed out of the car. A double-tap to each of their heads.

An untraceable gun and bullets.

He could be on a plane out first thing in the morning. Job done. Then on to South America. To the house he'd recently acquired in Cuenca, in Ecuador.

But instead of heading up the ramp to the parking levels, the Hyundai made a right, into the Sixt car rental area, and pulled up in a bay.

What were they doing?

Then he saw, under the weak overhead lighting, there was only one person in the car. Which puzzled him.

Red Shoes got out and headed towards the office.

Tooth reversed into an empty bay that gave him a view of the office through his mirrors. He watched Red Shoes approach the reception counter, with a bored-looking woman behind it.

And now he had a pretty good idea what was happening.

Leaving his Polo and keeping stealthily out of sight of the office, he hurried behind several rows of parked cars and over to the Hyundai. He crouched down behind it, felt underneath until he found the magnetic tracker, pulled it free and pocketed it.

61

Jules de Copeland drove away from Gatwick Airport in a new car, a small Kia, hired under a different name and card, from a different rental firm, Avis.

He was thinking about his vanished colleague. What a complete fool.

Jeopardizing their entire lucrative operation. Jesus.

His anger preoccupied him. Distracted him. Made him totally forget, as it had this past hour and a half, to properly check his mirrors.

Even if he had, he would have been unlikely to spot the headlights of the little VW Polo that followed him some distance back, staying several cars behind.

The Seekers were playing on the radio, 'I'll Never Find Another You'.

Oh yes I will. You, man, are history.

But all the same, he fretted. Kofi could give the whole game away if he was caught, and talked.

Hopefully, like himself, he'd been smart enough to get away.

Thirty minutes later, back in Brighton, he turned off the busy Dyke Road Avenue thoroughfare and down a short distance to leafy, secluded Withdean Road. He drove past the entrances to several houses, then halted at wrought-iron gates set between brick pillars and lowered the window to let the duty security guard in the control room see his face.

A twelve-foot-high, fortress-like brick wall protected the grounds and mansion beyond from prying eyes. The place served both as his residence and the headquarters of the JDC dating agency.

As the gates opened, he assured himself that Kofi would be there, in the private cinema, watching one of the crappy Netflix true-crime dramas he was addicted to.

He wasn't.

He wasn't in any of the toilets either.

Nor was he in his bedroom. The only occupant was the soul of the human skull sitting on a bookshelf. Kofi told him he'd stolen it from a grave, for his Sakawa fetish rituals. He could believe what he wanted, Copeland was fine with that, but he didn't go for all that stuff himself.

He didn't even like standing here alone in the room with the skull. It gave him the heebie-jeebies. Brought back too many memories, too many bad memories of too many skulls. Too many dead people. He had been a proud teenage warrior back then but he wasn't proud of his past any more. When you were a kid you believed what older people told you. It was easy to be brainwashed. He'd moved on from all that killing and mutilating, all that bullshit ideology fighting for a cause. All the futility. Kofi hadn't. Yeah, at times you had to be violent because that was the only thing some people understood. Kofi still got his rocks off being violent, but not himself, not any more. Now he got his bangs from seeing money in his bank accounts. *Kerrrrrchinggg!* The cash register ringing it all up in his head.

The day he reinvented himself several years ago as businessman Mr Jules de Copeland, open to do business between Ghana and the gullible Western world, with all its rich pickings to be had, was the day his life had changed. From his humble beginnings he was now a rich man, and getting richer all the time. Or at least he had been until tonight. Kofi had been a good and loyal lieutenant, but now, if he had been arrested – God forbid – he had to find a way to cut loose, fast.

He was a family man now, with his sweet wife, Ama, and a six-month-old son, Bobo, living in their farmhouse a short distance from Munich. He missed them and wanted to be back with them, soon. Please God Kofi wasn't going to mess all his plans up.

Down the end of a long corridor, in the large phone room, were six of his operatives whom he had brought over from Ghana, via Munich, for cultural training in UK ways. All were busily engaged emailing, FaceTiming or phoning 'loved ones'. Three males, three females, earning more each month here than they could have done in a lifetime back home.

But no Kofi.

Why had that stupid idiot gone back into the house? They'd already frightened the crap out of Seward – he would have been putty in their hands.

He sat down at his private workstation at the back of the room, elevated on a dais so it gave him a commanding view of his team. A bank of monitors in front of him enabled him to watch or listen in to any conversation any of his employees was having with a 'loved one' they'd met online.

He selected No. 5. Sisi Tawney. She was twenty-three, pretty.

He'd invested in a course of online elocution lessons for her, as he had with all his team.

Sisi's identity was Monique Dupres. Resident of Esher, Surrey. Widowed, tragically, at fifty-four when her late husband, a born-again middle-aged biker, was killed in a motorcycle accident, leaving huge debts. Looking to start her life over. And she had now found Mr Right.

Sisi was doing nicely. She had her hooks into a man called Guy Relph, a sixty-nine-year-old widower, eager to help his beloved in any way he could. He'd already transferred over £50,000 to help her clear her debts and keep her home. She was now playing him for a further £50,000 and it was going well.

The money was piling up!

Jules next hooked into his total star player, Esi Jabbar.

Esi had sucked in a seventy-nine-year-old widow who was besotted with him, or rather, the image she believed was him. A thirty-year-old black hunk he'd lifted from a past World's Strongest Man competitors' list.

She'd loaned him £28,000, and was now engaged with her bank, seeing if she could find a way to get an equity release on the last £100,000 of value in her house.

She was totally smitten with him, she told him. He was totally smitten with her, he'd replied.

As Jules logged on to his own workstation, a new email came in, which stood out amongst the dross and made him immediately focus. It was from his best prospect, a woman called Lynda Merrill. She was fifty-nine and attractive, with a sparkle in her eyes. He liked her. They'd been communicating for four months now, under the identity he was using of Richie Griffiths, a handsome silver-haired man, the film producer.

> **Hello, sexy beast, I've not heard from you all day. Have you gone off me? XXX**

She'd already paid over several small amounts, and now she was in the process of liquidating £450,000 to send him, to buy out his ex-wife's share of their home.

Or so she thought.

> **Go off you, my gorgeous? How could I ever, you're in my mind every second, driving me crazy for you. I've had one hell of a day. Laters, babe, yeah? I'm bursting for you. So can't wait to meet. XXXXXX**

He sent the email then put her momentarily out of his mind. He needed to find Kofi. Pulling an unused burner phone from a carefully labelled selection in his desk drawer, he set it on 'number withheld' and dialled his lieutenant's current phone. It rang. Once, twice, three times. Four times. Just as he thought it was going to voicemail, it picked up.

'Hello?' A male voice he did not recognize.

He hesitated in panic, wondering whether to hang up. Instead he asked, 'Who is this speaking?'

'Sussex Police. Who are you?'

He terminated the call instantly. His hand was shaking. He switched the phone off, and in his panic, stamped on it several times, crushing it, trying to destroy it.

His brain was racing. Could they trace the call? It was one of a bunch of burners he had bought in different stores around the Brighton area in the past months. And he'd withheld the number.

The bigger worry was why the police were answering Kofi's phone. Had the idiot dropped it, or – more likely – had he been arrested – and if so, what would he tell them? They'd long rehearsed the scenario of either of them being arrested. They both carried false identification with nothing to link them together. They had their cover story: they were travelling independently, tourists, come to visit England, the same as thousands of other visitors to Brighton.

But the British police were smart. Even if the jackass

didn't squeal, how long would it take the police to make the connections?

One statement from Toby Seward?

He thought about the £450,000. A big prize.

If he could get that quickly, then he could bail out, back to Germany or – even better – take Ama and Bobo home to the safety of Ghana, and screw Kofi. He could stew in his own mess.

Feeling a bit better, he went up to his room and began packing. Fortunately he had an emergency Plan B. A safe house he'd never told Kofi about. For just such a situation as this.

It was going to be fine.

Jules de Copeland was unaware of the car that had followed him back here from Gatwick Airport. The Polo was now parked a short distance along from the gates of this house, on the other side of the street, with an unobstructed view of the entrance.

He was unaware, too, of its occupant. A man trained by the US military in patience. A man who could go without food or water or sleep for days and still function sharply. A man who had learned to sit as motionless as a twig on a tree, for as many days as it took to do the job.

A man who had his car radio tuned in to Radio Sussex and was listening to it.

Who had just heard a newsflash about a suspected homophobic attack.

Who was waiting to kill him.

62

Tuesday 9 October

Wooky, lying on the floor, looked balefully up at her mistress. Then the miniature Schnauzer gave a little whine.

When that didn't work, she pawed at her jeans.

Fixated on her computer screen, Lynda Merrill reached down and scratched her fingers absently along her head. 'In a few minutes, darling, OK? We'll go for walkies. But Mummy's busy, OK?'

The internet was running dementingly slow tonight. A reply had come in from Richie but the text was taking an age to upload.

Finally it was there on her screen!

> Go off you, my gorgeous? How could I ever,
> you're in my mind every second, driving me
> crazy for you. I've had one hell of a day. Laters,
> babe, yeah? I'm bursting for you. So can't wait to
> meet. XXXXXX

Excitedly, Lynda Merrill picked up the bottle of Sainsbury's Riesling from the floor beside her and up-ended it into her empty wine glass on her desk, next to her keyboard.

Only a few drops trickled out.

'Oooh dear, naughty girl, you've drunk the whole bottle!'

she chided herself, aware she was feeling decidedly tipsy. *Blotto*.

Yes, that was the word dear Larry used to use whenever he – or both of them – were a bit smashed. 'Darling, I think I'm a tad blotto.'

Or, often as not, 'Darling, I think we're both a bit blotto.' They had fun getting blotto together on the fine wines he loved. She felt guilty about drinking this supermarket bargain. Larry would never have approved. He had such class, such good taste in wine. 'Some people live above their income – me, I just drink above it!' he used to say.

God, life had been hard in these years since he had died. She still missed him so much, thought about him constantly. Dreamed often that he was still alive. She remembered on their honeymoon in Capri, all those years ago, he'd leaned across the table with a glass of some very classy wine and clinked hers. 'My angel, if you live to be ninety-nine, I'd like to live to ninety-nine minus one day, so I never have to live without you.'

Her eyes moistened at the memory. Larry was staring at her now from a framed photograph on her desk. The archetypal gentleman, who had reminded her of Sean Connery when they had first met. He was always so perfectly dressed, as he was in this photograph, in which he was wearing a crisp white shirt, golf club cravat, dark hair immaculately groomed. Was it her imagination or was he looking at her disapprovingly?

Over her new romance?

The photograph was, suddenly, unnerving her. She moved it out of sight behind her computer screen.

Guilt?

She didn't need to feel guilt, she knew. Larry had told her repeatedly before he'd died that she was still a young woman and she shouldn't spend the rest of her life mourning him. That one day she would find someone else, that she should marry again and be happy again.

Maybe. She typed a reply, but the booze was playing havoc with the coordination of her arthritic fingers. It took several goes before the message was ready.

> **My beautiful Richie, you asked if I could get one hundred thou of the four hundred and fifty thou in cash. I'll have that together in a couple of days. Now, my naughty big boy, I have a real treat in store for you – and of course me! A very dear friend has gone away for a few days and she's asked me to keep an eye on her beautiful little cottage in a forest about twenty miles from here. I think it would be a very special place for us to spend a whole, uninterrupted weekend together. We could meet there in our own, very private love nest where we wouldn't be disturbed. And I could give you the cash! I desire you crazily! XXXXXXXX**

She read it through, having to concentrate hard to focus, realizing she was very definitely more than just a little tipsy.

She peered at the empty bottle again. 'Oh dear. Naughty me!' She looked down at the grey-and-white dog. 'Mummy's drunk a little bit too much tonight, hasn't she?'

The dog looked back at her, pricking her ears up. 'Shall we go for a little walkies?'

At the sound, Wooky went bonkers, tearing several times around the room, and then tried to jump on her lap.

'Down! Down!'

She stared at the screen, waiting for a reply. But nothing came.

She stood up and wobbled. 'Oh dear, Wooky, Mummy is *blotto!*' Somehow, holding the banister rail tightly, she made it down the stairs without stumbling or tripping over the animal, then went out into the back garden with her. She waited, patiently. When the dog had finished she headed back into the house, sobered a fraction by the breezy, salty night air, closed the door and locked it. Then, with the sound of Wooky lapping at her water bowl in the kitchen, she climbed the stairs and went back into her den. She sat down and hit the return key to bring the computer screen back to life.

No reply from Richie. Hmmm.

You don't know what you're missing, do you? You don't know what's in store, my hunky one!

Logging off, she crossed the landing into her bedroom and walked through into the en suite to prepare for bed. She stared into the mirror as she removed her make-up. The face of her thirty-seven-year-old daughter, Elizabeth, stared back for an instant before her own replaced it.

Not too many wrinkles.

Why did Elizabeth think it was disgusting that at just fifty-nine she was still interested in men? That, God forbid, her mother might have *sex* with a man. What was that about? Hadn't the actress, Helen Mirren, revealed rather a lot of her body in a recent photoshoot? *And mine is as fabulous!*

Girl, you are still a looker! You truly ain't bad!

And in truth she wasn't. Thanks to good genes from both her parents, a little help from a local plastic surgeon and regular botox treatments since she had 'met' Richie, plus workouts with her trainer at the gym, four days a week, she had retained her figure.

Sixty is the new forty!

She checked the laughter lines in her face.

Richie Griffiths, you are in for the surprise of your life!

63

Roy Grace, feeling exhausted, stood in the bathroom using his electric toothbrush. The toothache he'd had a week or so ago had gone away but was now back, and he needed to go and see his new dentist, Ian Pitman. He would phone for an appointment in the morning. The brush blip-blipped, telling him to move to his lower teeth.

Then Cleo called out to him. 'Your job phone's ringing!'

She brought it in. He switched off the toothbrush, hastily rinsed his mouth and answered. 'Roy Grace?'

It was Norman Potting. 'Chief, sorry to disturb you, we have a bit of a development.'

'No problem, Norman. Tell me?'

'The burner phone that was found on the suspect arrested near Toby Seward's house was sent for urgent analysis, as I think Notmuch told you?'

'He did.'

'Aiden Gilbert from Digital Forensics just contacted me. At 9.33 p.m. tonight he had a number-withheld call from a male. Due to the life-and-death nature of the investigation we are carrying out, he decided it justified answering the call. When he answered, the gentleman asked who was speaking, and as soon as he replied, "Sussex Police", the person hung up immediately. Gilbert said there was an O2

264

sim card in the phone. He put in an immediate RIPA request for a trace from the phone company.'

RIPA – the Regulation of Investigatory Powers Act of 2000 – gave the police the right to request immediate information about a phone call from the provider when there was a potential threat-to-life situation.

'What information have they provided, Norman?'

'We have the phone number – which is another burner – and the approximate location – within 250 square metres. It's somewhere in Withdean Road, or possibly one of the adjoining properties in Dyke Road Avenue immediately to the south.'

Grace knew Withdean Road well. It was one of the most expensive residential areas in the city. Large houses in substantial grounds. He'd investigated a case in the same street a while back. All mobile phones sent out signals, constantly, whether in active use or simply switched on. All the phone companies had masts at spaced-out intervals. Using simple triangulation, any phone company, such as O2, could tell the approximate area where a phone was – and in a city that would be in the 250-square-metre range.

In a densely populated part of a city, that kind of range could cover hundreds of terraced houses and apartment blocks – making any kind of house-to-house search a logistical nightmare. But in an area of large, secluded properties, such as Withdean Road, it could be maybe a dozen – or even fewer – properties.

His tiredness instantly gone, he felt fully alert and excited. 'I'm on my way, Norman. I'll be with you in half an hour. See what you can find out about the Withdean Road properties within the area O2 have given you.'

'It's getting towards midnight, chief.'

'So?'

'I'll get straight on it.'

'Google Earth runs 24/7, Norman. Just like the villains we're always trying to lock up. OK? And just like us, too. Put the kettle on, it's going to be a long night.'

'Yes, chief.'

As Grace walked out of the bathroom, ready to explain to Cleo, she was standing in the bedroom holding up a fresh pair of underpants in one hand and a crisp white shirt in the other. With a resigned look on her face.

'I love you,' he said.

'I know.' She gave him a strange look. 'I know.' She shrugged.

He stood for a moment, looking back at her. 'What?'

'Go clean up those mean streets,' she replied. 'As you always do.'

He kissed her. 'You OK?'

'I'm OK.'

'You're not, are you?'

'Maybe I could be more OK. Like, if you were coming to bed at midnight instead of going back out to work again. But that's not what I married into, and I'm never going to complain.' She shrugged again. 'It's just hard sometimes, you know, being the understanding wife, with a small baby and a South American dictator in the attic. That's all.'

64

Tuesday 9 October

Bright lights. Headlights. Lighting up the gates from the far side. A car was approaching from the house. It would take several seconds for the electric gates to open.

Ample time to cross the road and pump a double-tap into the driver's head.

Tooth weighed his options. He'd not been expecting any further movement until sometime tomorrow. Rush across now – or follow?

He decided on follow. Hopefully, Jules de Copeland would lead him to his colleague and he could despatch them both together. Job done. Then high-tail it out of here.

The Kia squeezed through the gates before they had finished opening. It turned right.

With his lights off, Tooth shadowed the car as it zigzagged through a network of residential streets, stopping twice – to check directions, perhaps? Then it joined a busy main road, Dyke Road Avenue. Tooth let a couple of cars pass then switched on his lights and pulled out behind them. They were crawling along and he was straining to keep an eye on the tail lights of the car he was following, which was pulling away.

It went over a green light. It was turning to amber.

Neither of the two idiots in front were going to make the light.

Recklessly, and gambling on no police cars being around, he accelerated hard past them.

The lights turned red a good two seconds before he reached them, approaching at over 60 mph. Holding his nerve, he shot across the junction, with headlights flashing at him and a horn blaring.

He glanced in his mirror. Nothing had followed him. The car was just a couple of hundred yards in front. It negotiated a roundabout, taking the third exit. Tooth followed, keeping well back, along a residential road and then down a sweeping hill beside Brighton railway station. It stopped at a red light and he pulled up well short.

When the light turned green, Tooth allowed the Kia to go on ahead for some seconds. Then he cursed as the lights changed again, much sooner than he had anticipated. Again he had to jump a red to keep up.

Where was Copeland going?

He followed the car down through the city centre towards the seafront, where it turned left. It passed the Palace Pier then carried on along Marine Parade, the upper seafront road, observing the 30 mph speed limit. Was he heading towards the channel port of Newhaven? A ferry to France? Or further, towards Folkestone and Eurotunnel, perhaps?

A mile on, still seemingly unaware of him, Copeland made a sharp left, without indicating, and drove into the entrance of a huge, old-fashioned apartment block overlooking Brighton Marina, called Marina Heights.

A rendezvous? With whom? Most likely, he figured, with Ogwang.

Tooth halted. He saw the Kia approach the underground car-park ramp. The gate opened upwards and the car went in, then halted just inside the entrance, brake lights on, engine running.

He knew what Copeland was doing. He was going to wait for the gate to close again behind him, to ensure no one followed him in.

So, he thought, Copeland had not rung any bell. No one had let him in, he must have used a remote that he had with him. Which meant he must be a regular visitor here. For what purposes?

The gate began lowering. The car waited until it was right down to the ground before continuing down the ramp.

Tooth drove around for a few minutes, until he spotted a good place to park on the street, behind a skip. He turned the car round, to give him a view of the car-park entrance and exit. Leaving the car, he sauntered towards the block, then when he was too close for anyone looking out of a window to be able to see him, he stood in the shadow of a tall shrub and waited. Hopefully another resident would drive in soon, and would be less vigilant with the garage door.

But half an hour passed and no vehicle arrived.

It was starting to rain. Deciding on Plan B, he strolled up to the main entrance and looked at the entry-phone panel, running his eye down the list of names and apartment numbers. Half just had a number and no name. There was no clue as to which one Jules de Copeland had gone to.

He pressed one bell at random. Nothing happened.

He tried another. Again, nothing.

Then a third. No. 23. After a short wait he heard a sleepy female voice.

'Yes?'

Putting on his best effort at a drunk English man trying to sound sober, he said, 'I'm sho shorry, John Michaels, one of your neighbours, Flat 39, keep putting in the code, not working. Could you let me in?'

There was a sharp click. Followed by an even sharper, 'Thanks for waking me, I'm trying to have an early night, OK?'

He pushed the door tentatively, opening it a short distance, then wider, and stepped into the hallway. It was surprisingly small for the size of the block and smelled sterile, institutional. A row of metal mailboxes lined the wall almost up to the single lift. The indicator on the panel above showed '5'.

Assuming no one else had used it since Jules de Copeland, he was on the fifth floor.

Returning to the front door, he held it open, studying the names and numbers on the entry-phone panel even more carefully than before. But they revealed no clue as to which fifth-floor flat Copeland had gone to, and there appeared to be twelve, if not more.

He closed the door behind him, walked past the lifts to a fire door and entered the stairwell. As he had expected, there were concrete steps up and down.

He went down and at the bottom pushed through another doorway into the underground car park. He smelled tyres and engine oil. Looking carefully around in the total silence, he could see no sign of any CCTV cameras. Good.

Striding along past the bays, he located the Kia quickly. He'd already memorized the number plate, but just to be sure he placed a hand on top of the engine compartment. It was warm.

What was Copeland doing here? Did he have a regular hooker? A girlfriend? Business associate? Was this his and Ogwang's bolt-hole? Might they leave together later or tomorrow?

Many apartment blocks had numbered parking bays corresponding to the apartment. But he was out of luck, there were no apparent number markings. It took him just a few seconds, kneeling behind the car, to place the magnetic tracker underneath and safely out of sight. Then, to buy himself enough time to go and grab something to eat, he let all the air out of the front right tyre, then put a deep slash into it with the Swiss Army penknife he carried in his pocket. Having done that, he crawled underneath the engine compartment and, using the metal file on his knife, he sawed through the fuel pipe, keeping his face away from the spray of petrol.

Next, he jammed wedges of Blu Tack into each end of the severed pipe and pressed them back together, winding tape around them. There'd be enough gas in the pipe, he figured, to get out of the car park, but to take it no more than a few hundred metres down the street before it ran out of gas, and its occupants ran out of luck.

They'd be sitting in the car, trying to restart it. The clatter of the starter motor would nicely mask the sound of the hit. With the engine turning over and over, any passer-by would not hear a thing. And by the time any police mechanic had figured out the problem, the two Africans would long be history.

As he walked back to the stairs, along the underground car park, he spotted a Polo, the same colour as his and the same model. Its tyres were soft and it was coated in dust. Clearly it hadn't been driven anywhere in many weeks, and more likely months. Perhaps its owner was working abroad.

He went back up into the lobby and checked for any other exits. There was just one, at the rear, which went into a side street. He walked back to the front and, using a torn-off corner of a Thai restaurant takeaway leaflet, which he picked up from the floor, he disabled the lock, in case he needed to return.

Two minutes later he was back in his car, wiping grease and oil spots off his face with his handkerchief, before heading towards Brighton. A quick cheeseburger and a coffee would set him up fine. After that, he decided, he'd check out that house in Withdean Road, just to make sure Ogwang wasn't still there.

65

Roy Grace drove in through the barrier of the Sussex Police headquarters shortly after midnight, feeling more awake now, having gulped a quick double espresso before leaving home.

Walking along the deserted corridor towards the Major Incident suite, he smelled the unappetizing aromas of microwaved ready-meals that were the all-too-familiar staple gastronomic delights of late-night investigations. He entered the room to see Simon, EJ, Alec, Arnie, Velvet and Vivi, the analyst, at their workstations. Norman was perched on a desktop, holding a foil container, spooning something lurid out of it into his mouth at high speed.

As soon as he saw him, Potting jumped up and hurried over to him like an eager puppy, orange stains around his lips. 'Thanks for coming in, chief. I think we're making progress. I'll show you.'

Grace went over to Potting's workstation. On the screen was a Google Earth aerial map of part of Withdean Road. 'There seem to be four houses where the call might have been made from,' Potting said. 'The analyst has identified, from an internet search, the occupants of three of them. One is owned by a female property developer, who has no previous with us. Another, an elderly widow, whose husband ran a building society. The third is a well-respected Brighton businessman, Ian Steel, a big charity benefactor.' He stabbed a finger at the screen, at a property between the last two, which appeared to Grace to be isolated in substantial grounds. 'This is the one that might be of interest to us, chief,' he said.

Grace peered closely at the part of the screen Potting's bitten fingernail was tapping. A substantial house, in a very large garden with a tennis court and pool.

'Apparently it's owned by a Swiss company, chief. We're unable tonight to find out more about them. But the managing agents are a Brighton firm called Rand and Co., who have been very helpful. We've phoned their office and got an out-of-hours emergency number. A short while ago DC Davies spoke to the proprietor, Graham Rand, who told him that the property was on a twelve-month rental. Mr Rand then rang the sales executive who handled the leasing and said it was a tall gentleman, a Jules de Copeland, he believed of African origin, currently domiciled in Germany. He said Mr Copeland paid twelve months in advance and had impeccable references. Then he added something that might be of real significance.'

'Yes?'

'Apparently he wore very shiny red shoes.'

Roy Grace stared back at him. 'Bingo!'

'That's what I thought, too, chief.' Potting beamed.

Grace immediately dialled the on-call Oscar-1 and requested an unmarked car to go straight to Withdean Road and take a discreet look around the vicinity of a property called Withdean Place.

When he had finished, he made a second call which gave him a great deal of pleasure. It was to Cassian Pewe's job phone. And hopefully it would wake him up.

It did.

'Apologies for calling so late, sir,' Grace said, breezily.

'This had better be good,' Pewe said, sounding bleary, as Roy Grace had hoped.

'I need a surveillance team, urgently,' Grace replied and quickly explained why. Whether Pewe was in the process of getting laid or trying to get a night's sleep, Roy Grace didn't give a monkey's. He just needed his boss's approval for the additional expenditure, as he'd been instructed.

He got it.

66

Wednesday 10 October

Tooth remembered a decent all-night café on Brighton seafront, called Buddies. To his irritation, it appeared the crew of a police patrol car, which was parked a short distance along, also liked it. He could see through the window two officers standing inside.

Although he'd changed his appearance from the last time he had been in this city, letting his hair grow back instead of shaving his head, wearing arty glasses and an ear stud, he didn't want to chance it. He was aware too many police here would have his description, which was circulated not that many months ago. It had also appeared in the local *Argus* newspaper in a photo parade of faces of the most wanted in the county.

He parked a couple of cars back and waited. The two officers seemed to be chatting with a man behind the counter. All jovial. Chatting. Chatting. Laughing, making small talk.

He continued watching. Waiting. The nodding heads. More laughter. He was anxious about being away from the apartment block in case Copeland slipped off. He checked his phone. The blue dot was still at the address, the car hadn't moved. Not that he was expecting it to.

Finally the officers came out into the street, holding

their dinner – or early breakfast – packages. Hopefully they wouldn't sit and eat them in their car, just here.

He was in luck. Within seconds of climbing in, they must have received a call.

They shot off at speed on blue lights.

Five minutes later, relieved that no more police had come in, he hurried out with his cheeseburger, fries and coffee, back to his car. He sat there in darkness to eat his meal and prised the plastic lid off his coffee cup. As soon as he had finished, he left and headed towards Withdean Road. On the way he pulled into a filling station in Dyke Road, went into the shop and loaded up with sandwiches, chocolate bars and bottles of water. Five minutes later he was out and heading on up the road in his car.

After half a mile he made a right turn, then a left into Withdean Road. The affluent area, lined with tall trees, felt more rural than urban, and it was, despite the street lighting, fairly dark. That had suited him well earlier, and it would suit his purposes even better now.

Most of the large, detached houses were partially or completely secluded behind tall hedges and walls, and those he could see were in darkness at this hour. He cruised along slowly until he reached the one, on his left, somewhere behind the high brick wall and wrought-iron gates. Withdean Place.

He carried on past, looking for somewhere to park. This end of the road was narrow and twisty. But it was late and no one was around. He put two wheels onto the pavement, secured the car, then walked back towards the house, looking up at the wall as he approached for any possible access point. He switched on his phone torch and ran the beam up the wall. Saw the glints of glass shards along the top.

He reached the gates and debated whether to scale them. No question they'd be covered by infra-red cameras on motion sensor. He switched the phone torch off and studied the Google Earth map on his screen. There was no rear access to the property because to the south was another house. That one fronted onto Dyke Road Avenue.

Maybe he could access this house from there?

He checked Maps on his phone. A short distance ahead was a side road that would take him to Dyke Road Avenue, and then another right turn would put him behind Withdean Place.

As he walked along, the street suddenly lit up with approaching headlights. He stepped behind a thick tree and watched a small, dark car with two people in it drive past, slowly.

Too slowly.

Two people inside. Looking for something? An address?

Midweek, mid-October, this was not party season. They sure weren't looking for a party – nor a rave. All his instincts pinned them as cops.

Were they simply patrolling the city's Nob Hill? In an unmarked car? Or, more likely, looking for something – or someone?

As he walked on, light built up behind him. A car.

The same car. Coming back.

It passed him as he stood, invisible, behind another tree. Had someone tipped them off?

What were they looking for? Him?

They'd have spotted his car for sure. Checked it out. Found it was a rental.

And hopefully left it at that.

Would they?

Or would they be wondering what a little rental Polo

was doing parked half on the sidewalk, in the middle of the night?

He abandoned any thoughts of breaking into the grounds of Withdean Place and walked as fast as he could, trying not to look obvious to any CCTV camera that might be clocking him, back to his car.

He set off, driving sedately, keeping carefully to the speed limits, and headed into a maze of residential streets, looking specifically for something. A Volkswagen Polo identical to his own.

After ten minutes, he found it, down a smart side street in Hove. A dark Polo, parked on the driveway of a detached house, which had clearly been there for some while, judging from its misted-up windows.

It took him less than five minutes to swap number plates.

When he arrived back outside Marina Heights, twenty minutes later, to further avoid possible detection by police cameras, he made a second number-plate swap, this time with the dusty one he had seen in the underground car park.

67

Roy Grace sipped a fresh mug of coffee he'd made as he read through the latest report from Kullen. The team there had established links between the suspects in the murder of Lena Welch – whom they had identified as Kofi Okonjo, alias Dunstan Ogwang, and Tunde Oganjimi, alias Jules de Copeland – to a Sakawa organization in Accra, Ghana. They had further established links to a British crime lord called Steven Barrey. Barrey was a Person of Interest to them in connection with a wide range of internet fraud schemes perpetrated out of Germany, and they were in the process of gathering more evidence on this. They believed Barrey might have relocated to the Channel Isles.

Kullen had also identified that Copeland had a wife and small baby residing near Munich.

Then, reading on, he was interested to see another piece of information from the German detective on the two suspects. Something which fitted with their behaviour and made them chillingly dangerous.

A shadow fell over him and he looked up to see the analyst Vivienne Crown standing in front of him, looking excited.

'You have something, Vivi?'

She handed him a printout. 'Take a look at this, sir. I

ran our suspect's biometrics, which I got from Custody, through the Home Office Border Control database.'

He read the document and sensed a breakthrough. 'Nice work!'

He immediately looked back at the report from Munich, which confirmed what she had brought him. He jotted down a number of notes and a reminder to himself to call Kullen in the morning. Then he yawned again, feeling exhausted. The best thing, he thought, was to send his team members still here home, to get some sleep and be fresh for the morning. He was about to stand up and tell them when DC Alec Davies came over to him, holding a small sheet of paper.

'Sir, I've just had a call from Oscar-1. The car sent to patrol Withdean Road has reported a suspicious vehicle, a Volkswagen Polo, parked near to the target house. They've checked it out and from the index it's a rental from Budget at Gatwick, hired on October 8th to a Mr John Jones.'

'Great name,' Grace said, sarcastically. 'We could narrow that down to around fifty thousand John Joneses. What licence did "Mr Jones" show?'

'A UK one.'

'Of course. With what address?'

'One in Brighton, sir, but I've since established it's fictitious.'

'What about the car – is it still there?'

'No, it left approximately ten minutes ago. The surveillance crew didn't see it leave. They did stop to check it out when they first saw it, and it was unoccupied. But the engine was warm so it hadn't been there that long.'

Grace was thinking. A rental car parked at this hour of the morning, then driving off, quite possibly spooked by the police car, was not likely to be there visiting friends. It could have been there casing properties for a potential burglary.

Or . . .

'Did whoever it was at the rental desk give a description of John Jones?'

'I just phoned Budget myself, sir, and spoke to a young lady there. She said he was in his fifties, short, wiry, with brown hair, green-rimmed glasses and a gold ear stud. He was dressed in a jacket and slacks. And he had what she thought was an American accent. She remembered him particularly because he was surly and walked with a limp.'

A fleeting thought crossed his mind. Could it possibly be?

No way. Forget it . . .

'Instruct Oscar-1 to put out an alert for the Polo. I don't want it stopped, just followed. Make that very clear.'

'Sir, I put in a request for any ANPR sightings of the vehicle.'

Automatic Number Plate Recognition cameras were in various strategic locations across the city and the county.

'Good man.'

'Between 11.30 p.m. and 11.45 p.m. the Polo was picked up by three cameras, the first heading down Dyke Road, the second heading south on West Street and the last one heading east along the seafront, Marine Parade. The next camera it would have pinged was at Rottingdean, but it didn't, indicating it either stopped or turned off somewhere before then. There were no further sightings until 12.15 a.m. when it travelled west on Marine Parade. At 12.45 a.m. it was sighted heading up Dyke Road. Then, coinciding with your timings, at 1.20 a.m. it was picked up travelling again on Dyke Road and turning down a number of side streets. It hasn't been clocked since.'

'A busy fellow,' Grace said.

'As he was earlier, sir, darting around the city.'

'No cameras have picked him up in any other direction?'

'No, sir.'

Roy Grace stood up, walked over to the whiteboard on which was pinned a map of the Brighton area of Sussex, showing the ANPR locations, and picked a red Sharpie pen from the rack at the base. He drew a circle, encompassing the Onslow Road area, as far as Brighton Marina and the immediate areas to the east and north, keeping the circle short of the other cameras. Then he turned to DC Hall. 'Kevin, have the local officers do a street-by-street search for the Polo, right away. Also ask Comms to get any unmarked vehicles available to do an area search.'

'Yes, sir.'

As Hall walked back to his workstation, Grace was thinking hard again. Withdean Road, with its houses beyond most people's dreams, would always be a prime target for burglars. There was bound to be CCTV surveillance outside most of them.

He glanced at his watch. It was almost 2 a.m. He was always mindful of the need to allow his team rest, in order for them to be fresh. But, equally, if you wanted to be an effective member of a major crime investigation, you had to understand that meant putting your normal life on hold.

He dialled Jack Alexander's number.

A young woman with an American accent answered, sleepily. Instantly Grace recognized the voice of their nanny, Kaitlynn. 'Yrrr, hello?'

He smiled, privately. 'Can I talk to Jack, please.'

A few seconds later he heard the young detective's slightly sheepish voice.

'Sorry to wake you, Jack, but we have a development.

I need your Outside Enquiry Team to crack into action at 6.30 a.m.'

'Of course, yes, sir,' he said, sounding more awake now.

Roy Grace told him about the parked rental car that had been spotted in Withdean Road, then added, 'We don't know why it was there, but the driver must have left it and walked along the street. If any of the houses have outward-facing CCTV cameras we need to get the footage between midnight and 1.30 a.m. checked out.'

'Leave it with me, sir.'

Grace ended the call, then finally told his team to go home and meet again at 7 a.m.

Then he left to grab a precious few hours of sleep.

68

Dawn had come in the form of an oppressive grey sea mist, coating the windscreen of Tooth's Polo in a film of moisture. From time to time he switched on the ignition and flicked the wipers to clear it. He listened on Radio Sussex for the news. But neither the 7 a.m. nor 8 a.m. bulletins carried any relevant updates.

There had been few signs of action in the apartment block. During the past hour, a handful of cars had driven out of the lot, but not the Kia, nor had any of them contained Jules de Copeland. A couple of people had left in taxis, one a weary-looking young woman – had she been the grumpy one he'd disturbed, he wondered, idly? The other, in a long dress, who looked like she was doing the walk of shame, had clambered hurriedly into the rear of a cab.

No Kia. No rush.

Take all the time you need, Jules de Copeland. Enjoy your last morning on earth, and tell your pal, Dunstan Ogwang, to enjoy his, too.

Tooth switched on the local radio, again, in time to catch the morning news.

To see if there was any update on the suspected homophobic attack of last night.

There was.

285

It was the second news item, after a concerned piece on the rise of Sussex burglary statistics and defensive sound-bites from an aggressive-sounding Assistant Chief Constable called Cassian Pewe.

'Following a brutal attack on Sussex motivational speaking expert, Toby Seward, Sussex Police have confirmed they have arrested a suspect. The events of last night are still unclear, but Sussex Police have announced that during the – possibly homophobic – attack, Mr Seward had his right hand severed. Trauma surgeon Robin Turner and his team worked through the night to reattach it. A hospital spokesman said the operation went well but it was too early to tell if it would be successful.'

Suspect, Tooth thought, with gloom as grey as the mist engulfing his car. Ogwang?

In custody?

He thought about his explicit instructions to eliminate Ogwang and Copeland.

Now one of his targets was possibly out of reach, in custody.

And if he was, for sure he would squeal. His paymaster, Steve Barrey, was not going to be happy.

Should he still go after Jules de Copeland? Or bail out while he could? The money from Barrey was in his bank account. Enough to live on comfortably for the retirement he had planned. Enough for the rest of his days.

He could fly out today and be in Ecuador tomorrow. End of.

Except, never in his life had he left a job unfinished. If you did that you would forever be looking over your shoulder. Because one day, whatever you left unfinished behind you, might instead come looking for you.

He was feeling lousy. Clammy. Giddy. Those flu-like symptoms again from that snake bite?

He dialled the number he had for Steve Barrey. It was answered after just one ring and Barrey did not sound happy.

'You've failed again, Mr Tooth, is that what you're phoning to tell me? I've made a mistake hiring you – you're a has-been, aren't you?'

Tooth bristled. But Barrey was right, he had screwed up. He'd lost the plot.

He was a has-been, it was time to quit. This was it, his last job. He'd had enough. 'I think Ogwang may be in custody,' he said. 'I'll try to find out.'

'Don't bother. I have contacts. If Ogwang is in custody I'll have someone I can trust take care of him. Just deal with Copeland.'

Barrey hung up.

Tooth needed air. He got out of the car and walked around in the salty breeze, as he had done every hour or so during the night, trying to fight the nausea that was overwhelming him. He felt unsteady, his balance all over the place. He clutched the car for support, then sat back in it again and lit a cigarette. Thinking. There had to be a caretaker or janitor or concierge on the premises here, of such a big apartment block. As soon as he felt better he would go and find him.

69

Wednesday 10 October

Jack Roberts sat at the oval table in his meeting room, dressed in a smart, brown open-neck shirt and suit trousers, listening intently to his client. Johnny Fordwater looked every inch the retired soldier and must have cut quite a dash when he was younger, Roberts thought.

Seated across the table from him with fine, military posture, the retired major still had all his hair, a good salt-and-pepper shade of grey and neatly groomed, if in an old-fashioned style. His clothes, too, were conservative. He wore a tweedy suit over a checked Viyella shirt and a club tie. Wrapped up in his anger, ignoring his steaming coffee, the bottles of water and the plate of expensive biscuits, Fordwater poured out his story from start to finish, while the red light on the recorder on the table blinked steadily.

It was the same story, with minor variations, Jack Roberts had been hearing all too often during the past couple of years. 'Four hundred thousand pounds?'

'More or less,' Johnny Fordwater said. Then, as if embarrassed to admit it, added, 'Perhaps a bit more.' He shrugged. 'Four hundred and fifty, actually.' His anger spent, he looked at the private investigator balefully. 'I've been a damn fool, haven't I?'

Roberts shook his head. He felt genuinely sad for his

client. This was a man who had made serving his country his career. No one went into the armed forces to get rich, and there were plenty of his equally well-educated contemporaries who would have taken a different path and gone for high-paying careers in the City or elsewhere. Fordwater had clearly been a fine soldier, honoured with one of the highest decorations for bravery the nation could give. He didn't deserve to be in this place now.

'No, Mr Fordwater, you haven't been a fool at all. You did what anyone might do in your situation, finding yourself alone, with very many active years in front of you.'

'You're kind. You see, the thing is I had a wonderful career in the army. There I was a somebody, I felt wanted. When I retired, for a while I had a focus – my wife, who became terminally ill. I retired early to look after her and for the next three years I was pretty much her nurse and carer, round the clock, until she passed away.' He gave a wan smile.

'And I suppose, looking back, that's when it all started, really. I found myself walking down a street, feeling no different from when I was in my twenties, but pretty girls didn't even bother looking at me. I tried to get a job, but no one was interested in a man of my age. I started to feel I was on the scrapheap, that this was it. I even toyed with joining the Scientologists, they at least were welcoming and wanted me. Then I bumped into an old army chum, Gerry, who reminded me he'd found the ideal woman through an internet dating site. He convinced me to have a go.'

'So you did?' Roberts asked.

'Yes, and I met Ingrid. She gave me back my feeling of self-worth and made me feel wanted again. She – or whoever it really was – is clever. Knew how to pull all the strings.' He looked wistful. 'You know, I believed her, I really did.'

'Mr Fordwater, my wife and I have a number of friends who've found love through internet dating agencies. Unfortunately, there are some extremely cunning scumbags out there – I think you might be surprised to know just how sophisticated their techniques are, thanks to digital technology. Yes, you are a victim, but please don't ever think you are a fool.'

'You're very kind,' he replied. 'I wish I could agree with you.'

Roberts knew from experience that all internet scammers had their subtle differences. Their specific MOs – modus operandi. Whether it was running banking scams, phoney retailer scams or romance fraud. The way they talked to their marks, the time spans over which they let everything play out, reeling in the victim little by little. Roberts employed an analyst who had created algorithms to spot any similarities between scams. Not that Jack Roberts needed a computer very often, he was an experienced enough PI to recognize patterns without the help of technology. And he was recognizing one now.

Without even running the case file through the algorithms, he was already certain that Johnny Fordwater and his US pal, Matthew Sorokin, were victims of the same scammers who had targeted his client Elizabeth Foster's mother, Lynda Merrill.

He was also recognizing something else in the quiet anger of the old soldier – a kindred spirit. He decided to test the water. 'Major, you told me when we started that you're aware it would be all but impossible to recover any of the money you've lost, and I'm afraid I would have to agree with you. So I'm not quite sure how my agency can help you?'

'You can help me by finding the scammers. Taking me to them. Then leave the rest to me.'

'You want to take the law into your own hands?'

'What law?' Johnny Fordwater said, defiantly. 'You know damned well that only the tiniest percentage of these bastards will ever be caught and brought to justice by the police, don't you?'

Roberts shrugged. 'I'm afraid so, yes. The majority are operating way out of UK jurisdiction, mostly in countries where the police are institutionally corrupt.'

'Exactly.'

There was a long pause before Fordwater continued.

'I've spent most of my life fighting enemies of our nation, Mr Roberts. The nature of the beast constantly changes. Eighty years ago, long before my time, it was the Nazis. More recently it's been the IRA, al-Qaeda, ISIS. You might not put internet scammers on the same footing, but they've destroyed my life and, from what I read, the lives of count-less others. These people are a scourge.'

'I can't disagree with you,' the PI replied.

'I still have a little bit of money left, Mr Roberts. We haven't discussed your fees yet, but so far as I'm concerned, every penny I have left in the world is yours – if you can get me the names of whoever did this to me. And an address where I can find them. I have some contacts at quite a high level in international policing – one is in a similar position to me.'

'I may be able to give you some leads,' the PI said. 'Although I'd be doing myself out of a lucrative part of my business if they were arrested.'

Johnny looked at him, unsure whether he was joking. 'Really?'

Roberts shook his head. 'No. I've seen too much misery. If I can help you bring even one of the bastards out there to justice, I would be very happy.'

70

A night alone in police custody was never going to be a happy one for anybody, Grace knew from long experience. The thin blue mattress and tiny, rock-hard pillow. The humiliating toilet facility in plain view. The light that stayed on, giving zero privacy. The deliberate hard slam of the steel door when you first entered the drab, comfortless cell. The frosted glass skylight high up, reminding you of the world beyond, all happening without you. The rubbish tracksuit and even worse shoes to humiliate you. Within hours, most people started to feel institutionalized.

It would make all but the most hardened of recidivists glad to see anyone in the morning. Even, he thought irreverently, the sight of Glenn Branson, all suited and booted in shiny designer gear, accompanied by a shaven-headed Norman Potting, seated across the hard, metal table of the interview room. Both detectives were looking as happy as pigs in the proverbial to be here, as if there wasn't anywhere on earth they'd rather be than this room.

Watching on a CCTV monitor from a tiny adjoining room, Roy Grace was focused on the thin black man with a tight, mean, scowling face and straggly hair, wearing a shapeless custody tracksuit, seated beside the solicitor. He was leaning forward on his elbows in an insolent, aggressive stance, diluted by a pallor of tiredness.

Glenn Branson addressed the camera, fixed high above them on the wall. 'The time is 9 a.m., Wednesday, October 10th. Detective Inspector Branson and Detective Sergeant Potting. Interviewing an unknown male using the name Donald Duck, in the presence of his solicitor, Alison Watts.'

Grace couldn't help grinning, glad no one could see him. 'If everyone in the room could please say their name for the benefit of the recording,' Branson continued.

They all did in turn except the suspect, who remained silent. After a brief pause Glenn asked, 'Would you like to tell us your real name?'

Ogwang looked at his lawyer. She was occupied with her phone. 'This my real name,' he replied.

Norman Potting, playing Mr Nice Guy, said, 'We do have a bit of a problem with that, with all due respect.'

Ogwang gave him a hostile, facing-off stare. 'Daz my name.'

'I'm afraid you are going to have to help us out here,' Potting said politely. 'You are from Accra, Ghana, right?'

He shrugged.

'You see, I've been in contact with your very helpful embassy. They've only been able to find one person named Donald Duck and they don't think that is his real name. He is ninety-two years old. I mean, let's face it, even if you'd taken some youth pills, it would be hard to swallow that you are really ninety-two.'

Grace saw the solicitor was struggling to keep a straight face.

'Yes, I took the pills.'

'The same ones as Mickey Mouse?'

There was an uncomfortable silence.

'I suggest you tell us your real name?' Glenn Branson said. 'We're going to find it out, and we've a pretty good idea what it is, so you might as well save us time and tell us.'

Ogwang consulted, in whispers, with his solicitor. He turned back to the two detectives.

'No comment.'

There was little Roy Grace liked less than a suspect who went 'no comment'. It was almost always a sure sign of guilt. And it was deeply frustrating.

'Could you tell us,' Norman Potting asked, 'what you are doing in Brighton?'

'Holiday,' he replied, immediately.

'Holiday? October's not the best month for a holiday in Brighton.' Potting looked at him dubiously. 'June, July, August, September perhaps. But you come from sunny Ghana to rainy, windy Brighton in October? I have a problem understanding that. Although good weather for ducks, I suppose.' He waved his hands in the air. 'Are you sure there isn't something else that's brought you here?'

Looking increasingly panicky, Ogwang again consulted with his solicitor. 'No comment.'

'There's another reason why we don't believe Donald Duck is your real name,' Glenn Branson said. 'We've checked with Immigration, and they have no record of anyone of this name entering the UK – and this gives us a bit of a problem. Either you are not telling us your real name or you've entered this country as an illegal immigrant. Would you like to explain this to us?'

'No comment.'

Branson and Potting exchanged a glance. 'Do you have a colleague, a gentleman with red shoes, Mr Okonjo?'

Branson said, immediately noticing the slight flicker of the man's eyes.

'No comment.'

'I want to make you aware,' Branson continued, 'that you have a legal right to stay silent. But it doesn't always do you any favours in court. Some judges take a dim view of accused people who come up in front of them who've gone "No Comment", when being interviewed. Just saying.'

Ogwang did not reply.

The solicitor looked as if she was going to say something, then appeared to change her mind.

'So,' Norman Potting said. 'You went clothes shopping yesterday. Did you buy anything nice?'

Ogwang did not react.

'You went to a boutique called OnTrend in Brighton's Lanes. There was a gentleman with you, wearing red shoes. Do you remember?'

Ogwang looked uncomfortable and consulted, again in whispers, with his solicitor.

'No comment.'

Branson took over. 'Mr Toby Seward, of fifty-seven North Gardens, Brighton, who had his right hand severed by a man with a machete last night, has described you, and this matches the description of a man we believe to be you, outside the boutique. We believe you and this other man were the two who came to Mr Seward's house and threatened him. And that after leaving, you returned, holding a machete, which you used to cut off his hand. You had that machete on your person when you were arrested last night. It had fresh blood on it, which has been sent for DNA analysis. We think it is likely to show that the blood was from Mr Seward. Can you give us an explanation of how you knew Mr Seward, and the reason for your actions?'

Again Ogwang consulted his lawyer. Again he said, 'No comment.' The two detectives looked at each other.

Glenn Branson said, 'You could be facing a very serious charge of Grievous Bodily Harm With Intent. This offence can carry a life sentence. You are not helping yourself in this interview. We cannot promise you any special treatment, but if you assist us with our enquiries, this would be taken into consideration by a judge sentencing you, if you were found guilty of any offences. I'd like to give you one more opportunity to tell us about your colleague, about how you know Mr Seward and why you may have committed this act of violence that you've been arrested for.'

Ogwang again glanced at his solicitor, who remained stony-faced. 'No comment.'

'OK. Would you consider yourself an intelligent man?' He gave a nod.

'Good. So let me cast your mind back a few weeks to Wednesday, September 26th. Biometrics matching yours, one hundred per cent, show a man who came into London Heathrow Airport on a Lufthansa flight from Munich. He was travelling on a Ghanaian passport which bore the name Dunstan Ogwang. Could this be an alias you use?'

Ogwang leaned over and whispered to his solicitor.

'My client says he has never heard of that person,' the solicitor said.

'OK, perhaps this might jog his mind,' Branson retorted. 'On May 17th, a gentleman by the name of Kofi Okonjo flew into London Gatwick Airport from Munich. Now, this is what makes me think our client is not as smart as he would like to think. You see, as is standard, Okonjo's biometrics were taken by the Border Control Officer. What's interesting to us is that the biometrics taken from your client, when he came into London Heathrow on September 26th under the name of Dunstan Ogwang, were an identical match to this Kofi Okonjo. This wasn't immediately picked up at the time because, luckily for him, the Border Control computer system had a software glitch. As a solicitor practising criminal law, I probably don't have to tell you the percentage chances of two sets of biometrics being a match, do I?'

'You probably don't,' she retorted, coolly.

Branson consulted his notes. 'Now there's another thing that intrigues us here. Back in May, at Gatwick Airport, the person who followed you into the Border Control desk was travelling on a Ghanaian passport, under the name of Tunde Oganjimi.' He paused. 'Does this name ring a bell?'

Ignoring the cautioning glare of his solicitor, Ogwang shook his head.

'It means nothing? You never heard of this gentleman?'
'No.'

'Have you ever heard the expression, "bang to rights"?'
'What's this got to do with anything?' Alison Watts asked.

'Quite a lot, if you'll allow me to continue,' Branson said. He leaned forward, suddenly, on his elbows, so he was virtually eyeballing the suspect. 'Now on September 26th, when you flew into London Heathrow Airport and arrived at the Border Control desk, the person who followed you was also travelling on a Ghanaian passport, under the name Jules de Copeland. Do you know this gentleman?'

'No.'

'OK,' Branson said. 'It must be a coincidence, then, but quite a big coincidence. Do you believe in coincidences, Mr Ogwang?'

Ogwang stared back at him in silence.

'Einstein called them *God's calling cards*. But hey, whatever. You see, the biometrics match identically those of Tunde Oganjimi, who followed you into the same Border

Control desk at Gatwick on May 17th, and was travelling on the same flight. Are you really sure you don't know him?'

Again Ogwang consulted in whispers with his solicitor. Again he replied, 'No comment.'

'Mr Ogwang, we've been busy since you were arrested last night, as we don't like our citizens having their hands hacked off.' He shrugged. 'It's just not a very nice thing to happen to them. We've been in touch with the police in Ghana. They tell us that a certain Mr Kofi Okonjo, who also goes under the name of Dunstan Ogwang, and a certain Mr Tunde Oganjimi, who also goes under the name of Jules de Copeland, are persons of interest to them. Believed to be major practitioners of Sakawa. My understanding of Sakawa is that it involves internet fraud combined with fetish rituals. Could you enlighten me on that?'

'That is a leading question,' Watts interrupted, sharply.

Branson acceded. 'OK, let's just say that two people arrived in England on May 17th. And two people, with those same biometrics, but under different names, arrived in England on September 26th. Any light you can shed on such an amazing coincidence, Mr Ogwang?'

'No comment.'

'Are you quite sure?'

'No comment.'

'OK,' Glenn Branson said, and produced his trump card, one that Roy Grace had fed him from intelligence received late in the night, from the police in Munich. 'I'd just like to make you aware that there is an international arrest warrant issued by the International Criminal Court in The Hague for a gentleman by the name of Dunstan Ogwang, believed also to use the name Kofi Okonjo, relating to a massacre in a village in Sierra Leone in 2002. As a matter of possible interest to you, there is also an arrest warrant, for the same offence, issued for a Tunde Oganjimi, believed to use the name Jules de Copeland. Are you aware of this?'

Ogwang stared ahead, looking, as Branson had hoped, totally blind-sided.

'Tell you what,' Glenn Branson said. 'We'll give you a little time to think about everything. Have a chat to your solicitor. We'll take a comfort break.'

He gave Potting a nod, and looked back up at the camera. 'Interview suspended at 09.28 a.m.'

The two detectives went out into the corridor, shutting the door behind them, and were joined, moments later, by Roy Grace.

71

'Interesting, don't you think, boss, that "biometrics" and "bang to rights" have the same first and last letter?' Branson said.

Grace frowned at him. '"Biometrics" is one word, Glenn. "Bang to rights" is three.'

'Three words, long sentence,' he replied.

Grace smiled.

'What do you think, chief?' Norman Potting said. 'Give Quack-Quack a little time to reflect after talking to his brief? Let him dwell on his potential sentence?'

Mindful of Cassian Pewe being on his back like an aggressive limpet, Grace said, 'What a little scumbag. He's clearly guilty, but I want to belt-and-braces this. And we need his accomplice.'

He checked his watch, calculating. A suspect could be held for thirty-six hours without being charged. Beyond that, an extension needed to be granted by a magistrate. Ogwang had been arrested at 7.30 p.m. last night, which meant their charging deadline was 7.30 a.m. tomorrow. 'We need to play him to reel the other in. We may need to go for a magistrate's extension to give us time to confirm his victim's blood on the machete, but with luck we'll get the DNA report from the lab before then. In the meantime we can undertake further interviews and carry out the ID procedures.'

Branson agreed.

'And while that's happening,' Grace said, 'I'll talk to the Crown Prosecution Service about charging him. We'll let him stew for a while. Give him time to preen. Think about his life as a millionaire internet scammer, compared to twenty years in a British slammer. Then we'll talk to him again later in the day, see if we can get him to squeal on his colleague. We're lucky with that Legal Aid brief – she doesn't seem particularly engaged.'

'I hope she never gets to defend me!' Potting said. 'Ugly cow.'

'I doubt she'd even want to represent you – ever!' Grace retorted.

Potting gave him a sideways look. 'I was talking about her attitude. But I'll tell you this, Roy. The day I can't say a woman – or a man – is plug ugly, that's the day I want to be taken out and shot.'

'That day's been here a while, Norman.'

'Just use a dumdum bullet, so it takes my brain clean out and doesn't leave me a vegetable. Promise me that one thing, chief.'

Grace put his arm on his shoulder. 'Norman, my dad always told me a person could choose to be offended – or not. It seems to me the world is in a strange place where everyone chooses to be offended all the time. First it was too far the other way. In my dad's time the police were institutionally racist, homophobic, sexist, you name it. That's all changed and for the better. Yes, I agree with you the pendulum's swung too far the other way, but that's the world we currently inhabit. It is what it is.'

Potting blinked and sighed. 'Sometimes I'm glad I'm not

a young man today, Roy, with all this crap in front of me – and probably going to get worse. At least we had fun in my day, right?'

Grace looked at him. Four failed marriages, each of the women fleeing him, his Thai bride the worst of all. Potting's idea of fun?

72

Just as he was about to enter the observation room again, Grace saw the tall figure of Jack Alexander hurrying towards him. 'Sir, one of my team has come up with CCTV footage from Withdean Road, from last night – outside the house next door to Withdean Place. The timing fits with the car that was spotted parked there.'

Grace hovered in the door, anxious not to miss the interview that was about to restart, but his interest piqued.

'Tell me?'

'It's very dark and blurry, sir, but distinct enough to make out a figure walking along past it. I thought it worth sending to Haydn Kelly. He came back very quickly – and very definitively – with a match from the person's gait.'

'OK? Someone known to us?'

'I'm not sure whether you are going to like this or not, sir.'

'Stop playing games, Jack. A match with who?'

'Your old pal, Mr Tooth.'

Grace's mind flashed back to the description from the woman at Budget. His wild thought then that it fitted the elusive Tooth, who had made a mockery of everyone in Sussex Police but, fortunately, most of all of Cassian Pewe, after escaping from hospital.

But still he could barely believe it. 'Tooth?'

'Yes, sir.'

'Haydn's sure?'

'He says he's as certain as if he had a one hundred per cent DNA match.'

Grace's brain was spinning. Tooth had first appeared on his radar after two murders in Sussex that followed the death of a cyclist in a road traffic collision. The unfortunate victim had turned out to be the son of a New York Mafia capo, and the murders of two of the parties involved were the result of a vendetta by the dead boy's parents. Tooth was the suspected hitman, who was later presumed drowned after disappearing in Shoreham Harbour. But he had then turned up months later on another killing spree. He'd been less lucky that time. He had been hospitalized, under arrest, after being bitten by a deadly snake as well as several other venomous creatures. But then, Houdini-like, he had once more escaped. He was like one of those bugs that wouldn't die, no matter what you sprayed at it, Grace thought.

He remembered intel from the FBI on Tooth's first appearance in Brighton. The man was a former US military sniper and commanded a fee of one million dollars, all paid upfront. He was, in the hitman world, a class act. Apparently considered the first choice for all the New York crime families. A man who delivered. Always.

And from his own experience when Tooth had been his prisoner, subsequently escaping, thanks to Cassian Pewe refusing to sanction a 24/7 guard on him, a very wily creature.

Could he really be back again?

One million dollars was big money in anyone's language. You would only pay that if much more was at stake.

Thirty million pounds had been scammed out of Sussex

residents by internet-based romance frauds last year. There were forty-eight counties in England alone.

Multiply that thirty million by forty-eight and Tooth was looking cheap. Very cheap. The Macy's bargain basement of hitmen. And in his experience of the man, Haydn Kelly was never wrong.

'Jack,' he said. 'Get someone to contact Budget and see if they have CCTV inside or outside – and if so to get the footage around the time of Mr "Jones" renting the Polo – let's see if we can confirm a positive ident on him.'

Although he was already pretty certain. Tooth was a master of disguise, but you couldn't disguise your height too much. The manager at the rental company had said Mr Jones was short and had an American accent. Tooth was short and American. He had been seen in Withdean Road last night around the same time the Polo was seen parked. Almost certainly it was Tooth's car.

If so, why was he here? What was he doing prowling around outside the house linked to the suspect who was being interviewed? Had Tooth been sent to kill him? Or the man who had made the phone call – or both?

73

'Interview with Dunstan Ogwang recommenced at 10.22 a.m., Wednesday 10 October, in the presence of his solicitor, Alison Watts, Detective Sergeant Potting and Detective Inspector Branson,' Glenn Branson announced to the camera. He turned to the suspect.

'Mr Ogwang, we are entitled to hold you in police custody for thirty-six hours without charging you,' Branson informed him. 'I don't know how much you know about the British custody system, so I suggest you have a chat with your brief here. What we're going to do now is give you some time to reflect on everything, then we'll have another chat a bit later on.' He gave him a big, humourless stare. 'OK?'

There was no response.

'The evidence against you so far relates to the identity and description of the two men at the shop, coupled together with the information from the victim, Toby Seward. In addition, we have your arrest and the recovery of the machete. We are also waiting for the DNA results and the identification procedures. All of this evidence is stacked against you and I would suggest that you need to think very carefully about your position.'

Branson then set out in detail the evidence against

Ogwang, warning him again that inferences could be drawn from his "no comment" responses.

Again there was no reply.

'After you've had a chat and you're back in your cell, have a good think about everything. If there's anything you'd like to tell us about your buddy, Jules de Copeland or Tunde Oganjimi or whatever other name you might know him under, I'm sure it would be helpful to you. That is of course if you do know him and we are not just dealing with a very big coincidence. Which of course is always possible. Yes?'

There was still no reaction from the suspect.

Branson leaned forward and laid a hand on the control panel, whilst looking up at the CCTV camera. 'Second interview with Dunstan Ogwang and his solicitor, Alison Watts, terminated at 10.45 a.m.'

74

Wednesday 10 October

Jules de Copeland stood by the south-facing window of his fifth-floor apartment, with its fine view over the road directly below and across to Brighton Marina and the English Channel beyond. It also gave him a commanding view along Marine Parade for a good mile, towards the Palace Pier to the west. What, he wondered, would Ogwang be telling the police? Would he squeal? Would the little fool attempt to do a deal by ratting him up?

He thanked the Good Lord for giving him the foresight to have rented this place without telling Ogwang. Because for sure he could not risk going back to Withdean Road. Too bad for everyone there if they got busted. No one knew where he was. So long as he kept cool he'd be fine. His current mark, Lynda Merrill, was gagging for him. He couldn't let that go before splitting. And he was pretty sure he could get more out of her before doing that. Then he'd get back to Bavaria, scoop up his beloved wife and their baby son, and hightail out and back to Ghana, where they would be safe.

God, he missed them so much. He'd never in his life before known what love really was. The love he felt for Ama and his son. He closed his eyes.

Please, God, bring us back together quickly.

There was just one small fly in the ointment. And at this moment that fly was behaving very strangely. Down in the street below he could see the little Volkswagen Polo that he'd seen parked shortly after he'd arrived here last night. The car had driven off some while later, then had returned. A man had sat in it all night long. Now that man was out of the car, walking around unsteadily as if he was drunk. He leaned against the front of the car and lit a cigarette.

Copeland picked up his binoculars and, discreetly, through a crack in the blinds, studied the man. A shortarse, with brown hair and glasses. He was dressed in a jacket, slacks and an open-neck shirt.

Cop?

Possibly. But there was something about his demeanour that made him doubt that.

If not a cop, who was he?

A private dick? Could just be coincidence and he was watching someone else altogether in this block. Someone suspicious of their partner?

Perhaps.

But perhaps not. Was he here to watch him? Who and why?

And looking like he was drunk?

There was only one person he could think of who would have put a tail on him.

His former business partner, Steve Barrey.

And if that was the case, he needed to be very wary.

Watch on, baby, you ain't gonna see nothing!

He went over to his desk, sat in front of his laptop, logged on and read again the email that Lynda Merrill had sent back to him at 11.15 p.m. last night, which he had still not replied to. Keeping her on tenterhooks.

My beautiful Richie, you asked if I could get one
hundred thou of the four hundred and fifty thou in
cash. I'll have that together in a couple of days. Now,
my naughty big boy, I have a real treat in store for
you – and of course me! A very dear friend has gone
away for a few days and she's asked me to keep an
eye on her beautiful little cottage in a forest about
twenty miles from here. I think it would be a very
special place for us to spend a whole, uninterrupted
weekend together. We could meet there in our own,
very private love nest where we wouldn't be
disturbed. And I could give you the cash! I desire
you crazily! XXXXXXXX

He composed a reply.

My darling, It makes me so hard just reading this!
Would have replied sooner but I've had some real
heavy shit from the ex to deal with – will tell you all
when we meet. This weekend? Am I able to really
believe we will finally be together this weekend?
Friday evening? I will bring the biggest bottle of
champagne you've ever seen. Although I'll be
packing something even bigger than that :-) Look, I
know I asked you for that loan of £100k, but the ex –
the bitch – has been playing games with me. I don't
know whether to believe her or not but she says she
knows someone who's prepared to put down a
deposit of £200k on the house. Somehow I have to
trump that. I know that if I walk in with £250k in
cash they won't have anywhere to go. Or maybe even
£300k to be safe. I hate to ask you, but any possibility you could go that distance? You'll have it back,
plus a minimum of 30% profit, within months, just

as soon as the house is sold, and this area of
Munich, Schwabing, is the place everyone wants to
be. No problem if you can't, I have a wealthy friend
who is desperate to give me the loan. But, my
gorgeous, because I love you and know we are going
to spend the rest of our lives together, I really want
to ask you first.

I love you.
XX

Less than five minutes later, a reply came in.

This Friday evening? Just two days away from my
prince's arms. I would hate you to lose the opportunity of your house. Bank interest rates are terrible,
30% is very very attractive. I'll find the money. Does
it need to be in cash? I love you too! Can't wait to be
with you. I'm starting a countdown of the hours,
minutes, seconds. XXXXXXX

He replied right away.

55 hours, maybe less!!! Yes, my sexy angel, my ex has
poisoned the lawyers against me. She's made up a
pack of lies that I have no money to buy the house,
and she is ready to close Monday. I've spoken to the
lawyer myself and I asked him if he saw the colour
of my money would that change his mind? He's
given me till midday Monday, otherwise he's closing
the deal with my ex's buyer. So if we are to secure
the property I need to walk in there with cash. That
way the lawyers will know the money is real. I'm
going to Munich Sunday evening, by when I know
I'm going to be all loved-up, my baby, and I'll be on

his doorstep 9 am Monday morning. Ready to ram the cash where the sun don't shine!

Love you.
XXXXXXXXXXXXX

Lynda Merrill replied.

How will you get the cash to Germany? Isn't £10,000 the maximum anyone can take out in cash? At least, without declaring it? Love you so much
XXXXXXXXXX

He typed back.

I have it all worked out. Trust me. XXXXXXXX

Moments later he added:

PS what is the address? XXXXXXXX

75

'Operation Lisbon has now been extended from the enquiry into the death of Susan Adele Driver to include the enquiry into the serious assault last night on Toby Antoine Seward,' Roy Grace informed his team. 'At the moment I'm treating this offence as GBH with Intent and we have strong evidence linking the offenders to both crimes.'

He went on to recap the events of the past twenty-four hours, the CCTV and the witness statement from Toby Seward. He also informed his team that surgeons were confident the operation to reattach Seward's hand would be successful, but it would be some time before they would know for sure if so and whether he'd ever have full use of it again. 'I'm also satisfied we have sufficient evidence to link the murders of Lena Welch in Munich with that of her sister, Suzy Driver, here in our city. CCTV footage, analysed by Haydn Kelly, gives us the positive identity of one man spotted at the scene of both crimes, whom we believe goes under the names of both Tunde Oganjimi and Jules de Copeland.' He pointed at photographs printed from the videotapes that were on one of the whiteboards behind him, alongside the passport photograph pages with the two different names.

He continued, 'This evidence together with the crime scene assessment and the postmortem result on Suzy Driver indicates she was murdered and did not commit suicide. I believe they panicked that their real identities would be disclosed, which is why they killed these women. We know, normally, that these types of fraudsters don't meet up with their victims.'

'They're not really that smart, are they, boss?' Simon Snape said.

'Copeland's smarter than his colleague who we're holding in custody at the moment,' Grace replied. 'Kofi Okonjo, also known as Dunstan Ogwang, also known as Donald Duck.' Again he pointed at the whiteboard, which showed photos lifted from the Munich CCTV, the man's Brighton and Hove Custody photograph and the two passport photo pages.

'Doesn't look much like the Donald Duck I remember from my childhood,' DC Boutwood said.

'I'm sure he'll quack up after a few days in a cell,' Norman Potting said.

There were several groans. As he always did after one of his jokes, Potting looked around for approval. He didn't see any.

'Any more gems where that came from, Norman?' Grace asked.

'There's probably one about the Old Bill in there somewhere, chief, but it's eluding me.'

'Luckily for all of us,' Snape murmured.

'Jack Alexander's Outside Enquiry Team has obtained two separate CCTV images of Copeland hurrying through Brighton, in the vicinity of North Gardens, straight after the attack – the timing fits. We have two prime suspects, who as we now know are the subjects of international arrest warrants for atrocities committed in the Sierra Leone war for independence at the start of this century.'

He turned to Glenn Branson. 'I'm holding a press conference later today at which I will be issuing the photographs we have of Tunde Oganjimi, alias Jules de Copeland, who is currently at large, appealing to the public for any sightings of him or for anyone who may know his whereabouts.'

He paused to drain his coffee cup before continuing. 'Our man in custody has gone "no comment" on us and is frankly pratting about. As soon as we get back the DNA analysis from Forensics, which I'm hoping will confirm the blood on the machete is a match with Seward, I intend that we charge him for the offence of Grievous Bodily Harm with Intent.'

'What name are you going to charge him under, chief?' Potting asked. 'Donald Duck?'

'I'm suggesting we charge him under the name he first used to come into this country, Kofi Okonjo. We can explain to the court that he is using at least two other names and I'll apply for him to be remanded in custody as a flight risk. With the international warrant out for him as well, I don't think we'll have a problem. Hopefully he'll be remanded to Lewes, which will make it logistically easy for interviewing him further regarding the murder of Suzy Driver – and, of course, the German police might want to speak to him in connection with their investigation into the death of Lena Welch. But it's possible in view of the international warrant he'll be moved to a high-security category-A prison – probably Belmarsh.'

Grace paused again to check his notes. 'Thanks to Haydn Kelly, we have something further to add to – and complicate – the mix. I'm sure you will all remember our very dear friend Mr Tooth? A gentleman as slippery as the saw-scale viper snake that bit him some months ago?'

There were several nods.

'He's done his best to mask his identity, but Haydn is one hundred per cent certain from his forensic gait analysis that this is the same man. Would any of you like to specu-late on what he was doing in Withdean Road last night, close to our prime suspect's residence, risking instant arrest and life imprisonment on a string of charges?'

No one responded.

'Me neither,' Grace said, 'but he was.' He paused. 'This is a professional hitman. A former US military sniper who survived the war in Afghanistan. This man is a survivor. I can safely say he wasn't prowling around Withdean Road late last night for any good reason and I'm guessing it wasn't a late-night stroll for his health. My hypothesis is that he is linked in some manner with our man in custody and Jules de Copeland. He must know the risks of being here. What's made it worthwhile for him?'

'Because he's all heart, gov?' Potting said.

'Yep, well since he nearly blew you to pieces with a car bomb, that's very generous of you, Norman.'

'That's cos I'm all heart, too, gov.'

'And if he'd had his way,' said Grace, 'you'd be liver, intestines and kidneys as well, all scattered around the road and pavement.'

'But not too much in the way of brains,' Glenn Branson chipped in. 'Would have needed the old Specialist Search Unit to find any trace of them.'

The whole team laughed.

'Right, this is what we have so far,' Grace said. 'A short time after Donald Duck or Kofi Okonjo or Dunstan Ogwang's arrest – let's go with Kofi Okonjo – a call comes into his phone, which is answered by Aiden Gilbert at Digital Forensics. The caller hangs up. Under RIPA powers, Gilbert requests from the phone provider, O2, a trace on the call. O2 reported that triangulation put the phone in the vicinity of Withdean Place in Withdean Road.'

'Could the caller have been Tooth, sir?' Simon Snape asked.

'Possibly, Simon,' Grace replied. 'Or someone inside the house. O2 have put a marker on the phone number and, from an update a short while ago, it has not transmitted any further signals since the time of that call, 21.33 p.m. That means it's been switched off or otherwise disabled. We have eliminated the immediate neighbouring houses from our enquiries as well as the ones on the other side of the road. We also have a confirmed sighting of Mr Tooth in the vicinity of Withdean Place, so yes, it is possible he made that call.' He turned to DC Davies. 'Alec, do you have anything new to report on the Polo?'

'Yes, sir, I do. Last night I asked Oscar-1 to put out an alert on its index. A response car spotted the vehicle on the forecourt of a house in Onslow Road, Hove, some while later. Turns out to be the home of a judge, His Honour Anthony Northcliffe, who wasn't too impressed about being woken at 3 a.m.'

'That bastard!' grumbled Potting. 'Serves him right, he gave me a right bollocking in Lewes Crown Court over my evidence a few years ago!'

'Norman!' Grace said. 'Is that comment helpful?'

Potting mumbled an apology.

Continuing, Alec Davies said, 'It looks like Tooth may have switched number plates with His Honour's wife's car. We requested an ANPR plot on that index and interestingly we got a similar route to the one taken by the Polo earlier. There were no further cameras pinged in any direction, which means he stopped pretty much within a mile or so of the Marine Parade camera and parked up – either outside or in a garage.'

'Back to the same area both times? Late at night?' Grace

said, pensively. 'I'd say that indicates he might be staying somewhere in that area. Alec, we need the house-to-house team to check with all hotels and boarding houses in that locale to see if there is any guest fitting his description.'

'There are hundreds, sir. Small hotels, bed-and-break-fasts, it will take days.'

'Make a start on it. Draft in some Specials if you need to.'

'Yes, sir.'

'OK,' Roy Grace said. 'So what we have so far is an address in Withdean Road that is linked to our suspects for three offences. And it is also linked to a person, Mr Tooth, who is pretty much at the top of our wanted person list. All the victims so far are connected to internet romance fraud. Are these suspects lining up another victim – or victims? We need to take an urgent look at this property.' He turned to Branson. 'Glenn, I'm putting you in charge of the raid.'

'Yes, boss.'

'DS Alexander will assist you. I'm tasking you with getting a warrant and putting together a plan for going in. We're going to need a Firearms Unit because of the potential for serious violence, the Local Support Team, Digital Forensics, a Police Search Advisor and search team. Surveillance is already in place. Something's up there that we need to know about, urgently. OK?'

'Yes, sir.'

'Do it in fast time. I want everyone ready in three hours. I'll speak to Gold to get someone appointed to lead the search for Tooth, working alongside our team.'

'Understood, sir.'

'Meantime, I'll handle our suspect. I want to speak to him myself.'

76

'Third interview with Dunstan Ogwang, in the presence of his solicitor, Alison Watts, Detective Superintendent Grace and Detective Sergeant Potting,' Roy Grace said to the camera. Then he addressed the suspect. 'Mr Ogwang, so far in your previous interviews you have remained silent, which you are entitled to do. I'll remind you that you are under caution. You have been arrested on suspicion of causing Grievous Bodily Harm with Intent. You do not have to say anything. But it may harm your defence if you do not mention when questioned something which you later rely on in court. Anything you do say may be given in evidence. Is that clear?'

Ogwang faced him off in sullen silence.

His solicitor said, 'Detective Superintendent, my client has told me that he will not answer any questions.'

'Understood, but I'm going to give your client one more chance to change his mind.' He turned back to Ogwang. 'When you were arrested last night, according to the arresting officer you had in your possession a machete. There was what appeared to be fresh blood on the blade. Would you like to say anything about that? Any explanation?'

'No comment.'

'I have just received from the Surrey and Sussex Police's

Forensic department the DNA analysis of the blood on your knife. It is an exact match with the blood of a gentleman who was attacked in his home a short while – in fact just minutes – before you were arrested. In this attack his hand was first pinned to a chopping board by a kitchen knife and subsequently it was severed by a machete. Are you following me?'

Again Ogwang faced him off.

'The victim has identified you. Is there anything you would like to tell me?'

Alison Watts said, sharply, 'I've already told you my client is not prepared to answer any questions.'

'I did hear you,' Grace said. 'I'm still entitled to ask him questions from which inferences may be drawn. Is your client aware of the gravity of this offence? That Grievous Bodily Harm with Intent carries a potentially similar sentence to murder? That he could be looking at twenty years or more in prison?'

'I will explain this to my client.'

'Ms Watts, just so we are under no illusions here about the situation, as has already been mentioned by my colleague Detective Inspector Branson in an earlier inter-view, Kofi Okonjo is the subject of an international arrest warrant issued by the International Criminal Court in The Hague for atrocities committed in the Sierra Leone war for independence at the start of this century. We have seen the photograph they have of him and I can confirm it is your client.'

Grace was enjoying the solicitor's clear discomfort. To her credit she remained poker-faced.

'I'm not prepared to disclose any confidential discus-sions I have had with my client,' she said.

Grace turned back to Ogwang. 'We believe you are

working with a colleague or an accomplice. We also believe that the pair of you are not working alone. I cannot promise you any kind of immunity or special treatment, but if you were willing to cooperate and give us information, I can tell you that a judge would take that into consideration in any future sentence you might receive if found guilty of this offence. Have a think, there's no rush.' He turned to Watts. 'Would you like to consider this? If you need further time with your client, we can suspend this interview.'

Ogwang glanced at his solicitor.

'As I've already made clear, my client will not answer any questions. Do what you need to do, which I presume will be to charge my client,' she said.

Grace looked once more at the big, round, dead eyes of Ogwang. Then he glanced at the clock and addressed the camera above them. 'Interview with Dunstan Ogwang terminated at 12.09 p.m.'

77

Wednesday 10 October

After the abortive interview with Dunstan Ogwang, Grace went down to the privacy of his ground-floor cubicle of an office. He first called Cassian Pewe, who had left a message wanting an update and insisting he attend the press conference himself. Determined, of course, to steal the limelight – and any future glory.

Ending the call to the ACC, he pondered on his lunch tomorrow in London with Alison Vosper. What did she have in mind for him? An escape from that plonker on the first floor of the building housing the brass?

He turned his attention to the reports he needed to read through before his meeting in London, tomorrow afternoon, with Emily Denyer and the prosecuting counsel on the so-called 'Black Widow', Jodie Bentley – one of the nastiest and most devious human beings he had ever had the dubious privilege to arrest. Responsible for the deaths of at least three rich lovers – and very nearly for the death of Norman Potting – Bentley deserved to be behind bars for the rest of her natural life. But, of course, thanks to the skewed justice system, that would never happen, he thought, gloomily.

There was a *rat-a-tat-tat* on his door, then Norman Potting blundered in, beaming. 'I've spoken to CPS, chief, and run through the evidence with them. They're happy for us to charge him with GBH with Intent.'

'Good – did you discuss with them his selection of names and which to charge him under?'

'Since he first came into this country as Kofi Okonjo, and that's the name on the international arrest warrant, they think that's the one we should use. Do you agree?'

'Yes. You can explain it to the magistrate in court when he appears, with luck this afternoon. I've checked and it's Juliet Smith who is the senior one on today. I doubt she'll be sympathetic towards him.'

Grace had a soft spot for her, because of all the magistrates he'd ever been in front of she was the most supportive towards the police, but always fair in her decisions.

'Do you want to do the honours, chief?'

'No, I have a ton of stuff to prepare for a meeting with counsel in London tomorrow, so the pleasure is all yours, Norman. With the severity of the charges and Okonjo clearly a flight risk, there shouldn't be any problem in getting the magistrate to agree to denying any bail application and remanding him in custody. So fill your boots.'

78

'Deputy Sheriff Sorokin,' Matt said, answering the phone in his freezing-cold office. 'How may I help you, ma'am?'

'I'm real worried,' the woman at the other end said. 'I haven't seen my Jean-Pierre in over four days. This is not like him, I've a real bad feeling about this.'

He clicked the keypad to open a file. 'OK, bear with me one second. May I have your full name, please.'

'Kathleen Jordan Martis.'

'And your address?'

He tapped it in as she recited it.

'And your relationship with Jean-Pierre – can you give me his last name?'

'He's a cat,' she said, indignantly. 'Don't have no last name.'

'Ma'am, with all due respect, you've called the homicide investigations number of the Sheriff's Department of the Hernando County Police. I'll give you another number to call.'

As he hung up, his phone rang again. It was Johnny Fordwater. 'Hey, pal, how you doing?' Sorokin said.

'Not great, but thanks for asking, Matt. I have some information you may be able to use. I've found a private investigator over here who has been specializing in so-called romance

324

fraud. I just had a call from him, giving the possible name of the mastermind behind the scams that caught us both.'

Sorokin sat up straight. 'OK?'

'He thinks he's a British criminal, known to the police here, who is involved in a wide number of internet scam operations and works with a Sakawa group from Ghana. His contacts within the police – don't ask – have told him that Barrey may have relocated to Jersey, in the Channel Islands. I wondered if your FBI connections might be able to take a look at this character?'

'Screw the Feds! If this is our man, I want to be the first in the line to bust his nose.'

'So long as I can be the second.'

'I like your style, pal. Leave it with me.'

79

Wednesday 10 October

Tooth was drenched in perspiration. His head seemed as if it was filled with water slopping around. He kept having to move the car, because of a son-of-a-bitch traffic warden on the prowl. He'd lost sight of the entrance/exit to the apartment block for several minutes on two occasions, but the blue dot on his phone remained reassuringly stationary.

There was very little activity – few cars driving in and out of the building and even fewer people coming out of the front door. A couple of food delivery drivers, an Amazon delivery from a white van and an Ocado delivery van some while ago. Now, with the overcast day, the light was beginning to fail. A bleached-haired man in a fur-collared overcoat, with a dog the size of a rat, appeared and headed off. They only got a few yards before the dog pooped. Wrinkling his face, and looking mostly the other way, he scooped it up with a plastic bag and knotted it deftly before setting off again, holding it daintily some distance from him.

A short while later a taxi pulled up, and Tooth watched with interest in case his mark was trying another route. But an elderly lady emerged with a wheeled shopping trolley, which the cabbie put in the trunk before holding the rear door for her.

A text pinged in on his encrypted phone.

Update?

He thought for some moments before he replied.

Nothing to report.

Another text followed.

Call me.

The traffic warden was approaching again. Tooth drove off, turned across the traffic and entered the drive of the apartment. He reversed into the visitor's parking bay he'd used a couple of times before during the past hours. It gave him a clear view of the garage door. Then he dialled the next number in the sequence of burner phones his employer was using.

Without the formalities of any greeting, Barrey said, 'While you're sitting with your thumb up your backside, there's been a development. Copeland's dickhead sidekick has been charged and remanded in custody by the magistrates' court to appear at Lewes Crown Court next Monday.'

'You sure?'

'I have contacts, I told you. I have them everywhere. This one's a bent prison officer. Ogwang has just arrived there on remand until Monday.'

'Will he get bail?' Tooth asked.

'He won't get as far as that hearing, Mr Tooth. As I've told you, don't worry about him. Just do your job and eliminate Copeland before he gets arrested, too, and starts squealing to save his bacon. Understand me?'

'I'm outside the building where he is. I've been here since last night.'

'Why the hell are you outside? Why aren't you inside?

Get in there. Eliminate him. Text me when you've done it. That's what I've paid you for. Or are you going to screw up again? If so, tell me now and pay me back my money.'

Barrey ended the call.

Tooth was sodden with sweat and could hardly keep his eyes open. He needed medication, he knew. Maybe he should be in hospital?

Not an option.

Somehow he had to get his act together and finish the job he had come to do. He sat back in his seat, hit the recline button and leaned further back, closing his eyes, gratefully.

He slept. Dreamed.

He was back in the calm blue waters of the Turks and Caicos, on his forty-two-foot boat, *Long Shot*, with its twin Mercedes engines that took him out hunting for his food, with his fishing rods, most days. Yossarian sitting on the prow, long tongue out, the wind riffling his fur, idiotic grin on his face.

He woke with a start.

Rain pattered down on the roof of the car. He was freezing cold.

Still sodden with perspiration.

The conversation with Steve Barrey vivid in his mind.

Barrey was right. He wasn't thinking straight. The goddam snake venom was messing with his brain.

Why was he outside when he should be in that building, hunting down his quarry? Finding him.

Then eliminating him.

This was going to be his last contract and he was as sure as hell not going to fail.

He didn't do failure.

80

Wednesday 10 October

Glenn Branson burst into Roy Grace's office, looking exhilarated. 'Wow!' he said.

'Ever heard of knocking on a door?'

'Dunno that film – was it on Netflix?'

'No, it was on Sky!'

Branson frowned then gave him a dubious, sideways look. 'I have an update for you from our raid on Withdean Place.'

Grace instantly switched his focus from the trial documents. 'Tell me?'

'You are going to like this, boss, seriously. Eight in custody. Enough IT hardware seized to keep Digital Forensics in business for the next decade. Looks like we've closed down Brighton's very own internet scamming call centre. Every single one of them of African origin – Ghana, from what one told me – and they are all on what looks like dodgy documentation – illegal immigrants. And we've found the phone that made the call last night that Aiden Gilbert answered – might get some prints off it. But what I think will interest you most is an online conversation Aiden's Digital Forensics Team found on a computer with a woman in Brighton. You said in the briefing we needed to look for the next victim – or victims – and I think we've found a big one.'

'How big?'

'Three hundred grand. Cash. She's due to hand it over to her lover boy on Friday night.'

'Where?'

'I don't know yet, boss. I'm waiting to hear. But Aiden thinks this is the overall mastermind of the outfit and that he scarpered some time before the raid. He's confident through what he has on the computer he can monitor any future communications between him and the victim. He's going through the RIPA formalities of an application to the Home Office. And, now, here's the golden nugget: Lover Boy is none other than Tunde Oganjimi, AKA Jules de Copeland.'

'Buddy of our suspect in custody, machete man Kofi Okonjo, and currently our Most Wanted?'

Grace was quiet for a moment, then said, 'This means we have the potential victim's email address and the ability to monitor her continued contact with Copeland. This might give us our best opportunity to catch him, so I don't want any contact with her at this stage.'

'Understood, boss,' Branson replied.

'Brilliant, Glenn, very nice work indeed.'

'I'll update you soonest. You're in London tomorrow, right?'

'Yes, pre-trial meeting with counsel on the Jodie Bentley case.'

'You missed out on the action today and you might miss out on further action tomorrow, boss.'

'Let me tell you something, matey: arresting suspects is just the beginning, the start of a very long journey. My old mentor, Nick Sloan, who's just retired, told me something that I've never forgotten. He said, "You can tell a good detective – a good one likes being in court."'

Branson patted his stomach.

'What's that meant to mean?'

'A good detective seems to like being in *restaurants*, too. You're putting on weight. Cushy married life, too much of Cleo's home-cooking? Middle-aged spread? Are you still going to be able to fit into your suit for my wedding?'

'Be nice to me, I'm organizing your stag-do – remember that guy who got put in a coffin on his?'

81

Wednesday 10 October

Kofi Okonjo had never been in prison before and he wasn't much liking the experience so far. He'd travelled in a van from Brighton magistrates' court with two other men who had been remanded, one an Eastern European and the other an Asian. None of them had spoken.

On arrival at Lewes Prison he'd been photographed again, face-on and side profiles, then stripped naked and a prison doctor had been called in to supervise an officer in blue gloves probing, roughly, inside his anus. It brought back painful flashbacks of being raped, repeatedly, at the age of ten, by male soldiers of the Revolutionary United Front in Sierra Leone.

His solicitor had told him he was entitled to wear his own clothes, rather than prison issue, as he had not been convicted of any offence. But when he'd requested them back, he'd been told that all the items of clothing he had been wearing when he had been arrested were being retained as possible evidence. He was handed an ill-fitting grey tracksuit that, although freshly laundered, had clearly been worn many times before, together with a pair of trainers, and told to get dressed.

His cash, along with his beloved Breitling watch, had been taken from him and he'd signed a receipt for them.

332

He was informed by a prison officer that his cash would be transferred into an account that would be set up for him, and any money he earned from wages doing jobs in the prison or any that was sent to him from family or friends would also go into this account. He would be allowed to spend a certain level a week depending on his earned privileges, and would receive the balance back, along with his watch, when he was released.

He was feeling humiliated. Burning with anger and resentment. Tunde should have agreed that they killed the gay guy, like they had killed the two women who had been threatening to expose them. Then they would have been fine. Instead of in this hole. At this moment he would happily have shopped his friend, given those cops his name, but he hadn't because he needed him to be free. Tunde would get him out, somehow, he always did. They'd always looked after each other. They were like brothers. But all the good life was making Tunde soft.

Twenty-one years ago the soldiers had come into his village. They'd raped his mother and sister in front of him. Then they shot his father and his younger brothers in the head. When they'd finished they told him either he could join their revolutionary army or be shot, too.

He'd met Tunde in the training camp a few days later. Both of them had been repeatedly abused by soldiers, and they were told that would stop if they proved their bravery. They learned how to shoot AK-47s and how to use machetes to behead enemies or mutilate and disable them by hacking off their arms. When the war ended, it was Tunde, who had close relatives who had fled as refugees to Ghana, who suggested they go there too, to safety.

It was Tunde's uncle who got him into school in Accra, and then, a few years later when they were both in their late teens, Tunde was told by a nineteen-year-old cousin, who drove a brand new Range Rover Sport, about Sakawa. Kofi could not believe it, but he saw for his own eyes it was true. Between them they could make vast riches, riches beyond their wildest ever dreams.

They enrolled in a Sakawa training school in the city of Tema. Kofi Okonjo had spent most of his schooldays before then bored by lessons. But now he trawled through images on his phone of the things that really excited him. Fancy watches and fast cars were at the top of his list. What he learned at Sakawa school, along with Tunde, enabled him to have all those things.

In the garage of the house Okonjo rented in Reutlingen, where he lived with his girlfriend, Julia, were parked his Porsche GT3 and his Lamborghini. He was sweet on Julia. Sweet like he'd never been on any woman before. The pretty, undemanding German girl with her fringe of brown hair and her big eyes. They'd met in a subterranean bar in Munich when he and Tunde had gone to see an unknown band playing, and she was now living with him. She was in the house alone with her Burmese cat, Minka, waiting for him to come back home. He texted her whenever he could, even though Tunde would have been mad if he found out – he wasn't supposed to have any communications that could risk them being traced. But he missed her. Although not as much as he was missing his cars and his watch, of course.

He had to see her, soon. He hadn't even got a message to her yet that he was in prison. Screw Tunde's concerns, he would have to do that.

Another prison officer, an unsmiling woman, came into the room holding a large bundle wrapped in cellophane, which she handed to him. 'Mr Okonjo, this is your bed pack and toiletries, which you will find inside. A safety razor, shampoo and soap.'

'What about cigarettes?' he asked, sullenly. 'Someone took them from me. I need cigarettes.'

'English prisons are smoke free, except in open prison at present. They're not available to buy.'

'I need cigarettes.'

'You'll be having your medical screening shortly. If you need patches, the medical officer will help access them for you and will also give you support to help you stop smoking.'

'Why can't I just smoke?'

'Because you are in prison. There are a lot of things you can't do in prison,' she said tartly.

She escorted him into a small room where another, more friendly officer sat behind a desk. The woman who had brought him in stood behind him. For the next twenty minutes the officer at the desk patiently asked him a series of questions.

He remembered Tunde's warning some while ago. Any question might be a trap. So he did not respond to any of them.

'Mr Okonjo,' the officer said, without losing his patience or friendliness, 'I'd just like to explain to you what will happen now that you are here in Lewes Prison. This is the First Night Centre, where all our new residents normally spend their first three days, to get used to the environment. You will then be moved to the remand wing, and one of our long-term residents will be allocated to you to show you the ropes. Do you have any questions?'

'How long I got to be here?'

'Until your trial, unless you are transferred to another prison, for any reason, before then. I'm sure you'll settle in fine.' He smiled.

Ogwang did not smile back.

Next he was interviewed by a nurse, who went through a checklist of medical conditions, asked him if he had any health problems, allergies, if he was on any medication, as well as asking him if he had ever, at any time of his life, contemplated committing suicide. Again, he refused to answer. The only time he spoke was to request nicotine patches. The nurse gave him some and told him she would put in a request for more to the doctor.

When his medical screening was over, the unsmiling woman officer escorted him to his cell for the night. It consisted of two bunk beds, and he had to share the cell with the Asian guy who had been in the van with him on the journey from the court. He was lounging on the top bed, watching football on the television. There was a plastic curtain between the bunks and a toilet and washbasin.

'Nice to see you again,' he said, politely.

'Yeah? I'll decide that,' the Asian guy replied. Then he added, 'You a Tottenham fan?'

Ogwang shrugged, then brightened a little – football was his big interest. 'Actually, Manchester United, they's my team.'

'Cunt,' his cellmate said.

82

Half an hour or so ago a doddery old man with a hearing aid the size of a golf ball, dressed in an overcoat and a tweed hat, emerged from the front door of the apartment building with two equally doddery-looking King Charles spaniels on leashes, and headed off through the falling drizzle in the direction of the seafront.

Still parked in the visitor's bay, where no one had bothered him, Tooth waited patiently, munching on a dried-up sandwich he'd bought at the filling station last night. He had no appetite and it tasted horrible, but he needed to eat something. The sickness he was feeling was sapping his strength, and his concentration. He forced himself to swallow. Then another bite. He chewed for some while before he felt he wouldn't throw up if he swallowed it. The other half of the sandwich he dropped back in the bag.

Sure enough, the old guy was now returning at an interminably slow, plodding walk, the dogs looking knackered.

As he reached the front door, Tooth slipped quietly out of the darkness and stood right behind him. Close enough to read the entry code he punched in. Neither dog reacted.

Tooth stood as the man and his dogs went in, allowing the door to click shut behind him, and watched through the glass as he waited at the lift, then dragged the dogs in. When the doors had shut on them, Tooth punched in the code and walked back into the building, feeling the reassuring weight of his gun in his inside jacket pocket.

First he went down to the car park, to check on the Kia and make sure he had not somehow been outsmarted. The engine compartment was stone cold. Good. He summoned the lift, entered the tired-feeling carriage and pressed the button for the fifth floor.

The doors opened onto a dimly lit corridor with a worn, patterned carpet. There was the faint sound of an opera aria, and a smell of cooking that reminded him of hospitals, which did not help his queasiness. Of course, Copeland could have taken the lift to the fifth floor as a blind, and then walked up or down to another one, but Tooth didn't think he had given the African any reason to believe he had been followed here last night.

He went to the end of the corridor, his story prepared, and rang the doorbell of flat 501, standing well clear of the spyhole.

After a brief wait, the door suddenly opened and he saw a middle-aged woman with long, fair hair in ringlets, in a revealing silk dressing gown, her breasts almost falling out of it, peering at him through glazed eyes.

'Oh,' she slurred. 'I thought it was—' She frowned. 'Who are you?'

'Sorry,' he said, slipping hastily away. 'Wrong flat.'

He tried the next one, directly across the corridor. It was where the opera was playing. There was no response. He tried again, then knocked. A dog yapped, a high-pitched *yip-yip-yip*.

The door opened with a ferocity that startled him. As did the face of the young man with the bleached hair and make-up who was looking at him. The one he had seen some hours earlier picking up the rat-like dog's poop. The creature came running out, yip-yip-yipping, towards him, and the man knelt to grab its collar. 'Goliath!' he said, sternly. 'Goliath, sit!'

'Sorry,' Tooth said. 'Wrong address.'

'Why don't you get the right one next time?' the young man said, standing up and slamming the door. It was followed by the rattle of a security chain.

Tooth was struggling, feeling dreadful and unsteady on his legs. Too many doors, too many flats.

Steve Barrey's stinging words rang in his ears.

Are you going to screw up again?

He knew he was letting too many people see his face but he had no choice but to persevere. He moved along to 503 and rang the bell. A male voice called out, in a very posh English accent, 'Hello, who is this?'

'It's Ricky!'

'Ricky who?'

'Ricky Sharp.'

'Who are you?'

'I may have the wrong flat. Are you James Pusey?'

'Sorry, you must have. Don't know anyone of that name.'

He next tried 504. There was no response to his repeated rings on the bell, followed by raps on the door. He clocked the number as a possibility and moved to 505. There was a faint smell of cigarette smoke coming from it. The door opened and the smell instantly became much stronger. He was greeted by a friendly woman in her mid-sixties wearing a grey onesie. The sound of a television was on, loudly, behind her.

'I'm sorry to disturb you,' he said, feigning a frown. 'I think I wrote the wrong apartment number down.'

'Who are you looking for, love?' she said in a kindly voice.

'James Pusey,' he replied. It was from a list of names he had memorized for moments like this.

She turned and called, 'Mick, do you know a James Pusey?'

A gruff voice called back, 'No!'

'A tall black guy – wears red shoes, usually?' Tooth prompted.

'Ah.' She looked pensive. 'Now I come to think of it, yes. We pretty much keep ourselves to ourselves here. But I've seen the chap you're describing, I think. Yes.' She pointed. 'Number 507, over there. I think, but I can't be sure.'

Tooth thanked her, waited for her to close the door then moved, stealthily, diagonally across the corridor. He stood outside the door, checking around for signs of anyone and listening hard.

He slipped his right hand under his jacket and gripped the heavy gun. Glancing around again in both directions, he switched off the safety catch; it was something he had practised endlessly in the long hours he'd had to kill waiting outside in his car.

He hadn't had a chance to properly test the gun which the rude moron had given him in the toilet of the Stag pub. Not a big problem if it failed to discharge. He had been studying the martial arts since his early teens. He rarely read books or watched movies or television. Mostly he'd filled the endless hours of the void since leaving the US military, in between fishing for food, hiking with his associate and occasionally visiting his hooker, by teaching himself every martial arts discipline there was.

If the gun which he was now holding in his hand, finger on the trigger, failed him, it wasn't a problem. Before Jules de Copeland even realized he hadn't been shot, his neck would have been severed and the top half of his spine would have been powered up through the base of his neck, through his brain and into the roof of his skull.

With his free left hand, Tooth pressed the doorbell.

83

Wednesday 10 October

'Healthy tonight, OK? Cod, quinoa, beetroot and goat's cheese salad.'

'Sure,' Roy Grace said. 'Sounds yum! Glenn told me I'm getting fat, so that would be good!'

'He said what?' Cleo peered at her husband. He was perched on the sofa, reading a paper, catching up on the news to switch off for a short while. 'Well, OK, maybe there's the tiniest bit of a tum visible.'

'Thanks a lot! Is that the reason for the salad?'

'No. We had the victims of a house fire in the PM room today,' Cleo said. 'You know how it always gets me.'

'From that one yesterday?'

'A chip pan on the gas hob. Two kids, the mother couldn't get them out of the house. Poor woman.'

'How do you ever recover from that?'

'You don't,' she said, simply.

He stood up and put a comforting arm around her. 'Poor love, you really are shaken, aren't you?'

There were tears in her eyes and she was fighting back a sob. 'It doesn't get to me, not normally. I always think nothing can shock me any more, that I've seen it all. Then something like this comes along.'

'It's not just you, it's every police officer and everyone

342

in the emergency services. Children, that's the one thing that gets us all.'

She sniffed. 'Yep.'

He kissed her tenderly on the cheek.

'Are you going to be working over this weekend?' she asked.

'I don't know yet. I'm not on call – are you?'

'No. It would be nice to do something with the boys on Sunday, perhaps. Bruno's at that party on Saturday – the one the boy at St Christopher's is having on a gaming bus.'

'It does sound an odd kind of party.'

'I think it sounds fun – very modern, very zeitgeist!'

'I guess anything that gets him out of his bedroom and mingling with other kids has to be a good thing. Zeitgeist or otherwise.'

She nodded in agreement. He stifled a yawn.

'You should have an early night, you've barely slept this week – and you want to be looking your best for lovely Alison Vosper tomorrow. Maybe she's going to tell you that she's secretly craved your body for years!'

'Ha ha – and now that I'm an old fatty, I'll have to somehow cushion her disappointment.'

'You will never be an old fatty,' she said. 'You take too much care of yourself.'

His phone rang. He glanced at the number before answering, 'Fat Bastard's phone.'

He heard Glenn Branson laughing at the other end. 'Where are you? Working out on a treadmill?'

'I'm giving my eyes a workout reading these trial documents. Did you just phone to insult me again or do you have anything interesting to tell me?'

'I just had a call from one of Aiden Gilbert's team. The burner Okonjo had on him when he was arrested has two numbers stored. They're from Germany and he's already passed them on to Marcel Kullen.'

Grace thanked him and immediately called the Munich detective.

84

Jules de Copeland heard the shrill ring of the doorbell. He'd been expecting that, or a knock on the door, for the past half-hour, ever since he had watched the man who'd been sat most of the day in his Volkswagen Polo parked in a visitor's bay enter the building.

Either he was a police officer – which he doubted from his erratic behaviour – or, more likely and more dangerously, he had been sent here, as he'd suspected, by his own former employer, Steve Barrey. Either way he was confident the unwelcome visitor could not know, for certain, which apartment he was in.

Since renting this place, some weeks back, he had been careful not to engage with any other resident, except for the caretaker, a bolshy Irishman called Joe, who lived in a ground-floor flat and vented spleen to him about the landlord not spending enough money on maintenance of the place, nor giving him a pay rise for the past three years.

A bung of £500, palmed to the grateful man, had, Joe assured Copeland, bought him his *omertà*.

When Copeland had looked puzzled, the caretaker explained. *Omertà* was the Mafia code of silence. His one previous visit here had been a quick in and out, to provision it with enough food to last him many days.

A few hours ago Joe had phoned him, as he had promised he would if anyone came sniffing around looking for him. 'A shortarse with an American accent just accosted me round the back of the building when I was putting out the wheelie bins. He said he was in town for a couple of days and trying to look up his old buddy, Jules de Copeland. He described you as a tall black fellow, but said he had lost your phone number and flat number. Said he wanted to surprise you. I told him there wasn't no one of that description living here, and that I knew everyone. He's a shifty-looking one. And if you want my opinion, he doesn't look right in the head.'

On his desk, Copeland had the most sophisticated voice-changing apparatus on the market. It gave him a whole range of male and female accents, and a whole range of regional ones in several languages. He selected the one he had prepared for just this situation now.

As he did, the bell rang again, followed by a rap on the door. He tiptoed in his socks and peered through the spyhole.

Although the lighting in the corridor was dim, and his face was distorted, there was no question it was the man who had been watching the building.

From the other side of the door, Tooth heard a haughty female voice call out. 'Yes, hello, who is this?'

Thrown, with his head spinning and see-sawing, he took a step back. Remembering the words of the woman in the grey onesie in the apartment diagonally opposite: *I think, but I can't be sure.*

Maybe she meant the one next door to it?

The giddiness was returning. The walls were moving. It felt like the floor was rising, pushing him up, then it dropped away beneath him and he fell, full length, onto the carpet. Fighting not to throw up.

He heard a door open and smelled a waft of perfume. Before he could get to his feet a voice said, 'Oh my God, are you all right?'

He peered up. A young, well-dressed Asian couple were staring down at him with concern.

'Yeah, I'm – I'm good.'

'Shall I call an ambulance?' the man asked. 'Do you need medical assistance?'

Tooth scrambled to his feet. Their faces were blurry. He tried to bring them into focus. He was swaying. 'I'm – I'm good.' He touched the wall to try to steady himself.

'Are you sure?' the woman said in a kindly voice.

'Yeah, I just tripped, you know.'

He was conscious they were looking at him oddly.

'I'm a doctor. You don't look right to me,' the man said.

'No, really, I'm good.'

They stared at each other in silence. Tooth wished they'd just go away.

'I just need some air.' Thinking fast and hard, he jerked a finger at the nearest door, saying, 'Just had a bit of an argument – you know – my girlfriend. Bit of air. Thought I'd go out and walk around for a bit.'

'We'll come down with you, make sure you're OK.'

'Right, yes.'

The lift took an interminable time to arrive. And even longer, it felt, to descend. All the time the couple were looking at him curiously.

'I don't smell alcohol,' the man said. 'Are you on any medication?'

'No, I'm – you know – just – you know – shock. Upset.'

The lift reached the ground floor. Tooth stepped out. 'We're going on down to the basement,' the woman said. 'Shall we come out with you?'

'Thank you, no, you are very kind. I'm fine, just need some air.' The doors closed on them, thankfully.

He hurried across the lobby, feeling like he was encased in a swirling mist. And walked straight into the glass front door with a bang that shook every bone in his body, shot agonizing pain through his nose and sent him reeling backwards.

He sensed warm liquid running from his nose. Put his hand to his face, pulled it away and saw blood on it.

He'd broken his nose, he realized. Then he saw the jagged crack in the glass.

'Jeez.'

He opened the door and stumbled out into the darkness and rain and strengthening sea breeze. His car was less than fifty metres away. It felt like it was at the other end of the planet as he zigzagged unsteadily towards it, like it was a homing beacon.

Finally reaching it, he clutched the front of the car to steady himself and worked his way along the side with his hands, like a drunk, until he reached the driver's door. He fumbled in his pocket for the key, hit the button and pulled the door open, then slumped gratefully inside, slamming the door shut against the elements.

Shivering, he turned on the engine and put the heating to full blast. As warmth seeped through him, he closed his eyes.

He was woken, moments later it seemed, by a sharp rap on the window. His instant reflex reaction was to go for his gun. He stopped himself just in time. A figure was standing by his window, barely visible in the ambient lighting from the building and the street lights.

He lowered the window. A bolshy-looking shaven-headed man with a missing front tooth was peering at him in hostile recognition.

'You?'

Tooth instantly recognized the Irish accent of the care-taker he'd spoken to by the wheelie bins. He stared back at him, helplessly.

'What the feck are you doing? This is visitors' parking. Get out of here before I call the police or the tow company. Clear off.'

85

Thursday 11 October

It seemed far longer than just two years since Roy Grace had last seen his former Assistant Chief Constable, Alison Vosper. There had been two further ACCs in charge of Major Crime since her departure. The first, Peter Rigg, had gone on to a Chief Constable role. The second, to Grace's chagrin, was still very much with him.

Rigg had been OK, he was a decent man. But compared to the current incumbent, vitriolic Cassian Pewe, Alison Vosper was Mother Teresa. Although every time Grace had faced her, back then, she'd made him feel like he was back, trembling, in his headmaster's study at school.

It didn't feel much different now as he entered the small Italian restaurant in Pimlico, near to Victoria Station. As the greeter led him through the room, he saw her, looking as starched as the pink linen tablecloth. She had her back to the far wall, of course, with a view of the whole establishment. The 'policeman's chair'.

He knew right away, even before he reached her, that she understood too what that meant for him. No copper would ever feel comfortable sitting with his back to the room and to the front door. She could have chosen one of the several empty side banquettes, where they could both have had this view, but instead she'd chosen the one that would put him at maximum discomfort.

He wondered if this was her regular lunchtime haunt and the table she always reserved, for tactical advantage.

In her mid-forties, with wispy blonde hair cut conservatively short, framing a hard but handsome face, Alison Vosper hadn't changed at all since they had last met. Even the powerful floral scent, with its acrid tinge, was the same as he remembered. As was her outfit. She was power-dressed, just as she always had been, in a black two-piece with a crisp white blouse. If anything, she seemed younger.

Rising to greet him, with uncharacteristic friendliness, she said, 'Roy! So very good to see you!'

'And you, ma'am.'

'*Alison*, please!'

They both sat down. A bottle of Perrier sat on the table and her glass was half full of sparkling water.

'What would you like to drink, Roy? A cocktail? Some wine?'

He felt like asking for a large Martini. Instead, he said, 'Perrier would be fine – I've a meeting with counsel this afternoon.'

She filled his glass for him, then looked at him more warmly than he ever remembered. 'So, how's everything in Sussex?'

'Domestically? Great. I've remarried since I last saw you, ma'am.'

'*Alison*.'

'Sorry, ma'am – *Alison*.'

She smiled, disarmingly.

'We have a baby son, Noah, and I've also found out I have a son from my previous marriage to Sandy.'

'Your wife who disappeared?' She looked puzzled.

'Long story.'

'Want to tell me? I know her disappearance had a big impact on your life – although professionally you never let it show, to your credit.'

As he brought her up to speed, he was thinking that Alison Vosper had softened since she left Sussex. Whilst she used to alternate between sweet and sour, now – at this moment anyway – she just seemed to be sweet. And compared to asshole Pewe, he now realized she had been a dream ticket.

When he had finished she encouraged him to look at the menu and order. 'What are you going to have?' he asked.

'Dover sole.'

The most expensive item. Clearly the austerity measures biting the police weren't affecting her expenses budget. 'That will do me fine,' he said.

They ordered, then she said, 'I can see you've been working hard, Roy, it's starting to show. A lot of stress?'

'A fair bit.'

'Maybe you need a change of scenery?'

Roy thought to himself, in mild panic, *Shit, I'm travelling in one direction and Alison Vosper in another. She looks five years younger and I'm looking a decade older.*

'If you want to know the truth, Alison, trying to get on with my job and having to answer to Cassian Pewe at the same time makes me feel like I'm a coconut in a two-sided shy.'

'I can see it, Roy. You don't look a happy man.'

He shrugged. 'I should look happy because I am happy. I love my family, I love my job. But . . .' He fell silent.

'But?'

'I love my job. It's my dream job. I'm doing what I always wanted to do.'

'And the *but*?'

'I don't know how much longer I can go on working for my current ACC.'

'Isn't he doing a good job. Roy?'

'A good job?'

'There seems to be a very high murder clear-up rate in Sussex – Cassian Pewe's track record is very impressive. Wouldn't you agree?'

Roy Grace bit his tongue. 'Cassian Pewe's track record?'

'It's not gone unnoticed.'

He stared at her, dumbfounded. '*His* track record?'

He saw the twinkle in her eyes. 'Roy,' she said, 'I'm not exactly here as your fairy godmother, but I want to offer you a possible alternative to your current – perhaps uncomfortable – situation. You're aware of the knife-crime epidemic we currently have in London?'

'Of course.'

'It's not so bad in Brighton, is it?'

'Not so far, touch wood.'

'I'm setting up a new dedicated team here in the Met,' she said. 'It will be a multi-agency team putting together a long-term strategy dealing with education, enforcement, investigation, the judicial process and rehabilitation. It's highly political, because knife crime is having a massive impact across the capital. It's harming confidence in the city, it's impacting on tourism and, very importantly, on the well-being of London's resident citizens. This is big politics, top down from the Prime Minister, the Mayor of London and the Commissioner of the Met. I want you for the Commander role. You won't ever get a bigger job opportunity than this. Initially for six months, it will be a temporary promotion to Commander, but who knows, you might decide to stay in the city.'

'Commander?' he replied.

'If it helps, that would put you on equal footing with ACC status, but more prestigious.'

'Cassian Pewe won't like that.'

'I thought that might appeal,' Vosper said.

He was thinking hard about the implications on his family life. The commute to London. Even longer hours than he was currently working.

Balanced against getting away from the clutches of Pewe. And being on his level. Or above him!

'I really want you to think about it, Roy. This could be a stepping stone for you to one day getting a top job in the Met. I know you are ambitious – and I know you have massive ability. Would you consider it?'

He looked at her, unsure for one of the few times in his life how to reply.

'It would be a big upheaval for you,' she said. 'I don't want to paint a rosy picture. It would be 24/7, full on, and if you got the job you would be in the national spotlight. Go home, talk it over with your wife, think about it. Personally, I can't think of anyone better for the job.'

'I'm very flattered,' he said.

The waiter reappeared. 'On the bone or off?' he asked in an Italian accent.

'Off for me, please,' she said.

'On the bone for me,' Grace said.

Alison Vosper said, without a hint of acidity, 'That's the Roy Grace I remember. Always up for a challenge!'

86

Thursday 11 October

Kofi Okonjo liked to work out. He let his lunch digest, then took his turn in the exercise yard, with its tall fence topped with two rolls of razor wire, and began running circuits in the pelting rain. No one else was out here and that was good.

As he ran he thought of his life back in Reutlingen. His cars. Julia. They'd had a similar background. She'd told him all about her father, an angry farmer, angry all the time at the EU subsidies, angry when she tried to read books to educate herself, angry at her mother. And who'd abused her throughout her childhood.

Kofi told her about his background, about stuff he'd done as a boy soldier, and it shocked and excited her. She understood. They were two of a kind. He dreamed of her now, her pale white skin. Her sexy mouth. Her bright-red nipples and her small but firm round breasts. The ring in her navel. The other ring, down below, that drove her crazy when he flipped it around with his tongue.

He felt himself growing stiff inside his loose grey track-suit as he ran. When he finished his circuits he'd whack off in the shower, perhaps, thinking of her. Imagining her voice. Talking him through it. Imagining her hand on him. Slow, slow, gently, then firmer. Harder. Faster.

An hour later, sodden with rain, he re-entered the First Night Centre, and the sour reek of disinfectant. He walked past the cells and went into his. His mean-looking cellmate wasn't there. No big loss. He stripped off his clothes, picked up his meagre towel, wrapped it round his midriff and headed off to the showers.

Entering, he slung his towel on one of a row of hooks and turned the tap, standing well back to check the temperature. Then stepped forward, immersing himself, feeling the jet of hot water, gratefully, on his face, body and hair. He washed his body and his hair thoroughly, rinsed off and stepped back, his eyes stinging from soap residue.

As he did so, a voice behind him startled him. 'Nice fresh towel, Dunstan?'

Who knew him by that name in here?

He spun round. To see a man with a towel over his head and face. Holding what looked like a home-made knife.

'Mr Barrey told me to take care of you.'

Before he could move, the man rammed the blade into his stomach. Okonjo felt for a second he had been punched by a fist. An instant later his stomach erupted with burning, searing pain. The towel fell away from his assailant's face. It was the silent Eastern European man who had been in the prison van with him from the magistrates' court.

'I'm told you like blades, don't you, Dunstan? Or should I call you Kofi?'

He moaned in agony.

The man held him against the wall with the hilt pressed against his stomach.

He was dimly aware that his bowels were evacuating. The man was eyeballing him.

'I've a message from Mr Barrey. He told me to take care of you in prison. Do you know anything of history? Those old medieval knights, in wars, had a code of honour. They would ask the knight who'd pierced them with a sword not to twist – it gave them a better chance of survival, because if they twisted the blade, it would tear their guts, ripping open their bowels, all that muck getting into the bloodstream. Sepsis would follow. Too far gone for doctors. A slow, agonizing death. Eh?'

Okonjo stared at him, shaking in agony and terror. 'No, please,' he mouthed, but the sound came out strange, distorted, lost inside another moan of agony.

'Plenty of time to think about your life, yes? All your loved ones. Got a girl you're sweet on waiting for you back home, have you? Julia, that her name?'

His assailant shot a quick, wary glance behind him. 'I could just twist the blade and then you'll have a few hours before you die. A few hours to think about Julia, yes? Or you would if I left you like this, but I can't take that chance. Sorry.' He withdrew the shank, Okonjo gasping as he did, blood and something darker and vile-smelling running from the wound. Okonjo jammed his hands over it, panting in pain. An instant later the man plunged the blade through Okonjo's chest. Pushing it in hard, right up to the makeshift hilt again. Then gave it a sharp twist.

The African jerked, once. A gurgling sound came from his throat, then he collapsed into the shower tray.

His assailant removed the shank. He rinsed it under the running water for some while, wiped it carefully with a towel and slipped away, taking the towel with him.

87

Thursday 11 October

Roy Grace had once been backstage at Brighton's Theatre Royal, some years ago when he was a young DS, and had never forgotten the experience. A stressed stage-door manager named Setch had called the police after the mysterious disappearance of an actress in a touring play who had failed to turn up for a performance and had subsequently been reported missing from her lodgings.

There had been reports of a creepily obsessive fan repeatedly hanging around outside the stage door – 'Stage Door Johnny', the staff had called him. Fortunately there had been a good outcome: it turned out she'd had a breakdown unrelated to this stalker, and had gone home to the north of England without bothering to inform any of the play's company.

What struck Roy, interviewing the stagehands, was the contrast between the opulence of the front-of-house, with its chandeliers, ornate decor and plush red velour seats, as well as the stage set of a Victorian drawing room, and the whole different world of darkness, shabbiness and seeming chaos of the cavernous dark spaces behind, with tangles of cables, ropes and pulleys, and props all over the place.

It was the same with barristers' chambers, he thought, as he left the tube station following his meeting with Alison

Vosper and walked along busy Fleet Street, past the imposing Gothic facade of the Royal Courts of Justice, then turned right, away from the hubbub, down through an archway into the sanctuary of Inner Temple, one of London's four Inns of Court, which housed barristers and their clerks. He was in a vast courtyard surrounded by tall, handsome red-brick terraced buildings, in front of which were gardens and a pond, as well as a car park containing a fair amount of expensive metal. Successful barristers, who acted as both prosecutors and defending counsel in the nation's antiquated legal system, were among the highest paid professionals in their field. Their clerks did pretty well, too. And yet he knew, as he stood on the doorstep of No. 82 and rang the bell marked G. Carrington QC, that just like front-of-house at the Theatre Royal, compared to the grandeur of the courts in which they performed, barristers' chambers tended to be in the main unimpressive and often quite cramped.

As the clerk on the third floor led him through into the small, legal-tome-lined office, it was little different from many he had been in before. George Carrington sat behind a desk, in front of which, in studded leather chairs, sat Financial Investigator Emily Denyer and Crown Prosecution solicitor Rodney Higgs.

Carrington, a Queen's Counsel who had a formidable reputation on both sides of the Bar, was in his early sixties, with a rubicund, well-lunched face. Dressed in a three-piece chalk-striped suit and looking out imperiously through half-frame glasses, he instantly reminded Grace of a television character, many years back, called Rumpole of the Bailey, played by the late Leo McKern.

As the barrister rose to greet him, Grace clocked the uncomfortable expressions on both Emily Denyer's and Rodney Higgs's faces, and apologized for being late.

'Detective Superintendent Grace,' Carrington greeted him in a deep, bass voice. 'Very good to meet you. Please take a seat.'

He pointed Grace to the third chair in front of him.

As he sat down, Roy Grace had the gut feeling this was not going to go well. He was right.

Carrington looked down for some moments at one of a pile of documents on his desk that were bound in coloured ribbon. 'So, Detective Superintendent, this very charming young lady, Miss Jodie Bentley – at least that's the name we are currently calling her, among many of her aliases – I believe you have given her the moniker of "Black Widow"?' He gave Grace a long, hard look. 'She's a tricky character, I think you might agree?'

'I'd say more than tricky, Mr Carrington,' Grace replied. 'Extremely well informed and cunning. She's been operating under a string of aliases, with bank accounts set up in different names around the world. I believe she was responsible for the deaths of at least three previous lovers, as well as, very nearly, the murder of one of my finest detectives, DS Norman Potting. She's a menace, a danger to society, and if there is any justice in the world, you'll see to it that she's locked behind bars for the rest of her life.'

Grace noted, uncomfortably, that both Denyer and Higgs were avoiding meeting his eye.

The QC steepled his hands. 'I can well understand your sentiments, and there is no doubt in my mind, from your extremely well-prepared trial documents, that she is very probably guilty of all you say. The problem we are faced with is the gap between what you are certain to be the case and what we would be able to get a jury to believe. I've been looking at the evidence you and your team have put together and playing devil's advocate with it.'

He tapped a pile of documents. 'There is no certainty that we would be able to use similar facts in the evidence to connect the deaths of her first husband and of Walt Klein. She has only been charged with the murder of her second husband, Rowley Carmichael. The defence had indicated this was to be a not-guilty plea, but in the last couple of days new evidence has been submitted which puts a different complexion on matters. The psychiatric reports obtained by the experts working for both the defence and the prosecution agree that at the time of killing him, her mind was adversely affected to the extent of amounting to diminished responsibility.'

'What?' Roy Grace had to restrain himself from shouting at the pompous man. He looked at his two colleagues and again they avoided meeting his eye.

The barrister continued. 'I've reviewed every salient detail of the evidence with the contents of the psychiatric reports and I have a number of concerns. But I also have a solution.'

'Good to hear,' Roy Grace said, barely masking his growing misgivings.

'As you know, Detective Superintendent,' Carrington continued, 'Jodie Bentley is due to appear at Lewes Crown Court tomorrow morning for a plea and direction hearing. My proposal is that she will plead guilty to manslaughter on the grounds of diminished responsibility, and be sectioned under Section 37 of the Mental Health Act. That means she can only ever be released under the orders of the Minister of Justice.'

Roy stared back at him in disbelief. 'You can't be serious?'

'I am very serious. I appreciate this may not be the day-in-court result you would like to see, but trust me, this is the best outcome. With the findings from the psychiatric reports and the experts' agreements on her mental state, there is no way the trial judge would proceed in any other way.'

'She's had everybody over, she's a serial killer, for God's sake!' Grace was almost shouting with frustration.

Carrington gave him a patronizing look that merely served to make Roy Grace even more angry. 'I appreciate all the work you and your team put into this case, and I've studied it long and hard. But I've been in front of juries for the best part of forty years and I know only too well just how unpredictable they can be. Too often it's not about right and wrong, justice and injustice.' He looked hard at the Detective Superintendent. 'This really is the right course of action, in the circumstances.'

Grace looked hard back at him. The QC carried on.

'To sum up, having reviewed all the evidence, Detective Superintendent, both from a prosecuting counsel point of view and from a defence counsel's, manslaughter is appropriate in this case.'

'And released in a few months by a well-meaning health worker?' Grace retorted.

Carrington shook his head. 'No, that's not going to happen.'

'How do you know?'

'I can assure you,' the barrister said. 'This is a good result. Trust me.'

Roy Grace stared back at him, thinking, but not saying, *Really? Trust you? Get real. Since when did letting a serial killer go free become a good result?*

88

Roy stormed out of the meeting, fuming. He felt let down by his legal team. In all his career, so far, he had encountered only a handful of people who could come close to Jodie Bentley for sheer evil. Why the hell didn't they get it?

Glancing up at the statue of Lady Justice, as he always did, he recalled that some other cultures depicted her holding a snake rather than a sword. Maybe along with her holding some dice, they were more appropriate, he thought. Justice so often seemed to be a slippery serpent. And that was never more apposite than with Jodie Bentley, who had used snake venom to kill at least one husband and possibly more.

As he headed back towards the tube station, his phone rang. It was Glenn Branson.

'How're you doing, boss?'

'Not great, actually. Got anything to cheer me up?'

'I've just heard back from your pal, Marcel Kullen. He organized a team to go to the house linked to one of the phone numbers in Germany. There is a young lady living there.'

'What do we know about her?'

'Not much – I'll – hang on a sec, can you? Kevin Hall's trying to get my attention, looks like something's up. Call you back in two?'

'Fine.'

It was nearly ten minutes later when Glenn called him back. 'Boss, we have a development this end.'

'Tell me?'

'Donald Duck's dead.'

'What?'

'He's dead. Donald Duck.'

'Awwwww, think about all the kids around the world.'

'This is serious, Roy. Kevin had a call from a deputy governor at Lewes Prison. Okonjo's been murdered.'

'What details do you have?'

'It sounds like he's been stabbed – shanked. Good and proper – in the stomach and the chest.'

When murders happened in prisons – relatively rare occurrences – they were mostly as a result of disputes. But just occasionally, in Grace's experience, there were contract killings to silence a potential witness. Okonjo hadn't been there long enough to have got into a murderous dispute, he was still in the First Night Centre. Had he been targeted by someone anxious to stop him talking – perhaps to stop him squealing on his accomplice who was still at large? But how did they access the First Night Centre?

Had his murder been masterminded by someone outside who knew how the remand-in-custody system worked?

At the magistrates' court hearing, such as the one Okonjo had attended yesterday, there would usually be more than one prisoner remanded in custody. Could someone, paid to kill Okonjo, have had themselves arrested deliberately for an offence serious enough to be remanded, so they would be in the same wing as Okonjo in the first few days?

His thoughts went to Tooth. The man had been positively identified outside the house in Withdean Road, where

Okonjo had been based, and now Okonjo was dead. Tooth was a contract killer. And Okonjo's death had all the hall-marks of a contract killing.

'OK, two things, Glenn,' Grace said. 'First, check out the duty SIO roster and get one assigned to the killing. Then check out if there were any other prisoners remanded along-side him and get their profiles. In particular, make sure Tooth wasn't one of them, under a bogus identity, although with what he knows that we have on him, he'd have to be nuts to allow himself to get processed through the prison system. But he's surprised us all more than once before.'

'On it, boss.'

89

Thursday 11 October

Jules de Copeland sat, dwarfing the small desk in the flat, his two large forefingers typing clumsily on the small keypad.

> **How's it going my gorgeous one? I'm getting all tingly with desire for you, thinking about tomorrow. Thinking about that first thing I'm going to do to you when I have you in my arms. I'm going to drive you more crazy than anyone ever drove you in all your life. I just want to hold you and take your clothes off and then I'm going to give you something so special. Tomorrow. It's too long. How can I wait? XXXXXXX**

As he finished the email, checked it through and sent it, the 6 p.m. news came on Radio Sussex. He always listened, as often as he could throughout the day. The first item was another scandal the US President was glossing over, and the second was the recent royal visit to Brighton of the Duke and Duchess of Sussex.

The third jolted him.

'A spokesman for Lewes Prison has just confirmed that a prisoner was found dead from apparent stab wounds earlier today. His identity has been withheld but we understand the dead man was in the First Night Centre, where recently admitted prisoners spend their first few days. We will bring you more news on this story as it comes in.'

Copeland switched off the radio. Thinking. The First Night Centre.

Kofi would have been there.

It could, of course, be another prisoner. But he had a bad feeling about this.

Real bad.

He walked over to the window and looked down at the parking bays below. No sign of the man or the Polo. The alert of an incoming email distracted him and he hurried over to his computer.

> My beautiful Richie, I have such good news! I've managed to put together £300,000 in cash. I'd completely forgotten my late husband traded a lot of high-end jewellery for cash. He hid a stash here in the house, because he was always worried about banks going under, and another in a deposit box, which I will collect tomorrow on my way to you! God, I can't wait to feel your hands all over my body. And to find out what it is you plan to do to me first??????? I'm tantalized beyond – anything. How will I sleep tonight? Your picture will be under my pillow, as it is every night. Love you. XXXXXX

He replied, distractedly.

> My dream is for both our heads to be on one pillow, together. My angel. Tomorrow at 6.30 pm that dream will come true! Love you even more than you love me! XXXXXXXXXX

Kofi? Was he the man whose name had not been released? Stabbed? Dead? His crazy bro? His heart heaved as he thought fleetingly about all that Kofi Okonjo had meant to him throughout their entwined lives. More than any friend. His bro. The closest he'd ever been with any human before his wife and son.

Shit, bro, are you OK?

But he wasn't OK. He knew it. Stabbed.

Was he taking too much of a risk staying here another day? Cut and run now? Forget Lynda Merrill and her £300k? Kofi had screwed up everything. Plus he had no idea what he might have said to the police when he was arrested. The police weren't stupid, either, they'd be piecing together connections. England. Germany. Ghana.

Someone had already pieced together connections ahead of the police. And he had a pretty shrewd idea who, too.

Someone angry enough to want Kofi dead. And himself. Someone powerful and connected enough to make it happen. There was only one person. When they'd split from him, he'd sworn to track them down and kill them both. Told them no one screwed him and lived.

Now it seemed his ugly threat was real. Steve Barrey.

If it was Kofi, he'd never get to see his girl, Julia, again. Nor his cars. The thought alarmed him. His own wife, Ama, and son, Bobo, living in their farmhouse near Munich. Waiting for his return. If Barrey had someone inside the prison, he could not risk being arrested.

Ama. Sweet Ama. He looked at her photograph now and kissed her pretty face. Then he kissed Bobo's too. There were tears in his eyes. Maybe he'd been stupid. Driven by greed. Maybe Barrey was right and they weren't smart enough to survive on their own. Kofi was too much of a wild card. And now he was dead?

He had to get back to Germany. Where she was waiting, patiently, trustingly, and lonely. She knew no one. Had no friends. He'd warned her against talking to people. Just her and Bobo isolated in the house in a foreign land, with a language she did not speak or understand. Waiting for him to take her back home to Ghana to all her family and friends. And not to have to go through another damp, cold, bitter winter, where she constantly felt like she was freezing to death. He'd made her that promise. Now it was October and winter was coming.

What if he got caught here? It would be years in jail – if he could even survive. What should he do? Cut and run now while he could? While he still, at least, had a chance?

From the back of the desk's bottom drawer he removed a thick brown envelope and shook out the contents: a Dutch passport and driving licence. Both carried his photograph. His name on the documents was Kees Vandegraff. He swapped them over with the British ones he currently carried in his pocket, put them in the envelope and pushed it to the back of the drawer. Closing it, he walked back over to the window. No sign of the man watching him.

That worried him. Where was he?

He heard the alert from another incoming email and went back over to his computer. It was from Lynda. The address and directions for tomorrow. Punctuated with exclamation marks and kisses.

He scrawled it down on a Post-it pad on his desk, then dutifully sent her a bunch of kisses back. Wondering how much of a fight she might put up. The cottage sounded really remote, no neighbours. The owners not returning until Monday. He needed enough time to get to Germany, and it would be too risky to take the cash on an airplane, with the sniffer dogs they had at airports. Which meant driving. A late Eurostar crossing tomorrow and he'd be in Munich by early Saturday morning. Visit the dealer who traded his cash for Bitcoins, then scoop up his family and get a flight to Accra.

Ama wouldn't be pleased she was going to have to pack in a rush and leave most of her stuff behind. But she would be happy that she was going home. That would outweigh everything. The look on her sweet face when he told her. He could barely wait to see her, to hold her. And Bobo.

He did some mental calculations. They should be safely back in Ghana by Sunday evening. Lynda Merrill's friends were not due back until Monday. It gave him a margin, but not a huge one in case of a delayed or cancelled flight. He didn't want to kill her, but he realized it might be the better option. If he tied her up, when her friends released her she would be able to give the police – Interpol or Europol or whatever they were – his description. Killing her would buy him more time.

He played out the scenario in his mind. Arms around her neck.

Snap.

90

The journey back down to Brighton was not doing anything for Roy's sour mood. The rush-hour commuter train out of London's Victoria Station was packed, with every seat already taken way before he boarded it, and he had to stand for the hour-long journey, wedged like a sardine, breathing in fumes of garlic, alcohol and rancid halitosis from the three men he was crushed between, as if he had suddenly found himself the hapless judge of a bad-breath competition.

At one point his phone rang. Extricating it from his pocket with difficulty, he saw from the display it was Glenn Branson.

'Got a development, boss.'

'Can't talk,' he murmured. 'Bell you back in half an hour.'

But he was talking into a dead phone, cut off as they roared through a tunnel.

When they were out the other side he sent Branson a brief text.

Finally, shortly before half past six, he jumped down onto the platform and into the relatively fresh evening air, jostling along with the crowds, most of whom, unlike himself, were probably heading home.

He called Cleo to warn her he would be back late. Then he dialled Glenn Branson as he approached the barrier.

'How was London, boss?'

'Don't ask,' he said, sticking his ticket into the machine and walking through into the concourse. 'What's the development?' He carried on, striding purposefully towards the car park.

'There's a resident in a block of flats in Kemp Town, Marina Heights, who's just returned from working abroad, and called in to report the number plates on his car have been stolen.'

'How is that a development for us?'

'A smart call-handler put two and two together when she took the call about the plates – she was aware of the marker on the car. Firstly, his car is a Volkswagen Polo, colour grey. The same model and year as the one we suspect Tooth is driving – which he had at Withdean Road last night, and which he swapped plates with His Honour Anthony Northcliffe's sometime after he left.'

'Interesting.'

'It gets better. DS Alexander obtained the CCTV footage from Budget at Gatwick of the man who rented the Polo. Haydn Kelly's viewed it and confirmed the man is Tooth. For sure.'

'Nice work,' Grace said. 'So what's his involvement with all of this? If he's involved?'

'Unlikely he's in Brighton for his holiday, boss.'

'Be nice to find him, have a friendly man-to-man chat with him – kind of thing.'

'I'm sure he'd appreciate that, he strikes me as that kind of a guy.'

'I'm on my way in, just leaving Brighton Station, be with you in half an hour or less.' Grace was thinking hard about the local geography. 'So what we know from the ANPR cameras is that Tooth's Polo was last seen early this morning heading east along Marine Parade and never pinged the next camera along at Rottingdean. You've put a marker on the new number plate and checked for any ANPR sightings?'

'Nothing's come up.'

Grace reached his car. 'So he's likely to still be in the area.'

'Unless he's dumped the car. But he wouldn't go to the trouble of switching plates if he was dumping it. This is a classic Tooth MO.'

'OK, speak to Silver and ensure Comms put out an all-ports description of the car and Tooth, and that all plain cars available do an area search.'

'I've already done it, boss.'

'Trying to make me redundant or something?'

'Just trying to take the pressure off an old man's shoulders.'

91

Ever since his confrontation with the irate caretaker of Marina Heights last night, Tooth had kept his distance, parked up behind another block of flats a few hundred metres to the east of the building, watching through night-vision binoculars.

Throughout the long hours of darkness and the whole of today, during which he'd fought his tiredness and nausea, he was certain that Copeland's Kia had not emerged from the building. Nor had anyone remotely resembling Copeland left the building on foot or in a taxi. It was almost dark again now. Good cover.

He wasn't comfortable that he'd remained in the same spot for almost twenty-four hours. Plenty of people had walked by him during this time, some with dogs, some just going or coming. A few he recognized for the second or third time. There was always the risk of someone like a Neighbourhood Watch coordinator, perhaps, phoning the police to report a suspicious person in a car. It was time to move.

He started the car and drove along, through the entrance marked with a large IN sign, past the warning notice, PRIVATE PROPERTY, that threatened dire consequence for any un-authorized parking, and found a bay close to the one he had occupied before, with a clear view of the front door to the block. He reversed into it.

Needing some energy, he forced himself to eat a dried-up vegetable wrap, knowing it was food that wouldn't go off as quickly as meat, fish or cheese, drank some water, then relieved his bladder by peeing into an empty litre water bottle. When he'd finished he opened the door, emptied the contents onto the ground and replaced the cap.

On the 6 p.m. news he'd heard an item about an inmate who had been found stabbed to death in the local prison, Lewes. The work of Steve Barrey? he immediately wondered. His mind went back to their phone conversation yesterday.

He won't get as far as that hearing, Mr Tooth. As I've told you, don't worry about him. Just do your job and eliminate Copeland before he gets arrested, too, and starts squealing to save his bacon. Understand me?

Tooth swallowed a couple of uppers from the pill box in his pocket. They would see him through the night and well into tomorrow morning.

Nausea swelled up inside him again. He took deep breaths. Lowered his window and breathed in the cold, damp air. Felt better. Just a little.

A taxi pulled up at the door. An elderly couple got in and the car drove off.

Jules de Copeland could not stay in his flat forever. At some point he had to emerge. In his rental car, most likely. Angry about the flat tyre. Distracted by his anger.

Then even more angry and distracted when it stopped a short distance away. Tooth glanced at the glovebox. At the gun it contained. A double-tap to Copeland's head. Then away.

But one thought nagged him. He'd been driving this Polo for too long. Much too long – it was dumb. *Shit, what's the matter with me?*

He'd lost it, he knew. *I used to be the best. The very best. I was a legend. Pull yourself together.*

Even with the change of number plates yet again, he wasn't safe. The police in this county, he knew from past experience, were smart. They might just start looking for dark-coloured VW Polos and checking them out regardless of their licence plates.

He had an idea, which had been simmering for some hours now. He had time. Copeland would not be able to fix the flat tyre, he'd have to call for assistance. At the very least he had an hour and, in all reality, longer than that.

Pulling out his phone, he did a Google search, trawled through a number of names, then picked one, a small local company, that offered a twenty-four-hour service.

92

Thursday 11 October

Grace arrived back at the Incident Room shortly before 7 p.m. It was a hive of activity and concentration, with several of his team busy on phone calls that were still coming in following the press briefing yesterday, or on their keyboards. He looked around, the buzz of adrenaline coursing through his veins momentarily eclipsing his anger at the legal team this afternoon. This was what he had signed up for and this was what he loved. The early days of a murder enquiry were a time of excitement and awesome responsibility in equal measures.

Glenn Branson strode over to him as he entered. 'So, what happened with the brief in London, boss?'

'One word, four letters. Begins with an S for Sierra, ends with a T for Tango. Or if you'd like the longer version, we've been one word, six letters, begins with F for Foxtrot, ends with D for Delta.'

'What? I mean – that bitch, Jodie Bentley – what happened?'

Grace shook his head. 'Why do we sodding bother? We do everything we can, risking our lives too often, only to get screwed by the system, time and time again. Long story, mate, I'll tell you the details later. So what's the latest here?'

'DI Henderson's on his way over from Lewes Prison to

377

give us an update on the murder. So far nothing on Tooth's car – we're—'

He was interrupted by DC Hall who was holding a phone in the air. 'Guv, Marcel Kullen for you.'

Grace went over to his workstation and picked up the receiver. Hall put him through.

'Marcel?'

'*Ja*, Roy. All is good?'

'Could be better.'

'So we have raided the house of the man, Kofi Okonjo – known also as Dunstan Ogwang – in Reutlingen. We have interviewed his girlfriend, Julia Schade, and our digital team has found on one of his computers – it is only an early examination – a link to an Englishman called Steve Barrey. He appears, from what they have found so far, to be living in the island of Jersey in the Channel Islands.'

'One of Germany's former colonies, Marcel.'

'Ha ha.'

'This is really helpful information. You obviously haven't been informed yet, but Okonjo is dead.'

'Dead?'

'He was murdered in prison this afternoon.'

'*Scheisse!* You're kidding?'

'Nope, I'm afraid not. You'd better tell his sweetheart he won't be coming home.'

Kullen was silent for an instant. 'Well, I have more for you from this lady. We have the address here in Germany of his suspected colleague, the man you are after, Jules de Copeland, also known as Tunde Oganjimi.'

'Brilliant, Marcel.'

'His Ghanaian wife and baby son are living there – they are in a village a short distance from Munich. Julia Schade told us Copeland is in England, with Okonjo.'

'We're doing all we can to find him, Marcel. We had positive sightings of him on Tuesday night, following the machete attack on Toby Seward, and we're on it.'

'OK, Roy, we are continuing with the investigation – I'll come back to you as soon as we know more.'

'Anything you have, Marcel, and as soon as you have it, please.' As he ended the call he glanced at his watch, then turned to Camping. 'John, get on to Jersey States Police and see if their Financial Crimes Unit have a Steve Barrey on their radar.'

'Interestingly, sir, his name is on a list my new contact there gave me,' the DS replied, flipping back a couple of pages of his notebook. 'Detective Inspector Nick Padden-berg of the Force Intelligence Bureau.'

'How many names of possibles did DI Paddenberg give you?'

'They're currently keeping four under surveillance. All of them potentially behind internet fraud schemes. I've also been liaising with the Jersey Financial Services Commission, because he's popped up on their radar, too.'

The tall, bearded figure of DI Henderson, who had been appointed SIO for the murder of Kofi Okonjo, came into the room and made a beeline for Grace.

'Just back from Lewes Prison, guv. Not exactly my favourite job of the year.'

Grace nodded, sympathetically. No cop liked entering a prison. In general there was a deep cultural dislike of all police officers by the inmates. And every officer entering a prison, for whatever business purposes, was always aware that if a riot kicked off while they were there, they could be both an instant hostage and a prime target for violence.

'What news, Phil?'

'Not a lot so far. The prison officers have done a good

job of sealing and protecting the crime scene for us. Looks like Okonjo was stabbed to death whilst showering, after he'd been for a run around the prison exercise yard. The suspected weapon was discarded in another part of the prison, a typical ingenious prison switchblade, made out of a filed-down plastic chair leg, I would guess. Wiped of prints, of course. I've interviewed both men remanded at the same time as him, and the officers. Neither of them admit to seeing anything.'

'Any indication that either of the prisoners remanded with him had had himself arrested deliberately, Phil?'

'No, guv. One in for GBH, the other arrested for repeated disqualified driving. The problem is that any of the other five hundred and eighty prisoners could have slipped into that area unnoticed and done it. And there's the other possibility of course – it could have been a bent officer.'

Grace well knew from his own experience just how hard it was to investigate a prison murder.

'I've left a Crime Scene Manager and two search officers there, as they need to get those showers freed up and back into use urgently. I'm going back tomorrow morning with a team and we'll set up camp, work our way through the bunch of charmers,' Henderson said. 'I decided there wasn't much point trying after lock-in this evening. The Prison Governor agreed.'

Grace thanked him, not envying Henderson his task. The DI told him he would report back later tomorrow, and left.

He then returned to his workstation, logged on and glanced through what was currently happening in Brighton and Hove to see if there was anything that might be connected to this current Operation Lisbon. But he saw nothing relevant to interest him.

An email from Cassian Pewe pinged in, asking for an immediate and urgent update.

But before he could reply, Glenn Branson came over. 'Just taken a call from Comms, boss. An RPU officer from Polegate, in a plain car, did a sweep of the Kemp Town area and has spotted our Polo parked up outside a block of flats, Marina Heights.'

'Yes? What else did he see?'

'He says the car appears to be empty.'

'*Appears* to be?'

'Because of the warning not to get too close and the darkness, he couldn't be one hundred per cent certain, but he's pretty sure.'

Grace clenched his fists. Was this the breakthrough he'd been hoping for?

Was it Tooth's car and, if so, would he be returning to it? 'Where exactly, Glenn?'

'In the visitors' parking area immediately in front of the building.'

'Where is this officer now?'

'His name's PC Trundle. I told him, as you instructed, to sit on it. He's parked up at a safe distance, keeping eyes on.'

Grace considered this development. Where might Tooth be now, if this was his car? In the building? Lurking nearby? Or had he abandoned it? Was there CCTV of the car park?

'When's Trundle's shift due to end?'

'Eleven tonight.'

'OK, either keep him on it or get another officer in a plain car to take over when his shift ends, if we don't have more resources by then.'

Two minutes later, Branson came back. 'Boss, the East and West Sussex Road Policing Units are all attending a double fatal near Chichester at the far end of the county. They've no resources currently to relieve PC Trundle.'

He told Branson to ask Trundle to hold his position and await further orders. Grace thought hard about everything they had on Tooth, mindful of his officers' safety. 'If it is Tooth's car he's very likely armed. Tell Comms to instruct Trundle to follow if he appears but not to stop the car, nor pursue him on foot if he leaves the vehicle. Request an Armed Response Vehicle on standby. But ensure it keeps well away and out of sight, we don't want Tooth doing yet another runner.'

'What might Tooth be doing at that building?'

'Waiting for someone to come out? Or inside it?'

'So who's in there that's so interesting to him?' Branson asked.

'The same person he'd gone along to see in Withdean Road before a marked car spooked him? The smart money's on a tall Ghanaian with shiny red shoes.'

'Yep.'

'I'll get a surveillance team in place. We also need some fast research on the building. There's bound to be a caretaker or concierge in a block of flats that large. Have someone get hold of them, and first thing check the CCTV to see if it is Tooth and in which direction he might have gone. See if they've noticed anyone of Copeland's description. Also find out who the managing agents are and whether they've let any of the flats to someone of his description – that will probably have to wait until office hours tomorrow. Likewise, in the morning, if nothing has changed, see what we can find out from the Council's relevant databases. In the meantime, check the electoral roll.'

'What about sending a couple of plain-clothes in to start doing door-to-door?' Branson suggested.

'I'm concerned that Copeland could be armed, as well as Tooth. We've seen what his colleague did. I don't want to put any of our team in unnecessary danger. Let's see what the caretaker comes up with first and then take a view.'

As Branson returned to his own workstation, Grace called the duty Gold and Silver Commanders and updated them.

They discussed a plan. When they had agreed it, together with the authority to continue deployment of armed officers, Grace stood up and called for the attention of everyone in the room. At that moment, Cassian Pewe phoned him.

93

Thursday 11 October

'Roy,' said a very irate-sounding ACC. 'What part of my email asking for an urgent update did you not understand? I expect to be kept informed, otherwise you make me look a bloody idiot to the Chief. The minimal feedback I keep getting from you lacks all granularity.'

Roy decided to give him back as good as he could muster, having recently trawled the internet himself for management gobbledygook with which to retaliate. Childish, he knew, but it gave him pleasure. 'With respect, sir,' he said, 'I appreciate you like to take the helicopter view. From forty thousand feet it may look one way, but it's very different down here in the weeds.'

For a brief while it seemed as if Pewe was stumped for a reply. 'What weeds are you talking about?'

'Sir, I'm in the middle of a fast-time situation, may I get back to you in a while?'

'Only if you have anything intelligible to say.' The phone went dead.

Grace concentrated back on his task. 'OK, for the benefit of all the team including new members, I'm going to provide a detailed update, so everyone knows where we are with the investigation. This is what we have so far on Operation Lisbon, the investigation into the murder of Suzy Driver, linked to the murder of her sister, Lena Welch, in Munich, and linked to the vicious attack on Toby Seward in this city two nights ago. We have two prime suspects for this attack, who are also our prime suspects for the murders of Suzy Driver and Lena Welch. They are linked to an internet romance fraud scamming outfit operating out of Germany, with further links to Ghana. We've established they have been operating from rented accommodation here in Brighton and we believe our suspects recently broke away from a much larger organization, possibly masterminded out of the Channel Isles. DS Camping is liaising with the Jersey States Police.' He paused to swig some water from a bottle.

'As you'll know, a major development today is that one of these suspects, Kofi Okonjo, also known as Dunstan Ogwang, who was arrested on Tuesday night shortly after the attack on Toby Seward and was remanded in custody in Lewes Prison yesterday, was found murdered in a shower block there earlier this afternoon.'

'Is anyone upset about the loss of such a fine, upstanding citizen, chief?' Norman Potting asked.

Roy Grace was not smiling. 'Norman!' he rebuked.

'Sorry, chief.'

'Our role is to solve crimes, not to act as vigilante judge and jury, OK, Norman?'

As Potting looked duly chastised, Grace would dearly love to have added, *more's the pity*. But he kept his focus.

'On Tuesday night, our dear long-lost friend, the amazing disappearing American hitman Tooth, was spotted in Withdean Road, close to the house where our two suspects were running their operation. We don't know what he was doing there, but it seems he may now be parked outside a block of flats in Kemp Town. Knowing what we do about Tooth's line of work, I suspect he may be linked to the killing of Okonjo in prison. It is extremely unlikely that Okonjo was murdered as a result of a fight, because in my view he'd not been in there long enough to have made enemies.'

Potting interrupted. 'Chief, we know from past experience that Tooth has Houdini-like qualities – but are you suggesting he somehow got into the prison, stabbed Okonjo and slipped out again?'

'I've no evidence to support that, Norman. But the presence of Tooth is very timely and indicates that he could be involved in some way. My hypothesis is that Okonjo was the victim of a contract killing – he was killed either to silence him or in retribution, or both. If Okonjo was killed to order, it is very possible there is a contract out on his partner, Jules de Copeland, too. We understand they were both working for Steve Barrey and split away from him to start on their own. Barrey's a ruthless man. It seems so far he's been like the old Mafia capo John Gotti, nicknamed the Teflon Don, who evaded prosecution and justice for decades.'

He took another swig of water. 'I'm going to continue with the surveillance team on Marina Heights, but in the meantime I want two of you to back up PC Trundle. Which of you are green permit holders?'

A green permit holder was a police officer with a driving licence that permitted engaging in a pursuit.

DC Wilde and DC Hall raised their hands.

'Right, Velvet and Kevin, take a car and go and remain in the area – but keep well clear and out of direct line of sight from anyone in the building. I'll get Comms to inform Trundle when you are in position.'

Both detectives immediately left the room.

Grace's phone rang. Apologizing to his team, he took the call. It was Aiden Gilbert from Digital Forensics.

'Boss, we have some more detail from Jules de Copeland's email. It's come as a result of the continuing monitoring of his email account we've been authorized to carry out. We don't have his present location, but he's made an RV with someone we've identified as a Mrs Lynda Merrill for tomorrow evening at an address near East Grinstead. It seems she is bringing a substantial amount of cash with her. At least £300,000.'

'What? Hang on, Aiden.' Grace told his team to stand down and hurried to his workstation. 'Tell me what you have?'

'From the email comms, this lady is all loved-up with a gentleman she believes to be called Richie Griffiths,' Gilbert said. 'We've identified this to be a false name given to her by Jules de Copeland. It looks like they've agreed to meet tomorrow evening at an isolated cottage for a romantic weekend.'

'Do you have the address?' Grace asked.

'I do, she's sent it to him with elaborate directions on finding it.'

'Nice work!'

Gilbert gave it to him and he wrote it down. Primrose Farm Cottage, Forest Row. Along with the directions.

'Sounds like they're planning to meet around 6.30 p.m. tomorrow evening, boss. You wouldn't want to go and spoil their beautiful tryst, would you?'

'An old romantic like me? Why would I even think about doing something like that, Aiden?'

'Glad to hear it, boss! I'd hate to be the one to blunt Cupid's arrow.'

As soon as he ended the call, Grace rang the Gold Commander, Detective Chief Superintendent Jason Tingley, and updated him.

They met a short while later, looking at a Google Earth map of the cottage and surrounding areas, and discussed a strategy for tomorrow evening, if there were no developments in the interim. Tingley asked Grace whether he'd considered speaking to Lynda Merrill, telling her the situation and replacing her with a police decoy.

Grace responded that he had already considered this, but it seemed from the intercepted emails that Lynda Merrill genuinely believed Richie Griffiths was real. He knew how reluctant victims of romance fraud often were to accept the truth, often going into complete denial. In his view, with the arrest – and now death – of his colleague, Copeland was a definite flight risk. His hypothesis was that Copeland was going to turn up, grab the money, convert it into a cyber currency and disappear. Back to Ghana, most likely, and then probably completely vanish.

Tingley saw his reasoning, but their primary concern was that Lynda Merrill could not be left exposed. Before policies had changed, some years back, they might have been able to consider using her as bait – like a tethered goat – but not now, when safeguarding victims had to be the priority.

The meandering driveway, over half a mile long from the road to the house, looked to be a major asset. If they had that covered, they both agreed, they could arrest Jules de Copeland before he got into the house. The Silver Command room would be set up at HQ, from which the operation would be run. Two CROPS – Covert Rural Surveillance officers – were to be deployed tonight to position themselves, under the cover of darkness, in observation posts covering Primrose Farm Cottage. They would report to a dedicated support team located in a concealed position close by, which would in turn liaise with the Silver Tactical

Command. To cover all likely contingencies, a vehicle containing two Armed Response officers would also be stationed close by, as well as additional police resources.

CROPS officers were trained in concealment. They wore combat fatigues made from Disruptive Pattern Material – DPM – selected for the terrain they were going into, with real vegetation attached to their garb and helmets. They carried provisions and equipment enabling them to stay in place motionless for hours and, if need be, days. Because once in situ they could not move for risk of being seen.

As further back-up, Silver would also request Home Office approval for a listening device to be placed in the cottage.

They agreed that the moment the CROPS saw Copeland coming down the drive, one ARV would carry out a high-threat enforced stop and arrest him in his car, with the second ARV coming up behind, both as back-up and to seal off the exit route for Copeland's car.

At 8.30 p.m., Grace decided that if his hypothesis was right and it was Jules de Copeland who Tooth was watching for, then nothing was likely to happen until later tomorrow, when Copeland made his next move. Grace set a rota of a skeleton team of his crew to stay during the night, and told the rest to go home and get some rest.

He left to go home, also, with instructions to the officers staying on to call him, no matter how late, if there were any developments.

He had a feeling that tomorrow was going to be a big and long day. In the meantime he had a serious discussion ahead with Cleo, about his job offer from Alison Vosper. He was flattered to be offered it, but he really didn't know how he felt about it, nor what Cleo's views would be.

But when he arrived home, Kaitlynn's car was outside

and Cleo's was gone. The nanny was dozing on the sofa in the living room in front of the television. There was a note on the kitchen table, confirming an earlier text from Cleo.

Just been called out to recover a body that's been washed up on the beach near the pier. Kaitlynn came over. Back as soon as I can, maybe with some fresh prawns and a lobster or two! Chicken casserole in the fridge – microwave four mins on full power and there are peas in the freezer. Love you. XXX

He loved her gallows humour. Opening the fridge, he put his food in the microwave and then chatted for a short while to Kaitlynn after she'd woken up apologetically. He was fast asleep long before Cleo came back home.

94

One lesson Tooth had learned during his many years in his chosen profession was how to remain invisible. In plain sight was often the best way.

Like wearing a yellow high-viz tabard. You were even more invisible if, wearing one, you carried a clipboard, and even more so if you held a surveyor's scope. You were invisible, too, if you drove a taxi – cabs could be anywhere, at any hour, without arousing suspicion. But you couldn't park up a taxi any place for too long.

A van was different.

You could park a van for hours and no one would take any notice. Which was why, at 3.02 a.m., Tooth was stationed across the road in a lay-by, two hundred metres east of Marina Heights, in a small white Renault van he had rented from a local company. He had a clear view of the garage entrance.

According to his phone, sunrise would be at 6.51 a.m. It had taken him less than an hour last night to cab it to the company's depot, rent the vehicle and return. Not enough time, for sure, for Copeland to have had his tyre fixed and depart.

During the long hours of the night, no one came in or out of the building – not through the front door, nor out of the garage.

He nibbled through a series of chocolate bars to give him energy, and they helped to quell the constant rising queasiness inside him. His temperature rose and fell between boiling hot and icy cold.

He needed a doctor. He needed to get back to Munich to see him. But that was not an option. Not right now.

What snake or scorpion or spider venom was still coursing through his system all these months on, he wondered, shaking a Lucky Strike out of the crumpled pack in his pocket and clicking his lighter, shielding the flame with his hand. Sucking in the smoke made him feel a little better.

Rain fell and then stopped. Wind blew for a while, rocking the car. An ambulance screamed past.

Tooth stared through the windscreen, occasionally switching on the wipers to clear his view. He was fine waiting. He'd waited days in way more hostile environments than this. At least no insects were biting him here, there were no landmines to be wary of and no enemies with AK-47s lurking. The cab of this Renault was close to luxury by comparison.

Five floors above, unable to sleep, Jules de Copeland peered through the blinds and down through the window towards the weakly lit parking bays. The Polo was still there. The darkness, rain and coating of salt on the window made it hard to see clearly. Was that the shape of the short man behind the wheel or just a shadow from one of the parking area lights?

Should he make his run for it now under the cover of darkness, he wondered? Hole up somewhere and wait until tomorrow afternoon, before heading towards Primrose Farm Cottage?

Or just stay put?

He checked his watch: 3.30 a.m. Maybe wait an hour or so till 4.30 a.m. That was the witching hour. He'd recently watched a television documentary about the human body clock. It seemed this was the time when people were at their lowest ebb. When sick people were most likely to die. Maybe the man in the Polo would be asleep then.

He made a list of what he needed to take with him, set his alarm and lay down on his bed, closed his eyes and tried to sleep.

95

Friday 12 October

Matt Sorokin downed two whiskies, followed by two miniature bottles of shit wine, closed his eyes and tried to sleep. The movie he had been watching on the transatlantic flight from JFK to London was shit. The seat he was in, sandwiched between a fat guy with bad BO, who was snoring loudly, and a woman on his left who smelled like she'd tried every perfume in the duty-free shop, was shit, too.

He'd pulled off the headphones and stuck them in the pocket in front of him, reclined his seat, ignoring the protest of someone behind him, and closed his eyes.

The Neanderthal behind him was now kicking the back of his seat. *Kick. Kick. Kick.*

Matt unbuckled his belt, turned round and leaned over his headrest, staring at the man, an angry-looking guy with bulging, thyroid eyes. 'You got a problem, buddy?'

'You put your seat back,' he said.

'Yeah. I put my seat back. I paid for my seat and I paid for the button that puts it back. You gotta problem with that?'

'I do.'

'Yeah?'

'It doesn't give me any room.'

'That's the airline's problem, not mine,' Sorokin said. He

turned away and let his seat back even further, as far as it would go.

The man behind him remained silent.

He closed his eyes again. Thought about his plans. His connecting flight to the island of Jersey. His lunch date at a fancy restaurant with Steve Barrey, whose name and contact details had been given to him by Jersey States Police Financial Crimes Unit. He'd approached Barrey in the guise of a bent cop, working in the NYPD Money Laundering Team, in the pay of a major New York crime family, and Barrey, who had fingers in the financial services world, had swallowed the bait. Sorokin was really looking forward to meeting the bastard.

And hey, the menu looked good, too. Shame, if his plan worked out, that he'd never get as far as ordering.

He drifted back into sleep, waking an hour later with a raging thirst and a blinding headache.

96

Roy Grace woke with a raging thirst and a blinding headache and glanced at the clock radio. It said 4.11 a.m. He gulped down the entire glass of water he kept at his bedside every night.

Cleo was sound asleep beside him. He hadn't heard her come back, although at some point in the night Humphrey had woken him, barking. His mind was whirring. Tooth. Jules de Copeland. Cassian Pewe. Alison Vosper. No one had called, so presumably there'd been no developments, so far.

Was he missing something? Something vital? What?

Slipping as quietly as he could out of bed, using the light of his phone and trying not to disturb Cleo, he went through into the bathroom, closing the door behind him. He ran the tap, waiting for the water to get cold, opened the cabinet and took out a couple of paracetamols. He swallowed them with another glass of water. He should try and grab a few hours more sleep, he knew.

Returning to bed, he lay there with his eyes closed. But he was too wired to go back to sleep. After fifteen minutes of raking over everything in his mind, he gave up, went back into the bathroom, showered and shaved. Using the minimum light possible, he got dressed in a fresh shirt and suit and tie. He kissed Cleo goodbye, but she didn't stir.

Fortunately Humphrey, downstairs, didn't stir either. He was snoring in his basket.

Grace made himself a double espresso, gobbled down a bowl of cereal and went out in the darkness to his car.

97

Two armed CROPS officers travelled in the small grey van, in the darkness, heading north towards the country town of East Grinstead along a winding rural road. The driver, borrowed at the last moment to replace a sick member of the team, was a pot-bellied old sweat of a uniform constable, seventeen shifts from retirement, he told them with pride and no hint of regret. He smelled of curry. For the past forty minutes since leaving Brighton he'd bored his passengers rigid, swinging the lantern as well as telling them how policing had changed since he'd first joined. Wasn't the same any more, no sir. You could call a spade a spade back then. Now you'd be up in front of Professional Standards for making a racist statement.

His passengers, CROPS officers PC Doug Riley and PC Lewis Hastings, politely humoured him, the CROPS knowing they would need him for transport later. Riley and Hastings were kitted out in their camouflage fatigues, with thermal underwear, black balaclavas and helmets with netting. They carried in their rucksacks water bottles, food rations, bottles to urinate in, bags to poo in, night-vision goggles, binoculars, cameras with long lenses and encrypted radios with earpieces. Each was armed with a Glock 17 handgun, in a holster.

Hastings, in the front seat, was watching the satnav on the dashboard, as well as the Google Maps app on his phone into which he had programmed Primrose Farm Cottage, Forest Row. The wipers, on the intermittent setting, swept away the light, misty drizzle from the screen. He was pleased at the mist, it gave them even more cover.

'Coming up, quarter of a mile, sharp left,' he instructed their driver.

The voice of the Silver Commander, Superintendent Julian Blazeby, came through the radio. 'Charlie Romeo Three Seven?'

Hastings reached forward and picked up the mike.

'Charlie Romeo Three Seven.'

'I have you on my screen close to the drop point. How is it looking?'

'Brilliant conditions, sir. Mist as well as darkness. Our ETA is five minutes.'

'Good. Let me know when you are both in position.'

'Yes yes, sir.'

The van turned into a wooded single-track lane, with overhanging trees forming a tunnel, and continued for a short while. They passed a sign for Primrose Farm on an open five-barred gate marking a potholed, metalled driveway. The driver slowed.

'The cottage is showing as further on,' Hastings said. An animal shot across in front of them.

'Deer,' the driver said. 'Lucky it wasn't a sabre-tooth tiger, eh?'

'Ha ha!' Riley, in the back seat, said.

'Did I tell you the time when I had to go looking for a reported tiger spotted in the woods at Stanmer Park?'

'No, but I expect you're about to,' Hastings said in a resigned voice.

'Turned out it had escaped from a circus! Do many of you CROPS guys get eaten by wild animals?' he asked.

'More likely to get eaten by boredom,' Hastings said.

'So what happens if you need to take a dump?'

'I don't,' Hastings said. 'I take Imodium before a job, bungs me up good and proper.'

'I once spent three days inside a fridge in the back of a van, parked up outside a crack den in Whitehawk, in Brighton,' Riley said. 'Had to piss into a bottle. Worth it, though, we got the scumbags.'

The headlights picked up the opening to another entrance, to the left. It was marked by rotting wooden gates, wide open and overgrown with brambles, which didn't look like they'd been closed in years, and a newer-looking oval wooden sign above a mailbox.

The driver slowed.

The letters read PRIMROSE FARM COTTAGE. He halted the car. 'Want me to drive down?'

'No,' Hastings said. 'Here's good.'

They rehearsed the code word they had agreed between them. *Rattlesnake.* If Hastings or Riley or the support team that would be stationed nearby said this word over the radio, it meant their cover was blown and the operation would switch instantly from covert to overt. The support team call sign was Romeo One.

As the two CROPS officers climbed out with their heavy rucksacks, the driver said, 'Abandon hope all ye who enter . . .'

'You're a regular cheerful Charlie, aren't you?' PC Riley said.

'Nah, I just like horror flicks. Have fun, lads!'

As the van drove off, the two officers pulled on their night-vision goggles and set off along the track, which dipped steeply at first down to the left, then levelled out. It was a long walk, three-quarters of a mile, lined on both sides with ferns and scrubby bushes, with the occasional mature rhododendron, and with dense forest beyond. Finally a house came into view. It was in pitch-darkness and showed up a ghostly green through their goggles.

It was a substantial brick building with three gables, a thatched roof and the front door off-set slightly. Attached to the right-hand side of the house, as if added on many years ago as an afterthought, was an ugly double garage that looked in a bad state of neglect. To Hastings, who'd worked in the building trade before joining the police, it looked like two – or possibly three – cottages had at some point in the past been knocked together and converted into a single dwelling. Ivy had grown up a large part of the facade, with almost bare branches of wisteria covering the rest.

A small off-roader was parked outside the front of the house, beyond an overgrown lawn with a brick wishing well bounded by an unpaved circular driveway. They slowed their pace. 'Proper Hansel and Gretel,' Hastings said, quietly.

'Mmmm. I'm kind of thinking *Texas Chainsaw Massacre*,' Riley retorted, also quietly.

'I'll make sure Leatherface gets you first!'

'And I always had you down as a gentleman!' Riley retorted. 'So what intel do we have?'

'Not much.'

'Dogs?'

'Just a cat.'

'If I lived here I'd have Rottweilers.'

'Me too, so I could keep out old plods with boring sodding stories!'

They began to move forward more slowly now, one step at a time, in case there were motion-sensor lights.

'Probably don't get too many Jehovah's Witnesses out here!' Riley whispered. Hastings sniggered.

The house was now fifty feet in front of them. A light came on in an upstairs window. The two officers melted into the trees.

The shadow of a woman crossed the window. Another light came on. Then another. An owl hooted somewhere nearby.

Twenty minutes later the upstairs lights went off and several came on downstairs.

At a few minutes before 4.15 a.m., all the lights went off. A woman emerged from the front door with a handbag and a large suitcase. She popped the tailgate of the off-roader, pulled out a squeegee and wiped the vehicle's windows clear of moisture. Then she hefted her suitcase into the rear and closed the tailgate. Firing up the rattling engine, she sat for some moments, then drove off past them, leaving behind a haze of diesel fumes.

Ten minutes later, Doug Riley had carved out a hide inside a dense rhododendron bush. He made sure both the front and rear were covered, then radioed the support team in the van. 'Romeo One, Mike Whisky One in situ.'

His colleague, Lewis Hastings, buried deep inside a hedge behind the house, radioed in a few seconds later. 'Romeo One, Mike Whisky Two in situ.'

Riley radioed again. 'Romeo One. A woman, looks like the householder, has just departed with luggage. What's the ETA of our weekend guests?'

'Early evening, Mike Whisky One,' the old sweat in the van replied. 'I'm afraid it's going to be a long day, chaps. Silver has requested as soon as it's light enough you take and email close-up shots of the front- and rear-door locks. He wants to get a listening device in the house ASAP.'

'Yes yes,' Riley said.

'Yes yes,' Hastings replied also.

98

At 4.30 a.m., dressed and heavily sprayed with cologne, Jules de Copeland peered down through the window at the parking area. The Polo was still there. The windscreen was wet and misted. Was that someone at the wheel?

Wait on, bro, Copeland thought.

He took the lift down to the underground car park, carrying two bags with him, one containing his passport and a few belongings, the other empty, big enough, he had calculated, for the cash Lynda Merrill was going to give him.

His plan was to leave here under the cover of darkness and head towards the rendezvous, then park up somewhere remote. En route he would buy a massive bunch of flowers, an impressive box of chocolates and a bottle of champagne.

He could imagine the look on her face. She would be expecting a handsome Richie Griffiths. Not him.

He had the spiel all prepared. '*Hi, Mrs Merrill, Richie got delayed, he sent me ahead to present you with these little gifts!*'

Then, depending how she reacted, he'd either knock her unconscious or more likely break the stupid bitch's neck.

The doors opened. He stepped out and walked across the silent, dimly lit car park, looking around warily while he made his way towards the dark-blue Kia, checking every shadow the way he used to as a kid during jungle warfare. As he approached, he pulled the key out of his pocket and pressed the unlock button. The indicators flashed and he heard the *clunk*.

Then he saw the front right tyre. Completely flat.

Shit, shit, shit.

This was so not part of the plan.

Putting the bags down on the ground, he opened the boot and peered inside for a toolkit and spare wheel. There wasn't one – instead he saw a bag labelled 'Tyre Inflation Kit'. He opened it and studied the instructions. He removed the cylinder, knelt and removed the dust cap from the valve. Then he screwed in the nozzle and pressed the trigger.

There was a sharp hiss and to his relief the tyre began inflating. Then, as the air in the cylinder ran out, he heard a further hiss. Coming from another part of the tyre.

In front of his eyes, it fully deflated again in seconds. He swore, feeling a flash of panic.

Opening the passenger door, he flipped down the lid of the glovebox, pulled out the rental document and scanned it, looking for an emergency contact number. He found it and dialled. It was answered after a few rings. He explained the problem to a polite, weary-sounding male. He would get a breakdown vehicle to him as soon as possible, he assured Copeland. But it might take a while because it was the middle of the night.

Copeland locked the bags in the boot of the car and went back up to his flat. Over two hours later, his phone rang. A chirpy-sounding man from the breakdown company told him he was five minutes away with a spare tyre for him in case the puncture could not be fixed; could he let him into the underground car park?

Copeland hurried back down.

99

Now parked just behind a bus stop lay-by on the far side of the clifftop road above Brighton Marina, two hundred yards to the east of the apartment block, where he had moved over two hours ago, Tooth maintained his vigil in the van. Oblivious to the cold, he sat pretty much motionless, just occasionally switching on the wipers. He was still nauseous.

The only thing that gave him any pleasure was the red NO SMOKING roundel fixed to the van's dash. He shook out yet another Lucky Strike and lit it. After a few drags he flicked the ash into the footwell, where it fell on the pile of butts that had accumulated during the night.

A few hundred yards to the west, DC Hall and DC Wilde sat in their silver Ford Focus, in the parking bay of another, smaller block of flats, with a clear view but out of sight of the Polo parked at Marina Heights. They had relieved the Road Policing Officer, PC Trundle, almost eight hours earlier. In the breaking light they could see the skeletal structure of a gasometer a short distance to their left.

Kevin Hall, struggling to keep awake, periodically ran the engine to crank the heating up and drained the last of the coffee, that had long gone cold, from his thermos flask. Beside him, DC Wilde mostly occupied herself with her phone, exchanging texts with her partner who was a nurse on night shift in West Sussex, and occasionally showing him jokes and videos that a friend was sending her on WhatsApp. Several of them were of questionable political correctness, but they sure helped pass the time.

He winced at one she showed him, captioned, 'If you ever moan about a splinter . . .' It showed a young man, lying on what looked like a hospital trolley, with the sharp, thin shoot of a tree branch lancing his scrotum and emerging from his stomach just above his navel.

'Yech! How did the poor sod end up like that, Velvet?' Hall asked her.

She shrugged, then in her rich Belfast accent said, 'Guess he branched out from whatever he was doing.'

He laughed. 'You are one sick puppy!'

She replied, 'I'm taking that as a compliment.'

A few minutes later they saw a flatbed truck, with a winch in the rear, pull up at the entrance to the underground car park of Marina Heights. On the side of the vehicle were emblazoned the words, Sussex Tyre & Breakdown Services.

Hall was hoping against hope that an arrest would be made today. Tomorrow his team, Reading, were playing a crucial game against Queens Park Rangers and he wanted to be there in the crowd to lend his voluble support.

The garage doors opened and the truck drove down the ramp.

He called Comms and asked for the duty Oscar-1. Inspector Mark Evans came on the line. 'Charlie Romeo Six Four Zero?'

'Sir, a truck has just entered Marina Heights underground car park, from a company called Sussex Tyre and Breakdown Services. Can you find out who has requested it?'

'Sussex Tyre and Breakdown Services?'

'Yes yes.'

'I'll get it checked and come back to you, Charlie Romeo Six Four Zero.'

'Thank you, sir.'

Tooth watched as the garage door lowered seconds after the breakdown truck had descended. Wondering. Had it been called to fix a flat tyre?

He put his hand into his inside pocket, pulled out his gun and deactivated the safety catch. If he was right in his assumption, Copeland would be emerging soon. And he would be ready. The fuel would carry Copeland no more than a few hundred yards from the entrance – if that far.

100

Jules de Copeland, standing in the car park in the glare of the breakdown truck's headlights, directed the driver. He stood, watching, as the man in overalls got out and examined the Kia's front right tyre. After just a few seconds he shook his head. 'Wouldn't be clever to repair that, sir,' he said. 'That's a bad tear.'

'What can you do?' Copeland asked. 'I'll pay whatever's necessary.'

'No need, not a problem, it's down to the hire company. I'll just replace it. I brought a spare, just in case.'

Copeland gave him a high-five. He watched him drop a ramp at the rear of his truck and, expertly, roll down a heavy-duty jack. He cranked up the front of the car and set to work. Fifteen minutes later there was a brand-new tyre on the wheel. He dropped the car back down, produced a form for Copeland to sign, rejected the fifty-pound note he was offered as a tip and jumped back into his cab.

Copeland pressed the clicker to open the garage door and the truck drove up the steep exit and out into the grey, early-morning light.

As soon as the door clattered back down, Copeland hurried back up to the fifth floor, switching off his phone and dropping it down the rubbish chute on the way. He went into his flat and peered down through the window.

101

The radio in Kevin Hall's phone crackled briefly. 'Charlie Romeo Six Four Zero?'

'Charlie Romeo Six Four Zero,' he answered. It was Oscar-1.

'Charlie Romeo Six Four Zero, I have information on the car that the truck from Sussex Tyre and Breakdown Services was called to attend. It is an Avis rental vehicle, a Kia, index Mike Victor, One Nine, Bravo November Zulu, rented to a Samuel Jackson on October 9th. There is a marker on this car. Samuel Jackson is believed to be one of the aliases of a wanted suspect, Jules de Copeland, who also goes under the name of Tunde Oganjimi. He is believed to be armed and extremely dangerous.'

As Oscar-1 spoke, Hall and Wilde watched the truck make a left turn, east, away from Brighton. Hall noted there was just one man in the cab, but was it the same man who had been there when it arrived?

'Sir,' Hall said, 'it's possible Copeland could be riding, hidden, in this truck – that he might have hijacked it? Permission to leave station and interrogate the breakdown vehicle? We've just been relieved by another team to continue the surveillance.'

'Charlie Romeo Six Four Zero, leave station and follow

411

discreetly at a safe distance but do not attempt to stop it. I'll get an Armed Response Vehicle to you – there is one ten minutes away. Repeat, do not attempt to stop it. Understood?'

'Do not attempt to stop,' Hall repeated. 'Yes yes.'

'Go for it,' came the reply. 'But maintain a safe distance.'

Hall started the car, drove out of the parking area and stopped at the main road. The morning rush hour had started and a line of cars went past. Obeying the instruction to be discreet, he pulled out into a gap, heading east, without switching on the blue lights, and accelerated hard. He rapidly overtook several vehicles that were sticking to the 50 mph limit. Within moments, through the misty rain, he could just make out faint red tail lights and the silhouette of the truck directly ahead in the distance.

Hall quickly narrowed the gap to the vehicle along the clifftop dual carriageway, passing the renowned girl's school Roedean and then the home for blind veterans. He slowed as they went downhill towards the village of Rottingdean, where the breakdown truck had stopped at traffic lights. Hall braked to a halt and both he and Velvet Wilde looked hard at the vehicle. There was no sign of anyone through the rear window of the cab except for the driver. He told Velvet Wilde to radio Oscar-1.

'Charlie Romeo Six Four Zero, sir,' she said to Mark Evans. 'We are behind the breakdown truck, continuing east.'

'The ARV is heading west towards you from Newhaven. ETA two minutes. Maintain your position. They will do the stop.'

'Yes yes.'

As they drove down into a sweeping dip and up the other side, they saw strobing blue lights approaching from the opposite direction at speed. Seconds later a dark, unmarked Audi, with lights still flashing, made a sharp U-turn in front of them and accelerated towards the truck, gaining on it rapidly.

It tucked in behind the vehicle, flashing its headlights and whup-whupping the siren. The truck immediately braked and pulled into the roadside.

Hall pulled up a short distance behind them. He and Wilde watched two uniformed officers in body armour climb out of the Audi, crouching low, each holding an automatic rifle. They advanced slowly and purposefully.

The two detectives got out, staying back as instructed.

One armed officer checked out the rear of the truck with his torch, while the other walked up to the cab, keeping his gun low but visible.

Hall and Wilde moved to within earshot.

The driver lowered his window. 'Good morning, officer,' the driver said. 'Can I help you?'

'Can you tell me where you've just been?'

'Delivering and fitting a new tyre to an Avis rental vehicle at Marina Heights – a Kia. We work under contract for them.'

'What was the problem with the tyre?' the Armed Response Unit officer asked.

'A flat – unrepairable. Been slashed. Might have been a pothole – or vandals.'

'Who was it rented to?'

The driver looked at his call sheet, attached to a clipboard on his dash. 'The customer's name was Samuel Jackson.'

'Can you describe him?'

'He was a tall black guy. Not as good-looking as the actor!' Then he added, as an afterthought, 'And he smelled nice.'

'Do you remember what colour his shoes were?'

'Oh, yes – they were red.'

'Did you speak to him?'

'A little – he seemed agitated but very polite. He tried to give me a fifty-pound tip, but I told him we're not allowed to accept tips.'

Deciding it was safe now to step forward, Kevin Hall held up his warrant card and asked the driver, 'Do you have his flat number?'

The driver shook his head. 'Just the address of the building and his mobile phone.'

'Can you give me the number?' Hall wrote it down on his pad.

'Is there a problem, officers?' the driver asked, looking bewildered and overwhelmed.

After a brief discussion with the Armed Response officers, Hall said to him, 'No, thanks for your help. You are free to go on your way.'

Hurrying back to his car, Hall phoned the Incident Room and gave the phone number to Arnie Crown, who answered, telling him to check it out urgently.

102

Jules de Copeland stood by the window of his apartment, up on the fifth floor, watching the progress of the breakdown truck as it headed east along Marine Parade. He saw the small saloon suddenly appear from seemingly nowhere and accelerate hard in the same direction.

Cops?

Moments later he lost sight of it in the mist.

Cops who had been waiting somewhere outside, out of his view? Watching the building? Watching him? What would the breakdown truck driver tell them? The man had turned down his attempt to bribe him. Would he give them his phone number?

Of course he would. The phone which he had dropped down the chute. It was a burner, but he did not know how much information they could pull from it. His address?

He looked at his watch: 7.25 a.m.

How accurately could GPS triangulation on his phone call pinpoint him? To the building? The floor? The apartment?

Even more urgent to make a run for it.

103

In his van across the road from Marina Heights, Tooth watched the breakdown truck emerge from the car park and turn east. Moments later he was startled by the sight of a small, silver Ford, with two people in the front, moving fast in the same direction as the truck, racing past other vehicles and vanishing into the mist.

Where had it sprung from?

Had Copeland escaped in the rear of the truck? Should he chase after it, too, and see? But what if he was wrong? What if he did that and Copeland left the building in his car, with the tyre replaced, and he lost him?

It was a gamble either way. Stay put, he decided.

A few minutes later he would see he had made the right decision.

104

Jules de Copeland did a frantic last-minute check of his flat. Was there anything he had missed that could give the police any leads to him if they raided it?

He ran through into the bedroom, the spare room, the bathroom, then back into the large, open-plan living area.

His laptop!

Duh! How could he have missed it? Jesus, calm down. How shot were his nerves?

Cool it, man! Take a chill pill, wasn't that what they said these days? Chill! Calm it all down. Hold your nerve, hang tight. Tonight you are going to scoop up £300,000 in cash from that dumb bitch. Tomorrow morning you'll be in Germany. And by Sunday you'll be back with Ama and Bobo. And rolling in cash!

Buoyed by the thought, he reached the front door, opened it, gave the room one final sweep with his jumpy eyes, turned the master switch off and closed the door behind him. Then, to be safe, he took the fire-escape stairs down to the basement.

All four tyres of the Kia looked nicely inflated. He put the laptop in one of the cases in the boot then jumped in, holding the key, and for a moment couldn't find where to insert it. Was it to the right or the left of the steering wheel?

His hand was shaking like a jackhammer. Calm down, dude!

His vision was blurry. Nerves. He took several deep breaths. They didn't calm him the way they usually did.

It took him three stabs to insert the damned key into the ignition slot. He twisted it. A whole bunch of dash lights and dials came to life. But nothing more.

No!

No, no, no!

He switched it off and tried again, twisting it so hard he was worried the key would snap.

NO! Don't do this to me!

He tried again. Again. Then, to his relief, the car finally started.

Thank you, God!

He released the handbrake, reversed out of the bay, then accelerated forward and up the steep exit ramp. Shaking. In a total state, his eyes not even seeming to focus properly.

Get a grip!

The car-park door rose steadily upwards. As soon as it was well clear of his roof, he drove out and turned left through the visitors' parking area, passing the Polo with its windscreen all misted and wondering if there was anyone inside it, but no longer caring. He was focused on just one thing, now. Getting away from here.

He drove past the EXIT sign and stopped at the main road. A steady stream of traffic was passing, at speed. Anxiously he peered in his mirrors. Any sign of the Polo moving? Nothing.

Good.

The traffic was relentless. Car. Car. Car. Taxi. Van. Bus. Truck. Car. Car. Car. Truck.

Come on, give us a break!

A short gap opened up. A large van, headlights on, was bearing down, but he had time if he floored it.

He pulled out sharply into the road. Halfway, the engine stalled.

Died.

No, not now!

Frantically he pumped the accelerator. Heard the scream of brakes and tyres and—

Suddenly he was inside a cocktail shaker. Or a tumble dryer. Spinning.

In slow motion and fast motion simultaneously.

105

Friday 12 October

Tooth, fingers closed around the handgrip of his gun, was scarcely able to believe what he was seeing. He was watching a scene from a horror movie playing in front of his eyes in slow motion.

The Kia pulling out into the busy road, then stopping dead. His doing, he realized.

An instant later, the Kia being T-boned, just behind the passenger compartment, the van sending it spinning around and into the oncoming traffic, where it was hit again by a Mini. The Kia rolled onto its roof and then, somehow, righted itself, landing on its wheels, stationary, in the middle of the road.

All the traffic, in both directions, halted.

People were jumping out of their vehicles and running towards the scene. The driver of the Mini, a woman, wasn't moving.

Tooth maintained his grip on his gun. Watching through the windscreen of his van.

He saw, to his dismay, the tall black guy, looking dazed, climb out of the car.

Copeland stared around, lost, like an astronaut who'd landed on the wrong planet.

Tooth rapidly considered his options. Rush to the gathering crowd, half of whom were filming the scene on their phones, and in the chaos put two quick shots into Copeland and sprint away before anyone figured what was happening?

Then he heard a siren. Louder.

Saw blue lights in the distance approaching along the seafront, from the west.

He cursed, put the safety catch back on and pocketed the gun, watching the unfolding scene. Maybe they'd take Copeland to hospital. He knew that place, knew it extremely well. He'd have no problem hitting Copeland there.

His head swam again, another bout of nausea engulfing him. He needed to be in hospital himself, he knew. One for tropical diseases. He needed urgently to see a specialist in venomous bites again, like the one in Munich, to get all this crap happening inside him sorted out. He'd find one in Ecuador, for sure.

Then he stiffened as he watched a new development. Something was up.

He tried to focus.

106

Jules de Copeland, trying desperately to focus, to gather his wits, saw a bearded man in paint-spattered overalls striding angrily towards him. A phone camera flashed.

'You stupid twat!' the man yelled. 'You pulled right out in front of me. Jesus, are you all right? You stupid moron! I thought I'd killed you!'

Another camera flashed.

The man pushed through the crowd, fists clenched, and reached him. 'You pulled right out in front of me!' He grabbed Copeland's coat lapels. 'Look what you've done to my van – that's my whole livelihood!'

Instinctively, without even thinking about it, Copeland took a swing at him, striking him under the jaw and decking him.

As the van driver staggered backwards and fell to the ground, Copeland ran to the rear of his car, barely clocking the shocked faces all around, wrenched open the boot lid, pulled out his two cases and ran, pushing through them, ignoring the shouts.

As he ran, he looked in desperation in both directions. Which way? Left? Right? They were his only options.

Tooth saw his chance. Copeland making a break for it. The roundabouts were coming on again inside his head.

422

He opened the driver's door and, as he climbed out, his foot caught in the seat belt and he fell flat on the hard, wet tarmac. He lay there, stunned, for some seconds, then vomited.

Copeland reached the far pavement and stopped for an instant, his brain feeling like it had been through a blender. The siren was getting closer. His right leg was hurting badly and his chest felt as if a sword was sticking into it. Busted rib? No time to think about it. To his right, the main road stretched endlessly away into the distance along the clifftop. He'd be completely exposed. His only option was left. A couple of hundred yards to his left another main road joined it. If he could reach that he could head up it, north and away.

He ran, limping, swinging the cases, every step agony, then turned right and carried on up the main road. Over to the left was an underpass and, beyond that, a gasometer. After a short distance he stopped and turned. No one was following him. A marked police car, lights flashing, shot past the junction.

How long before someone told the police which direction he'd run off in?

He had to hide. Where? There was a housing estate over to the right with a large car park in front. Could he hide behind one of the vehicles? He was about to make a dash for it when, unbelievably, he saw a turquoise-and-white taxi coming down the hill with the FOR HIRE sign lit up.

He dropped the cases and jumped out in front of it, holding up a hand, and to his relief the taxi stopped. The Asian driver lowered the nearside window and Copeland leaned in. 'Oh man, you've saved my life! I've got to catch a flight from Gatwick and my bloody car won't start!'

The driver climbed out, all happy. 'No problem!' Then

he peered closely at Copeland's face. 'You've got a nasty gash.'

Copeland put his hand to his cheek and felt something sticky. He pulled it away and saw blood on his fingers. 'Yeah, the bonnet caught me in the face when I lifted it to see if I could fix the problem.'

'You ought to get that attended to, it might need stitching – do you want to go via the hospital?'

'No, no time. And it's nothing like the injury I'm going to be getting from my wife if I don't catch that plane. It's our wedding anniversary!'

'All right, jump in, please. I'll take care of the bags. I'll give you some tissues – don't let any blood get on the uphol-stery, please, it's not my cab and the guy who owns it is well fussy.'

Copeland got into the rear and pulled the door shut while the driver put the cases in the boot. Moments later they were under way. He sat back, dabbing his face with a tissue and putting on his seat belt. They went over a pothole and he stifled a scream as the rib dug painfully into his chest.

Seconds later the taxi halted at the junction with the main seafront road. 'Nasty-looking accident over there,' the driver said.

Peering through his window, Copeland saw the police car stopped a short distance from the smashed Kia, van and Mini, and the crowd of people who had left their vehicles, from both directions. 'Ah,' he said. 'That's what the noise was. I heard a loud bang.'

'Looks a big one!' The driver pulled out, turning right, to Copeland's relief, and away from the scene.

'Where you from?' he asked.

'Scotland,' Copeland replied, randomly.

'Always raining there?'

'Always.'

'North or South Terminal?'

'North,' he said.

'Are you sure? What airline?'

'British Airways.'

'They go from the South Terminal to Scotland.'

'Ah, right, thank you. South, please.'

Copeland closed his eyes. Jesus. What a mess. What a mess.

'I've got a mate who moved to Edinburgh, married a girl from there. Said it's flipping cold.'

'Yeah,' Copeland said distantly, tuning him out. He was thinking. Police had been watching the flat. Someone else had also. Kofi had been murdered in prison. Steve Barrey's doing? Almost certainly, that was his style, his reach – Barrey had long tentacles. And if he'd ordered Kofi dead, he would have ordered him dead, too. If he was sensible he'd forget the cash, just cut and run now. If the police and Barrey were after him, it could only be a matter of time.

But £300,000 was too much to walk away from. There had to be a way to grab the money and go, if need be from right under the nose of anyone watching – police or friends of Mr Steven Barrey.

An idea was forming. The police had raided his Withdean Place business premises, but there were only a few of his staff there. Most of them had gone home to their rented accommodation in the city. He hit the speed dial on his back-up phone of his trusted manager, a fellow Ghanaian, Lucius Orji, hoping and praying this was still his current number. He encouraged all his team to ditch their burners every three days and replace them.

It rang and moments later Orji answered.

'Man, am I glad to hear your voice,' Copeland said.

'You too, boss. You OK? I mean I heard about Kofi.'

'Meet me at Gatwick Airport, get there as quickly as you can. Bring your driving licence. South Terminal arrivals hall, there's a Costa. I'll see you there.'

For the next twenty minutes Copeland sat in silence, planning. He made a list of what he required.

107

There was a tradition within the Sussex Police Major Crime Unit of a member of an operation team anonymously sticking a cartoon, relevant to the enquiry, on the inside of the Incident Room door. Despite their collaboration some while back now with Surrey Police Major Crime Team, the tradition still held good.

Roy Grace, hunched over his workstation, stared with amusement at the one that had appeared overnight. It had been clipped from a newspaper. The headline above said,

INTERNET FRAUD AT RECORD LEVELS

and below was an image of a cash register spewing out money like a fruit machine.

Serious again, he focused back on his task of trying to piece together everything he currently had on Operation Lisbon. He read through his notes, carefully, on the pad in front of him, beside his Policy Book.

Lena Welch. Suzy Driver. Marina Heights. Lynda Merrill. Jules de Copeland/Tunde Oganjimi bringing £300,000 to Primrose Farm Cottage, Forest Row? Tooth. Ghana – Sakawa. Dunstan Ogwang/Kofi Okonjo (deceased – murdered?). Two CROPS in situ at Forest Row. To the list he added the latest development of the breakdown truck attending the vehicle and subsequently being stopped and searched. And the driver's description of the man who had rented the Kia car he had attended, the tyre of which he had replaced.

A call came through from an officer at the Silver command office. 'Sir, the CROPS officers have sent through images of the front- and rear-door locks. Two covert surveillance officers are on their way to the house to install listening devices.'

Grace thanked her, asking her to inform him as soon as the listening devices were in place and live. As he ended the call, Arnie Crown came over. 'Sir, intel back from Daniel Salter at Digital Forensics on the phone number used to call the Avis breakdown service. They've traced it to Marina Heights, Kemp Town. But they're not able to pinpoint the address any closer.'

'Good work, Arnie.'

The information didn't take Roy Grace any further.

Moments later, Norman Potting hurried over. 'Chief, just in from Oscar-1. There's been a three-vehicle crash outside Marina Heights. One of them is a Kia car, rented from Avis at Gatwick on Tuesday, October 9th. Witnesses reported that a tall black man, who they say was driving the Kia, fled the scene carrying two suitcases after assaulting the driver of the van that hit his car. One witness reported he was wearing red shoes.'

'Sounds like Fancy Boy,' Grace said. 'That's a top-end building, expensive flats, a good chance they'll have outward-facing CCTV. Have someone check and also the city's TV.'

'I will, but there's more, chief,' Potting said, looking pleased as Punch. 'I just ran the Kia's licence plate against ANPR records. It pinged the same ones, just a few seconds ahead of the ones that clocked Tooth's suspected car shortly

428

after 11.30 p.m. on Tuesday. The last one that clocked it was on Marine Parade, when both vehicles headed east and were not picked up on ANPR.'

Grace processed this. 'Which means . . . ?'

'That either Tooth and Copeland are working together. Or—'

'That Tooth is following him,' Grace said. 'With the intention of killing him. I think that's the more likely scenario.'

'Yes, chief, I agree.'

'Good work, Norman. What we know so far is that Copeland is due to rendezvous at Primrose Farm Cottage, Forest Row, early this evening. Now his plans will be in disarray after the accident. He's done a runner – where? And where is Tooth in all this? Still in his car close to Marina Heights?'

Yet again he privately cursed Cassian Pewe for lifting the guard on Tooth all those months back, allowing him to escape. Which Tooth had done very neatly and was now back to haunt them.

'I don't know, chief,' Potting replied.

'OK. Copeland's gone AWOL. Have the ARV go to Tooth's car, and if he's in it, nick him. He's no further use to us – we know where Copeland's going to show up later today, let's focus on that now. And if Copeland's been staying in that building, we need to find out which flat and get it searched. Hopefully the caretaker will know, if he's back in his flat.'

As Potting went back to his workstation, Grace again studied his notepad. To make a conviction stick, they needed to catch Copeland red-handed. Which meant letting him meet with Lynda Merrill for their planned love-in.

But that was dangerous.

Under current guidelines, some of which were over-cautious in Roy Grace's view, there needed to be a risk assessment prior to any action. These guidelines were created by civil servants with little comprehension of what frontline policing was about, and who were primarily concerned with protecting the police from expensive lawsuits.

He'd always tended to take the view that it was easier to beg forgiveness than ask for permission.

But he did need to be pragmatic, however much that went against the grain. He had to weigh up Copeland's known and suspected history of violence against the risk of him harming the woman. And it didn't look good on the scales.

Pewe would have a field day if it went wrong. The ACC would have his guts for garters for allowing a member of the public to put her life on the line. He knew what the ACC would say. Pewe was only interested in protecting his backside, keeping his nose clean for the next step up, God forbid, his career ambition to be a Chief Constable – and beyond.

And it would be putting his own career on the line, too.

But, equally, Copeland and his team needed to be stopped in their tracks before they ruined even more people's lives. And he had a golden opportunity to catch this nasty criminal red-handed.

Could he take the risk that Lynda Merrill might be harmed?

One option was to pull her out and replace her with a decoy. But that could create all kinds of problems down the line. He could imagine a smart brief, like that arrogant twat, Carrington, claiming entrapment.

It was a massive risk. But he did have Alison Vosper's offer from yesterday, however unattractive it might be – and uncertain – as a potential backstop, if it all went tits up.

Throughout his career he'd taken risks. Always in the interests of what he believed to be justice. One time it had nearly got his best friend, Glenn Branson, killed – he had been shot and wounded in a raid. But wasn't that part of being a police officer? The risk of injury or death was one all officers knew they were taking on when they signed up. In the words of a former Chief of the Metropolitan Police, 'When everyone else is running away from danger, we – and the other emergency services – are the ones running towards it.'

Could he live with himself if Lynda Merrill got harmed? On the other hand, could he live with the knowledge he'd failed to arrest an internet fraud mastermind, who had destroyed countless lives, because he'd been too scared of the possible consequences?

He stood up and walked over to Potting. 'Know what this whole thing is, Norman?' he said. 'It's a ball of shit dipped in wasps.'

108

Two ambulances were now on the scene, as well as several police cars. Vultures were holding cameras up with outstretched arms, recording whatever they could, to post on whatever social media trash they followed.

Tooth climbed to his feet, feeling better after throwing up. Thinking more clearly. He'd missed his opportunity and now he had no idea where Jules de Copeland was headed. Or when – or even *if* – he would return here.

A thought struck him. One that should have occurred many hours earlier, if the insides of his head weren't so messed up.

A crowd had gathered behind the blue-and-white tape sealing off the three wrecked vehicles. Leaving the van and striding around them, he crossed over to Marina Heights, walked up the driveway and rang the intercom button for the caretaker.

After a pause, the man answered through the crackly speaker in a grumpy Irish accent.

'I've a Fed-Ex delivery for Mr Jules Copeland that requires his signature. Can you tell me where I can find him?'

'Flat 507,' came the curt reply.

Flat 507, Tooth thought. That was the one where the woman's voice had come from, when he'd rung the front doorbell last night. Now he rang the intercom bell. Silence. He tried again. Still silence.

Good.

He punched in the door code and entered. The intercom panel said the caretaker was in Flat 2. He'd just answered so Tooth presumed he was in residence. Very good. He could get two bits of business done in one visit.

Following the numbers along the corridor, past the lift, he saw the door to Flat 2 facing him at the end. There was a smell of burnt toast. He stopped in front of it and glanced behind him, checking there was no one, then pressed the buzzer. There was a sharp rasping sound. After a few seconds Tooth heard the man call out.

'Hold on a sec, I got fecking toast on fire here!'

It was another minute or so before the door opened and the stench was much stronger now. Wisps of smoke drifted out. The shaven-headed caretaker, barefoot in a T-shirt and jeans, peered at him, bolshily. The flat looked typical of the poky little ratholes they gave caretakers – he'd been one himself for a couple of years after he left the military. He could see a kitchen just beyond with smoke wafting in it.

'My hours are eight thirty to five, it says so outside, come back in half an hour.' He was about to shut the door in Tooth's face, when he peered at him more closely, with recognition. 'I know you, don't I – we met before?'

'Wednesday night, seven thirty. Out of your office hours. You must have been putting in overtime – saving up for some dental work?' Tooth replied, rapidly trying to assess whether anyone was here with him. From the slovenly look of the place he doubted it. 'You're going to have to save a bit harder.'

'Huh?'

Tooth headbutted him, straight in the mouth, relieving him of the teeth either side of the missing one, sending the man staggering back across his small hall and crashing against the wall.

As the caretaker groaned, covering his bleeding mouth with a tattooed hand, Tooth shoved the door shut behind him, simultaneously launching himself forward and aiming a disabling kick at the man's groin, instantly shooting all the wind out of him. The man doubled up in agony, gasping. As he did so, Tooth seized his forearm and threw him over his shoulder, still gripping the arm, which snapped clean in two.

The caretaker lay on his back on the carpeted floor, staring at him fearfully, blood over his chin and neck, half his radius bone sticking out through the skin of his forearm. Gasping in agony, he cried, 'What is this, what do you want?'

'I don't like you.'

'Huh?'

'You're a very rude man.'

'Rude – ah – ah – you're the fekker that was parked outside.'

Tooth saw what he needed, hanging on the wall by the door. No need for the caretaker any more. He knelt and put a hand under the base of the man's chin, staring him in the eyes. 'If I was a politer guy than you, I'd apologize for what I'm about to do. But I'm not and I don't like you, so I won't.' He jerked the janitor's chin up sharply with his left hand, simultaneously smashing a karate chop with his right into his neck, shattering his windpipe. As the man's head slumped forward, his throat rattling in his struggle for oxygen, Tooth cracked the side of his hand into the rear of his neck, severing the spinal cord.

The caretaker spasmed, then lay still.

Tooth stood back up, went over to the board by the door, which looked like it had keys to every flat in the building hanging on numbered hooks, and found No. 507. As he removed the key and pocketed it, the doorbell rasped.

He froze, thinking. Waiting.

It rasped again.

A resident – or police? There was no damned spyhole to look through and see.

Shit.

He knelt, grabbed the dead man under the armpits and dragged him through into the little kitchen. Then he went back out into the hall and closed the kitchen door, softly. He stood waiting. One minute. Two. Three.

Was someone still out there? He pulled out his gun, removed the safety catch and put it back in his pocket. He waited a short while longer, then, braced to take down anyone standing there, he pulled the door wide open.

The corridor was empty.

But as he stepped out and closed the door, a man in a business suit, holding a smart laptop bag, appeared at the end of the corridor and strode up to Tooth, smiling.

'Hi, are you the caretaker?' he asked politely in a South African accent. Tooth nodded. Ready to tackle him if he needed to.

'I'm Dave Allen – my partner, Nicky, and I have just moved into No. 402. The hot water's not coming on – could you see if you could fix it or let me know the name of a plumber?'

'Sure,' Tooth said, disarmingly pleasant. 'I'm just dealing with a problem in another flat. Can you give me half an hour?'

'We're both just off to work – I think you have a key?'

'I do. Flat 402. I'll go and investigate, Mr Allen, and if I can't find the problem I'll call the plumber in right away.'

'You're American?'

'Uh-huh, but I've been here a long while.'

Dave Allen thanked him, then went through the door to the underground car park.

Tooth took the fire-escape staircase up to the fifth floor.

109

Closing the door of Flat 507 behind him, Tooth stood in a wide, luxuriously appointed hallway. As a precaution, he called out, 'Hello! Caretaker!'

There was no response.

He called out again louder, to make sure, then walked along the hallway and into a large, open-plan living-dining area. Picture windows gave panoramic views to the east and south, all with full-length blinds, fully lowered and opened at an angle that would allow the occupant to look out but not be seen.

It was some pad. Clearly Jules de Copeland didn't stint himself, lavishing some of the money he conned from his internet dating scam business on a nice lifestyle. Smart, modern furnishings, with a fancy Bang and Olufsen hi-fi and a vast flat-screen television.

He walked across thick, white broadloom to the south-facing windows and peered down at the road. The fire brigade were in attendance now, applying heavy cutting gear to the Mini, the driver still inside. There were three ambulances. Police everywhere. His van was still parked across the road in the bus stop, no one seemingly paying it any attention.

He turned away and looked around. Somewhere in here,

he hoped he'd find a clue as to where Copeland might be heading.

And if he didn't?

Tough shit, Steven Barrey. This was his last contract. For the first time since he had started his business he decided to throw his principles to the wind. Take his chances on the burnt-face bastard ever tracking him down in South America.

Over against the far wall, where there was no window, was a fancy walnut desk and white leather chair. He went over to it. There was a Mac charging cable, a phone charger and a mouse. He looked around more carefully. In the waste-paper basket he saw a screwed-up yellow Post-it note that had some scribble on it. Curious, he retrieved it and opened out the small yellow square of paper. The words were barely legible.

Lynda. Primrose Farm Cottage.
Forest Row. 6.30 pm. 300K

He pocketed it, then left the apartment, making his way back down the stairwell. There was a non-alarmed fire-escape door out onto the street at the back of the building. He took it. Too risky to return to his van, he decided. No doubt it would be clamped or towed sometime later this morning. But with all the chaos happening in the street in front of it, he doubted anyone would be paying it too much attention for some while. With luck it would be removed to a car pound and, long before anyone started looking for the man who had rented it, he would be out of the country.

A light drizzle was falling again. He walked along the street, with an underpass to the left and the gasometer beyond, thinking, planning. Feeling very much better, suddenly, although he knew that would not last. Sometime soon again the nausea would return.

When he was a fair distance away from the seafront road he stopped and did a Google search for van rental companies in the area. In his search yesterday, he'd found several. He pressed the link for the phone number of the one that had been second on his list, and dialled the firm. They had a vehicle which suited his purposes fine. He told them he would be with them within the next two hours.

Perfect. He still had two unused identities on him – passports and driving licences in different names. He would collect the rental, drive to his hotel near Gatwick, pick up his bag, then head over towards Primrose Farm Cottage, Forest Row. Copeland and his beloved Lynda were due to rendezvous at 6.30 p.m. He would get there nice and early. Later he would drive to Ashford and catch a late Eurostar to Paris with his one remaining identity.

He was thinking about the lyrics of one of the few musicians he liked listening to, John Lennon, and one of his favourite tracks, 'Beautiful Boy' – 'Life is what happens to you while you're busy making other plans.'

Oh yes.

Jules de Copeland, think about that. It's not going to happen.

110

Shortly before 9 a.m., partly through hunger and partly to relieve the monotony, Doug Riley opened his rucksack, removed the lid of the plastic box inside and ate a breakfast of the egg sandwich, tomatoes and cucumber his wife had prepared for him. Just as he finished, his earpiece crackled.

'Mike Whisky One?'

'Mike Whisky One,' Riley replied to the support van.

'Two covert entry officers approaching in a white Ford van, index Juliet Foxtrot, Five Nine, Papa November Echo. They said to thank you for the photographs.'

'Glad we had the time to fit them in,' Riley answered, facetiously.

Moments later the van passed him and halted outside the house. Two officers in forensic protective suits climbed out and hurried to the front door, one carrying a toolbox.

Riley watched through his binoculars as the one with the toolbox opened the lid, selected a device that looked like a pocketknife and inserted a rod into the lock. Within seconds the door opened and they went in.

Ten minutes later they came back out, closing the door, and drove off. Riley radioed in what he had seen.

His earpiece crackled into life again. 'Mike Whisky One,' he said.

'Mike Whisky Two. An overweight British Blue cat has just appeared through the rear-door flap.'

'Thanks for that information, Mike Whisky Two.'

'Just thought you'd like to know.'

'Sure it's not a cat burglar?'

'Might be going cat-fishing,' Hastings retorted.

Riley groaned. 'Just don't let it piss on you.'

Half an hour later there was another break in the monotony when a post van appeared. The driver pulled up, got out, shoved several envelopes through the letter box in the door and drove off.

Riley radioed his colleague to tell him.

'Any mail for me?' Hastings asked.

111

Pinned to a whiteboard in the Incident Room was an aerial map of Primrose Farm Cottage and the immediate surrounding area. Two red circles marked the positions of the CROPS officers, logged from their transponders.

Below was pinned a floorplan of the cottage, obtained from council records, from when a planning application to extend the building had been put in twenty years back. Roy Grace had virtually memorized it. There was no hallway; the front door opened straight onto an open living area, with a dining area to the left and kitchen beyond, and a door out to the rear. To the right was the snug area, with an inglenook fireplace. A staircase, facing the front door, went up to the first floor where there were four bedrooms and two bathrooms, and what looked like a narrower staircase up to an attic. In the kitchen was a trapdoor, with steps down to what was marked on the plan as a wine cellar.

Also pinned to the whiteboard was a section of an Ordnance Survey map of the area. Grace had marked a circle of approximately five miles radius from Primrose Farm Cottage and was now staring at it, noting the terrain, studying the grid of roads, lanes, bridleways, footpaths. He needed to have a ring of steel around the property. The ability to check out every approaching vehicle from any direction.

There was so much potential for this to go badly wrong. Maybe he should take the safe option, after all, he wondered, and put in a decoy?

His thoughts were interrupted by DS Alexander, standing beside him. 'Sir, we've found a Streamline taxi that picked up a man matching Copeland's description. He flagged the car down a short distance from Marina Heights at 7.45 a.m. – the time fits.'

'Nice work. Where did it drop him?'

'Gatwick Airport – South Terminal.'

Grace looked at him. 'Does that mean he's bailing out? Are they looking for him at the airport?'

'Yes, sir, security has a full description of him and his alias. Inspector Biggs is the duty commander there today. He's checked with security and is pretty sure no one of that description has passed through so far. He has officers checking the departure areas.'

'Make sure he checks the lounges, too.'

'That's happening, sir, and the CCTV. There is one strange thing the taxi driver reported. He had two suitcases with him – one was reasonably heavy but the other, a large one, felt empty.'

Grace thought fast. Was Copeland doing a runner? With an empty suitcase? Ignoring £300,000? Maybe, in the scheme of things, that was small beer to him. But could that amount of money, in cash, be insignificant to anyone?

Why else would he be carrying an empty suitcase, unless he intended putting something in it?

Something as bulky as the cash?

Gatwick Airport wasn't just a hub for flights.

While Alexander stood in front of him, Grace pulled up

the calculator on his computer. On a previous case he'd had to check the weight of £1 million in fifty-pound notes, which was about twenty-six kilograms; £300,000 would be about eight kilos. Well within an airline weight limit.

But with a legal limit of £10,000 being the most anyone could take out of the country without an explanation, would anyone in their right mind take a punt on £300,000? Although, as was becoming increasingly common now, villains were converting cash into crypto-currencies.

'Jack, I'm hypothesizing that Copeland isn't doing a runner. He has that suitcase for a reason. Circulate his description to all car-hire companies in the Gatwick area, and to all the taxi and limousine companies. We can't assume he's trying to flee the country.'

'Yes, sir.'

He turned to Glenn Branson.

'Want to come for a drive in the countryside?'

'To take in the autumn colours? Sounds idyllic, boss.'

As Branson stood up, DS John Camping approached Grace with a clutch of documents in his hand. 'Sir, I have an update from Jersey. Their States Police Financial Crimes Unit have come back with some potentially useful intel. Our enquiry links with something they've been working on for many months. A network of internet fraudsters, focused on internet dating, operating throughout Europe, but mostly Germany. And here's the best bit!' Camping gave him a broad smile. 'It tallies with information we already have. Mr Big – the mastermind – they suspect is none other than Steven Barrey.'

Grace banged the desk. 'Yes!'

'How confident are they, John?' Branson asked.

'Confident enough to put him on 24/7 surveillance, sir.' He looked at Branson, then Grace. 'They've also put a phone tap on his landline and listening devices to try to capture any mobile phones he uses. My contact over there, DC Vanessa Forde, says they are particularly anxious to stamp out this operation because of the importance to Jersey of being a secure financial centre.'

'Are they planning to arrest Barrey?'

'They are still information gathering, sir,' Camping said. 'But if he tries to leave the island they will stop him.'

'Good.' Then Grace turned back to his immediate situation. In less than seven hours, if he was right, Jules de Copeland, with an empty suitcase and potentially murderous intent, was meeting Lynda Merrill, who had romance in mind, in the remote rural location on the whiteboard in front of him.

There was one possible good outcome. And one very bad one.

112

Roy Grace let Glenn Branson drive, to give him time to think and to study the roads and terrain around Primrose Farm Cottage. But they'd barely travelled a couple of miles from Police HQ before he remembered why it was that, last time Glenn had driven him, he'd vowed never again. He gripped the grab handle above him in scared silence, stabbing an imaginary brake pedal in the footwell in front of him, willing Glenn to slow as he was driving far too fast, in his opinion, for the wet road. Glenn overtook a car and pulled into a tight gap shortly before an oncoming lorry thundered past.

'A bit close, matey,' Grace said, grimly.

'Nah, plenty of time. It's all about judgement.'

'And the Collision Investigation Unit and the mortuary. Didn't they teach you the principles of driving on blue lights at police driving school?' Grace asked.

'Yeah, get there fast!'

'Really? The key message I took away was *drive to arrive*.'

Glenn, as ever when he drove, had the focus and grim determination of Lewis Hamilton, but without the Formula One driver's skill.

'Road death statistics are badly up in East Sussex this year,' Grace added by way of a more subtle hint.

'Many back-seat drivers among them?' Branson retorted.

Grace, with a copy of the Ordnance Survey map on his knees, looked at the satnav screen. He consoled himself with the knowledge that there were now less than nine miles to go. A further comfort was the statistic a traffic officer had given him, that most accidents take place within one mile of starting a journey. At least, some small relief, they were out of that danger zone.

He tried to focus on his task. Could he really allow Lynda Merrill to go to the cottage – at least without putting armed officers inside with her? But it came back to his concerns that she might inadvertently alert Copeland and panic him into doing a runner. No, he had to press on with his plan, but that plan had, first and foremost, to ensure she was fully protected.

It was just coming up to 1 p.m. when they found the tumbledown gates that marked the entrance to the cottage, fallen leaves carpeting the drive. He told Branson to pull over, then climbed out of the car and walked some yards down the steep drive to the point where it levelled out, but he couldn't see the house from here. The first CROPS officer would be much further along. Both the ferns and shrubbery either side, and the forest beyond, were dense. There was clearly no other route to the house from here, for a vehicle, other than this driveway.

Grace got back into the car and directed his colleague to take the first right. They turned into an even narrower lane, beneath a guard of honour of overhanging trees. Much of the road surface was covered in fallen leaves.

'Amazing colours,' Branson said, staring at the autumnal golds around them.

'So you do actually notice the beauty of the countryside sometimes?' Grace ribbed.

'When it's autumn, yeah – all dying, decaying. That's our bag, isn't it, death?'

Grace scanned both sides of the lane as they drove. They passed an occasional cottage and one very large house set a short distance behind a five-barred gate, with a horsebox in the driveway. Carrying on, the landscape dipped sharply down to their right. They passed a fallen tree at the roadside, then saw a sign for Southern Water and a reservoir. A short distance on was a sign by a narrow, unmade track for a sailing club. On their right, a barrier made from a small tree blocked off the entrance to another track into the forest.

Endless places for a car to hide, he thought. You could hide an entire army here.

'You're in a cheerful mood,' he said to Branson. 'Is this how being about to get married makes you feel?'

Branson shrugged. 'Maybe I've been around dead bodies too long.' He carried on driving, following Grace's directions along a series of roads and lanes that eventually took them a full 360 degrees around the property.

Roy Grace marked every junction and indentation where a vehicle might be concealed as they went. He didn't spot where the CROPS support vehicle was hiding – clearly they'd done a good job of concealment. They drove back round to the far side of the property and explored a track that went into the forest. But it stopped after a short distance, opening up into a picnic area.

Grace sat studying the map for some while, discussing with Branson the number of vehicles they would need to check anything approaching. They could put a car at each end of the lane, either side of the entrance. But that wouldn't give them enough time to have the registration checked. If they made the net wider, he calculated it would need a minimum of a further seven cars to ring fence the place. A resource, even for a major operation such as this, that would be hard to put together quickly, if at all, and he only had a few hours at most.

A new Silver Commander had relieved Julian Blazeby a few hours earlier. Superintendent Terry Novak was an officer after Grace's own heart because, like himself, Novak was willing to take risks – something that was becoming increasingly rare in the force. Grace phoned him and told him his concerns. Would they be wiser after all to approach Lynda Merrill and take a gamble on losing Copeland, he posited?

'And leave that scumbag free to carry on wiping out the savings and destroying the lives of decent people with his internet scams, Roy?' Novak said, with deep bitterness in his voice.

Grace remembered now. Novak had told him only a few weeks back how his elderly mother had been conned out of £12,000 by a scammer pretending to be her bank. It was almost every penny she and his father had in the world. His eighty-seven-year-old father was so distressed, he'd been unable to sleep and lost his appetite, causing him to end up in hospital suffering from exhaustion. According to the medics, so Terry Novak had said, this was common for victims. The husband would feel consumed with guilt, anger and a sense of utter helplessness – as well as anguish at the irreplaceable loss itself.

Novak went on. 'Roy, we have two armed CROPS covering the house and we'll have ARVs in place. Copeland hasn't a cat in hell's chance of making it through that front door.'

'I like your attitude.'

'Sometimes, Roy, in this world gone crazy, where we police officers spend more time watching our backs than looking for villains, attitude is necessary.'

113

Friday 12 October

It was a fine, almost cloudless day in Jersey and the bright, low sun was shining straight into Steve Barrey's eyes. Sorokin, with his back to the window, could see, to his pleasure, that his guest was clearly uncomfortable. That was exactly the reason he had requested this window table, and he'd made sure he got there early, ahead of his guest, to secure the seat he wanted.

The former New York detective had been told that because of Barrey's facial disfigurement, he preferred corner tables and low lighting levels, to be away from gawkers. Where the man sat now, bang in front of the window, in plain view, and with the dazzling light on him, he was like an actor placed centre-stage. The Stetson he had tilted low and his dark glasses completed the theatrical image.

Barrey was dressed in a loud suit, a tieless shirt buttoned to the neck and bling Louboutin brogues with silver toecaps. Sorokin found it hard to look at his ravaged and scarred face, framed by wisps of hair from his blond wig, but equally hard to look away.

'I can see you're wondering whether it's polite to look or not, Mr Sorokin – or rather, Detective Sorokin, aren't you?' Without waiting for an answer, he said, 'Feel free, look away, I know I'm not a pretty sight, am I? My friends all call me

449

Crispy.' He smiled with a decent set of teeth that looked strange against the tiny slivers of pink that were what remained of his lips. Then he jabbed a finger downwards. 'But the good news is, all's OK from the waist down!'

'Glad to hear it,' Sorokin said. He was conscious of the occasional glances from other diners – whether it was curiosity at Barrey's disfigurement or the man's local reputation as a crime overlord, he didn't know.

Barrey was struggling against the glare, despite his dark glasses. 'Great view, isn't it?' Sorokin said. And it was a very fine view down across the yacht basin and the ocean beyond. The Quayside was a smart restaurant, too, all glass and modern furniture, elegant staff. Situated close to the banking and financial services district of the island's capital, St Helier, the busy lunchtime crowd were well dressed, talking quietly and earnestly. 'I thought I'd let you have the view.'

'You're the visitor,' Barrey said. 'You should have the view.' He shook his head. 'You didn't tell them it was me coming when you booked, like I told you to – they know me here, they always put me in a corner table at the back where we can't be overheard.' He looked around him and signalled to a waitress. 'Drop that blind, would you?'

As she moved towards it, Sorokin put up an arm, halting her. 'I'm enjoying the sun on my back, leave it, it's fine.'

Barrey bristled, but said nothing. From what this guy had told him over the phone, with his background in the Mafia-busting team of the NYPD, his organized crime connections in the US could be of real value to him, both for money laundering and for expanding his internet romance fraud business into that country. Yet there was something about Sorokin that didn't sit quite right. The guy was cocky and arrogant, as if he knew he held a full hand of the cards he wanted.

A waiter appeared with menus. 'Will you be having wine, gentlemen?' he asked.

Sorokin gestured to his guest. 'A glass of wine?'

'I think we should have a bottle of champagne to celebrate – on me,' Barrey said expansively. 'Bottle of Bolly,' he instructed the waiter, but signalled him not to go away. He turned back to Sorokin. 'You like oysters?'

'Uh-huh.'

'Bring us a dozen each, grilled,' he said to the waiter. 'Then we'll look at the menu.'

As the waiter went off, Barrey said, 'Their grilled oysters are to die for.'

'OK.'

Barrey glanced around, as if desperately seeking another table, out of the sun, more out of earshot, but the place was full. He checked out the diners on either side. On the left was a table for two, with a couple of lovers canoodling over lobster thermidors. On the right were four businessmen having a lunch meeting. He leaned forward and lowered his voice. 'So, OK, you have a proposition for me, I'm all ears. What's left of them anyway,' he added with a strange little laugh.

'I kind of left it a little late in life to go into business but I thought, you know, hey, too late is when you're dead! Maybe I still have time to cash in on my experiences – and in particular the contacts that I've made over my years in law enforcement.'

'As you told me over the phone. And you know, don't you, that Colonel Sanders didn't start his fried chicken business until he was in his seventies. You look like you've got a few years on him, yet.'

'Know that old gardening joke?' Sorokin replied. 'A guy asks a landscaping expert when's the best time to plant a tree. The expert replies, "Twenty years ago."'

Barrey gave him a meagre apology for a smile, shelling it out like he was dropping a coin into a homeless person's cap. They were distracted as the champagne arrived and they waited until it was poured before resuming. This time Sorokin's voice was quieter.

'A former golfing buddy in the US got badly rinsed by a lady he met on an internet dating site. Six hundred and fifty thousand bucks.' He watched Barrey's face but it was impossible, with his eyes behind the dark lenses, to read it. 'He asked me to use my police connections to look into the world of internet romance scammers and I found they're mostly out of Ghana and Eastern Europe. To my surprise, I found there are few real players in the US. That's when the idea first popped for me. I realized with all the organized crime connections I'd made over the years that there was a real business opportunity, both to set up a scamming business myself and, hand in hand with it, a money-laundering channel.'

He could still read nothing in Barrey's face.

'Then your name came up on an FBI list of persons of interest in the cybercrime fraud world.'

Barrey still gave no visible reaction at all.

'So, I'm here to offer you the opportunity to expand your empire into the United States, if that's of interest?'

'How do I know I can trust you?'

'I guess I should ask you the same question, Mr Barrey.'

'The future in internet romance is vast, Mr Sorokin. There's a limitless supply of mostly older people desperate for love. We're talking a market worth billions. If you opened up the US for me, we could be making more money than either of us could ever spend.'

'And how do we stay out of jail?'

'By being untraceable of course – as I am.'

'Really? If you are so untraceable, how come I found you so easily?'

'You might have found me, Mr Sorokin, but have you found any evidence that I've committed any crime?' Barrey looked at him intently and triumphantly. 'Well?'

'Clearly you've hidden your activities very cleverly.'

Two large dishes with hot oysters grilled in their shells in a cream sauce arrived. Barrey tucked his napkin into the top of his shirt, all focus, momentarily, on his food. 'You like turbot?' he asked Sorokin.

'Sure.'

He told the waiter to bring them both turbot and a bowl of Jersey Royal potatoes. As the waiter moved away, he addressed Sorokin again.

'As you know, I operate through a network of nominee companies around the world, all springing from my bases in Ghana and Nigeria. The internet fraud and the money laundering run in parallel. I've a string of legitimate financial services companies that everything's fronted through.'

'So is PerfectPartners.net one of your targets?'

After a moment's hesitation, Barrey said, 'One of. Why do you ask about that one in particular – is that the one that your buddy got caught on? Maybe if we do business, I can find a way to get your buddy paid back – how much was it?'

'Six hundred and fifty thousand bucks, give or take.'

'No big deal.'

'It is to him. It's everything he has – or had – in the world.'

Barrey's phone made a soft, staccato noise. Raising an apologetic hand, he answered the call. 'Yeah? What? That's – that's – is he just having a laugh on me?' His voice was becoming increasingly loud. 'Jesus H – Christ, I don't believe this. Sort it!' He killed the call, shoving his phone back in his pocket, looking furious.

'Bad news?' Sorokin asked.

'What's that got to do with you?'

'Quite a lot, actually.'

Barrey stared at him. 'Huh?'

'You see, Mr Barrey, it wasn't just my pal who got screwed out of money on your website scam, it was me, also.' Sorokin looked at him levelly. 'Ninety-seven thousand and sixty-three bucks and forty-two cents, to be precise. Are you going to give that back to me, too?'

Barrey's whole demeanour suddenly changed, his lips forming an ugly snarl. His body shifted and Sorokin saw his arm, with his hand concealed by his napkin, drop below the table. 'Just what is your game, Mr Sorokin?'

'I've come here to get even with you, you fat bastard. To level the score.'

'Is that so?'

'Yep, that's about the size of it.'

For an instant, Barrey's confidence evaporated and he looked wracked with uncertainty. 'You've not invited me here to discuss a business deal at all, have you?'

'You're catching on, fatso. I've come here to nail you and see you brought to justice.'

'And how exactly do you intend doing that?'

'Quite simply. Down in the street below, this place is surrounded by Jersey States Police officers.' Sorokin pulled open his suit jacket to reveal his wiretap.

Barrey stared at him in disbelief and rising anger. 'You've fucking tricked me, you sack of shit.'

'That's pretty rich, coming from you, Barrey. How many hundreds of people have you tricked out of their savings?'

'I'll tell you something you don't know, Mr Smartass

former New York cop. There's no law in Jersey preventing ownership of handguns – just like in your country. I have one under the table now, pointed at your crotch. Call off the cops this second or I'll blow your nuts off.' Looking panic-stricken, he turned and signalled to a table where two large men were seated.

They rose and began walking over.

Sorokin seized the opportunity and upended the table into Barrey's lap, at the same time lunging forward, putting his arm round the back of Barrey's head and pulling his face into a bowl of scalding oysters, hearing the crunch of breaking glasses and shells.

Barrey twisted away, more agilely than Sorokin had anticipated, and rolled into the table of the two lovers, sending their lobsters and wine glasses flying.

As Sorokin lunged after him he saw the two henchmen closing on him. He spun, headbutting one and kicking the other, hard, shattering his knee. Barrey clambered to his feet, stumbled and crashed into a table, sending a seafood tower flying. As the former detective reached him, oblivious to the shocked faces of diners and waiters, Barrey grabbed a bottle from an ice bucket and swung it at him. Sorokin ducked. Barrey swung it again, this time catching him a glancing blow in the face with it, dazing him and propelling him reeling into yet another table, sending more glasses and dishes to the floor.

As he crawled back onto his hands and knees, half blinded with pain, he saw Barrey, minus his Stetson, wig askew, lumbering towards the exit. He reached it several seconds after Barrey had vanished through it, determined, totally determined, the bastard wasn't getting away. As he ran down the first flight of stairs he heard a voice below him yell, 'Stop, police! Put your gun down. Put your gun down or we shoot! Drop your gun and put your hands in the air where we can see them.'

Turning a corner in the stairwell he saw Barrey below him drop his gun, and it clattered down the steps.

Directly below were four police officers in body armour, helmets and vizors, two aiming automatic rifles, two pointing handguns.

Barrey raised his arms in the air.

Sorokin stood still for a moment. Then, he couldn't resist it, he carried on down until he was right behind Barrey, leaned forward and spoke quietly into his ear. 'Guess I'm never going to see my money back now. But I tell you what – this moment, it's worth every damned cent just to see this. And if you want the really bad news, I'm told they don't serve grilled oysters in British jails, so eat the one that's still stuck to your forehead and savour the taste – you're gonna have to make that last a while.'

114

Friday 12 October

The drizzle finally let up and, to the relief of PC Doug Riley who was drenched to the skin, the sun came out. He pulled a flapjack from his rucksack and took a bite. Then he froze as he heard the sound of an approaching vehicle.

Hastily swallowing and replacing the rest, he zipped the bag up and waited. A taxi bumped along the cart track past him, headed around the driveway and pulled up outside the front door. With the smell of exhaust fumes in his nostrils, Riley watched through his binoculars as the rear door opened and the passenger climbed out.

Not the tall black man he'd been briefed to expect.

The man paying the driver looked to be in his late fifties. He was dressed in a tweedy jacket, checked shirt and blue cords, with well-groomed grey hair. As the taxi drove off the man looked around, seemingly getting his bearings, then walked to the front door. He had no luggage, just a coat over his arm.

Riley lowered the binoculars, raised his camera, zoomed in and took a series of photographs as the man let himself in with a key.

As soon as the front door closed, Riley spoke into his radio. 'Mike Whisky One to Mike Whisky Two.'

'Mike Whisky Two,' the response came almost instantly

from his colleague, from his hideout somewhere beyond the rear of the house.

'An IC1 – white male – late fifties, has just arrived in a taxi and entered the house, using a key,' Riley informed him.

'Workman?'

'No, he looks posh.'

'Port out, starboard home,' Hastings said.

'What?'

'Just being facetious.'

'Save it,' Riley said. 'This man's not on our brief or radar. We're waiting for an IC1 female, late fifties, a tall IC3 in his thirties and the possibility of another IC1, a short, thin guy, might be walking with a limp. So any idea who this visitor might be?'

'A burglar?'

'With his own front-door key?'

'Good point!'

Riley radioed the support team, asking if there was intel on anyone else expected at the house.

Moments later a request was radioed back, asking him to ping the photographs, urgently, to the Silver command team.

115

Roy Grace, at his desk, looked at his watch. Under four hours to the rendezvous. The Armed Response and the Local Support Team officers would be in situ by 4.30 p.m., with all vehicles removed from the immediate area.

His adrenaline was surging. He was excited, but nervous. Troubled by one constant thought: where did the wild card, Tooth, fit into all of this?

The Outside Enquiry Team had reported that Tooth's rental Polo, which had been found in the car park of the apartment block along the street from Marina Heights, appeared to have been abandoned. Further, a small van, illegally parked in a bus stop lay-by across the street from Marina Heights, also appeared to have been abandoned. An alert traffic officer had connected the dots, tracing the van to a local rental company. The name it had been rented under meant nothing, but the description of the hirer fitted Tooth, although they had no CCTV to verify this.

So, Grace speculated, had wily Tooth left the car as a false trail, then rented the van? Then, realizing he was unable to move the van, because of the road being sealed off after the accident, abandoned that vehicle, too?

Had he rented another? He leaned back, closing his

eyes, thinking. Why had Tooth been watching the building? For Copeland? It was the obvious link to why Tooth had been in Withdean Road in the early hours of Wednesday morning, outside the property where Copeland had been operating from.

Someone coughed in front of him as if to get his attention. He opened his eyes and saw Glenn Branson peering at him. 'Having an old person's nap, are you?'

'Yeah, yeah. You know what? I'm doing something you've never done in your entire life. I'm *thinking*.'

'It's worn you out, obviously.'

'So have you just woken me up to piss me off?'

'No, as your mate I was getting pretty worried about your score on the Glasgow Coma Scale. I was about to put you down for a One.'

'A *One*?'

'Yeah. *Does not open eyes. Makes no sounds. Makes no movements*. I was wondering whether to call an undertaker.'

'Do you have anything useful to say – or can I go back to my *old person's nap*?'

'Actually, I do. No one's been able to get hold of the Marina Heights caretaker all day, but EJ contacted the managing agents for the building and got a list of all tenants – none so far match Copeland.'

'How many flats are there in the building?'

'Eighty-six.'

'Send as many Outside Enquiry officers in to start door-to-door as you can muster. Copeland's a distinctive-looking fellow – if he's been staying there someone will have seen him. We need to find which flat and have it searched.'

As Branson returned to his desk, Grace's phone rang. It was the new duty Silver Commander, Helene Scott.

'Roy,' she said. 'CROPS officer Mike Whisky One has just

called in a man arriving by taxi at Primrose Farm Cottage. He appears to be a key holder.'

'What's his description?'

'IC1, about six foot tall, grey hair, well dressed, age approximately late fifties.' Grace frowned. The description fitted neither Jules de Copeland nor Tooth.

'Any idea who he is or what he's doing at the property?'

'No, just that he entered and closed the front door. The taxi left. The CROPS wonders if we can ID him. He's emailing photographs but he's in a rubbish reception area, with a poor signal. Hopefully they'll come through in a few minutes.'

'Can you send them to me as soon as you get them, please,' Grace said.

Ending the call, he again lapsed into thought. Who was this man who'd gone into the cottage? Something felt seriously off-kilter here.

Recapping on his intel, Lynda Merrill had set up what she believed would be a romantic weekend in an isolated cottage she had been loaned with the man she had been conned into believing was her soulmate. And she was about to be in for a rude shock.

His phone rang. It was Silver, telling him she'd just sent him a few photographs.

Grace immediately looked at the email which came through. Opening the files, he saw a series of images of the man he was pretty sure he recognized from his photographs as Johnny Fordwater, approaching the house and looking around as if surveying the surroundings.

'Norman!' he called out. 'Can you come here a sec.'

Potting ambled over and stopped beside him. He looked at the screen, then peered closer. 'That's Johnny Fordwater,' he said.

'I thought it was. You're sure that's him?'

Potting peered closer. 'Absolutely. No question.'

'Remind me what we know about him.'

'He's a widower. Some months ago he joined the German internet dating agency, ZweitesMal.de, and met a woman – or so he thought – who gave her name as Ingrid – um – Ingrid Ostermann. They had an online romance for several months, during which time he became deeply infatuated with her – whoever she really was. He paid out over four hundred grand, most of which was for what turned out to be a bogus property purchase. Where are these pictures from?'

'Taken just now by a CROPS officer outside the house where a woman's about to meet this guy who's been romancing her on PerfectPartners.net, and hand over three hundred grand in folding to him.'

Potting frowned. 'So what is Major Fordwater doing there?'

'I was hoping you might be able to tell me.'

Potting shook his head. 'I'm baffled, chief.'

Roy Grace's phone rang. Signalling an apology to the DS, he answered it. 'Detective Superintendent Roy Grace.'

He instantly recognized the Brooklyn accent of his old friend New York Detective Investigator Pat Lanigan.

'Hey, pal, it's been a while!' Lanigan said. 'How you doing?'

'Busy, Pat. Thanks to the ceaseless ingenuity of villains and human gullibility. You? How's Francene?'

'She's great. Cleo good?'

'She is, thanks.'

'Meant to call you a few days back, but likewise, it's been a crazy time here. This may not be your bag, but I thought you ought to know, as the guy involved is on your patch.

And he's pretty angry, know what I mean – dangerously angry?'

Covering the mouthpiece, Grace told Potting he'd catch up with him in a few minutes. As the DS returned to his workstation, Grace said, 'Dangerously angry?'

'Well, here's the thing, pal. One of my old work buddies, Matthew Sorokin – remember Matt?'

'Of course, very well. How is he?'

'He took retirement and now lives in Florida – went back to work again because he got bored – he's now with a county sheriff's office down there. Here's the thing, pal. Matt has a bit of a train wreck of a love life. He recently joined an online dating agency, on the recommendation of an old buddy, name of Gerald – or Gerry – Ronson, and ended up getting conned out of a shedload of money.'

'Tell me more.'

'Well, seems like Gerry and Matt met soon after Gerry had left the military and joined the New York Fire Brigade – on the morning of 9/11. They kind of bonded in the aftermath of the hell that it was and kept in touch. Gerry moved to Minnesota and met – and married – a lady through an internet dating agency.'

'And recommended the agency to Matt?' Grace checked.

'Uh-huh. Gerry raved about it to him. At the time, Matt was lonely and morose. So he joined. This is where you come in. Gerry has another buddy, a Brit he met out in Iraq, called Johnny Fordwater – who got promoted to major. The way I understand it is that Johnny's wife died and he spent several lonely years. Until Gerry talked him into online dating.'

'And he joined ZweitesMal.de, right?'

'Yep,' Lanigan said. 'You should be a detective!'

Grace suppressed a grin. Then a cold chill rippled

through him. He looked back at his screen. At the image on it. The former major, who had been conned out of over £400,000. Just what was he doing entering Primrose Farm Cottage, and with a key? This was beyond a coincidence.

Who had given him a key?

'You still there, pal?' Lanigan said, breaking into his thoughts.

'I am. Your call is very timely, Pat.' What was Fordwater up to?

'Timely?' Lanigan quizzed.

'Tell me what you know about this character, Major Johnny Fordwater, Pat?'

'Sure, that's why I was calling you. Johnny Fordwater flew over from London to see me this week. I met with him and Matt Sorokin in my office. Fordwater's a nice guy, I felt kind of sorry for him, you know. He recognized he didn't have a cat in hell's chance of recovering a cent, but he wanted to find some way of hitting back at the bastards who'd rinsed him. Both guys asked if I could use any of my contacts here in the NYPD or the FBI or the Secret Service Homeland Security teams.'

Grace felt a prickle of anxiety at what he was hearing. 'Were you able to, Pat?'

'I told them I'd been doing some digging around and it seemed the ringleaders are almost all based either out of Africa or Eastern Europe. I gave them a name I'd been given, of someone on your patch, Roy. Someone the FBI cyber-crime unit has worked with in the past. This is one smart guy – he's been an advisor to both Apple and Microsoft on cybersecurity. Recently retired from the Sussex Police Digital Forensics Team due to a health issue. Set himself up as an independent consultant investigating internet fraud. I'm told he's the man.'

'That's Ray Packham!'

'You're kidding! You know him?'

'I've used him many times – he's been a huge help in a number of my investigations. We'll get in contact with him right away. I really appreciate your help, Pat.'

'No worries, pal. Any plans to be in New York?'

'Well, actually Cleo did say a while back she'd love to go Christmas shopping there this year, if we had the time – and I have a load of annual leave owing. So maybe.'

'Just let me know. I'll pick you guys up from the airport, show you around, give you a great time.'

'For sure!'

'You got it.'

The moment he ended the call, Roy Grace opened the address book on his phone and looked for Packham's number, thinking that the last thing he needed was a vigilante.

116

'Roy!' Ray Packham answered, sounding genuinely pleased to hear from him.

Grace cut to the chase. 'I've got a fast-time situation, Ray. Can you tell me if a Major Johnny Fordwater has been in touch with you – he was given your details by a detective in the NYPD on Monday.'

'Hmmm,' Packham replied. 'Not sure whether I should be pleading client confidentiality.'

Grace was unsure from the tone of his voice whether he was joking or not. 'There's possibly life at stake here, Ray.'

'Mate, I'll always give you priority over any client. Yes, he's been in touch, came to see me on Tuesday. He's a pretty angry man – and with good reason. He wanted to pay me every penny he has left in the world to track down the scammers who'd targeted him. I told him he's up against very smart operators, who hide behind a virtually untrace-able digital trail, and the best thing he could do was write off what he had lost, put it down to experience and try to enjoy the rest of his life and what money he had left. But he wasn't having it. He's just dead set on revenge.'

'So how did you leave it with him?'

'He wanted to hire me to have a go at finding them. But I genuinely felt I couldn't help him. Frankly, if I'd taken his money I would have been conning him, too, and I wouldn't do that to anyone. I gave him the name of a contact I've had some dealings with, who's made something of a speciality in the internet romance field, and told him he'd be better off spending his money with him.'

'Who's that, Ray?'

'A PI called Jack Roberts – has a company called Global Investigations.'

'Interesting.'

'You know this character?'

'I do, yes.'

'Roberts has a great reputation – seems to be able to do a lot more for his clients than any of the current police forces around Europe.'

'By taking the law into his own hands, Ray?'

'I couldn't possibly comment on his methods.'

Once again, Grace was unsure whether Packham was joking or not. But he was starting to have an idea what Major Johnny Fordwater might be doing at Primrose Farm Cottage.

And it wasn't to enjoy a few hours of autumnal Sussex countryside.

Thanking Packham, he ended the call, then sat, absorbing what he had just been told. Thinking back to last week when he and Glenn Branson had met Jack Roberts in his company's Kingston offices. When Roberts had, none too subtly, made clear his views on the ability of the police, with current resources, to effectively tackle internet fraud. And his chilling words.

I'll give you one piece of advice. You'd better act fast and hard on this. Otherwise you're going to find vigilantes doing your job for you.

So, he thought, Major Johnny Fordwater had gone to

see Jack Roberts. Fordwater was angry, wanting to hit back at the scammers. Was Lynda Merrill also, possibly, a client of Roberts? Had Fordwater gone to Primrose Farm Cottage to protect her – or with the intention of confronting Jules de Copeland?

The bloody idiot was in danger of messing up his whole planned operation. He looked at his watch: 3.40 p.m. There was time. Should he send someone in to tell Fordwater to get the hell out of there?

He weighed up the pros and cons, and realized there was a definite pro to letting Fordwater remain in situ. If the retired major was in cahoots with Lynda Merrill and was planning to confront Jules de Copeland when he entered, he would be giving her protection until the police went in. The con was—

He was interrupted by a call from an officer at the Silver command centre. 'Sir, Mike Whisky One has just called in a woman, fitting the description of Mrs Lynda Merrill, arriving at the cottage. The front door was opened by our mystery man and he has helped her unload several bunches of flowers and Waitrose carrier bags from her car, into the house.'

Grace began to panic. Could the intelligence he'd received be wrong? Were Lynda Merrill and Johnny Fordwater now lovers, having a romantic weekend together?

He'd put together this entire, huge and costly operation on the information from Aiden Gilbert's team at Digital Forensics. What if they'd got it wrong and Copeland had slipped the net and left the country?

He didn't even want to think about what Cassian Pewe would have to say. And yet.

He had to hold his nerve.

Had to remind himself that £300,000, in cash, was a lot

of money. An amount worth taking a risk for. And from his past history, Copeland was a risk taker.

'What else has happened during the day – have the CROPS reported any other activity?'

'Nothing significant since the covert entry team, only the arrival of the postman around 1 p.m., and another van dropping what looks like an Amazon delivery, who left a package on the doorstep, about 2 p.m., sir.'

'OK, patch the listening devices in the house through to me. Are the CROPS hearing it, too?'

'They are, sir.'

Moments later, Grace followed the very clear dialogue between the couple.

It wasn't the conversation of intimate lovers.

The woman said, 'We need to find somewhere for you to hide.'

The man, in an upmarket voice, said, 'What time is this runt meant to be arriving?'

'Around 6.30.'

'I'll be ready. Just keep him sweet-talking. Tell him you're going to fetch the cash and make him a drink. Whatever he wants.'

'You're not going to attack him?'

'No, I just want to see the bastard face to face. See what he has to say. I'm wearing the wiretap Jack Roberts put on me. My goal is to get him to confess.'

'Are we sure about what we're doing? It's not worth getting hurt for, Johnny.'

'That, my dear lady,' Fordwater said, 'is a matter of opinion.'

117

Friday 12 October

Roy Grace, worried, removed his earpiece, riffled through his notes and found the number he was looking for. He dialled it.

A friendly-sounding woman answered after two rings. 'Global Investigations. How can I help you?'

'May I speak to Jack Roberts, please?'

'I'm sorry, he's out of the office for the rest of the afternoon.'

'Can you give me his mobile number?'

'I'm very sorry, sir, I'm not able to give that out.'

'I'm Detective Superintendent Roy Grace of the Surrey and Sussex Major Crime Team. I met with Mr Roberts on Tuesday of last week. I need to speak with him very urgently – there is potentially a life at stake.'

'Are you able to verify who you are, sir?'

'I can send you through a scan of my warrant card. But you saw me in your office last week.'

Hesitantly, she gave him the number. Grace wrote it down. Immediately he rang the Digital Forensics Team and read out the number to one of its members, Daniel Salter, who answered. He asked Salter to locate the current position of the phone, as a matter of extreme urgency.

Ten minutes later, Salter called Roy Grace back with the

GPS coordinates. The detective plotted them on his phone, then to double-check, looked at them on the map on the whiteboard.

Jack Roberts was less than two miles away from Primrose Farm Cottage. What was he doing?

Grace dialled the number.

'Jack Roberts,' the private investigator answered, almost instantly.

'Mr Roberts, it's Detective Superintendent Grace.'

He sounded hesitant. 'Detective Superintendent – how can I help you?'

'Can you tell me where you are and what you are doing?'

'I'm afraid not. I'm on a covert operation for some clients. I think I'm about to have some very good news for you, but I can't tell you where I am yet.'

'Two miles west of the village of Forest Row in East Sussex?'

'Very accurate, Detective Superintendent.'

'Mr Roberts, I've a pretty good idea who your clients are and they are both in very considerable danger.'

'That's why I'm here, ready to go to their assistance.'

'I appreciate your concern, but we have a major armed police operation in progress following several days of surveillance and intelligence gathering. I'd be very grateful for your cooperation. We both want the same thing.'

'Of course, what do you need me to do?'

'The best thing you can do for both your clients' safety and your own would be to go back to your office. This may not be what you want to hear. I know your views on the police from what you told me when we met, but I need you to trust me.'

'I'm sorry, Detective Superintendent, I promised Mrs Merrill and Major Fordwater I would be close to hand. I want to stay involved – it's not often I get the chance of a live one, and it would be good for my business. I won't go any closer and I won't interfere. Is there any more information you need?'

'Not at the moment, but stay in contact. I'm not happy about this but it's too late to change things now,' Grace replied. 'We'll stay in touch.'

'I'd appreciate that.'

Grace ended the call and immediately updated Silver. 'Can you trust Roberts to stay out of this?' Helene Scott asked.

'I hope so,' he said.

And silently thought, *So long as this doesn't all go tits up.*

118

Tooth, a baseball cap pulled low over his face, was fighting off another attack of giddiness as he drove his rental van up the high street of Forest Row, observing everything. Ahead was a church with a steeple at which he needed to turn right. Immediately to his right was a delivery truck unloading supplies into a deli. To his left an old red van, then a wide forecourt in front of Java & Jazz café and the Chequers Inn. Several cars were parked tail-out, except for one, a dark Ford saloon, which had reversed in.

He clocked two people inside it. Cops for sure, he could always spot them – he could smell them, the way a wildebeest scents a lion or a jackal. The third lot of cops he'd seen in the past ten minutes – one marked, the others plain, in separate lay-bys on the approach to the village. Watching. Hunting. He was well aware from stuff on the news and in the papers how short of resources the British police were, currently. To have deployed three vehicles – six officers – to a small village meant one distinct and dangerous possibility to him. That they had intel on Copeland.

Waiting for him to arrive?

From what he could see from his maps they'd been cleverly located, as anyone coming from the Brighton area

473

would have a very long detour if they didn't take one of the three directions these cars were covering.

He'd survived in this game for as long as he had by never taking chances. British police cars were now fitted with number-plate recognition kit, which meant that almost certainly they'd be running the plates of every passing vehicle. Rental vehicles would be of particular interest to them. There was every likelihood the caretaker at Marina Heights had been found.

One phone call to the company where he'd rented this van from two hours ago, from one of these cop cars, and there was a high probability they'd be looking for him, too.

A high probability, also, that the entrance to Primrose Farm Cottage was being watched.

He tried for a moment to put himself in the mind of the police behind whatever was going on. They would know Copeland was extremely violent and dangerous. Would they let him get as far as the cottage itself? He was on a mission to pick up £300,000 – surely they'd want to catch him red-handed? Maybe they already had undercover officers inside the house? As well as a decoy for the woman?

He needed to find out, get himself inside that cottage. How?

He navigated a small roundabout, forking right in the direction he had memorized. Parked on the pavement a short distance along on his right, outside a house, was a white van, bearing the name SOUTHERN WATER and a small blue logo. Its rear doors were open and two men in high-viz jackets and hard hats were standing on the lawn of the house. One was wearing what looked like ear defenders, until he looked more closely as he passed them and saw they were headphones. The workmen had a metal rod inserted into the lawn, with a cable running to the headset.

He realized what they were doing, they were listening to a buried water pipe. Looking for a leak, he guessed.

A short distance on, passing a lychgate set in a flint wall, with a cemetery beyond, he saw a small field adjoining two houses under construction, but with no sign of activity. To the left was a large warehouse and beyond the field was wooded countryside. But what drew his attention was a second Southern Water van, parked up a track between the field and the first house. Two more men in yellow jackets and hard hats stood in the middle of the field, occupied with inserting a listening rod into the ground.

Definitely a leak, he decided, slowing down. How many more vans like this were in the area? Was it a major leak they were trying to trace?

He hoped it was. Very major.

He hoped it would be as big as leaks get.

119

As soon as he could find a place to turn, Tooth circled back, fast, and was relieved to see the two men were still occupied with the rod in the middle of the field. He pulled the van into the small car park for the cemetery, jumped out and locked it, then stood by the road while several cars passed, before running across.

He was feeling better now. The adrenaline coursing through him had nixed the nausea and hopefully would keep it at bay. He felt alert, back in the army, in the jungle, alone, surviving on his wits. The thrill. It was moments like this when he felt truly alive, as if all the rest of his life was padding.

This was the last time, he reminded himself. Savour it, enjoy the moment.

Could he really retire? Spend his days fishing and walking his dog? The mutt wouldn't live for ever and he had no idea how old the creature was, anyhow – seven, ten? Whatever, he had a few years in him yet. But retirement meant not having to deal with punks like Steve Barrey, and all the others who'd employed him before. In his line of work, he wasn't ever going to get hired by anyone decent.

He switched his mind back to his task. Stalking mode. Instinctively he crouched a fraction, keeping below behind the hedgerow until he reached the rear of the van. Obligingly, the workmen had reversed the vehicle in here. Which meant no one from the road could see him. Good.

He slipped along the far side of the van, which was out of sight to the men in the field, and around to the rear of the vehicle. The doors had been pushed to, but not closed. Perfect. He took another glance at the workmen, then pulled open one door, wincing at the loud creak of its hinge, but the men were too far away to hear it, and one had headphones on anyway. He peered in. It was cluttered with equipment – traffic cones, meters, gauges, a box of valves, a large toolkit, a pump and, to his joy, a tarpaulin that lay under a jumble of road signs, right behind the driver and passenger seats.

He scrambled in, pulled the door shut behind him, then trod his way carefully in the semi-darkness towards the front. Reaching the tarpaulin, he knelt and wormed his way under the heavy sheet, which smelled of damp and plastic. He lay on his back on the hard metal floor, right up against the seats, checking to ensure his legs were concealed by the signs lying on top of the tarp. Then he pulled out his gun, removed the safety catch and settled down to wait.

120

Roy Grace sat, worriedly, at his workstation in MIR-1, staring at the clock on his screen: 5.01 p.m. Less than ninety minutes, if their intel was correct, until Jules Copeland was due to arrive at Primrose Farm Cottage for a loved-up weekend with Lynda Merrill – not.

He had been toying with alternative possibilities. Had Copeland boarded a flight at Gatwick Airport? The Ghanaian was distinctive-looking and had two large suitcases with him. But no CCTV cameras had picked him up. Sure, they didn't cover every square inch of the passenger areas, but the average person walking through the departure lounges of either the South or North Terminals would be picked up several times. Inspector Biggs's team had shown Copeland's photograph to all check-in staff and no one there had recognized him either, nor had any security staff. The Gatwick Hilton hotel had also been checked.

The Kia that had crashed outside Marina Heights this morning had been rented from a firm at Gatwick on Tuesday night to a man fitting Copeland's description, using one of his aliases, Samuel Jackson. He'd assaulted the driver of the van he'd collided with and done a runner. The cab he'd taken to Gatwick Airport would have dropped him there around 8.45 a.m. So where had he spent the past eight and a half hours?

Was he still within the vicinity of the airport? Grace suspected not.

Was he still in the country?

Grace wrote down on his pad what he knew of the man. *Resourceful. Ruthless. Driven by greed. Wife and child in Bavaria. £300,000 for the taking.*

Then after a few moments further mulling over, he thought about Copeland's red shoes and added *vain* to his list. And then:

Vain = arrogant = brazen
= Hubris

A man who was happy to murder two people who'd threatened to expose him, and to maim a third for daring to warn people about internet romance scammers.

Copeland, he decided, almost certainly was not going to let that money go. He was going to turn up.

121

Tooth heard the men returning to the van. He sensed the interior brightening a little as the rear doors were opened, heard the clatter of equipment being laid down in the rear, close to him, as he held his breath. Then the slam of the doors. Moments later the van rocked as the two men climbed into the front.

'You OK to work on, Bob?' one said.

'Yeah, nice bit of overtime – you, Rog?'

'The missus wants a new kitchen, the more the better – and it's bloody Christmas coming up and all. Got fifteen more properties on our list, we'll keep going?'

'Big game at the Amex tomorrow, got my season ticket – I'd rather work on tonight than have to come in tomorrow and miss the footy.'

'How many other teams out there this afternoon?'

'There's eight vans.'

'So it's a big leak, you reckon, Bob?'

'Very big. Head office are concerned, they need it found ASAP. Problem is, a lot of the pipework around here's ancient – could be a break anywhere.'

'We haven't had a frost yet.'

'Could just be a valve's let go. Or a builder or a farmer's dug through some pipework without realizing.'

'Have the traffic police been alerted to look for standing water in an unusual place?'

'I believe so.'

'OK, so where's next?'

Tooth heard the click of their seat belts. It was followed by the rustle of paper – maybe a map or plans. He waited, silently, until the starter motor whirred. As the engine fired, he rose up behind the driver's seat and was pleased to see the driver had removed his hard hat. Tooth chopped him hard in the back of his neck with his left hand and, instantly, he slumped forward, unconscious.

His startled colleague, still wearing his hat, spun round and found himself looking down the barrel of an automatic pistol.

'Hello, Bob,' Tooth said, calmly.

The man had fair hair and a tattooed neck. He stared at Tooth with petrified eyes behind rimless lenses. 'Wh— what – who – who – what do you – please – please don't shoot.'

'Well, Bob, that's all going to depend on how you and I get on.' Tooth transferred the gun to his left hand. 'Undo your pal's seat belt.'

Shaking with terror, the man leaned over and, a second later, Tooth heard the click of the buckle releasing. 'We don't have any money. Is that what you want?'

Keeping the gun trained on the man in the passenger seat, Tooth crooked an arm around the unconscious driver's neck, then using a taekwondo movement, jerked hard, pulling the man upwards over the top of his seat, with its built-in headrest, and catapulting him over his head, striking the ceiling of the van, then falling on his back onto some of the equipment lying around in the rear of the vehicle.

The man's work buddy stared on, paralysed with fear.

Behind him, Tooth heard groans. He cursed. He'd not hit him hard enough. 'Get in the driver's seat,' he said.

The man clambered over.

'I'm going to give you directions,' Tooth said. 'You're going to follow them, nice and easy. You with me?'

The man nodded several times, urgently.

Tooth jabbed the muzzle of the gun into the back of his neck.

'Please – I – I've got two kids – two young kids,' the man jabbered. 'Two and four. Please don't shoot me.'

'I got a dog,' Tooth replied.

'You've got a dog? I – I've got a dog, too.'

'You're going to drive down to the road and make a left.'

'Yes – yes – what kind of dog? You know? What kind of dog do you have?'

Tooth was silent. There was a loud moan behind him, then a voice called out, 'Jesus, who are you?'

The man tried to stand, as if making a lunge for Tooth. 'Who are—?' Then he cried out in pain, clutching the back of his ribcage.

'I'm the man with the gun,' Tooth said. 'You're in pain, right, Rog?'

He saw the man's right hand moving stealthily but clumsily towards a metal rod on the floor. Maybe the one they'd just been using. Then he launched himself at Tooth, raising the rod to strike him.

Tooth fired two near-silent shots in rapid succession into his forehead. His head jerked, then he fell on his back and lay still for a second. Then twitched.

His colleague screamed in shock and terror.

'Shut the fuck up!' Tooth said, loudly and firmly.

The man was shaking uncontrollably. 'You shot him. You shot him! Oh my God, you shot him.'

'It's a mutt,' Tooth said, staring at the man he'd just shot. He was twitching the way he often saw a caught fish twitch after he'd smashed its head with a priest.

'What?' the man said.

'My associate.'

'Associate?'

'It's a mutt. I was just walking along a street in Beverly Hills and it started following me.'

'I – I – I—' His eyes were bulging. 'Started following you? What did?'

'My dog,' Tooth replied. 'You asked about my dog. He's my associate.'

The man was staring past him at his colleague who was now motionless, with blood running from the two holes in his forehead. He tried to say something but nothing came out. He tried again. 'I – I – you – you shot him.'

'His name's Yossarian.'

He looked at Tooth, bewildered. 'Yossarian?'

'Turn around, put your seat belt on and drive.' Tooth raised the gun, putting it right up close to his face. 'Drive.'

The man continued staring at Tooth as if too frozen with terror to think or move.

'You want me to shoot you, too? I don't mind, I'll drive myself.'

'N-n-n-n-n-no, please.'

The man spun round as if a plug had been pushed into a socket, sat down, clicked on his belt and put the vehicle in gear. They lurched forward and stalled.

'Sorry,' he said. 'Sorry. Please don't kill me, please, please, I'll drive.' He restarted, they lurched forward again and this time they kept going.

'Left at the road,' Tooth said.

'Left. Left at the road,' the driver repeated.

'He has different-coloured eyes. One's kind of red, the other sort of grey. Depends on the light.'

'Different eyes?'

'My dog. Make the next right.'

They turned into a narrow lane. There were damp leaves on the road surface and the trees formed a tunnel overhead, blotting out the sky.

'W-what kind of d-dog did you say you have?' He was struggling to speak through his fear.

'Anyone stops us, anyone asks you any questions, you tell them what you're doing, hunting a leak, right? Hunting a big leak. You're working late like a lot of your colleagues tonight, hunting a big leak. Saving the environment, saving natural resources. Understand what I'm saying?' He pressed the barrel into the man's neck for emphasis.

'Yes, yes, I do!' the man yammered, jerking in terror, and the van swerved, momentarily losing grip on the slippery surface as he fought with the wheel to steady it.

'Drive more carefully, asshole.'

'Yes, sorry, sorry.'

'Or you want me to put you in the back with your friend?'

'No, please, please, please.'

'You make a left at the T-junction.'

The driver turned left at the T-junction. He was shaking and nodding his head at the same time.

'I don't know what kind. It's a dog,' Tooth said. 'I don't give a shit what kind.'

They passed a row of cottages with a couple of cars parked outside. Then a large house to the left, with a horsebox in the driveway. They continued past a sign to a sailing club and to waterworks, then Tooth instructed him to slow right down and turn into another single-track lane.

The light was beginning to fail, and Tooth was happy

about that. He told the driver to slow again as they reached an open gate and read the sign.

Primrose Farm

'Carry on,' he instructed.

A quarter of a mile further, Tooth saw rotten wooden gates that were open. And the oval sign, Primrose Farm Cottage, with a cart-track of a driveway dipping steeply down.

'Turn in here,' Tooth said.

122

Riley, deep in his hide in the rhododendron bush, heard the sound of an approaching vehicle. Immediately, the CROPS officer radioed the support team.

Moments later the van came into view.

'Mike Whisky One, do you have visual contact?'

'Romeo One, a Ford Transit van with Southern Water markings, heading towards target house.'

'Southern Water?'

'Yes yes.'

'Hold station, we are checking.'

'Hold station, yes yes.'

Riley watched the van drive around the bumpy driveway and pull up in front of the house.

Inside the rear of the van, Tooth, now wearing the dead man's yellow high-viz jacket, crawled up behind the driver and chopped him hard in the back of his neck, knocking him out. He hauled him over the seat and onto the floor, where he gagged him and tied him up securely with cable from a reel and wound duct tape round his mouth.

He then climbed over the driver's seat and, as an added precaution, pulled the keys from the ignition.

'You don't move, Bob. Understand?' he said to the

unconscious man. He opened the door and stepped out into near darkness.

Doug Riley's radio crackled. 'Romeo One to Mike Whisky One.'

'Romeo One, this is Mike Whisky One.'

'Mike Whisky One, we've just spoken to Southern Water. There is a serious leak in the Forest Row area causing localized water pressure issues. They currently have a number of vehicles out working into the night, checking the pipes and meters of properties in the area, trying to locate and isolate the problem.'

Riley checked his watch as he replied. 'Romeo One, any idea how long they have to spend at each property?'

'Five to ten minutes, maximum, Mike Whisky One.'

'Roger that, Romeo One.'

123

Tooth, holding a clipboard, which he knew was always a good prop, looked for a bell, but couldn't see one. So he rapped hard on the oak door with his knuckles. He found some British accents hard to master, but others came easily. At this particular moment, he was a Welshman.

It was opened by a woman with silver hair, and all dolled-up for lover boy. She wore a low-cut blouse revealing a large amount of cleavage, a short green skirt, knee-high patent-leather boots and reeked of dense, musky perfume. She looked at him with undisguised irritation, clearly not wanting anyone around at this moment queering the pitch.

He flashed the dead man's identity card, keeping his finger over the photograph. 'I am so very sorry to be bothering you, like. I'm from Southern Water and we are investigating a major leak. Would you mind if I checked your water meter – it might be saving you money, you know.'

'Is this going to take long?' she asked, unsmiling and clearly anxious.

'Oh no, madam, just a few minutes. Can you direct me to the water meter?'

'I'm afraid I have absolutely no idea – I'm house-sitting for a friend.'

'All right then if I have a quick look for it?'

'Be my guest.' She glanced at her watch, then out of the window, past the van, at the drive beyond.

Tooth frowned. But he took it as licence to check the place out.

Lady, he thought, *if you knew why I was really here, you'd be throwing your arms around me in gratitude. I'm your freakin' guardian angel, lady.*

'Do you have a loft?'

'Yes, there's a hatch up on the landing. I saw a pole with a hook against the wall. I'll show you.'

He followed her up the stairs, and she pointed to the hatch and then the pole. He reached up with the pole and pushed the hatch, which dropped down on a hinge to reveal a folding ladder. He hooked the bottom rung and pulled it down.

'I'll leave you to it,' she said.

As he began climbing she went back downstairs.

124

Friday 12 October

'Mike Whisky One to Romeo One. For information, Southern Water official has now been inside target house for ten minutes.'

'Romeo One to Mike Whisky One. Did you say he is *inside* the house?' The support officer sounded concerned.

'Inside the house, yes yes.'

'Mike Whisky One, Southern Water say that all water meters are external. There is no need for anyone to enter a property, other than to ask where the stopcock and meter are.'

Doug Riley was distracted by the sound of another vehicle turning into the drive. A dark-grey Mercedes coupe drove past him, travelling slowly on the bumpy track. Slowly enough to make out the identity of the driver through his binoculars.

'Romeo One,' Riley said, urgently. 'A Mercedes coupe is approaching target house. Driver is a male IC3.'

'A black man, Mike Whisky One?'

'Affirmative.'

'Can you positively identify him as Jules de Copeland?'

'I can't positively.'

'ARVs to carry out enforced stop,' came the command. The Mercedes suddenly stopped. Doug Riley, bits of shrubbery tumbling from his clothes and helmet, stood a short distance from the car, his Glock drawn and aimed. He was joined by his colleague, Lewis Hastings, also showering vegetation from his clothes, gun in his hand.

An instant later an ARV raced up behind the Mercedes. A second blocked the exit onto the road.

The first ARV officer stopped at the driver's door, as his colleague reached the passenger side.

'Police!' the first one yelled. 'Hands in the air! Show me your hands!' The man behind the wheel, looking scared, raised his arms.

The officer yanked open the door. 'Keep your hands up and get out!' The driver tried to move but his seat belt restrained him.

Standing back, holding both hands on the gun, the officer yelled, 'Unbuckle and get out, out, out!'

The man obeyed and climbed out, raising his arms as high as he could. He was short, wearing a hoodie, jeans and trainers.

Doug Riley instinctively felt something was wrong. That this was not his man. Not from his height, for sure. 'What's your name?' he yelled.

'Lucius Orji,' the man said, with some reluctance.

Hastings came round, stood behind the man and frisked him thoroughly. Then he jerked his arms down behind his back and snapped on handcuffs, as Riley peered carefully into the empty rear of the car.

'Where's Jules de Copeland?' Riley demanded as he saw, out of the corner of his eye, the support van followed by the second ARV approaching at speed.

'Who?'

'Jules de Copeland. Don't try playing innocent. Did he send you?'

'I don't know any *Jules de Copeland*.'

'No? So what are you doing here? Taking a drive in the country? Admiring the autumn colours?'

Lucius Orji nodded. 'Yeah, just taking a drive – must have took a wrong turning.'

From the look in the man's eyes, Riley knew he was lying. 'Are you sure? It wasn't Jules de Copeland who asked you to come here tonight?'

'I don't know no one of that name,' he said, sounding angry and insolent.

'Really?'

'Well, maybe.'

'Maybe?'

The van and the car pulled up behind them. The support officers, also guns in hand, got out of the van. Two ARV officers, in vizors and full body armour, jumped out of the car, brandishing Heckler and Koch sub-machine guns, further covering the handcuffed man.

Riley conferred with the support officers, who then began searching the Mercedes. Glancing around, he suddenly saw that the driverless Southern Water van was rocking. He sprinted towards it.

125

Jules de Copeland, for once in many years not wearing red shoes, stood in the woods, shielded by a tree, a short distance to the west of Primrose Farm Cottage, watching the unfolding events, the empty suitcase by his side. His car, which he had rented from a company twenty miles from Gatwick Airport, was concealed up a forest track fifteen minutes' trek through the woods from here.

Good man, Lucius!

His most trusted senior employee had done exactly what he had planned – to flush out any cops that might be watching the house and distract them.

Keep it going!

Copeland was dressed, head to foot, in dark camouflage gear, black boots and a black balaclava over his head. For the past half-hour he'd worked his way steadily through the dense woods and even denser undergrowth. He was feeling pleased, and not a little smug, that his plan had worked out. The police officers he had suspected might be watching the house were now all occupied out front.

Through a downstairs window he could see a woman, standing alone, looking out at the commotion. Dressed to kill.

Lynda Merrill.

With the £300,000 in cash for him!

He had to trust that Lucius Orji would hold his nerve and stick to the script.

Out of sight from everyone at the front of the house, a hunting knife in his hand, he sprinted the hundred yards to the flimsy-looking side door. Not wanting to take a chance on whether or not it was locked, he hurled his full weight against it, splintering it open and stumbling in.

The woman spun towards him, shock and fear and bewilderment in her eyes. 'Lynda! I have a message from your darling Richie!' he said, reaching her in two fast steps and holding the blade out of sight. 'Don't be scared, my love. Just get the money, quick, quick, quick, and let's go!' He knelt and clicked open the suitcase. 'Quick!'

She pointed at a cupboard under the stairs. 'It's in there.'

'Get it! I'm taking you away to Richie! He is waiting! Quick, quick!'

Calmly, she walked over to the cupboard, opened the door and knelt. As she did, he heard a voice behind him.

'Freeze, you scammer bastard!'

He spun round.

A silver-haired man in his late fifties had appeared from seemingly nowhere, with a gun in his hand.

Copeland's mind went into overdrive.

Had he walked, dumbly, into a trap? 'Who are you?' he demanded.

'You should know me, you and your friends have relieved me of over £400,000,' Fordwater replied.

Copeland looked at him, patronizingly. 'Put the gun down, I'm sure we can sort something out.'

'Really?'

Suddenly, the old guy raised his aim, away from him, at something behind him.

Copeland turned. He saw a short man, halfway down the stairs, crouched, holding a handgun in a double-grip, aiming straight at him. Then he heard what sounded like a gunshot from behind him. A chunk of plaster flew out of the wall beside the short man's head. Followed by another gunshot. This time the man was flung backwards. Then another shot and he tumbled down the staircase, head first, spurting blood from his shoulder.

Copeland, frozen in panic like a rabbit in headlights, smelled the pungent reek of cordite.

Tooth disorientated, his brain swirling, aimed through the banisters and fired at Copeland. The bullet hit his thigh, sending him reeling back. Tooth fired again and the bullet went wide. Saw the blurry shape of the silver-haired man standing on the far side of the kitchen, aiming at him. Tooth fired again. Missed.

Then all hell broke loose as the front door caved in, and with the warning shouts, 'ARMED POLICE, ARMED POLICE, DROP YOUR WEAPONS!', he saw two vizored officers, sub-machine guns in hand, crash into the room, sweeping in every direction with their guns. They were followed by more officers wearing baseball hats marked, SUSSEX POLICE.

It seemed to him, for an instant, that the pause button on a video had been pressed. The silver-haired guy dropped his gun. The woman and Copeland both froze. For an instant.

Giving him the chance to finish his task. Against all his training, which was to shoot at the body because that made a bigger target, he aimed at the balaclava. He wanted to bring that big bastard down with a headshot. Finish the job he'd come here to do. Finish his career with one final success. It seemed, in this moment, that he had all the time in the world.

'DROP YOUR GUN!' someone shouted.

Tooth fired. Shit. Fabric and blood flew from Copeland's left arm and he lurched back. Instantaneously Tooth saw muzzle flashes in the periphery of his vision and heard a volley of shots. In the same instant, it seemed, he was kicked in the chest by what felt like the boots of an entire football team, slamming him back against the wall.

The gun fell from his hand.

His vision blurred. Light faded from his eyes as if a dimmer switch was being turned.

He saw Yossarian. He was sitting on the prow of *Long Shot* as they skimmed across the azure Caribbean Sea, heading out of Turtle Cove Marina on Providenciales Island for a day of deep-sea fishing. Hoping his master might catch a yellowtail snapper or some other tasty morsel which he might throw his way.

But the sun was already setting and he hadn't yet put out his lines.

Yossarian stared at him with disappointment showing in his two different-coloured eyes. Stared at him as the sun set and darkness fell.

Tooth tried to mouth the word, 'Sorry'. But the darkness struck first.

126

Jules de Copeland, his thigh and arm stinging in agonizing pain, looked around, bewildered.

Someone took hold of him, restraining his arms behind his back.

He heard a voice radioing urgently for an ambulance. And overhead the *thwock-thwock-thwock* of a helicopter.

Then a man in camouflage fatigues, wearing a helmet covered in netting with bits of greenery intertwined, faced him. 'Tunde Oganjimi, alias Jules de Copeland, I am arresting you on suspicion of the murder of Susan Adele Driver in Brighton and on suspicion of causing grievous bodily harm with intent to Toby Seward in Brighton. You do not have to say anything, but it may harm your defence if you do not mention when questioned something which you later rely on in court. Anything you do say may be given in evidence. Is that clear?'

Copeland grimaced in pain at him. 'Can you and I talk in private for a moment, officer?'

Lewis Hastings made a pretend show of switching off his radio's microphone. 'OK, we're private now.'

'I need more private than this.'

Hastings looked around. The silver-haired man was hand-cuffed and covered by one police officer with an automatic pistol. Another was standing, protectively, by the scared-looking woman.

'This is as private as it's going to get, OK?'

Copeland leaned forward and whispered into Hastings's ear. 'I'm a very rich man, officer. Name your price.'

Hastings looked him squarely in the eye. 'Mr Copeland, my price is beyond anything you can afford or ever will be able to afford. It's called morality. That's probably not a word in your limited lexicon.'

127

Roy Grace, sitting in his car outside Primrose Farm Cottage, surrounded by police vehicles, two ambulances and the Coroner's van, called Jack Roberts as he had promised.

'Your clients are both safe,' he informed him. 'Major Fordwater has been arrested for illegal possession of a firearm and may face more serious charges. Copeland is currently in an ambulance, under arrest, being treated for gunshot wounds.' He said nothing about the dead American contract killer.

'That's good to hear, Detective Superintendent,' Roberts said. 'I appreciate your updating me.'

'There's quite a lot to take in at this moment, as I'm sure you can understand, Mr Roberts,' Grace continued. 'But from what I know so far, I would say you've sailed pretty close to the wind. Fortunately we've had a result. It could have been a very different outcome.'

'I'm taking that as a positive,' Roberts replied.

Grace pursed his lips, not wanting to give the PI any encouragement. 'When we met in your office, you gave me the impression you are not too enamoured with the police. I hope this might help change your mind.'

'I'll reserve judgement on that,' Roberts replied. 'You

might be scooping the glory, but you need to remember who teed it up for you.'

As Grace ended the call, his phone rang. It was Cassian Pewe.

'What's going on, Roy?' he demanded. 'Where are you? Media Relations are being bombarded by the press for information on what's happening. A caretaker's been found dead in the apartment block you had under surveillance. Do you have anything I can tell them? Any bones I can throw for them to gnaw on?'

'I was made aware of the caretaker just a couple of hours ago, sir.'

'Well, really, I'm so pleased to know you are aware of something that's happening in this county, where you are supposed to be the Head of Major Crime. Do we have any more dead bodies or is one enough for today?'

'I'm afraid we have two more,' Grace replied. 'But I think you might be happy to know the second is the American, Tooth, who, as you know, has long been on our radar.' He nearly added, *Longer than need be, thanks to your intervention months back*, but he held his tongue. 'Tooth was shot by firearms officers and we will of course notify the Independent Office for Police Conduct.'

There was a brief silence from Pewe. Then he said, sarcastically, 'I'm sure the Chief Constable will be very pleased, Roy. Thrilled to bits, I would say, when I inform him.'

'Talking of chiefs, sir, I had lunch with Alison Vosper.'

'Alison Vosper, did you say?' Pewe sounded thrown.

'Yes.'

'Why didn't you tell me you were seeing her?'

'You didn't ask,' Grace retorted, smugly. 'I had an interesting conversation with her, in which she told me about all the major cases in Sussex that you've taken credit for. Maybe my memory is going, but I honestly don't recall your involvement in quite a number of them.'

'Is that so?' Pewe said acidly. 'So what was the purpose of this lunch?'

'She offered me a job in London. It would put me on the same rank as you if I accepted.'

'Over my dead body.'

'Well, if that's what it takes, sir.'

Ignoring the comment, Pewe said, 'Be in my office at 9 a.m. tomorrow.'

'It's Saturday tomorrow.'

'Yes, Roy, quite correct. Saturday follows Friday in the Gregorian calendar. Although perhaps in the weird bubble you inhabit, you are still on the Julian calendar, which was started by Julius Caesar? In case you're not up to date, we switched to the Gregorian calendar in this country in 1752, so we'll go by that one, shall we?' he said in his most patronizing tone.

128

Roy Grace drove up to the barrier at the entrance to the Police HQ a few minutes before 9 a.m. As he waited for it to rise, he noticed Cassian Pewe's classic black Jaguar XJS sports car, which was usually as spick and span as the ACC himself, parked outside the handsome Queen Anne mansion that housed the offices of the Sussex Police top brass, and the East Sussex Fire and Rescue chiefs.

Grace couldn't help smiling as he noticed also that the Jaguar's paintwork was splattered, like a patterned carpet, with messy white blobs. Clearly a passing flock of migrating birds held the same opinion of the man as he did.

Five minutes later he knocked on the door of Pewe's office and was summoned in. Despite it being the weekend, Pewe was attired in his full dress uniform. Grace hadn't bothered to make the same effort himself. He was unshaven and he was dressed in a leather bomber jacket over a quilted gilet, T-shirt, jeans and trainers. His casual appearance had the desired effect, clearly throwing Pewe off his guard.

'Very kind of you to make space in your valuable downtime to meet me, Roy,' he said, briefly frowning disapproval at his appearance as he stood up and shook the Detective Superintendent's hand, his signet ring glinting in the morning sunlight. He had a cold, damp and limp grip that always felt, to Roy Grace, like shaking hands with a corpse.

'I see you've been attracting birds with your car, sir,' Grace quipped.

Pewe gave him a sickly look. Then, without replying, said, 'I'm afraid my assistant and staff officer are both off today, but I could make you a coffee myself if you'd like one?'

'I'm fine, thank you, sir.' Grace sat in one of the two imposing chairs in front of his desk. To his surprise, Pewe was actually looking friendly, which put him even more on guard than usual.

'So, Roy, quite a showdown yesterday, eh? Gunfight at the OK Corral!'

Grace replied, hesitantly. 'I wouldn't say that exactly.'

'Well, it's been quite a time, these past couple of weeks, Roy, for our supposed Head of Major Crime, hasn't it? The murder of Mrs Susan Driver. The caretaker of the Marina Heights apartment complex. The murder of the Southern Water employee. And now the shooting of Mr Tooth. Not to mention the gunshot wounding of the – admittedly dubious character – Mr Jules de Copeland. And the brutal murder in custody of your prisoner, Mr Kofi Okonjo.' Pewe was no longer smiling.

'Meaning, sir?'

'Meaning, Roy, that our Chief Constable and our Police and Crime Commissioner are not happy bunnies. Brighton got rid of its title of Murder Capital of Europe back in the 1930s. Under your watch it looks like it's about to regain it.'

'I hardly think so, sir, when you compare the number of murders in London this year, and you can hardly put all of these deaths at my door.'

'You and I need to meet with Media Relations first thing

Monday, Roy, and get a pretty reassuring press release out. What you have to think about is just how safe does all this mayhem make the citizens of our county feel?'

'I'm not sure I can answer that. I have a job to do, which is to investigate crimes and to try to lock up the villains. I'm pretty satisfied, despite the tragic deaths of Mrs Driver and the caretaker of Marina Heights, that Operation Lisbon has succeeded. We've smashed a major internet romance network and we have its local ringleader and several of his minions in custody. A man we believe to be the major mastermind for a massive European internet romance fraud network is currently in custody in Jersey. On top of that we finally have the American hitman, Tooth, who has been responsible for at least two murders that we are aware of, as well as coming close to murdering DS Potting, no longer a threat.'

'No longer a threat?' Pewe's lips formed an almost rictus smile. 'But no thanks to you, Roy. And you are sure Tooth really is dead, are you?'

Grace again resisted the temptation to remind the ACC it was his insistence on removing Tooth's hospital guard that had enabled the contract killer to evade justice earlier in the year. 'I don't think he's going to be coming back from the dead anytime soon.'

'Really? Are you sure about that?'

'The world wasn't big enough for Alexander the Great,' Grace retorted. 'But a coffin was.'

'What?'

'Juvenal.'

'Who?'

'A Roman poet of the first century AD. My wife's doing a degree in philosophy at the Open University. Very apt for Tooth.'

'What's apt about that?'

'Think about it, sir.'

Pewe shook his head. 'Roy, I'm your line manager. You don't tell me what I should and should not think about. Do you understand?'

'Actually, Cassian,' he said, clocking Pewe's startled expression as he used the familiarity of his first name, 'last night, after speaking with the Chief Constable, I accepted Alison Vosper's offer. For the next six months I'm going to be heading up a new initiative to tackle knife crime in London, set up by the Prime Minister, the Mayor of London and the Commissioner of the Met – the National Knife Crimes Task Force. My title will be Commander, initially on a temporary basis, which means I will be of the same rank as you, and I trust you will respect that.'

There was a long silence. He saw Pewe's face struggling to absorb this. Finally Pewe said, his tone very conciliatory, 'Look, Roy, I – I know we've had our differences. But I would hate to lose you from Sussex Police. I mean – I – we – we can't afford to lose you.'

'Is that so? You've never given me that impression.'

'Roy, let's put our cards on the table. I don't want to lose you. I may not like you, and I know you don't like me, but I recognize that you are a bloody good police officer.'

Grace stared him back, levelly. 'What you actually mean, Cassian – sorry – *sir* – is that I make you look good.'

Grace stood up and walked out of the room, slamming the door behind him. Slamming it on a chapter of his life.

129

'I can't believe it!' Cleo said, snuggling up beside him on the sofa in front of the television. Noah toddled across his play mat, stumbled and giggled, then began pressing buttons on a toy, each of which was in the shape of an animal. He stabbed an elephant, which trumpeted. Then a cat, which miaowed, followed by a sheep, which baaed. He giggled again.

'Believe what?'

'That you are actually here, at home on a Saturday after-noon, watching rugby – instead of working. And looking like the cat that got the cream!'

'Maybe I did get it.'

She looked at him, quizzically. 'You've not had any second thoughts since last night? You really think fighting knife crime in London is going to be an easier gig than your current job?'

'Anything that doesn't have Cassian Pewe involved is going to be an easier gig.'

'Really? Commuting to London daily – that's going to be easier?'

'It's only a six-month posting.'

'What if they want to extend it and keep you on a year, two years? Permanently?'

Grace watched, hope rising as an England player sprinted with the ball towards the touchline, then he grimaced as the player was felled by a tackle.

'Darling, my heart's here in Brighton,' he said. 'I wouldn't ever want a permanent posting away. But I'd be very happy to have a six-month break from Cassian Pewe.'

'Well, if it's going to make you less stressed than what you're currently doing, I guess that's a good thing.'

'Less stressed and a higher pay scale. What's not to like? It'll help towards the cost of Bruno's bathroom!'

She smiled, fleetingly, then looked him in the eye. 'It'll help towards another cost, too.'

'Oh yes?'

She patted her midriff, looking both happy and sheepish at the same time. 'I think I'm pregnant!'

'You are?' He put his arms around her and kissed her. 'Oh my God, fantastic! Are you sure?'

'I've got an appointment with the doctor on Monday, but I did a second test this morning and it's positive!'

'Brilliant, I can't believe it!' He sat for some moments, holding her tightly. 'Just amazing news.'

'Let's celebrate properly after it's confirmed on Monday – and don't let's tell anyone yet, in case—' She shrugged, and the unspoken words hung in the air.

'Sure, of course.'

Cleo glanced at her watch. 'I'll have to go and pick Bruno up in a few minutes, from his party bus. He was so excited when I dropped him off. I really hope he's had a good time with his school friends. Maybe this will be the break-through.'

'Let's hope so. I can go if you want – a pregnant lady should have plenty of rest!'

'You're the one who needs it this weekend,' she replied.

'I wish! I have to go in tomorrow morning for a team debrief.'

'Will you be there all day?'

'Most of it, I'm afraid.'

'So tell me more about yesterday – what's going to happen to that poor army guy who got conned out of every penny he has in the world?'

'Fordwater?'

'Will he go to prison?'

'We're putting a file together for the Coroner, and I've spoken to the CPS. He will be charged with illegal possession of a firearm, and I can't do anything about that. He's being interviewed under caution this morning, with his solicitor. I feel sorry for him, but I'm not sure what he had in mind going to that house – whether he was just planning to frighten Jules de Copeland or actually shoot him. He says he was acting in self-defence, protecting himself, and – ironically – de Copeland. Ultimately it will be for the CPS to decide what to charge him with.'

'The poor guy,' she said, 'I feel sorry for him. His life's destroyed.'

'I'm afraid he's a member of a very big club. Men and women looking for love on the internet in this country have been scammed out of an estimated £300 million in the past twelve months. Most of them are in their sixties, seventies, eighties and even nineties. Many of them, like Fordwater, have lost their homes and every penny they have in the world. And with no chance of ever recovering any of it. It's tragic.'

'So Major Fordwater should get a medal, not a prison sentence.'

'If there was any justice in the world.'

130

At half past five, Roy Grace was on the phone to Glenn Branson, who was updating him on the interviews with Fordwater and with Lynda Merrill, when he heard the sound of Cleo's car pulling up outside the cottage.

Humphrey ran to the front door, barking, waking Noah, who for the past hour had been sound asleep on the floor.

'Go to your room!' he heard Cleo bellow, sounding uncharacteristically furious.

Moments later she stormed into the living room, her face a thundercloud.

'Call you back in a few minutes,' Grace said, and put the phone down as Cleo stood in front of him, shaking her head.

He looked up at her. 'What? What's happened?'

'Our – sorry – *your* – darling son. That's what's happened.'

He stood up. 'Tell me?' She was close to tears and he put his arms around her.

'I need a stiff drink.'

'Is that wise?'

'No, it's not wise, and I know I can't have any. But my mother drank all through her pregnancy with me and I survived.'

509

He poured two glasses of sparkling water and they sat down. 'So, what's happened?'

She burst into tears. Noah began bawling.

Glancing down, as if torn between him and her husband, she said, 'I've never been so embarrassed in my life. God.' She sniffed, composing herself a little. 'I arrived at this very posh house in Hove, which had a large bus parked in the driveway. The parents of the boy who'd invited Bruno looked at me like I was something the cat brought in. Other parents, too, were looking at me like I'm some kind of monster.'

'Why, what had he done?'

'Bruno had completely ruined the party, for fourteen children.'

'What happened? What on earth happened?'

'They'd hired the gaming bus, right – for all the children. At some point, Bruno locked himself inside the bus and wouldn't let any of the other children in. That's what happened.'

'You're not serious?'

'He – just like – barricaded himself inside, halfway through the party. He locked the doors so that none of the kids, nor the driver who'd gone to stretch his legs, could get in. And he spent the rest of the time in there by himself, ignoring everyone hammering on the doors and the windows.'

Grace felt his heart plummeting. 'What – I mean – how – why? What was going through his mind?'

'He told me why in the car. He said, *Because they were too slow. They were at a completely different level to me, slowing me down.*'

Grace stared at her in numb silence. 'He did that?'

'The whole party was ruined. By Bruno. He's got no concept at all of socialization. He alienated himself from every boy and girl there. He's a bully, Roy, he's a bloody bully. We can't have him behaving like that.'

'I'll go up and speak to him.'

She shook her head. 'No, not now. I've tried telling him on the way home that what he's done is just not acceptable. He knows how angry I am. Leave him tonight and let's both speak to him tomorrow. I don't think there's anything you're going to get from him tonight.'

They sat in silence.

'I'm sorry,' Roy Grace said, finally. 'This is all my fault. Maybe I shouldn't have brought Bruno here to live with us.'

'Of course you should – he's your son. He drives me mad, too, but I honestly think there's a decent person inside his – his persona or whatever. From what you've said about his mother, he's had a pretty strange upbringing to say the least. The son of a heroin addict can't be expected to immediately adopt other values.'

'You really think that?'

'Yes.'

'Remember what we talked about not all that long ago, about when we first met?'

'Yep, over the corpse in the mortuary. And you were turned on by my scrubs, right?'

He gave her a teasing look. 'Well, apart from those, what also turned me on was something you said as you looked down at the body. It was a twenty-two-year-old male who'd been stabbed eleven times. He was known to Sussex Police as a local drugs dealer who'd been in and out of prison since his teens. You said that someone, once, must have loved him and perhaps still did. And that he'd started life as an innocent baby. And you wondered what had happened in those years in between to change him. That's the first thing I fell in love with. Your humanity. The way you could always see the good in people, unlike in my job, where we mostly only ever see the bad.'

'So it wasn't my legs or my boobs?'

'They helped.' He grinned.

She grinned back and held his gaze. There was such deep trust and intense love in her eyes that it made Roy, momentarily, feel shallow. He knew he could never be as good and compassionate a person as Cleo truly was. There were times, too, when he worried that she thought he was a better person than he really was. Perhaps it was too many years as a copper, only ever seeing the worst of people, that had done that to him.

'We *will* change Bruno,' she said. 'Whatever it takes. Yes?'

'Yes!'

'So tell me,' she said, changing the subject. 'Do you know much about Tooth's background?'

'Not really – not beyond his criminal past, anyway.'

'Are you sorry?' she asked, suddenly.

'Sorry? About what?'

'That he's dead?'

'I'm sorry in the sense that I'd like to have had the chance to talk to him, to see what made him tick. I heard from the NYPD that at the last count he'd been responsible for over thirty-six contract killings.'

'What do you think shaped his life to get him to the point where he could kill like that?'

'Drill down into the background of almost any criminal I've ever dealt with and you'll find the same blueprint.' He shrugged.

'I suppose a lot more would have come out if he'd gone to trial. Does it make you feel a bit cheated?'

Grace shook his head. 'No.' Then he said, with a smile, 'I have a feeling that Tooth didn't do trials.'

GLOSSARY

ANPR – Automatic Number Plate Recognition. Roadside or mobile cameras that automatically capture the registration number of all cars that pass. It can be used to historically track which cars went past a certain camera, and can also create a signal for cars which are stolen, have no insurance or have an alert attached to them.

CAD – Computer Aided Dispatch. The system where all calls from the public are logged and, if they require police attendance, the live time record of who is attending, how it is developing and what the outcome is.

CID – Criminal Investigation Department. Usually refers to the divisional detectives rather than the specialist squads.

CIM – Critical Incident Manager. A Chief Inspector who has responsibility for the response to and management of all critical incidents within the force area during their tour of duty.

CSI – Was SOCO. Crime Scene Investigators (Scenes of Crime Officers). They are the people who attend crime scenes to search for fingerprints, DNA samples etc.

DIGITAL FORENSICS – The unit which examines and investigates computers and other digital devices. Part of SCC.

FLUM – Flash Unsolicited Message. A direct short message sent between computer screens, mainly in the control room, to alert other controllers or supervisors to either a significant incident or an important update on an ongoing incident. It flashes up, alerting the recipient to its content immediately.

HOLMES – Home Office Large Major Enquiry System. The national computer database used on all murders. It provides a repository of all messages, actions, decisions and statements, allowing the analysis of intelligence and the tracking and auditing of the whole enquiry. Can enable enquiries to be linked across force areas where necessary.

IC1 – White – North European.

IC3 – Black.

IFA – Independent Financial Advisor.

IMEI code – A fifteen-digit number used by a mobile network to identify valid devices and therefore can be used for stopping a stolen phone from accessing that network or to trace phones used with any SIM card.

LST – Local Support Team. The standing unit of officers who provide public order, search and low-level surveillance tactics on a division.

MO – Modus Operandi (method of operation). The manner by which the offender has committed the offence. Often this can reveal unique features which allow crimes to be linked or suspects to be identified.

NaCTSO – National Counter Terrorism Security Office. A national police unit that leads the fight against terrorism.

NPAS 15 – The call sign for the helicopter that provides air support to Sussex Police.

NPT – Neighbourhood Policing Team. A team of officers and Police Community Support Officers (PCSOs) who are dedicated to a particular geographical area, primarily to reduce crime and improve people's feelings of safety.

OSCAR-1 – The call sign of the Force Control Duty Inspector, who has oversight and command of all critical incidents in the initial stages.

PM – Post-mortem.

Priest – A tool or implement for killing game or fish.

QR Code – A form of barcode which, when scanned, diverts the reading device being used to a website.

RPU – Roads Policing Unit. The name for the Traffic Division.

RTC – Road Traffic Collision (commonly known as an 'accident' by the public, but this term is not used as it implies no one is at fault when usually someone is).

RV Point – Rendezvous Point. The designated location where emergency services meet prior to deploying to the scene of a crime or major incident. Used when it would be too dangerous or unwieldy for everyone to arrive at the scene at the same time in an uncoordinated way.

SECAMB – South East Coast Ambulance Service.

Section 17 PACE Powers – A power of entry under the Police and Criminal Evidence Act 1984 which allows officers to enter premises without a warrant to make an arrest, to save life or limb, or to prevent serious damage to property.

SIO – Senior Investigating Officer. Usually a Detective Chief Inspector who is in overall charge of the investigation of a major crime such as murder, kidnap or rape.

SLANG AND PHRASES

All-ports alert – A nationwide alert for all air and seaports to be on the lookout for a particular person, vehicle etc.

Bosher – The heavy metal handheld ram used to force open doors and allow officers to enter a locked premises or room swiftly and with the advantage of surprise.

Burner phone – Slang for a pay-as-you-go mobile phone, which is used once then disposed of to avoid the user being traced.

Golden hour – The first hour after a crime has been committed or reported, when the best chances of seizing evidence and/or identifying witnesses exist.

Q word/Q day – Short for 'quiet'. Emergency services personnel never say the word 'quiet', as it invariably is a bad omen, causing chaos to reign!

CHART OF POLICE RANKS

Police ranks are consistent across all disciplines and the addition of prefixes such as 'detective' (e.g. detective constable) does not affect seniority relative to others of the same rank (e.g. police constable).

ACKNOWLEDGEMENTS

For me, every book has a trigger, a starting point that fires my imagination. In this case it was an article in the *Sunday Times*, featuring handsome Brighton motivational speaker, Steve Bustin. From a phone call out of the blue, Steve discovered that his identity was being used to scam women on eleven different dating sites. We had met some years before when Steve had interviewed me for a Brighton Chamber of Commerce event, and he readily agreed to meet up for a coffee. The information he so generously gave me, and the introduction to Constance Wood, who had first alerted him to what was happening, helped me to shape my story and I am immensely grateful to both of them.

Another I must single out among all those who gave me invaluable research help is PC Bernadette Lawrie BEM, who opened my eyes to the sheer scale of internet romance fraud across not just Sussex, but the whole of the UK and the entire Western world, with countless lives ruined every day. The majority of the victims are in the upper age brackets – often vulnerable people who have lost their life partner and are now seeking love and companionship for their final years. People who are about to find out that the person they've met online, have been communicating with, and have fallen in love with, does not exist. The double whammy facing victims is that not only have they lost what they thought was the love of their life, they are going to find out they've been rinsed of almost every penny they have in the world. All their savings for a comfortable retirement. And all too often their homes, which they've re-mortgaged in order to send money to the scammers.

I've also had quite exceptional help from Jack Roberts of Global Investigations and Dick Smith QPM of the Association of British Investigators, an organization of which I am proud to be Patron.

As always, I'm indebted to many officers and support staff of the police services. In particular in this book, Surrey and Sussex Police, the Metropolitan Police, the City of London Police, Jersey States Police and the Brooklyn Department of the DA. A big thank-you to Sussex Police & Crime Commissioner Katy Bourne; Chief Constable Giles York QPM; Julian Blazeby, Director General Justice and Home Affairs, States of Jersey Government; DCO James Wileman, Jersey States Police; Detective Chief Superintendent Jason Tingley; Chief Superintendent Lisa Bell; Detective Superintendent Mike Ashcroft; Detective Superintendent Steve Boniface; Superintendent Paula Light; Superintendent Simon Nelson; DCI Stuart Hale; DCI Andy Richardson; DCI Lee Turner; DI Pete Billin; DI Richard Haycock; DI Emma Vickers; DI Bill Warner; DI Mark Warren; Acting DI Lawrence Courtness; Inspector James Biggs; Inspector Jason Cummings; Inspector Paul Davey; Inspector Mark Evans; Inspector Dan Hiles; DS Phil Taylor; DC Vanessa Forde; DC Martin Light; Acting DC Ben Nield; PC Jen Dunn; PC Pip Edwards; PC Richard Trundle; PC Lee Williams. Katie Perkins, Jill Pedersen and Suzanne Heard from Sussex Police Corporate Communications; Emily Denyer, Financial Investigator; Maria O'Brien, James Gartrell, Chris Gee and James Stather from Forensic Services. Annabel Galsworthy, Aiden Gilbert, Joseph Langford, Graham Lewendon, Shaun Robbins and Daniel Salter from the Digital Forensics Unit. Barry Faudemer and Emma Vickers of the Jersey Financial Services Commission; Investigator Mark Grieve from the Attorney General's Office, Jersey. Detective Investigator Patrick Lanigan of the Brooklyn DA's office, Deputy Sheriff Dennis Bootle of the Lake County Sheriff's Office and Detective Stephen Beeman of Key West Police.

Also to the following retired officers: Chief Superintendent Graham Bartlett, Detective Chief Inspector Trevor Bowles, Inspector Keith Ellis, Inspector Andy Kille, PC Jon Bennion-Jones, PC Pete Gear and PC David Rowlands.

A very special thank-you also to: Theresa Adams; Dave Allen; Steve Barrey; Tony Cooper (Southern Water); Kaye Fontaine; Jonathan Gready; James Hodge; Haydn Kelly; Marcel Kullen; Steve Lampard; Kevin Lemasney; John Lynch; Bob Norgrove (Southern Water); Ken Owen; Ray Packham; Alan Setterington; Juliet Smith JP; Hans Jurgen Stockerl; Orlando Trujillo; Mark Tuckwell; John Tupperwares (Southern Water); Tom Vautier; Michelle Websdale; Richard White and Mr Christopher R. P. Williams.

Although writing itself is a solitary task, the act of creating a finished novel ready for publication involves elaborate teamwork, many of the members playing vital roles at various key stages. My UK agents, Isobel Dixon, Julian Friedmann, Conrad Williams, James Pusey, Hana Murrell, Hattie Grunewald and all the team at Blake Friedmann. My US agent, Richard Pine of Inkwell. My mentor and good friend, Geoff Duffield. My fabulous editor Wayne Brookes and all at Pan Macmillan. Singling out just a few: Sarah Arratoon, Jonathan Atkins, Anna Bond, Stuart Dwyer, Lucy Hines, Daniel Jenkins, Sara Lloyd, Alex Saunders, Jade Tolley, Jeremy Trevathan, Charlotte Williams, Natalie Young. My structural editor, Susan Opie. My publicists at Riot Communications, Preena Gadher, Caitlin Allen, Emily Souders and my US publicists, Elena Stokes, Tanya Farrell and Sabrina Tenteromano at Wunderkind.

Everything starts with the book (writing the pages) and my brilliant and hard-working Team James help me to hone the manuscript into shape long before it reaches my agent and publishers. My amazing PA, Linda Buckley, who runs our lives (!) and who never lets a fact go unchecked; my book-keeper Sarah

Middle, Danielle Brown who manages my social media, and my crucial first-look editorial team who give me so much guidance; Anna Hancock, Susan Ansell, Helen Shenston, Martin and Jane Diplock.

A very special thank-you goes to my task-master extraordinaire, my 'real-life' Roy Grace, former Detective Chief Superintendent David Gaylor, who has a brilliantly creative and analytical mind, as well as being able to juggle half a dozen sets of editorial notes in his head. Without him, the editorial process would take me way longer.

My biggest thank-you of all is to my beloved wife, Lara. She is my rock, my smartest and most trusted critic, my best friend and she always keeps my spirits up.

And my final thanks to our adorable menagerie, including our dogs, Oscar, Spooky and Wally; our kitten, Madam Woo; our alpacas, Al Pacino, Fortescue, Jean-Luc, Boris and Keith, and our emus, Spike, Wolfie and Dorothy. However dark a day may be, they brighten it with their goofy grins, their lopsided smiles, and their antics.

You, my readers, have a special place in my heart – without you I'd be nothing! Your emails, blog posts, tweets, Facebook, Instagram, and YouTube comments are always wonderful to read. Keep them coming, I love to hear from you!

Peter James

contact@peterjames.com
www.peterjames.com
www.peterjames.com/youtube
www.facebook.com/peterjames.roygrace
www.twitter.com/peterjamesuk
www.instagram.com/peterjamesuk
www.instagram.com/peterjamesukpets

1

'There are, of course, no skeletons in this attic!' the estate agent said with a wink, as she threw open the door with a flourish and ushered her clients into the loft space.

'Wow!' said Mike Diamond.

'Wow!' his wife Julie echoed.

'It sure has the *wow* factor, wouldn't you say, Mr and Mrs Diamond?'

'It sure has,' Mike replied.

And it sure did.

The young couple stared around in wonder as they entered the high-ceilinged room. Painted all in white, it covered almost the entire top-floor area of the brand-new house, and was flooded with light from gable windows at each end. The view to the north was across the long, newly turfed garden ending at the lake, the fields and the hill that rose beyond, and to the south across the partially completed housing estate and down to the village of Cold Hill, half a mile below them. There was a rich smell of fresh paint and timber.

'I can tell you, this is a far superior property to the show house, which was sold in the first hour it was on sale. Far superior.' The agent pointed out the four Sonos speakers and the voice-activated electric blinds, then showed them the equally teched-up en suite bathroom. 'This would make a great master bedroom, or an office,' she enthused. 'It's rare to find a room so well equipped, even in a modern home, you'd have to agree.'

Mike and Julie looked at each other. He pulled a face and his wife grinned at the signal. This estate agent was already irritating them, and they'd only been in the house for a few minutes. An elegant woman in her thirties, with short, dark hair, power-dressed in a black suit, white blouse and court shoes, she marched in front of them, brandishing the particulars as if she was about to present them with a certificate. *Future Owners Extraordinaire of Lake House, No. 47 Lakeview Drive!*

They followed her back down the spiral staircase to the first floor and along a short landing, where she opened another door with an equal flourish, onto a small bedroom. 'This will make a great room for your baby,' she said.

Again, the couple shot another secret glance at each other. Mike frowning and Julie frowning back a *what?* Her pregnancy had only been confirmed yesterday by their doctor, and there was no possible way it could be showing yet.

They followed the agent into two further small bedrooms – perfect spare rooms for guests, she enthused, or maybe one of them a den? Then into the master bedroom. 'You'd have to admit, this is pretty much a *wow* room, too!' She strode confidently across it, unlocked French windows and opened them onto a wide Juliet balcony.

'Can you imagine, on a fine day like today, Mrs Diamond? The two of you sitting out here, having an early morning coffee, looking across the lake?'

'It's north-facing,' Mike said. 'So, no morning sunlight.'

'Who wants morning sunlight in a bedroom?' the agent said. 'Not me! But of course, if that's a concern, then you could make the upstairs space your bedroom.' She gave them a conspiratorial look. 'I tell you, if it was me – and I could afford a house this beautiful – I'd make that loft space my master bedroom. It would make anyone feel they were masters of the universe, just like you two truly are – I can tell!' She glanced at her watch. 'I'm so sorry, we'll have to hurry, I have viewings of this place every twenty minutes today. It won't be staying on the market for long, that's for sure. Not with the shortage of quality new-build stock there is today, believe you me.'

She hurried them through the downstairs: the open-plan kitchen and family room, stacked with smart-gadgets, including the memory fridge; the dining room; the small office; the spacious hall; and then the piece-de-résistance – the large, luxuriously carpeted living room with a photochromic-glass conservatory at the rear, overlooking the wide lawn running down to the lake. 'Of course, it would be easy to fence off the lawn part way down, to make it safe for your baby.'

The Diamonds looked at each other. *How does she know about the baby?*

Then, profusely apologetic, she ushered them to the front door. Her next clients were due any moment. If they wished to make an offer, she most strongly advised them to do it sooner rather than later. This was the first day of viewings and this property, priced to sell, would not be hanging around on the market for long.

As she opened the door she said, 'Mr and Mrs Diamond, I can *so* see you living here – in your forever home! And your baby son – what a wonderful environment for him to grow up in. But please, I urge you, don't think about it for too long.'

As they stepped out into the bright, mid-morning sunlight, and the front door closed behind them, Mike and Julie

Diamond stood on the path, with the newly turfed lawn on either side, as a car came along the road. They looked at each other. The same look.

What the fuck?

Our 'son'?

A Mini emblazoned with the logo of RICHWARDS ESTATE AGENTS pulled up behind their parked Mercedes. A tubby, smiling man in his forties, in a flamboyant suit, clambered out and hurried across to them, holding a bunch of keys like a gaoler.

'Mr and Mrs Diamond?'

'Yes,' Mike said, hesitantly.

'Paul Jordan, I do apologize for being late – I had a viewing of another property that ran over.' He shook hands with each of them, once again apologizing profusely. 'You are going to love this house, I promise you. It is really quite special. On the whole of the Cold Hill Park development, this is my very favourite, by a country mile.'

As he rummaged through his keys, Julie Diamond said, 'Yes, it is very lovely.'

'Wait until you view the inside! And let me show you the technology – wow!'

'We've actually just seen it,' Mike Diamond said.

Jordan looked at both of them, puzzled. 'Seen it?'

'Your colleague just showed us around.'

'Colleague?'

'Yes.'

The agent frowned. 'I'm sorry – we are the sole agents for this development, and none of my associates are here today.' He looked hesitant. 'Someone showed you around?'

'Yes,' Julie replied. 'A lady, she said she had viewings back to back all day and could only allocate twenty minutes to us.'

'It isn't possible,' Jordan said. 'I – I don't understand. What was her name?'

The couple looked at each other, then Mike shrugged. 'Well, she didn't give us her name. To be honest, she was a bit odd.'

'Can you excuse me?' Jordan asked. 'Please, just a couple of minutes?'

Reluctantly, the couple nodded.

He let himself into the house, walked through the hallway and called out, 'Hello! Hello! It's Paul Jordan – hello!'

He went into each of the downstairs rooms, then up to the first floor, checking each of the rooms there. Then up to the loft, being sure to check the bathroom.

There was no one.

Frowning, he hurried back downstairs and out the front door. And caught a glimpse of the Diamond's Mercedes, already several hundred yards away.

2

Saturday 27 October

'I love it!'

'You do?'

'Don't you?'

'No!' he said, beaming. 'I don't *love* it – I FUCKING love it!'

Standing in the huge loft, with autumn sunlight streaming in through the south-facing window, Jason put his arm around his wife and hugged her. 'I abso-fucking-lutely love it!'

'You'll have to excuse my husband's language!' Emily said to the estate agent.

'Oh, please, Mrs Danes,' Paul Jordan beamed. 'Artistic licence with language is permitted, for such a famous *artist* as your husband!'

'I'm hardly famous, but thank you,' Jason Danes replied.

'Oh, I would question your modesty, Mr Danes. I took the liberty of looking you up on Wikipedia, and imagine my excitement when I realized I have one of your oil paintings hanging in our living room – a wonderful picture of an old man in an armchair with a spaniel at his feet. So full of charm. My wife bought it for me for Christmas a couple of years ago, from a gallery in Lewes. In the Jordan household, you are indeed famous! And I'm quite certain that should you decide to buy this beautiful, unique home, one day there will be a blue plaque with your name on the wall outside.'

'Not too soon, I hope,' Jason Danes replied. 'You have to be dead for that to happen.'

Jordan smiled. 'Well, don't they say that death is always a good career move for an artist?'

As if given a cue, the sunlight faded behind a cloud. The room darkened, and the expressions on the faces of Jordan's two clients darkened with it. Their enthusiasm for the property suddenly seemed to be draining away.

'Only joking!' Jordan said quickly, trying to recover the situation.

'Of course,' the painter replied. 'I'm only thirty-nine – I hope to have a few more years yet.'

His wife, five years his junior, gave the agent an awkward smile.

Neither of them, looking out at the views in turn, noticed the nervous glance the agent suddenly shot at the doorway.

Jason stared out through the rear gable at the huge lake, and the sloping field beyond, and the soft round contour of the hill rising up steeply beyond that. He watched ducks – Mallards and Indian Runners – on the lake. It was so tranquil. 'I could work here, I know I could – it's just, wow, so inspiring! Well, this view to the north is, anyway. It is north I'm looking at?'

'Yes indeed, Mr Danes, and that is part of the South Downs National Park, so it can never be built on.'

'Unlike the other directions?'

The view to the south looked down at the brand-new houses directly opposite, and the rows of houses beyond, most of which were just shells still under construction. To the west was a vast, muddy site, on which there were bull-dozers, diggers, men in yellow hard hats with theodolites, and marked-out plots. To the east was a huge empty and overgrown field.

'I'll show you the shape of the whole plan,' the estate agent said, kneeling and unrolling a large map on the bare oak floor.

It was headed, COLD HILL PARK DEVELOPMENT – PHASE 1, PHASE 2, PHASE 3.

'The whole site comprises just over twenty-five acres, Mr and Mrs Danes. Now this, where we are, is part of phase one, which is, frankly, the most exclusive area, with the largest homes, the very best of which – and of which this house is the *very* best – have the lake and rural views. The position is, frankly, superlative – you see, phase one is built on the curtilage of the original mansion that was here; Cold Hill House. Whatever your views on aristocracy and gentry, you have to admit they all knew a thing or two about position and views. And all the infrastructure is already in place – the roads, drains, utilities and of course, the all-important super-fast fibre broadband. The area to the west, which you can see, is phase two, which will be smaller buildings; town-houses, a few two-storey apartment buildings and some affordable housing.'

'You mean council houses?' Emily quizzed.

Jordan looked a little awkward. 'Well, in all but name, yes. But you'll never even know they're there, with their separate road network. And then to the east, that field, that will also be detached homes, very classy ones.'

'How many residences in total will there be here?' Jason Danes asked.

'When phase three is completed, there will be one hundred and thirty altogether.'

'So, this place will be a building site for the next two years?'

'Yes, Mr and Mrs Danes, but honestly you'll scarcely

notice. There's very little phase one left, and of course the price of this house reflects the temporary inconvenience.'

Jordan noticed the flicker of doubt between the couple and went on, hastily. 'Let me show you a feature that is very rare in modern houses.' He strode over to one window, unlocked it and pulled it up. 'Genuine sash windows, in every room! A true Georgian feature. You see, this house has been designed almost as a miniature model of Cold Hill House, which once stood here. Sash windows, I tell you – no expense was spared by the builders on this beautiful home.' He smiled. 'For your catering business, Mrs Danes, I don't think you'll find a more magnificent kitchen on the market anywhere in Sussex.'

'Let's take another look at it,' she said.

'Please follow me,' Jordan said, checking his watch, mindful that the Danes had already overrun their allotted thirty minutes and another couple would be arriving for a viewing shortly. But hell, they could wait. He had a good feeling about Mr and Mrs Danes. He could get them over the line.

He rolled up the plan, tucked it under his arm, and led the way down the staircase to the first-floor landing. 'Note how wonderfully light the house feels everywhere, from the clever use of mirrors.'

Jason and Emily looked around, and he was right. Mirrors along the landing walls, and down in the hall, created both light and the illusion of even greater space. Entering the expansive kitchen, Jordan said, 'It's almost as if the architect designed this house with you two in mind. The kitchen perfect for your catering business; the attic a truly divine artist's studio!'

'It is perfect,' Emily said, regaining her former enthusiasm as she strode around. 'So much storage, and how rare to have a walk-in pantry!'

PETER JAMES

'Not to mention the technology,' Paul Jordan added. 'All the houses on this development have this feature.' He pointed at a small cylindrical device with a glowing green light, sitting on the kitchen unit. 'All the switches and controls and taps throughout the house are voice activated from that one command box – and its satellite units around the house. You each have to get it to learn your voices. Then anything you want – heating turning up or down, appliances switched on or off, curtains and blinds opened or closed, can be done by simply saying, for instance, "Command! Kitchen blinds down!"'

There was a whirr. The kitchen darkened as blinds lowered over each window.

Again, unnoticed by the couple, Jordan shot another wary glance around, before saying, 'Command! Kitchen blinds up!'

Immediately they rose, and light returned.

'You can even open the fridge and freezer doors by voice command! So hygienic, never needing germ-infected hands to touch any switch or control.'

'Presumably there's a manual override?' Emily asked.

'Absolutely.' He walked over and pressed a button. The command box light turned red. 'Now everything is operated manually, or by remote controls.'

'No one realizes quite how many germs are spread by hands,' Jason Danes said, solemnly. 'The average bowl of peanuts sitting on a pub bar counter contains twelve different traces of urine and five of human faeces.'

Jordan blanched slightly. 'I think I've just developed a peanut allergy!' He rapidly changed the subject. 'And of course you can set up your phones to operate anything in this house remotely – just a simple app – from wherever you are in the country, or indeed the world! You can even be lying on a beach in Greece and check the contents of your fridge if you like!'

Emily opened the integral door to the double garage and utility and went in, followed by her husband and the agent. The lights flickered on automatically. 'I could make this into my catering kitchen. It would work, don't you think, darling?'

Jason nodded. 'It could.'

'It *really* could!' she insisted. 'I could get all the fridges, freezers and ovens I need into here.'

'Of course,' Jordan said, 'some people – especially an artist of your calibre, Mr Danes – might prefer something old, quaint, historic. Rustic, perhaps? If you would rather view an Edwardian property, or Victorian or even Georgian – I do have some very attractive houses within your price range I could show you. But of course, along with their beauty, old and historic properties come with a raft of maintenance issues. Here, with a totally new build, you get the builder's ten-year guarantee. Ten years maintenance free! You don't have to worry about draughts or leaks or doors sticking. When you buy new, you are buying worry-free.'

'And germ-free,' Jason Danes added.

'Absolutely, quite right! Germ-free. Ah, yes, indeed, germs are of course not included in the purchase price – they are extra!' Jordan chuckled, but his clients stared blankly at him.

'It's an important consideration,' Emily Danes said. 'Germs.'

'Ah, of course, indeed. In the catering business, you cannot be too careful, I'm sure. Old buildings can be full of bugs and all kind of things. *Yechh!* All of them lying beneath the floorboards and in crevices for years, decades, centuries even, waiting to pounce! Here, in addition to hygienic switch activation, we have the very latest in state-of-the-art insulation. I tell you what, if I found a cockroach in here, I'd name it Houdini.' Behind him, he heard the sound of running water.

'It's actually more for my husband,' she said. 'He doesn't do germs, bugs, dirt.'

'Quite right, who does, eh?' Jordan turned to see his client running his hands under a tap in one of the twin sinks and washing them with liquid soap from an electronic dispenser. 'Germs, eh, Mr Danes – nasty little buggers.'

Absorbed in the ritual of cleaning his hands, Jason did not appear to notice the comment.

Jordan frowned. There was something different about the man, something that was pushing him, just a little, out of his comfort zone. But at the same time, he genuinely did love that painting of the old man with the dog. Every time he looked at it, he wondered what the man was thinking, what his life was – and had been. Clearly Mr Danes was a genius, and weren't all geniuses just a bit eccentric? But would an artistic genius really want to live in a sterile, new-build house?

'The houses on either side of this, Mr Jordan – are they sold?' Emily asked.

'No, not yet, although I believe a couple – a very nice couple, with two children – are going to buy number forty-five – that's the house to the east – if the sale of their house goes through.' He crossed his fingers.

'Children?' Jason said, dubiously. 'What age?'

The agent smiled. 'I know what you're thinking; what a nightmare when you're trying to paint, having screaming children next door. I don't think you need to worry – they are twelve and fourteen. We've not had any couples with young, screaming children looking at any of the properties so far. And there's quite an elderly couple, retired, who are very interested in number forty-nine. They're moving down from Yorkshire to be closer to their daughter, who lives just outside Lewes.'

'How many other people are living on the estate at present?' Emily asked.

'Well . . .' he hesitated, smiling uncomfortably. 'At this moment, there's just the very nice couple diagonally opposite – they've been here a month or so now – and there's a family due to move in opposite you, in number thirty-four, soon. Elsewhere, no one at the moment. But the properties are selling like hot cakes – it's just such a fine development; so near to Brighton and to Lewes, close to rail links to London – just fifty minutes on the Brighton line. And surrounded by beautiful countryside. This is a very special position – quite unique.'

Jordan glanced at his watch again. 'Look, I'm very sorry, but I have another couple arriving for a viewing. If you'd like to have a think about it and come back to me, we can always book a further appointment. But I do have to warn you, we have so much interest in this property – indeed in the whole estate. We've already sold over half the properties off-plan, and this one, which is the real jewel in the crown, is not going to be on the market for long, I can tell you. And of course, I can help you with a mortgage should you require. But I really would advise you, if you are interested, to move quickly. The couple I'm waiting for now are coming for their second viewing, and I'm told they don't have any property to sell – they are cash buyers.'

'We'll take it,' Jason said decisively, rinsing his hands then soaping them once again. 'We'll pay the full asking price.' He looked at his wife, who nodded.

Jordan beamed. 'Well! What can I say? I don't think it is a decision you could ever possibly regret. This is the finest house in the best property development I've ever been privileged to handle – and I've handled many, I can tell you. The location, the sheer build quality. The views. You could not have a better investment!'

'So, what do you need from us to take it off the market, immediately, this minute?' Jason Danes asked. 'We're cash buyers, too. We sold our previous home and we're currently renting, and we don't need a mortgage.'

'Good, excellent.' The agent was pensive for a moment. 'It's Saturday, nothing can happen until Monday when solicitors are back at work. If you would like to go to my office and put down a ten thousand-pound deposit – entirely refundable – as a show of good faith, I'll tell the couple who are coming that the house is under offer. I'd be prepared to give you a four to six week window to exchange contracts. How does that sound?'

The Danes looked at each other. 'We might be able to move in before Christmas!' Emily said.

Rinsing then soaping his hands again, Jason Danes nodded enthusiastically and said, 'Very fair.'

'I'll even throw in some containers of soap!'

Neither of them smiled.

After an awkward moment, Jordan beamed again. 'In which case, Mr and Mrs Danes, I look forward to handing you the keys and to formally welcoming you to your new home. You won't regret this, I can assure you. This is a very special house. You are going to find it very creative, very creative indeed.'

3

Friday 14 December

Maurice and Claudette Penze-Weedell peered out through the slats of the blinds of Arden Lodge, 36 Lakeview Drive, watching the activity going on across the street at number forty-seven. They were happy that, after two months, they would no longer be the only people living in the Cold Hill Park development. They were also very curious to catch a glimpse of their new neighbours.

'Not too wide, dear,' Maurice said. 'They'll notice, and we don't want to seem like nosey.' Maurice had originally suggested changing to net curtains, like the ones they'd had in their previous home, which prevented passers-by from seeing in while still enabling them to see out. But Mrs P-W – as he referred to his wife – had put her foot down, saying net curtains were far too common. As owners of the grand show house – and the first residents of Cold Hill Park – she insisted they had to set standards. Blinds it had to be, and vertical ones, in her view, were so much more elegant than horizontal ones.

Maurice agreed with Mrs P-W, or 'High Command', as he called her when with his friends. He always agreed with her. It was, he had learned over their years together – the very *many* years – the route to a happy marriage. 'Happy wife, happy life,' he had already told all the regulars, several times, at his new local the Crown, down in the village. Well perhaps more accurately, he reflected, a *tolerable* life. Although his joke at their housewarming party – which, coincidentally and economically, had doubled as their thirtieth wedding anniversary celebration – that he would have got less than thirty years for murder, had fallen somewhat flat.

'It's a rather *grand* design for a not very grand-sized house, don't you think, Maurice?'

'I think it's quite attractive.'

'Quite attractive? It's like a sort of bonsai stately home. Gables in the attic and that ludicrous chimney, like the house is wearing a top hat – it's just *sooooo* pretentious. And with the lake behind it and all. Honestly!'

Unlike its rather uninspired neighbours on both sides, which were rather squat, red-brick houses with pantiled roofs, like a million others on new-build estates, number forty-seven stood proud and aloof. It was a Georgian-style house on three storeys, with large, gabled dormers. The exterior walls were fawn-coloured and the door, framed by a handsome porch, navy blue. The front garden was a short lawn behind black railings, with a wide drive and parking area and attached double garage to one side.

'I think the estate agent said the house was a nod to the original ruined mansion that was here – that the architect had taken his inspiration from it.'

'So, which grand house did the architect take his inspiration from for ours?'

'I don't know, my love.'

A removals van the size of an ocean liner had pulled up outside the house some ten minutes earlier and the removals men were milling around, two of them smoking, one onhis phone. But it was when a silver BMW drove onto the driveway and pulled up in front of the garage that both the Penze-Weedells had taken up position by the window. The driver remained in it, seemingly talking on his phone.

'That car's just like ours!' Claudette Penze-Weedell said with relief in her voice. 'Identical!'

'I'm afraid not,' her husband said, gloomily. 'Ours is a 520; that one is a 540i.'

'Is that more expensive?'

'Much.'

Claudette stared at the car across the street venomously. 'It's probably time to upgrade, isn't it, Maurice?'

Only weeks after moving in, Maurice Penze-Weedell had been made redundant by the insurance company in Brighton which had employed him for twenty-eight years. He had risen from the post-room to become its Chief Operating Officer. Although given a substantial pay-off, a new car for either of them at this moment was out of the question.

He hadn't yet told his wife just how serious their financial situation was and that – heaven forbid – she might actually have to actually get up off her backside, which seemed to widen every day like the flow of volcanic lava, and get a job. They only had sufficient reserve funds to cover the mortgage for another twelve months, and he had been finding out to his dismay that the jobs market for a fifty-five-year-old in twenty-first century Britain was pretty shitty. 'My dearest, our BMW is only eleven months old. It's fine, we don't need to upgrade it for a few years.'

'In that case we should upgrade my car. I think the Lady of the Manor should have a dignified motor car and not a child's toy. Really, I feel like Noddy every time I get in it.' She was referring to her little Japanese runaround, currently in the garage, plugged into the charger. It was a regular bone of contention between them.

'I hardly think we're the Lord and Lady of the Manor, dear.

We've bought the very nice show house on a very nice estate, but I don't think the other residents are going to be queuing at our front door to pay their annual tithe of chickens, bushels of corn and God knows what else.' He hesitated and smiled. 'Although I suppose, of course, *droit du seigneur* might be rather nice.'

'Droit de what?'

He smiled again. 'The ancient right of the Lord of the Manor to deflower any local virgin.'

'Dream on, you wouldn't know what to do with a virgin.' She tried to stop herself in mid-sentence, but it was too late, it came out.

'Quite right – I never had that experience, my dear.' He delivered the trump-card smile she could not defend against. She'd lost her virginity to his original best man three weeks before their wedding. Maurice had caught them himself, in flagrante. It was a hold over her that had served him well for three decades.

'Anyhow,' he added, defensively. 'You hate parking and your Leaf has self-park. You said you liked that feature.'

'Only because I can do it when I'm outside the car, so no one can see me in it.'

Across the road, a tall, gangly man in his late-thirties climbed out of the BMW and tossed his head, shaking his mop of fair hair from his eyes. Dressed in a leather jacket over a black polo-neck jumper, skinny jeans and boots, and arty glasses, he stood looking approvingly up at the front of his house, which was bathed in winter sunlight, then around and across the street. He clocked the twitch of the blinds in the large, rather ugly house over the road, with the flashing blue and green Christmas lights adorning the porch and the hideous Santa's grotto that covered most of the garden.

'That must be him,' Mrs P-W said. 'The painter!'

'Could come in handy when we need to redecorate.'

'Ha ha,' she said. 'Jason Danes is famous. He's the talk of the village shop.' She smiled, coquettishly, at her husband. 'Just a thought – why don't you commission him to do a portrait of me for my birthday?'

'Why would I want that? I've got plenty of photographs of you.'

'That's not the same. God, you used to be so romantic, Maurice! Don't you think a portrait would be a romantic gesture?'

He looked at her. She wasn't quite the svelte beauty he'd first dated, although if he was honest, neither was he still the dashing cavalier of his youth. Both of them now sported double chins that were visual testament to the laws of gravity.

'Hmmmn,' he grunted. 'I imagine he charges a fortune.'

'And I'm not worth it?' She peered through the blinds again, very cautiously this time. Then she gasped. 'Please tell me that belongs to the removals company and not to these . . . these people?'

A small, bright-pink refrigerated van, emblazoned with the legend, TASTE SENSATIONS – EMILY'S PANTRY, the words separated by a floral logo, pulled up alongside the BMW. An attractive, red-headed woman in her early thirties got out, wearing a baggy crimson parka over black tights and calf-length boots.

'What does she have in there, then, Danish pastries?' Maurice said.

'Huh?' his wife said blankly.

'The Danes. Danish pastries. Geddit?'

'You're full of humour today – you been on the sauce or something?'

The Penze-Weedells watched as the couple kissed, then

hugged, then kissed again before heading towards the front door. Then Claudette turned to her husband.

'Maurice,' she said, sternly. 'You are not going to permit them to leave that van parked on their driveway, are you?'

'What do you mean?'

'You know *exactly* what I mean. We're not going to sit here and allow the value of our house to be diminished by a hideous van parked outside a neighbour's property.'

'I really don't see what business it is of ours. It's advertising her business, surely?'

'Yes, well, there's an awful lot you don't seem to see these days. Perhaps you should go to Specsavers and check you don't have cataracts.'

'Don't be absurd, my love. My vision is perfectly good – 6/6 at my recent check-up.'

Releasing the blinds again, she said, 'Don't you remember when we bought this house, the restrictive covenants? One of them said that no commercial vehicles were permitted to be parked on the estate overnight.' She pointed across the road. 'That is a commercial vehicle.'

'It's only a small van.'

'*Small?* It's hideous.'

'I'm getting a little bit confused.' He stroked his threadbare dome with his right hand. 'Do you want me to ask him to paint you, or to put his wife's van inside their garage?'

'Both!' she said emphatically.

'I think we need to be a little diplomatic. I'm not even sure that covenant applies to vehicles owned by residents.'

'Don't be ridiculous. Of course it does. Let me tell you, I do not intend to spend the rest of my life staring out of my drawing room window at a pink van. If you're not man enough to tell them, I certainly will. I'll go over tomorrow and tell them, very politely of course.'

'Perhaps give them a few days,' he suggested.

'A few days?'

He turned and pointed at their Christmas tree. Gaily wrapped presents lay around the base, and fairy lights twinkled in the branches of plastic pine needles. 'Isn't this meant to be the season of goodwill?'

She again parted the blinds, peering at the removals men, who were starting to carry furniture towards the front door of the Danes' house. 'Yes, Maurice, *goodwill*. Which means respecting what this estate is all about. *Aspirational homes.* There are people with a tatty camper van moving in at the end of our road soon – probably travellers – and now we have a pink van opposite. This is all just ghastly. I don't care if he is bloody Rembrandt reincarnated, they are not leaving a pink van on their driveway.' She paused. 'Oh look, a piano, well that's something, I suppose.'

'The people at the end of the road are not *travellers*,' he said.

'No?' she rounded on him. 'They came in a Volkswagen camper with a yellow roundel in the rear window saying, *Nuclear Power – Nein Danke!* They're not *travellers*?'

'No, they're *New Age* people. Probably lovely and very gentle. You have to remember, my love, that this whole estate will have a mix of people, which is no bad thing.'

'Yes, well, I'm beginning to think we've made a terrible mistake moving here.'

All the warmth drained from the room. Maurice and Mrs P-W shivered, suddenly. Inexplicably.

A woman stood right behind them, watching them. She was wearing a long blue dress with yellow shoes, and had an angry, shrivelled face.

Parvenus.

She did not like them, nor their ridiculous name.

Penze-Weedell.

Each of them, as if drawn by a magnet, turned their heads.

All they saw was the flashing Christmas tree, and the cards on the mantelpiece above the electric dancing flames of the simulated coal fire in the fake grate.

'Has the heating gone off?' she said, giving her husband a sharp look. Are you economizing again?'

He shivered again. 'No, it's set for all day.' He hurried through into the kitchen and then into the utility room. The boiler was blazing away.

4

'Oh my God!' Emily Danes said. 'I hadn't realized just how hideous it is – daylight sort of masked it!' She stared out from the front window of the living room through the falling darkness at number thirty-six. At the illuminated Santa's grotto in the front garden, complete with Santa rocking from side to side and with flashing lights for eyes, and a string of elves frozen in mid-dance. 'Can you imagine, we're going to have to look at this until – the sixth of January, isn't it, the date when you have to take decorations down or its unlucky? God!'

'The curtains shouldn't be too long,'

Emily leaned against a packing case and looked at her checklist. 'Right. I've rung the window cleaner we were recommended and he's going to try to fit us in before Christmas. He asked if we'd mind him coming at the weekend, this once – what do you think?'

'Be good to get them done, they're quite grimy.'

'Probably dust from the construction going on all around us.' She peered at the list again. 'I've called Sky and that's sorted. I've also gone on the council's website and found what day the bins go out – recycling is every other Monday, but it's all going to change after the New Year, so I'll have to check again then. Oh, and there's a post office counter in the village shop that's open to eight p.m.!'

546

'That's better than in town.'

'I know, brilliant!'

'Oh, and I've finally found the stopcock,' Jason said.

'You'd better show me.'

'Tomorrow, when it's daylight. It's out down the side of the house behind the bin store.'

'OK.'

'Right, time for a celebration, methinks!'

'You said the curtains shouldn't be too long – how long did she say?'

'I spoke to the woman a few days ago – she thought about a month,' he said, coming back in with two champagne flutes. He set them down on the glass coffee table in front of the two huge sofas they had splashed out on, and which were put together in an L-shape.

He went back to the kitchen and returned with a cold bottle of champagne that the estate agent had left them in the fridge. 'That's a bit snobby, darling – I think we should at least give them a chance!'

'With Christmas decorations like that? Hmmm. Perhaps we could hang a blackout sheet up in the meantime,' she said with a grin. 'Although I guess that wouldn't exactly be very neighbourly – they might think we were doing it to stop them spying on us.'

'They are spying on us,' he replied.

'What?'

'They are, darling. I saw their blinds move when I got out of the car this morning, and every time I look across, I keep seeing the blinds in the same downstairs window twitching.'

'Perhaps they're curious, like we are, to see who their new neighbours are. They must be happy to have another couple on the estate. The agent said we're only the second owners to move in. It must have felt like living in a ghost town.'

Jason frowned. 'I think – what's his name – Paul Jordan must be mistaken; there are people in the house directly opposite us – the one that looks like a small child's drawing. I saw a couple and two children through one of the windows this morning.'

'Oh, so my husband is a peeping Tom, is he?' she said, peering across at it. 'It's a funny-looking house – two windows upstairs, two down, either side of the front door, and a pointy roof. You're right, like something a child would draw.' She hesitated. 'Are you sure you saw people there?

'Yes, in one of upstairs rooms.'

'But there are no lights on, and no car outside.'

'Perhaps they're out.'

'More likely they haven't moved in yet, and were just there measuring up, or whatever,' she said.

'There! Number thirty-six, they're looking at us again, I saw the blinds move!'

'Shall I flash at them?'

'Might be a lechy old perv living there who'd get off on that.'

'Doesn't look much like a lechy old perv's house to me.'

He peered out. 'No, too naff. It's actually horrible – I mean, how did the same architect who designed this place ever think that house was a good idea? Or the one opposite. I mean, ours is a really pretty house – it's like he designed this, got drunk, and came back to his drawing board and did that one and the Grotties'.'

'The Grotties! I like that. I think one of us should go over tomorrow and say hi, put them out of their misery so they can see we're actually human. And tell them how much we like their Christmas lights.'

'I'd like to see you do that with a straight face.' He raised the bottle in the air. 'Grrrrrrrrrr, we're your new neighbours, we're the cousins of the Munsters and we are very, very, very weird!'

Emily giggled.

He set the bottle on top of an unopened packing case the removals men had plonked there and began working on the foil.

'Maybe he was just having a laugh,' Emily said, flopping down on one of the sofas. 'Like food critics every now and then describing something utterly disgusting as the most wonderful thing they've ever put in their mouth. Like, what is the most horrible house he could design that someone would buy. Or that portrait you painted of that politician whom you didn't like, deliberately making him look about two hundred years old.'

'I was just trying to show the wisdom of his years etched into his face.' He held the bottle facing safely away from her as he untwisted the wire.

'Of course you were.' She lay back and kicked her legs in the air. 'Woweeee, this sofa is sooooo comfy!'

There was a massive pop and the cork flew out, ricocheting off the ceiling, the champagne squirting and foaming out as if the bottle had been vigorously shaken. He stared at it, startled. Over half the contents had gone by the time it settled.

'Bloody hell!' he said. 'This is a lively one.'

Looking up, she said, 'It's made a mark on the ceiling!'

'We should leave it there – our house christening mark! Our *forever* home.'

'I like that!'

He filled their glasses and handed her one. Then he picked up his and, staring her in the eye said, 'Cheers, to our *forever* home.'

PETER JAMES
ON STAGE

PETER JAMES'
DEAD SIMPLE

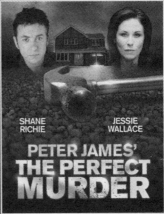

SHANE RICHIE

JESSIE WALLACE

PETER JAMES'
THE PERFECT MURDER

SHANE RICHIE
LAURA WHITMORE

PETER JAMES'
NOT DEAD ENOUGH

STEPHEN BILLINGTON

JOE McFADDEN .. RITA SIMONS

PETER JAMES'
THE HOUSE ON COLD HILL

LOOKING GOOD DEAD - coming to the stage in 2021

For performance licensing of the above plays
please contact peterjames@stage-rights.com

@PeterJamesStage